PLANTANIMUS

PLANTANIMUS

The Holographic Saint

Joseph M. Armillas

PLANTANIMUS
THE HOLOGRAPHIC SAINT

iUniverse books may be ordered through booksellers or by contacting:

iUniverse
1663 Liberty Drive
Bloomington, IN 47403
www.iuniverse.com
1-800-Authors (1-800-288-4677)

ISBN: 978-1-5320-9448-4 (sc)
ISBN: 978-1-5320-9449-1 (e)

Print information available on the last page.

iUniverse rev. date: 02/06/2020

Table of Contents

ACKNOWLEDGEMENTS. ix

PROLOGUE xiii

GALACTIC YEAR 9,931

CHAPTER 1   Sales Pitch 1

GALACTIC YEAR 10,023

CHAPTER 2   The Novice Allondra Velmador 15

CHAPTER 3   The Kelemite Curia 22

CHAPTER 4   Ogram Zepol. 30

CHAPTER 5   A Meeting at the top of a Pyramid. 36

CHAPTER 6   Desperate Measures 43

CHAPTER 7   The Enemy Appears. 46

CHAPTER 8   A Rescue from the Storm. 48

CHAPTER 9   The Reboot Uncovers a Mystery 53

CHAPTER 10   Infiltration. 59

CHAPTER 11   Saved by the Saint 64

CHAPTER 12   Sleeping with the Lights On. 72

CHAPTER 13   Of Religion, Science and Politics 76

CHAPTER 14　On the Voyage to New Jerusalem. 80

CHAPTER 15　Ogram Meets Sister Allondra. 86

CHAPTER 16　A Late Dinner with the Matriarch 94

CHAPTER 17　On the Planet Kāla Kōṭharī 105

CHAPTER 18　Revelation 108

CHAPTER 19　A Growth Chamber on the Venus Fly Trap 114

CHAPTER 20　Nobius-72527 118

CHAPTER 21　Camp Zurk 122

CHAPTER 22　Into the Mouth of Eternity 125

CHAPTER 23　An Interesting Conversation 127

CHAPTER 24　The Retrieval Goes Bad 136

CHAPTER 25　Arrival, Confusion and First Absorption 140

CHAPTER 26　A Disturbance in the Quantum Tide 145

CHAPTER 27　The Invasion Begins. 150

CHAPTER 28　The Far End of the Carina Sagittarius Arm 156

CHAPTER 29　Arrival 161

CHAPTER 30　A Surprise in the Jungle 166

CHAPTER 31　A Quiet Dinner with the Saint. 172

CHAPTER 32　The Gospel According to St. Kelem Part I 178

CHAPTER 33　Allondra's Moment of Doubt and Fear. 189

CHAPTER 34　The Gospel According to St. Kelem Part II 193

CHAPTER 35　The New Apostles 202

CHAPTER 36　Plots within the Curia 207

CHAPTER 37　A Public Declaration of Faith. 211

CHAPTER 38　An Unholy Alliance 213

CHAPTER 39   A Wedding in Sister Ornata's Chapel 219

CHAPTER 40   The Plantanimus CUBE is Destroyed 221

CHAPTER 41   Pandemonium in the Galaxy 229

CHAPTER 42   Ogram is Arrested, Allondra Escapes 231

CHAPTER 43   The Men's Holding Facility in Latonga 234

CHAPTER 44   Rendezvous with the Trinity. 240

CHAPTER 45   Kalpanā Bhūmi (Fantasy Land) 246

CHAPTER 46   The Attack on the Old Factory 257

CHAPTER 47   Termination. 265

CHAPTER 48   The Kren Arrive. 276

CHAPTER 49   Queen Harriett II (The Second) 282

CHAPTER 50   The Drums of War. 289

CHAPTER 51   Ogram's Moment of Doubt and Fear 294

CHAPTER 52   A Daring and Risky Plan 299

CHAPTER 53   The War Begins 301

CHAPTER 54   Through the Gauntlet – Part 1. 305

CHAPTER 55   Through the Gauntlet – Part 2. 310

CHAPTER 56   The Miracle at the Heavenly Temple 321

CHAPTER 57   The End of a Very Long Relationship 335

GALACTIC YEAR 10,148

CHAPTER 58   Kelem's Ascension 345

Epilogue. 353

About the Author. 355

Acknowledgements

To Barbara, my light in the world and the teacher of much wisdom.
To my mother and my spiritual guides who gifted me this book.

"God has no religion."
— <u>Mahatma Gandhi</u>

Prologue

The Holographic Saint is the last book in the Plantanimus series, concluding the eight thousand year saga of the story's main character, Kelem Rogeston.

Books one through four, have prologues, with the prologues of book two, Plantanimus "Return to Mars", book three, "Plantanimus The Gulax War" and book four, "Reunion", containing enough background of the story as it developed from book to book.

The story, by now, has become rather complex and detailed to give a prologue its due, so we've decided to forego a description of the previous books and encourage you, (the reader) to please purchase the entire series. You won't be disappointed!

The author has worked hard to make sure that if you were to read any of the books in the pentalogy out of order or just one, that you would be able to enjoy that one book without having read the others.

Thank you for your patience and enjoy the last novel of the Plantanimus saga.

GALACTIC YEAR 9,931

CHAPTER I

Sales Pitch

Cristoph Naragan was being escorted by a platoon of militia men taking him to the stronghold of Chasson Zamundi, the most powerful warlord in Ibira III, the planet that he'd been assigned to negotiate with, on behalf of the Secundo Vita Corporation. The company he worked for was one of the biggest body shop corporations in the Guild.

Nowadays, Ibira III, originally settled by Terrans during the Third Millennium, was considered a backwater planet situated on the outer edges of the galaxy, many thousands of light years from the cluster of civilized worlds that comprised the Galactic Council. It was located even further out than the Kren sector, which the Galactic Council and the Church of St. Kelem avoided with caution.

The Kelemites had tried to proselytize the insectoid species and found that, not only were the Kren impossible to evangelize, their queens claimed that their society had been transformed by Kelem Rogeston himself during the Second Millennium. Their account of Kelem Rogeston's involvement with their species contradicted the Church's mythology and timeline.

During the Kelemite Crusades of the Fourth Millennium, the Kelemite Church declared that the Kren were too alien and totally incompatible with humanoid logic and spirituality and should therefore be considered outcasts and pariahs. They were officially proclaimed angels of Satan by Matriarch Castilia, the then leader of the Church.

From that point in time, any contact with the Kren was considered sacrilegious and punishable by discommendation, followed by exile from all the Galactic Council planets.

The truth was that the Church and the Council had sent a large armada to defeat, and then convert the Kren to the Kelemite religion but the force was completely wiped out in a battle that lasted all of twenty minutes. The insectoid's technology and weapons were far advanced than those of the crusader's. Fortunately for the rest of the galaxy, the Kren were not interested in either revenge or conquest. They just wanted to be left alone.

It was these and other factors that motivated the Body Shop Guild to establish business in planetary systems that were considered too remote, unprofitable or dangerous for The Realm, and therefore the Church of St. Kelem.

Cristoph Naragan, a Terran in his forties with an athlete's body and military training, was a superb salesman and negotiator. Considered the best troubleshooter in Secundo Vita, he was always the point man whenever the company faced a tough prospective client like Ibira III. The planet had been plagued by war and poverty for thousands of years and was ripe for the type of takeover that the Guild specialized in. A victim of the isolation brought about by the Kelemite Crusades, the planet had languished in poverty, violence and political strife for millennia.

Secundo Vita had placed a stealth spy satellite over the planet six months earlier and sociologists at the company had come to the conclusion that the best chance of reaching an agreement with the people of Ibira III was to negotiate with Chasson Zamundi, the leader of the Wamcha tribe, the largest and most powerful military power on the planet. The man was reputedly a violent psychopath who treated his enemies as well as his people with an iron hand. Cristoph Naragan was putting his life in peril by coming in contact with Zamundi and the Wamchas, but he knew that it was the only way to negotiate a successful treaty with the inhabitants of Ibira III. Once Naragan had Zamundi's signature on the treaty, the rest of the planet would follow. The trick was not to become a prisoner, be tortured or killed in the process.

Wamcha society was a strange mix of the ancient and the new. They had modern weapons and machinery that the tribe occasionally acquired from traders that came out to do business this far from the center of the galaxy. Their religion was a bizarre combination of Christianity and polytheistic idolatry called Hansurak. The men decorated their clothing with the bones of their enemies and sported fancy tattoos on their bodies. However, they lived in modern buildings with electricity and plumbing and were fastidious about their cleanliness. The women were just as violent and dangerous as the men.

No foreigner had visited the Wamchas in decades. His appearance in the city drew quite a bit of attention. The crowd surrounding the men who were bringing the newcomer to their chieftain, got so big and out of control with curiosity that one of the militia men took out his weapon and fired it into the air to disperse the crowd. Naragan's heart was racing, wondering if the next shot would be aimed at his head.

Cristoph Naragan was a highly trained troubleshooter who'd risked his life for his company many times in the past. But this particular assignment was the most dangerous of all. The spy satellite that Secundo Vita had placed in orbit around the planet had recorded many instances of the Wamcha's savagery and disregard for human life.

The platoon escorting him entered an official looking building, the largest in this part of the city. Zamundi's men pushed back the crowd, and after Naragan and the platoon entered, guards closed the large wooden gates to the building and the crowd's noise subsided. They passed through a double door and Naragan found himself in a large semi-dark assembly hall resembling an old theater. He was brought to the middle of the center isle of the orchestra seats facing the stage. Chasson Zamundi was center stage in a huge, ornate throne-like chair, sitting atop a dais, decorated with human skulls that had been painted black. Above the man, who appeared to weigh about two hundred and fifty, or perhaps as much as three hundred kilos, was a light fixture shining down on him. The theatrical setting made Zamundi appear as if he were a deity.

Chasson Zamundi was a giant blob of a man who probably couldn't walk on his own and most likely had to be carried around in the dais on which he sat. Naragan was surprised to discover that the most powerful man on the planet was an enormously obese man who resembled a giant toad sitting on a lily pad.

In spite of the contradiction in appearance, Naragan knew that regardless of what Zamundi looked like, his life was still very much in danger. One of the men in the platoon leaned close and whispered in his ear.

"You are to address him as Great Leader."

Naragan nodded and whispered back, "May I approach him?"

"Only if he asks you to," the militiaman replied sternly.

Naragan cleared his throat and addressed Zamundi. "Great Leader, my name is Cristoph Naragan. I represent a group of businessmen who would like to invest a great deal of money in your planet."

"I know who you are. We were warned that you were coming," Zamundi replied in a strangely high pitched voice, carrying a hint of sarcasm.

Naragan was startled by the warlord's revelation that his visit was not a surprise and wondered if the Galactic Council had gotten there ahead of him. Perhaps the Council had already made a deal with Zamundi, in which case, he'd never leave this planet alive. He took a chance and continued.

"Well then, Great leader, you have been the victim of lies, deceit and manipulation."

"That's what the other ones said about you!" Zamundi replied laughing and was then joined by the others in the assembly hall.

Naragan swallowed hard and tried to maintain his calm demeanor. The goddamned Kelemites had gotten there ahead of the Guild!

Naragan began to laugh himself, using every ounce of thespian knowhow in his salesman's bag of tricks. He had to appear as if he was highly amused, even though his laughter could be interpreted as an insult to the 'Great Leader', thereby risking imminent death.

Zamundi's men stopped laughing the instant Naragan began to laugh and their expressions revealed that indeed Naragan's attempt at humor might backfire on him, but he continued laughing anyway. He knew that he had to outthink these barbarians if he was to survive and make his deal.

"You think this is funny foreigner?" Zamundi said, in a threatening tone.

"Forgive me Great Leader!" Naragan answered, looking as if he was having a hard time hiding his amusement. "I was told that you were a man of great intellect and wisdom. I find it difficult to believe that those snakes from the Galactic Council were able to deceive you so easily!"

Zamundi's guards and the militiamen that had brought Naragan to this place, suddenly cocked their weapons and aimed them at him. He shook his head as if in disbelief and forged ahead in spite of the fact that he was terrified.

Zamundi reached into the folds of the large robe that covered his immense body and produced two bone-white human skulls that he held in one of his beefy hands. "These are the skulls of the two infidels that, like you, tried to; ... how was it you put it? Ah yes! To deceive me so easily!" he concluded, with a twisted smile.

Zamundi's use of the term 'infidels' signaled to Naragan that the Wamchas, and perhaps many of the people in Ibira III, were much more religious than the Secundo Vita sociologists had believed. Perhaps one of the skulls belonged to a representative or a cleric from the Church of St. Kelem. If this was the case, Naragan's hope for success suddenly improved! He knew how arrogant and insensitive to native cultures many of the Kelemite missionaries were. Changing his demeanor to that of a penitent man, Naragan threw himself on his knees bowing respectfully, hoping that his next move would prove to be the right one.

"Forgive me Great Leader, I was wrong in assuming that your wisdom was lacking! I now realize that you and your people are very devout and trustworthy. I can assure you that the people that I work for are not in any way interested in converting your great nation to a new religion."

Zamundi put the skulls back into his robe and leaned back, rubbing his chin pensively. He made a subtle gesture with his left hand and one of the militiamen grabbed Naragan by his right armpit and lifted him to his feet brusquely. At that moment, he wondered if he was about to be executed, but the man simply pushed him forward and motioned for him to approach the stage. Slowly, and as respectfully as he could, he walked forward, head bent down until Zamundi stopped him a couple of meters from the stage.

"That's close enough foreigner!" the warlord said, sternly.

Naragan froze where he stood and a militiaman brought a chair and placed it behind him, while a second one pushed him down into it. Though he was still being treated roughly, he knew that he had, at least, bought some time for himself. Now all his training in the psychology of primitive cultures and the fine art of negotiating treaties with warlords, tyrants and madmen, came into play.

From his new position near the stage, Naragan had to crane his neck up to look at the corpulent form of Chasson Zamundi and realized that he'd been given an audience with the authoritarian dictator of Ibira III. The setup was meant to intimidate and impress the individual sitting down on the orchestra floor. From Naragan's point of view, the spectacle of Zamundi's leviathan mass, sitting atop the large throne, lit dramatically from above, did indeed look quite intimidating.

"Tell me why I should listen to your business proposal and why I shouldn't add your skull to my collection," Zamundi demanded, pointing to the many skulls decorating his throne.

"As far as my skull is concerned, I'm very fond of it and I wish to remain attached to it for a very long time," Naragan replied.

Zamundi and the men laughed at his joke and had the effect that he'd hoped for.

"What my employers are offering is the opportunity for you to gain complete control of the planet. That means all of your enemies' territories and resources."

"That's exactly what the man from the Galactic Council and the priestess offered me," Zamundi argued dismissively.

"I'm sure they did, but their offer came with a price didn't it? And that price was religious conversion. And am I right in assuming that their skulls are in your possession because they insulted you by demanding that you and your entire population convert to their religion in exchange for their . . ., so called, help?"

Zamundi leaned forward and looked at Naragan with distrust in his dark eyes. "You have the tongue of a clever merchant who is trying to sell his wares for profit. What's to prevent your people from giving me the appearance of power for a period of time and then taking over? And what is it that your employer wants from us for their . . . ., so called, help?"

Naragan was impressed with Zamundi's insightful question. Inside that giant blob of a man lay the intellect of a discerning politician. He'd have to up his game with this one.

"First of all, we're not interested in conquest. We are not a political or patriotic organization. We're a business conglomerate interested only in profit. And although we can provide you with powerful weapons and military technology, we ourselves do not use them and have no standing military forces, save for a small cadre of guards that protect our headquarters. Second, the only thing that we want from you is the license to operate business establishments on your planet and your guarantee that you will provide us with security and protect us from the Galactic Council and the Kelemite Church."

"The Kelemite priestess claimed that your businesses deal with the corruption of the human body and that you perform wicked and immoral procedures on people."

Cristoph Naragan lowered his head and shook it, demonstrating his incredulity of the Kelemite Church's accusations. At the same time, he was bidding for time, trying to come up with a safe, non-descript explanation of what Secundo Vita's main business was, the re-incarnation of people's consciousness into manufactured bodies. Unfortunately, the company's sociologists had not been able to fully investigate the Hansurak religion and ascertain what their taboos were.

"Tell me Great Leader, did the Kelemite priestess tell you what the Church of St. Kelem's main source of income is?"

"No. Like you, they offered me wealth and power, but I stopped listening to her the moment that she demanded that we all convert to her religion."

"Well, the Church owns a galaxy wide business called The Realm. The Realm specializes in putting people's minds into a box. In other words, after you die, everything that you know, think, remember or have ever experienced will remain trapped in a magic box for all time."

Zamundi and his men laughed at the very idea that a person's consciousness could be put inside a box. "You are indeed a merchant trying to sell worthless trinkets at the market!" Zamundi said, amidst fits of laughter that made the fat layers in his body jiggle like blubber.

Naragan laughed along with the rest for effect. "Yes it does sound preposterous! I myself had the same reaction when I first heard of this. But I swear to you Great Leader, that everything I am telling you is true. The Kelemites made a pact with the Devil and learned this magic from him."

The room fell silent and Naragan wondered if he'd made a *faux pas* by mentioning the Devil as an accomplice of the Kelemites. Perhaps in the Hansurak religion, the Devil had a sacred connotation.

"You have proof of this white man? How do I know that it isn't you and your people that are in league with Satan?" Zamundi demanded, raising his voice.

"I can't prove that it isn't so without taking you off planet and letting you see this evil with your own eyes. The Kelemites promise immortality with this witchery and enough people in the galaxy have believed it and paid huge sums of money in the hopes of living forever. This is how the Church of St. Kelem has grown so rich and powerful. They've been at it for millennia. As a matter of fact, the Kelemite Crusades are the main reason why your planet and your people are so isolated from the rest of the Galaxy and why you have to rely on pirates and questionable merchants for many of your goods."

"Your tongue is sleek and yet, I'm not convinced. You still haven't explained what your employer's business is," Zamundi demanded, staring Naragan down with his fierce dark eyes.

"It's simple. The guild that I work for represents a large conglomerate of medical technology companies that specialize in prolonging life. We do not offer immortality as the Kelemites do, but we are able to extend a person's life by about fifty to eighty solar years."

"Hah! It sounds very similar to what you say the Kelemites offer!" the fat man argued.

"Only in that we can give our clients a longer life, though it is by no means immortality! We do this by means of science. Say for example, that a child or perhaps one of your warriors loses a leg during a battle. What happens to the child or the man afterwards?" Naragan asked, hoping to hear a certain answer. Certain primitive cultures tended to discard those with handicaps.

"If the child survives the loss of a leg and if it's a female, she can go on to marry and bear children. If it's a boy, he'll do women's work for the rest of his life. If it's a man who can't fight any longer, he commits Shalmeru."

Naragan nodded. He understood that Shalmeru was the name for ritual suicide.

"What if that child or man could be given a brand new leg? And by that I don't mean a wooden leg or an artificial limb. I mean a real honest to goodness leg, grown from the very tissues of that person's own body?"

"That's impossible! It still sounds like the Devil's work to me!" Zamundi argued.

"No sir!" Naragan replied forcefully, neglecting to use Zamundi's title for the first time. "I can demonstrate this technology to you. It is done by means of machines made by men made of flesh and blood like you and me, not by witchery."

Zamundi leaned back against his ornate throne and rubbed his chin once again. He was weighing the foreigner's proposal with great care. If somehow this salesman's words were truthful, having the ability to repair his warrior's bodies was an advantage that could indeed, give him absolute control of Ibira III.

"Supposing I believed you, how could you demonstrate this ability? I certainly will not ask any of my people to chop off a leg or an arm to test your theory," Zamundi replied as a challenge.

Naragan, gulped slightly. Although in the past he had successfully proven to other prospective clients that a man could indeed grow a new limb by cutting one of his own, he was not looking forward to doing it again. The experience was harrowing and even though his right arm had been replaced with an identical twin, and nowadays one could not see the line of demarcation between the original and the copy, he dreaded the prospect. But, he was Cristoph Naragan 'the legend'. In his twenty year career as Secundo Vita's top salesman, he'd never failed to close a deal yet!

Naragan took a deep breath. "I will prove it to you, by having my left arm cut off. I'm even willing to have one of your warriors do it!"

Zamundi leaned forward, looking surprised as well as his men, who suddenly regarded Naragan with great respect.

"You will do this here, in front of our eyes?" Zamundi asked, sounding incredulous.

"Yes, but I must first radio my ship and have four technicians and some equipment brought down," Naragan replied, having already accepted the ordeal he was about to endure. "And unlike myself, who landed at the edge of the city, my men will have to land on the plaza in front of this building because the equipment needed is too large and heavy to carry such a long distance."

"You are indeed a merchant and not a religious zealot! Only a money-lover would go to such lengths to make a sale! Zamundi exclaimed, shaking his head with a mixture of amazement and disdain in his voice.

Naragan squeezed his left ear lobe. "Thermopolis, this is Naragan. Send down a limb recovery team ASAP. Touch down in the main plaza of the city as close to the central fountain as you can."

"Are you alright boss?" came the reply from Thermopolis, the company's ship in orbit above the planet.

"I'm fine. Just bring down the team and have everyone ready to spend a week, planet side."

"Come again?" the com officer asked, surprised by Naragan's request.

"Just do what I said Thermopolis, Naragan out." Naragan turned to Zamundi, "I will have to remain in this place until my new arm grows back. May I set up a bed here in the middle of the isle? I have to remain attached to the machines for seven to ten days."

Zamundi simply nodded.

The limb recovery team, consisting of three men and a woman, landed an hour later and set up their equipment in the middle of the assembly hall, surrounded by the many curious guards and militiamen of the Wamcha tribe. The men had never seen such advanced electronic equipment, but they were just as fascinated by the single female member of the team. Naragan worried that Zamundi or one of his men might take a fancy to the female medical tech, but fortunately the subject never came up.

The word got around that the foreigner that had come to their city was about to have one of his arms chopped. So, by the time Naragan and his team had everything ready, the assembly hall was filled to capacity.

Naragan sat on the same chair that he had used to talk to Zamundi with his left arm resting on what looked like a butcher's block table. The thing smelled foul and there were unwashed blood stains on it. Naragan steeled himself for what was coming, hoping that whatever bacteria were on the disgusting table would not end up killing him in the end.

One of Zamundi's guards, a large warrior with muscles to spare, held a large broad axe in his hands. The man was smiling at Naragan, obviously looking forward to doing his job. The blade's metal was shiny and looked very sharp which Naragan thought a blessing. Better to suffer a clean cut from a sharp weapon than a blunt one which would end up causing more damage to bone and tissue.

One of the limb recovery team members brought a roll of gauze and put it in Naragan's mouth. He bit down on it, and with sweat pouring down his brow, he nodded at the Wamcha warrior and held his breath. The man lifted the axe high above his head as the crowd roared with excitement. Naragan closed his eyes.

The axe came down and cut off his arm cleanly just below the shoulder with one quick motion. Naragan screamed in agony as blood spurted on the butcher's table. The crowd roared with approval and applauded. The medical team rushed in and quickly stopped the bleeding. One of them gave Naragan a fast acting anesthetic rendering him unconscious immediately and attached a tube-like device at the end of the stump. They laid him down on a med-bed and began the procedure of growing a new left arm.

The crowd soon dispersed looking somewhat dissapointed by the lack of gore. Many had hoped to see the straw haired stranger suffer in pain for a while. As the place began emptying, an old woman came by the butcher's table, grabbed Naragan's newly disconnected limb and carried it out like a trophy.

A week later, Chasson Zamundi signed the contract giving Secundo Vita unlimited rights to conduct business on Ibira III. As the shuttle carrying Cristoph Naragan back to the company's mother ship began lifting from the village plaza, the best salesman in Secundo Vita smiled as he unconsciously rubbed his newly grown left arm.

He turned to the pilot smiling. "These primitives won't know what hit them when we take over their stinking planet!"

GALACTIC YEAR 10,023

CHAPTER 2

The Novice Allondra Velmador

Cardinal Matuch Richelieux gazed out of the passenger window of the winged chariot taking him to the Heavenly Temple of the Kelemite Church. The giant spherical structure, floating above New Jerusalem, was gleaming brightly in the vacuum of space. Illuminated by the sun of the Tal system, the temple's white spires and gold decorations reflected the sun's light in shades of pink and purple, giving the station the appearance of a finely crafted jewel. Inside, thousands of Kelemite nuns, priests and church employees worked day and night managing the largest religious organization in the galaxy.

He'd come here many times before, but the Holy See never failed to impress and inspire him. This time however, his appreciation of the grandeur and beauty of the physical and spiritual center of the Kelemite Church was diminished by the nature of the financial report he was bringing to the Matriarch.

The church had been steadily losing income over the last few decades due to the many 'body shops' that had become direct competitors with the church in the 'immortality trade', the church's main source of income. The Realm, a galaxy wide corporation that offered life after death by downloading an individual's consciousness into a realistic virtual environment, was suffering huge losses.

The company provided a continuing life after death experience by downloading an individual's soul into a gigantic net of super holographic quantum computers known collectively and individually as the CUBE. The body shops instead, transferred an individual's life long memories, consciousness and personality into a genetically lab-grown body guaranteed to last more than a century, all, at a very competitive price.

The 'after life' experience within the CUBE was a close facsimile to the real thing, but in spite of its sophisticated technology, it had its limitations. By contrast, the experience of continuing life in a genetically lab-grown body was indistinguishable from the previous mode of existence. In addition to this important difference, some clients chose different bodies than their original ones or asked for gender re-assignment and continued their lives as members of the opposite sex, which the Kelemite Church deemed a sin against nature.

Declared a heretical abomination by the previous Matriarch a century earlier, the Church of St. Kelem had persuaded the governments of the many planets under its influence to expel body shop businesses from their worlds. But the industry organized itself by creating a powerful guild and quickly established business on planets that were not part of the Galactic Council and therefore, free from the Church's powerful reach.

For the first time in millennia, The Realm was experiencing diminishing profits, which meant that the Kelemite Church's influence and power was slowly and steadily eroding.

The winged chariot approaching the Heavenly Temple fired its retros and let the gravitational field of the moon-sized sphere pull it toward the entrance of one of its cavernous hangars. Once inside, the ship, designed to look like a golden bird, folded its gilded wings and settled gently on the hangar's deck.

Richelieux, tall, thin, with long braided black hair, showing a few wisps of grey around his temples, closed the upper buttons of his vermillion cassock, picked up his small carry-on luggage and exited the craft. As he stepped off the winged chariot's metal plank, a young Tarsian novice nun, dressed in a white habit, was waiting for him.

"Welcome Monsignor Richelieux, you bless us with your presence," the green skinned nun declared, bowing respectfully.

"Thank you Sister Allondra," the Cardinal replied, quickly reading the young nun's name tag. "I assume that I'll be staying in Seventh Heaven?"

"Of course, your Eminence, you are *primus sacerdos'* (prime priest)," she replied, as they headed toward the elevators, making their way through the many splendidly ornamented winged chariots parked in the hangar's deck.

At thirty five years of age, Cardinal Matuch Richelieux, was the youngest cleric, or male, for that matter, to achieve the rank of cardinal in the Church's history. He would have preferred to stay in one of the simpler lower level apartments in the Heavenly Temple, but now that he was *primus sacerdos'*, church protocol dictated that he'd be billeted at Seventh heaven, the most luxurious deck in the Heavenly Temple, reserved for senior clergy of the Church of St. Kelem.

Upper rank male clerics were rare within the church, and Richelieux's meteoric rise to "Cardinal Counselor to the Matriarch" had garnered him many enemies in the Kelemite Curia. Many of those enemies were the oldest female Cardinals, who resented him, for both being male and having reached the highest possible status within the Church (except for the Matriarch herself), at such a young age. In addition, Richelieux's disregard for the pomp and circumstance of his position, further enraged his opponents. Many believed that his humility and openness to those below him, was pure political subterfuge.

Matuch Richelieux could never become head of the Kelemite Church, for that position had been traditionally held by a female Matriarch since the Church's beginnings in the Second Millennium. But that fact did little to diminish the resentment and enmity of the senior cardinals.

As the elevator began climbing toward the living quarters' deck, the novice spoke. "The Matriarch's secretary, Bishop Kalduwan, has arranged for a visit to the Temple's spa, should you desire it."

"Thank the bishop for me, but I've had a very long journey and wish to retire for the evening, though I would like to visit St. Ornata's chapel and spend a few minutes of quiet meditation before going to my quarters."

"Ah yes! I often go to Mother Ornata's chapel myself. Local time is 12:30 AM, so the sanctuary should be very quiet right now," the Tarsian novice commented, walking up to the panel and changing the elevator's floor stop.

Richelieux glanced briefly at the young nun, wondering if she was the proxy of one of the female cardinals who considered him unworthy. Young novices were not supposed to make personal statements unless asked. He wondered if this novice nun was pushing the boundaries of church etiquette in order to draw him out, hoping that he'd say something inappropriate. He studied her and noticed her youth. The Tarsian couldn't have been more than eighteen years old. Sister Allondra was rather tall for a Tarsian and the upward obliqueness of her green eyes was very slight, giving her face an almost human quality.

"If I remember correctly, the chapel is on level 23, right?" he asked, looking at her from the corner of his eye.

"Yes, your Eminence,' the girl said demurely.

"Tell me Allondra, what brought you to the church?" the cardinal suddenly asked, watching her intently. Something about this young novice intrigued him.

The girl blinked and couldn't help but show her surprise at Richelieux's question. She hesitated for a moment. "I grew up on Tarsia Prime. Both my older sisters entered the order before me. Many in my family have served the church in the past. There was never a question in my mind as to what I would do with my life."

"So, service to the church is a tradition in your family?"

"Yes your Eminence, dating back to the beginning of the tenth millennium," she answered nervously. Perhaps the Cardinal was testing her faith.

"Ah, here we are," Richelieux announced, as the elevator doors opened to the 23rd level.

The cardinal exited first and turned left heading for the chapel. She followed him and would wait outside until the Cardinal finished his prayers.

When they reached the chapel the cardinal opened the pressure door and then unexpectedly, waited by the threshold. "Well? Aren't you coming in?" he asked her.

The request shocked her. Church protocol dictated that a senior cardinal's private meditation be exactly that; private. Allondra hesitated for a fraction of a second and entered the chapel after him. Richelieux put his bag down by the door and walked up to the holographic statue of Sister Ornata Rogeston, the first Mother of the Church of St. Kelem. He knelt down, and then placed his head and hands on the floor in front of him. In the rear of the chapel, Allondra was debating whether she should go up to the saint's statue and perform her greeting now, or wait for the Cardinal to get up and then do it. To her relief, the Cardinal got up and motioned for her to pay her respects. She rushed to the statue and knelt down quickly.

When she got up, she noticed that the Cardinal was already sitting in the first row of pews to the left, facing the chapel's altar. She started walking toward the pews on the right, when Richelieux motioned with his hand for her to sit by him.

Kelemite novices were not allowed to sit in the same section of a sanctuary as ordained nuns, priests or any other superior rank of clergy. This man was the second most powerful cleric in the church and here she was, about to sit next to him in prayer. With her legs shaking, she walked up to the pew and sat down next to Richelieux.

Afraid to meet the Cardinal's eyes, Allondra stared at the lifelike statue of Sister Ornata as a young woman. The founder of the church stood at the front of the altar with a beatific smile on her lips, looking straight ahead. Her red hair was encircled by a pulsing, shimmering halo and her maroon habit glowed brightly under the light fixture above her.

The Cardinal looked at her for a few seconds and then smiled. "Don't be nervous Allondra, in Sister Ornata's eyes we're all equal."

Surprised once again by Richelieux's casual manner, the young novice could only nod respectfully in his direction.

He closed his eyes and began to meditate. Young Allondra Velmador, one of the youngest novices currently residing in the Heavenly Temple, closed her eyes and prayed with all her might that she could enter Samadhi and connect with the Universal Mind God. For a few desperate seconds, she tried to empty her mind of thought, but her intellect kept distracting her with the knowledge of who she was sitting next to. But her faith was true and powerful and eventually, her eyes rolled upwards and she went into a deep meditation.

Sometime later, a gentle tap on her left shoulder brought her out of Samadhi and she felt somewhat embarrassed that she might have lingered in meditation for too long.

"I'm sorry your Eminence! I didn't mean to delay you in any way!" she apologized to Richelieux and then jumped up and straightened her habit.

The Cardinal laughed softly and shook his head. "Not at all, we've only been here about twenty minutes. At first I could hear you heart racing and wondered if your mind would keep you from entering Samadhi, but you quieted the Beast and eventually went in quite deep."

"I'm . . . I'm sorry your Eminence, I didn't mean to . . .," she stuttered nervously, feeling that she had revealed herself to be unworthy of ordainment. She had heard rumors that some of the older members of the Curia were able to hear people's heart beats at a distance and know if an individual was really in Samadhi or not. The Cardinal Counselor to the Matriarch had just informed her that he could indeed hear her heartbeat without touching her.

"Sit down Allondra," he said patting the space next to him. She obliged and sat down again, feeling vulnerable and somewhat intimidated.

"I have to confess something," he continued. "I was testing you before, when I asked you what brought you to the church. I wanted to know if your heart was that of a faithful Kelemite, and after praying next to you, I knew that you were a true believer. Your faith is quite strong for someone your age."

Allondra nodded, feeling relieved that Richelieux had tested her and that she had passed the test. At the same time, she wondered why the second in command of the Kelemite Church would care so much about a low rank novice's faith in the first place.

As if he had heard her thought, he answered her question. "I'm sure that you're unaware that although Kelemite nuns and priests are good people, some of us fall prey to the temptations of politics and other human foibles. A male cardinal in my position is not without detractors and there are those within the church that wouldn't mind seeing me fail at my job. Do you understand?"

"I'm not sure I understand your Eminence, but I would never do anything to harm you in any way!" Allondra protested, feeling somewhat offended by Richelieux's statement.

"I know that now. But I had to make sure that you weren't assigned to escort me in order to inform on me to one of the cardinals in the Curia. Such things do go on sometimes."

"I . . I don't know what to say!" the young novice replied, stunned by the knowledge that members of the church could be capable of spying on one another.

"I can see that you're shocked to learn that deception and subterfuge are part of the Church's culture, but as in any endeavor that involves sentient beings, especially humanoids, there's bound to be jealousy and competitiveness. But, as I said before, most of us are good people, just trying to live our lives in faithful service to the church."

Allondra nodded quietly, trying to assimilate the Cardinal's revelation. Her concept of the church's hierarchy had been changed, suddenly exposing her to the weaknesses of the adult world. She felt confused and wondered what it all meant. She was a sophisticated youngster, and knew that Cardinal Richelieux's conversation with her was out of the ordinary. She would pray to Sister Ornata for clarity and meaning in the days to come.

"Come, let us pay our respects to the first Mother and be on our way," Richelieux suggested, getting up.

This time Allondra did not hesitate to follow the Cardinal and prostrate herself next to him by Sister Ornata's statue. They rose together and walked out of the chapel.

A few minutes later, after escorting the Cardinal to his suite on the Seventh Heaven deck, sister Allondra headed for the novice's quarters sixty five levels below. In the elevator on the way down, the young nun knew that she would have a hard time going to sleep tonight.

CHAPTER 3

The Kelemite Curia

At the north pole of the Heavenly Temple sat The Garden of Eden, the most beautiful manicured gardens in the entire galaxy. Encompassing twenty hectares covered by a gigantic plastic bubble, the grounds were a tribute to the technical and artistic talents of humanoids. Though the design was highly reminiscent of famous gardens from Terra Prime, humanity's birthplace, other species, such as Nevarans, Tarsians, Gulax and the Dolmeki, had also contributed to the beauty and diversity of the garden.

The Garden of Eden was actually several gardens, one hundred and eighty to be precise. Each was as wondrous and exquisite as the next. But the central garden, the one where the Matriarch's palace was located, was the most awe inspiring and majestic of all.

Sitting in the middle of the bowl-shaped valley atop Mount Sinai, the highest elevation in the garden, was the Holy Residence, a palatial structure built out of green marble from Tarsia Prime. Surrounded by green rolling hills covered with the most exotic and beautiful plant life from planets belonging to the Galactic Council, the Holy Residence stood above the land, its towers, ramparts and promenades shining brightly in the sunlight of the Tal system.

Though the sun gave its chlorophyll based plant life the right environment for photosynthesis. Water flowed from the top of Mount Sinai from several artificial waterfalls that turned into rivers that meandered through the gardens. When the rivers' waters reached the edge of the valley, a network of powerful pumps recycled the water back to Mount Sinai.

Considered one of the most beautiful wonders of the galaxy, The Garden of Eden was a popular tourist attraction that drew millions of pilgrims and tourists every year. The fees collected from the many visitors that flocked to the artificial moon, along with profits from the food and entertainment franchises and hotels located on the lower levels of The Heavenly Temple, were a considerable part of the Church's income.

It was this crass commercialism that irked Cardinal Richelieux the most. Although a faithful devotee of St. Kelem, Richelieux wished that the church would follow its own doctrine of humility and modesty, instead of having its leaders live in such extravagant luxury, while profiting from this place as well. But he learned early on in his career, that his views were considered radical and unpopular. He had long ceased to voice his concerns, knowing that it only made his job more difficult.

As he ascended to the roof of the Holy Residence in a public elevator accompanied by nuns, priests and church employees on their way to attend the weekly Curia meeting, he kept his thoughts to himself. Now more than ever, with the church's finances in peril, his opinions of the church's commercialism would be even more out of step than usual with the majority of the cardinals.

The elevator's door opened to the bright morning sunlight on the residence's roof. From here, one could see the entire valley 360 degrees. He was greeted by Bishop Kalduwan, the Matriarch's personal secretary. Kalduwan was in her forties, a native of Centralia, the Galaxy Council's home world. She came from a wealthy family and was well connected with the Council. Richelieux suspected that the woman was one of his detractors, though she always treated him with apparent grace and respect.

"Welcome your Eminence. The Matriarch is anxious to meet with you in private right after the Curia. She asks however, that you sit next to her during the meeting," Kalduwan informed him.

Richelieux knew that when the Matriarch 'asked' for something, it was meant as an order. He always avoided attending the Curia, but this time he had no choice but to be there.

"Of course Bishop," Richelieux answered politely.

"Brother Mathias here," Kalduwan said, pointing to a young male priest that appeared by Richelieux's left shoulder as they walked along, "has a list of the subjects covered in todays' meeting."

Richelieux nodded at the young man, who bowed politely at him.

"I leave you in Brother Mathias' capable hands. I have to supervise the Curia's lunch break. Enjoy your stay Cardinal," Kalduwan said, bowing slightly as she walked away.

Brother Mathias pressed a button on his cassock and a list of subjects appeared in Richelieux's ocular implant. The list was the usual collection of mundane matters that the Curia dealt with, mostly having to do with the management of various parishes throughout the galaxy and the usual litany of requests and complaints from bishops and monsignors.

"Do you have it, your Eminence?" the young priest asked, referring to the list.

"Yes Brother Mathias, thank you."

"If you will follow me your Eminence, I will escort you to the Matriarch."

The two men walked together and stepped onto one of the many people movers in the palace's roof. As they glided gently on their way to the Curia's amphitheater located at the center of the palace's top level, many nodded to him politely as they passed him by on the opposite moving platforms. Richelieux nodded ever so slightly at as many nuns as priests as he could, knowing by experience that one could very quickly get a sore neck repeating this motion over and over. He was thankful when they reached the Matriarchs' private entrance at the amphitheater. From now on, one only bowed to the Matriarch once, while at the meeting.

Brother Mathias led him through the tunnel that led directly behind the Matriarch's throne. When they came out to daylight once again, the young priest waved goodbye and Richelieux proceeded to walk around the throne and make himself present.

As he came into view of the entire Curia, the eyes of three hundred and seventy-five cardinals focused on him as he stepped in front of the Matriarch and bowed respectfully in front of her. In the upper seats of the amphitheater, the lower echelon nuns and priests could be heard whispering to each other in response to his appearance.

"It is good to see you again, Cardinal Counselor. Please sit at my right side and be my light in the dark," Matriarch Vasilia Bentara Rogeston said with a smile on her lips. All Matriarchs of the Church of St. Kelem took on the Rogeston surname once they ascended to the position. Vasilia Bentara was a female human in her early forties who looked much younger than her age. She was an attractive woman who had the looks and beauty of a famous actress or performer. Although she'd been born a brunette, by tradition, all matriarchs had their hair color genetically altered to auburn red in honor of Sister Ornata Rogeston, the Church's first matriarch.

Richelieux nodded and sat on the throne to the Matriarch's right. On the opposite side was an empty throne, that of St. Kelem himself, who always sat to the left of the Church's mother, in spirit.

Matriarch Vasilia turned to Richelieux and squeezed his left hand affectionately. Richelieux smiled at her and nodded once more, feeling a rush of emotion course through him. Physical touch from the Matriarch was considered a blessing from high above and in his case, it legitimatized his position in the eyes of the Curia. The Matriarch was aware of Richelieux's detractors and she always took the opportunity to show her affection and trust in the man.

The meeting went on for another mind bending five hours until, thankfully, lunch was called and the entire Curia went down one level below the amphitheater to the common hall, where the food was served. The Matriarch recited a prayer of thanks for the food they were about to receive and afterwards, all sat down to eat the midday meal.

Surrounded by senior cardinals at the table, Richelieux and the Matriarch only exchanged polite conversation during the meal, knowing well, that it was best to keep their business private. After dessert, the Matriarch once again, recited another prayer of thanks and Richelieux and the Matriarch were escorted to her private quarters. The Curia would continue for another five hours, but thankfully, the Matriarch only attended the morning session. Bishop Kalduwan escorted them to the Matriarch's private residence and after having tea and aperitifs served in the residence's main salon, the two top leaders of the Church of St. Kelem were finally left alone.

Matriarch Vasilia waited until the door closed behind Bishop Kalduwan, promptly took her top hassock off, and walked over to a wet bar near the center of the room.

Wearing her long white undergarment only and smiling like a school girl who just got away with doing something naughty, she looked at Richelieux with an expression of relief.

"Thank the Saint that we can relax for a while! Will you join me in an aperitif Cardinal?"

Richelieux nodded and accepted a small goblet of Cointreau from the Matriarch. The two sat in silence for a while enjoying the sweet fire from the liqueur.

"Alright Richelieux, let's have it, I know you don't have good news."

"I'm sorry your Holiness, I wish that it weren't so, but you're right. The body shops are springing up everywhere the Council doesn't have authority. As a result, The Realm's numbers will be affected severely this next quarter."

The Matriarch stood up and began pacing back and forth. "How do we stop this Matuch? My legacy will be that of the Matriarch that led the Church to ruin!"

The Heavenly Temple's rotation was moving toward late afternoon, and the sun's rays were now streaming through the salon's large windows. The light passed through the church leader's undergarment revealing her feminine shape.

Richelieux looked at Vasilia Bentara's female form and smiled inwardly, not in a perverted way but in recognition of the fact that like him, she was just a young human who had ascended to the leadership of the largest religious organization in the galaxy at a very young age. He knew the pressure that she was under and sympathized with her plight.

"Your Holiness, the Church has had its bad periods before and no one blamed those matriarchs for the Church's history during their reigns."

"Don't sugar coat this Cardinal!" the Matriarch countered with frustration. "This situation is nothing like the Church has ever encountered before. The Galactic Council's Revenue Office is not going away and The Realm's corporate taxes have to be paid on time every quarter. We're bleeding Kredits like never before and unless something's done soon, we're going to have to start closing facilities in large numbers. The Realm's board of directors is threatening to fire Hubert Longsdale, the company's CEO and you know what that means don't you?" the Matriarch exclaimed, looking at Richelieux with angst.

"You think that the board would make a deal with the Body Shop Guild?" Richelieux asked, surprised that the Papissa of the Church of St. Kelem would project such a dire consequence to the current problem.

"Why not? They are all capitalists first and foremost. What's to keep the board from changing allegiances once they see that the Church's power is unable to protect their interests?"

"Your Holiness, I've spoken to the board of directors, and it's true that they're worried about The Realm's future. But we're a long way from having Hubert Longsdale fired from the company and the board deciding to go into the body shop business!"

"Aaagh!" the Matriarch uttered, as she sank back into one of the large sofas. She tossed her long hair around, momentarily covering her entire head with her red mane. She sat there for a while, the image of frustration personified.

"Tell me something good, wise Richelieux. Tell me that you know of a way to fix this!" she said from behind her hair.

Richelieux looked down at the ornate Oriental rug at his feet and pondered whether he should speak frankly. He knew his answer would be considered heresy by the church, but his affection for the Matriarch was such that he decided to risk it.

"A long time ago on Earth, the Christian churches only elected males as their leaders. But after the Dark Period of the 22nd century things changed. As a result you are now the beneficiary of the actions taken by those with courage and vision who advanced the history of human religion."

Matriarch Vasilia lifted her head and looked at Richelieux with curiosity. "You're intimating that the Church of St. Kelem should change its long standing edict that the body shops are a sin against nature?"

"Once, a female pope would have caused a schism in the Christian Church," Richelieux replied quietly.

"You're treading on dangerous ground Cardinal!" The Matriarch cautioned, turning away and looking at the darkening landscape of The Garden of Eden through the large windows of the salon.

"You chose me as Cardinal Counselor to the Matriarch because you knew that I would always be honest with you no matter what the cost. You may demote me or expel me from the church madam, but at least you know that I'll never veer from the truth. And right now your Holiness, you need people around you who will always tell you the truth, no matter how painful or distasteful it might be!"

"You're right Matuch. I picked you as my Counselor because of your reputation for honesty. But what you're proposing could be considered heresy. A reformation of Kelemite law would certainly cause a schism in the Church and most likely destroy it from the inside out. Please never mention this subject again."

Matriarch Vasilia returned to the center of the room and sat next to him. "Have you spoken again to the techs at the company about improving the after-life experience inside The Realm?"

"Yes, your Holiness, and as they've stated many times before, quantum holographic computers have reached their maximum capability. Unless a new more advanced memory and processing hardware is developed, the CUBE is the best technology available at present."

"I pray to St. Kelem and Sister Ornata every night that they may shine their blessing upon us in this time of need Matuch. Tonight I shall spend more time in Samadhi, perhaps I haven't gone deep enough to reach their heavenly souls," the Matriarch whispered in a soft voice.

"I will double my efforts as well your Holiness. Perhaps together we might reach their spirits and receive their blessing," Richelieux offered, holding the Matriarch's right hand.

She smiled at him and seemed to regain her youthful upbeat personality for a moment, but Richelieux could tell that she was putting on a brave front.

"You have had a long day and should retire soon your Holiness. I've taken too much of your time and you need your rest to deal with tomorrow's challenges. With your permission, I shall leave and continue my search for an answer to our problem."

"Thank you Matuch, Cardinal Counselor to the Matriarch," the Matriarch replied, smiling back at him, grateful for his honesty and support. "I have had a long day as you said and I will turn in soon. Will you have breakfast with me tomorrow morning before you depart for Centralia?"

"Absolutely your Holiness. Nothing would please me more!"

"I shall tell Bishop Kalduwan to have my cook make some of those blueberry muffins that you love so much!"

"That will be excellent! Perhaps your cook can make a few extra muffins for me to take with me on my voyage home?"

The Matriarch smiled genuinely this time, cheered by Richelieux's humor. "I will have him make two dozen. Will that be enough to keep you company on your voyage?" she replied with a smirk.

"Hmmm, two days travel and two dozen muffins. . . . that sounds about right!" he answered, smiling back at the Matriarch, happy to see her feeling better.

"Very well your Eminence. I shall see you early tomorrow morning," she said smiling.

She hugged the cardinal and exited the salon. Richelieux left the Matriarch's residence and descended to the Seventh Heaven level soon after. On the way down to his quarters, he fell into a slight depression as he thought of the huge difficulties facing the Church of St. Kelem. Then his mood worsened when he remembered that the Kelemite Crusades of the Fourth Millennium were partially a result of financial pressures on the Church.

CHAPTER 4

Ogram Zepol

A single-passenger orbital taxi disengaged itself from the Terran cruiser Apollo and plummeted down toward Plantanimus. Inside, Ogram Zepol, a Terran computer systems specialist hired by The Realm to troubleshoot the company's quantum holographic computer known as the CUBE, leaned back on the passenger seat and gazed at the planet below.

The young Terran smiled as the east coast of Ranes, the largest continent on the planet, came into view. Plantanimus had a special meaning for him. He had read every book and article about the planet since childhood. He chuckled at the thought of The Realm hiring him of all people. Ogram Zepol was not only well known as one of the premiere computer scientists in the galaxy, but also as a self-described agnostic. He realized that the Church of St. Kelem had to be very desperate to allow The Realm to hire him as a consultant.

At age twenty three, Ogram Zepol had reached near cult-like status among his peers and the galaxy at large. Considered one of the three top computer scientists alive, the fair haired young man from Earth commanded astronomical fees for his technical advice. But this time however, he was more than happy to provide his services to The Realm for free.

The Kelemite church considered him *persona non grata*, and he thought that charging The Realm for his advice would only aggravate the situation. And here he was, about to land on Plantanimus, the legendary planet where Kelem Rogeston supposedly took his last breath. Eight millennia ago, Sister Ornata Rogeston had claimed that Kelem Rogeston was a divine messiah sent to Mars by God to liberate the Martian people. Nowadays, the man, now known only as St. Kelem, was considered as significant as Jesus Christ, Buddha and Mohamed. Though the Christian religion still held sway in many places in the galaxy, it was the Kelemite church that was the most powerful and popular. The Galactic Council, the ruling political power in the Milky Way, located in the planet Centralia, was practically a subsidiary of the Church of St. Kelem.

Plantanimus had once been the seat of the Kelemite Holy See. Though the religion had originated on Mars, the Church did not gain its true popularity until it relocated its headquarters to Plantanimus in the first half of the fourth millennium. It was from here that the church launched its holy crusades in 3896 and it was here also, that The Realm built its first CUBE, the first super computer that allowed the transfer of human consciousness into digital data.

All the CUBE computers were interconnected via quantum entanglement, so Ogram Zepol could have consulted at any of the hundreds of planets that housed CUBE computers for The Realm. But his presence at Centralia's or New Jerusalem's CUBE facilities would have caused a public relations nightmare for the Church. Plantanimus had long been forgotten as the former home of the Kelemite Holy See. The church knew that Ogram Zepol's presence here would not garner any attention.

The taxi fired its retros and the window shields closed. For the next few minutes, the small craft would be enveloped in a bubble of hot plasma created by the hull's friction against the planet's atmosphere. Soon, the windows reopened and Ogram Zepol could see the Eastern Plantanimus Sea approaching from below. Ranes was now to the orbital taxi's left, heading north and he knew that his destination would not be the planet's capital but somewhere on its north pole.

All of The Realm's CUBE computers were located in their respective planets' coldest regions or their north or south poles. The reason was simple. The company's galaxy-wide network of quantum holographic computers were gigantic structures measuring several square kilometers that were buried underground and whose circuits had to be maintained at the freezing temperature of absolute zero, (minus 273 degrees Celsius). The Realm's computers were built with super conducting conduits that operated at maximum efficiency only when the ambient temperature was at absolute zero, at which point its components offered no resistance to electricity. The Realm saved big on the gargantuan expense of keeping the giant machines cold by situating each CUBE in a cold region.

Ogram Zepol adjusted his clothes' settings to cold weather and prepared to land at The Realm's facility, now growing larger in the craft's front window as it descended. The term 'facility' however, was a misnomer. The area above the CUBE computer could really be considered a large megalopolis with huge skyscrapers, highways and living residences with a variety of businesses that catered to the many individuals who maintained the giant quantum machines that transferred consciousness into digital data. Each CUBE required a staff of thousands to operate and maintain it year round.

The taxi glided above the city-like scape and landed smoothly on the roof of a huge pyramid shaped building bearing the emblem of The Realm, a white infinity symbol ∞, surrounded by a bright yellow sun.

As the noise of the landing turbines wound down, a group of four men dressed in business attire approached the craft. Ogram Zepol looked out the window and was surprised to see Hubert Longsdale among them. It was at that moment that he realized how desperate the company had to be to, not only to have hired a publicly acknowledged agnostic as a consultant, but in addition, have the fabled CEO of The Realm meet that agnostic in person.

The taxi's door opened and Ogram Zepol stepped on the building's roof.

"Welcome Mr. Zepol, I hope you had a pleasant trip?" Hubert Longsdale said in a very mellow baritone.

"Yes I did Mr. Longsdale, thank you very much," replied the Terran.

"Please follow us Mr. Zepol. We'll take you directly to your quarters where you can relax and get a goodnight sleep before you start working tomorrow."

Ogram Zepol looked back at the tall, lanky dark haired Longsdale as he followed the quartet. "First of all, Mr. Longsdale, please call me Ogram, and second, I would like to get started right away if you don't mind. I have a very active mind and I never feel the need to 'relax'."

Hubert Longsdale smiled back. He was pleased by the Terran's no-nonsense approach. "Very well, Ogram, we'll take you directly to our control center where we will familiarize you with our system."

"Please don't take this as an insult or a disparagement of your technology and your staff, but I'm probably more familiar with the inner workings of the CUBE than most of your technicians," the Terran said, interrupting the CEO's words.

Hubert Longsdale shrugged and smiled inwardly. Everything that he had heard about Ogram Zepol's personality rang true. The young man had a reputation as an narcissistic, eccentric genius whose intellect and personality were known as sharp, acidic and to the point.

"This is Vardo McCallan," Longsdale said, pointing to the man on his right, a tall lanky human with grey hair and a long face with a sour expression. "He's our facility manager. You will be working closely with him during your consultation."

The Terran ignored the introduction and continued walking while looking straight ahead. "I hope you realize that I need all of your security codes, including your backups if you expect any results from my consult."

Longsdale and McCallan exchanged a look of great concern. Giving a stranger the company's security codes was tantamount to treason, in addition to the Church of St. Kelem considering the act a sacrilege.

"Ogram, you must realize that what you're asking is impossible. Surely you can perform your job without such extreme access to our security," Longsdale protested.

Ogram Zepol stopped walking and waited for the quartet to do the same. A few steps further they noticed he wasn't following.

"Mr. Longsdale, unless I have complete access to your system, I will not be able to help you fix whatever serious problem has forced your company to resort to contracting an agnostic. The Church of St. Kelem and The Realm must be in a desperate state to call on an individual like me for help. There are only two other individuals in the galaxy with skill sets like mine, but one is a Buddhist and the other is an atheist. So I suppose that an agnostic is the least offensive of the two. Either you accede to my demand or I'll turn around right now and go back to Earth and continue my practice."

Longsdale and McCallan looked distressed and nervous, their facial expressions almost bordering on panic. The other two men, who had remained silent all along, looked unhappy as well.

"Ogram, please, let me and the others take some time to think about your request. You must understand that we're constrained by the rules and regulations of our corporate charter, not to mention the wellbeing of all our stock holders who would scream holy hell if it was revealed that we gave an outsider free reign of our system!"

Ogram Zepol knew that 'taking some time to think about your request', meant that Longsdale and the others would have to ask the Church of St. Kelem for permission to allow him such unprecedented access to the company's security codes.

"I will give you until tomorrow at this time to either accept or deny my request. If the answer is no, I already have a return reservation on the Apollo bound for Earth, day after tomorrow."

Hubert Longsdale, looking ashen faced and fatigued, nodded silently and pointed the way to the building's interior. Once inside, he and McCallan excused themselves, surely to call on the Kelemite Holy See. Ogram Zepol was then escorted to his private suite by the two silent company men whose expressions couldn't hide their dislike for this pretentious unbeliever who dared ask for The Realm's security codes.

As soon as the door to his suite closed silently behind him, Ogram Zepol relaxed, took his outer tunic off and walked straight into the apartment's spa-room, and after undressing completely, proceeded to take a long dip in the whirlpool tub.

Later that night as he laid in the large king size bed in the apartment's bedroom staring at the ceiling in the darkness, he suddenly felt a strange uneasiness, as if a hidden danger lay just beneath his awareness. Something unpleasant was gnawing at the edge of his consciousness. It was a feeling that he'd never experienced before. He had always wanted to visit the legendary home of the Dreamers and Kelem Rogeston's legacy, but now the planet felt more like an unwelcome place, almost as if Plantanimus itself didn't want him there. He fell into an uneasy sleep and had a dream about shadowy forms hiding within the circuits of the CUBE.

CHAPTER 5

A Meeting at the top of a Pyramid

"Mr. Zepol, wake up please. You have visitors at the door," the apartment's A.I. announced in a female contralto voice.

The bedroom's shutters opened automatically letting the morning sunlight in. Ogram Zepol opened his eyes, squinting at the brightness of the light enhanced by the white snowy mountains in the distance. He jumped out of bed and started for the door when he remembered that he was buck naked as was his practice when going to bed. He turned around and put on his clothes and went out to the living room. When he opened the door he was met by the stone face of one of the men that had escorted him here last night.

"Mr. Zepol, please make yourself presentable as soon as possible. Cardinal Richelieux has arrived and wishes to speak to you. I'll be waiting out here ready to escort you to the meeting."

"Richelieux, really?" the Terran exclaimed, amused by the turn of events.

The man's face remained static and Ogram laughed inwardly at the employee's stance. "Very well, I'll be out in a few minutes," he said, closing the door and shaking his head. He stepped into the spa and asked the A.I. to provide him with a proper business outfit. He washed himself, combed his hair, got dressed and ten minutes later he and the stone-faced men were on their way to meet Cardinal Richelieux, the second most powerful person in the galaxy.

The pyramid shaped monolith that was the central headquarters for the CUBE, was so big, that the pair had to board a small rail line that ran within the facility. The conveyance ferried them to the part of the building where the meeting was to take place.

"You will address the Cardinal as 'your Eminence' or 'Cardinal' and please, do not use the pronoun 'you' at any time," one of the men advised him as the rail car slowed down.

The Terran nodded absently as he contemplated this new development in his present situation. He followed the stoic-faced employees after they exited the rail car. The pyramid was actually several buildings within buildings and the two had to pass through several security check points before arriving at what Ogram took to be, the central inner *sanctum sanctorum* of the complex. He passed through a large ornate wooden double door and found himself in a pyramid shaped pavilion, several meters tall with wide floors and ceilings made of white marble. This had to be the very top of the huge building. Above, a gigantic skylight illuminated the space with sunlight. The sight was impressive and awe inspiring. In the very middle, sat Cardinal Richelieux dressed in his vermillion cassock, in one of two white chairs situated in the center of the floor. Ogram Zepol did not miss the obvious purpose of the visual contrast between the whiteness of the place and Richelieux's red outfit. In the Kelemite tradition, white represented the sanctity of the church and vermillion the physicality of the real world. He approached the man, and Richelieux stood up and extended his right hand when he arrived.

"Welcome Mr. Zepol. I wanted to meet you personally and have a conversation with you. I hope you don't mind," he said shaking Ogram's hand.

"Not at all your Eminence. It's not every day that one gets to meet the Cardinal Counselor to the Matriarch of the Kelemite Church," the Terran replied.

Richelieux smiled politely and pointed to the empty chair across from him. Both men sat down, each measuring the other quietly for a few seconds.

"I guess I've 'muddied the waters a mite', as we Terrans used to say in the olden days!" Ogram pronounced, breaking the silence.

The cardinal smiled, genuinely amused by Terran's ancient colloquialism, then nodded in response.

"I suppose the big question in everyone's minds, including yours, is; can this man be trusted with The Realm's most sacred information?" Ogram proposed, looking straight into the cleric's eyes.

Richelieux continued studying the young man's face with great interest and then asked a strange question.

"Have we met before?"

"Never . . ., do I look familiar to you? Perhaps you've seen me through the media. I'm not very famous but I'm somewhat of a celebrity in certain circles."

"No, I've been aware of your public persona for some time, but after meeting you in person, something about you seems very familiar to me."

The Terran pursed his lips trying to make light of the cardinal's unusual comment. For a moment he wondered if this very powerful man whose authority was only second to the Church's Matriarch and who presided over trillions of Kelemite followers, would use the ruse of perceived familiarity to gain his trust. But no, somehow, he knew that the man was being honest.

"I hope that your sensing that we've met before is indicative of your willingness to trust me with The Realm's security codes," Ogram stated, hoping for a positive answer.

"Yes and, no," the cleric answered, assuming his regal persona again. "That is to be decided after we discuss certain matters that are of great concern to the church and to The Realm."

"Please, let us both save time and trouble your Eminence. Number one, I know for a fact that my being hired by The Realm at the current moment has nothing to do with either expanding or improving the efficiency of the CUBE system. I know, because I was among the members of the scientific committee that The Realm consulted with on that subject more than ten years ago and the judgment of the entire group was that quantum holographic computers had reached their maximum efficiency, a fact that remains true today. So if may continue," the young Terran said, "whatever problem it is that The Realm is dealing with now, has to be of an unusual nature and I surmise that some sort of anomaly has manifested within the system, and that your technicians have no idea what in hell they're dealing with. Am I right so far?"

Richelieux remained calm and nodded ever so slightly in agreement. "You're right of course. May I ask how you reached that conclusion?"

"It's simple really, I knew that The Realm would not be satisfied with the committee's judgment, and because of financial pressures from the body shops, the company's computer technicians would continue experimenting with ways to improve the CUBE's processing powers. I'm sure that your Eminence is aware of the fact that no one really understands how a quantum computer truly works, including individuals such as myself and a few others, in spite of all our knowledge. Quantum holography is as close to hocus-pocus magic as science can come. I think that your technicians have created a problem by fiddling with the CUBE's operating system asking it to do something that it is not capable of doing and therefore have created a sort of 'processing conundrum' which the A.I. avatars cannot resolve."

"By artificial intelligence avatars I suppose you mean to describe what we call 'guardian angels'?"

"Yes. Your 'guardian angels' are artificial intelligence programs originally designed to welcome and guide newcomers to the system and help them adjust to life inside the CUBE, like a staff of heavenly receptionists. The designers gave the guardian angels tremendous capability, autonomy wise. They were given the ability to counsel newly arrived individuals with very sophisticated psychological techniques, especially if such individuals entered The Realm after suffering terminal illness for a long period of time or had perished after a violent accident. And because such avatars were given so much power by the designers, I'm sure that one or more of your technicians decided to modify their programming thinking that re-tasking the avatars to help with the processing capability of the CUBE was a brilliant idea."

"You're right Mr. Zepol. That is exactly what the technicians have told me. You think that this re-tasking of the guardian angels is what has caused the malfunction in the system?"

"Yes of course! Asking an avatar . . ., I mean one of your guardian angels to perform processing tasks, is like asking a highly trained surgeon to wash laundry while transplanting an organ," Ogram Zepol said with sarcasm.

Cardinal Richelieux rubbed his chin while looking down and remained pensive for a few seconds. "Tell me Mr. Zepol, what are your views of the Kelemite Church?"

"Before I got into physics and computer science I thought I would be a historian. I'm probably one of the very few individuals alive today with extensive knowledge of the galaxy's history, going back millennia. In my opinion your Eminence, organized religion has been responsible for more pain and misery than any other fact throughout history. Having said that, I do not bear any malice toward the Kelemite church or any other major religion. My beliefs are personal and I do not share them with the media or anyone else, except with you right now. I know I must be one hundred percent honest with you if you are to trust me."

"Thank you for your honesty Mr. Zepol, I appreciate it. And yes, I do believe you when you say that you bear no malice toward the Church. But I must now convince Hubert Longsdale and quite a few others that they should let you have complete access to the CUBE's security codes."

"Forgive me your Eminence, but isn't that akin to the parent asking the child for permission to redecorate the house?" Ogram asked, surprised that Richelieux would have to plead his case with the company's executives.

Richelieux smiled and shook his head lightly. "Mr. Zepol, I know that many believe that the Kelemite Church has complete authority over The Realm, but the truth is that over time, The Realm has become more and more autonomous. Though the Church is still the majority stock holder in the company, the total number of stock holders is so huge and politically influential, that quite often, we (the Church), are at odds with the board of directors."

"I apologize for my ignorance Cardinal. I didn't realize that was the case."

"No apologies necessary Mr. Zepol, but the Matriarch and I would appreciate it if you did not divulge such facts to others."

"I never divulge confidential information given to me by my employers and even though I'm not charging a fee for my services, I consider The Realm and the Church of St. Kelem my employers."

"I knew that you were the right person to hire Mr. Zepol. I'm the one that suggested that you should be brought in as a consultant," Richelieux admitted, surprising the Terran completely.

"You asked for me . . . ? I have to admit that I'm completely taken aback!"

"I was a young priest assigned to my first parish when I heard about you and your amazing accomplishments at such a young age. I'm a bit of a history buff myself and I clearly remember hearing you talk about Earth's past and history and the diaspora that followed the invention of *n'time* travel. You attributed much of mankind's progress to Kelem Rogeston, and of course, being a Kelemite priest I took notice of your words."

"I'm pleased that you've followed my development all these years, but even though I still think Rogeston is a major influential figure in human history, I'm wondering why you suggested me for this job even though I'm an agnostic."

"I don't usually do things by instinct, but in this case I did. Your agnosticism was a bit of a challenge when it came to the Matriarch, but I managed to convince her that you were the right person for the job, though I have to admit that you asking for full access to our security codes was a bit of a shock. When Longsdale called to tell me about your request, I decided to come here in person."

"Well Cardinal, I hope that your faith in me will prove you right, though I'm afraid that my findings and technical report will ruffle quite a few feathers here and throughout The Realm. My guess is that I'm as welcome here as a snake in a sleeping bag, and with my reputation as an agnostic, you'll have a hell of a time trying to convince Longsdale and the others to agree to give me those codes."

"I must ask you, is it absolutely necessary that you have those codes in order to do your job?"

"One thing that I've learned about large organizations is that those in positions of power tend to see outsiders as intruders, potential enemies and trouble makers. It's normal for Longsdale and the others to try to keep their corporate privacy. But no, your Eminence, I cannot do my job if I can't peer into the innards of your system without any reservations."

Richelieux laughed and nodded. "You are wise beyond your years my young friend. You seem well acquainted with the politics of large organizations."

CHAPTER 6

Desperate Measures

"Goddamn that Terran infidel!" Hubert Longsdale yelled, as he paced back and forth in his plush executive office. Outside, the sky was getting dark and the large floor to ceiling windows facing a long chain of mountains in the distance were beginning to be covered with snow. Plantanimus' North Pole didn't usually produce many blizzards, but today it did. The storm was just another bad omen in a series of damaging events that had been plaguing The Realm for the last few months.

Vardo McCallan was sitting on a large sofa facing the windows, holding a glass full of vodka in his hand. He looked just as unhappy as Longsdale. "How do we stop this?" he asked, following Longsdale with his eyes as the man walked frantically back and forth along the length of the wall of windows.

Longsdale didn't respond to McCallan's query. "I'm trying to figure out why Richelieux, of all people, would have asked a god-damned agnostic to come here and stick his nose in our business!" he complained, absorbed in his own misery.

"Do you think he suspects something and brought in Zepol because he has no ties to us and the Church?" McCallan asked.

"I never liked Richelieux! I don't understand how the Curia elected him as Cardinal Counselor in the first place! I don't trust him. I think

43

he's a heretic trying to ruin us and the Church!" Longsdale declared indignantly, still engrossed in his troubles.

"I don't like him either Hubert, but right now our problem is Zepol. We can't give that son of a bitch the codes. You know what he'll find. We've got to do something!"

"For St. Kelem's sake! What do you propose we do Vardo? Kill Zepol? Tell Richelieux that he fell out of a window or something?" Longsdale bellowed, stopping his pacing and then collapsing on another couch facing McCallan as a growing panic took hold of him.

"We've got to do something," McCallan muttered under his breath, his mind thinking furiously.

Outside, the wind was howling, louder than either man had ever heard on Plantanimus' North Pole before.

"Listen to that!" Longsdale said, pointing at the swirling snow beginning to blanket the windows. "It's the apocalypse . . . we're done Vardo, this is it for us! After tomorrow, Richelieux will have us both arrested and thrown in prison!"

McCallan, who had been looking at the floor, raised his head and seeing the unusual power of the polar storm, an idea came to him. It was a terrible idea, one that he dreaded even thinking about. It was desperate and wrong, but he and Longsdale were in a very desperate place. He downed the rest of the vodka, got up, straightened his jacket, and walked up to Longsdale who was holding his head in his hands.

"I think I have a way to save us Hubert. I'm going up to the central matrix to check on something."

Longsdale raised his head and looked at McCallan. He always relied on Vardo McCallan and trusted him implicitly. "You've figured out something Vardo? Something technical that will prevent Zepol from discovering our secret?" he asked, with hope in his voice.

"Yes Hubert, something technical. Don't worry about anything, I'll take care of this," McCallan replied, patting Longsdale's shoulder and then turning towards the door.

"Do you want me to help you? I'm not without technical skills," Longsdale offered.

"No, it's better if you're not involved Hubert. If this goes bad, you can claim ignorance and put it all on me," McCallan replied.

"You're not going to hurt the Terran are you? Because if you do I won't have it!" Longsdale warned McCallan.

"I promise that neither I nor anyone else will touch a hair on Zepol's head, Hubert. Have a stiff drink, then a dip in the whirlpool and go to sleep. By tomorrow all our problems will be over, I promise you. Goodnight!" McCallan said, as the door slid closed behind him.

Outside Longsdale's office the two stoned faced security men from the day before were waiting for McCallan. "Come with me, I have a special job for you two," he ordered, as he walked toward the elevators.

CHAPTER 7

The Enemy Appears

Ogram was dreaming of being chased by a dark formless shadow that followed him everywhere. He was running for his life and the evil presence relentlessly pursuing him reached for his legs with long tentacles that felt like ice. The thing grabbed him and dragged him toward a dark gaping hole at the center of its black mass, surely to devour him. Shivering with cold and beggining to lose feeling in his extremities, he was crawling on the floor, desperately trying to get away from death. He dug his nails down with all his might to keep from being eaten alive, but the demonic black monster was too powerful and began to pull him toward its mouth. As the monster's tentacles drew him near, Ogram Zepol saw the image of an angel appear momentarily, then become the monster's mouth again.

"Heeelp!" he yelled, at the top of his lungs, hoping that someone would save him from this horror.

He opened his eyes and was shocked to realize that he was in his apartment at the pyramid. His body was covered with a thin layer of frost and when he exhaled, a puff of condensed breath formed in the air.

"What the hell?" he exclaimed, shocked to find that he was lying on the floor next to the bed, freezing to death.

All the automatic windows facing the exterior were open. Several centimeters of snow had piled near the windows and the wind was swirling the snow, sending it deeper into the apartment. "Avatar, what is happening?" he called out to the A.I., but there was no response and the bedroom's night lights didn't come on. With difficulty he stood up feeling severe pain in his extremities from the cold. "How long have I been like this?" he asked himself, trying to make sense of what was happening. The apartment was dark, save for the faint glow of the snow storm, occasionally interrupted by sheets of snow that were coming down in waves.

He looked out into the open and realized that the entire area was in the dark. Somehow, the CUBE, which also powered the city-like complex, had been shut down! For the first time in millennia, a CUBE in The Realm's quantum computer network had gone off grid!

He reached for his clothes but couldn't find them anywhere. He needed to cover his body to keep from freezing, but even the bed's sheets were missing. Stepping into the living room he called out again for the apartment's avatar, but the A.I. had obviously been damaged by the cold, or someone had purposely shut it off. He made his way to the spa-bathroom hoping to wrap towels around his body that was growing colder and stiffer by the minute, but the automatic door leading to it was frozen shut.

It suddenly occurred to him that this was not an accident and realized that his life was in danger. He yelled out into the dark, cursing himself for not paying attention to his feelings the night before, that something bad was about to happen. He stumbled over to the front door and pressed the operating button, but as he feared, the thing didn't work. He began pounding on the door hoping that someone would hear the noise and come by to investigate, but each time his fists made contact with its surface, they felt as if they were going to shatter. He continued pounding the door bravely for a while, but eventually, the cold was too much and he collapsed unconscious on the floor, curled in a fetal position.

As his body began shutting down, he knew he was hallucinating when he saw the image of the angel again, this time laughing at him with a cruel expression on its beautiful face.

CHAPTER 8

A Rescue from the Storm

"Pavitraam, Pavitraam!" Rek, the leader of Richelieux's Gulax personal guard said with angst, trying to revive his beloved master. Pavitraam was a bastardized version of the Hindi term, *Pavitra ādamī*, which meant 'holy man'. The Gulax had a fancy for Hindi because it rolled off their tongues far more easily than any other humanoid language.

The Gulax was wearing his vermillion battle armor which was strangely emitting vapor from its surface. Richelieux opened his eyes and looked upon Rek's yellow reptilian eyes with confusion. He was shivering with cold and was having difficulty getting his bearings.

"What . . . what's going on?" he asked, looking around. Three other Gulax guards were in his room, all wearing their battle armor, their suits also emitting vapor.

"The CUBE's been shut down Pavitraam. We have a shuttle ready to take you to safety!" the Gulax informed him, as he pulled the cardinal from his bed. One of the other Gulax guards brought a heavy winter coat and threw it over Richelieux's shoulder.

Still groggy from the effects of the cold, Richelieux spoke. "Why are all your armor suits steaming?"

"It's forty degrees below Celsius, Pavitraam, the entire city is in a blackout. The pyramid's environmental systems are off and our suits are set to maximum heat because it's the only way we can continue guarding you!" Rek explained.

Gulax were a desert species. The mean temperature in their home planet was fifty degrees Celsius. At minus forty degrees, their armored suits were barely keeping the lizards able to function. Rek was as close to a panic as a Gulax was capable of experiencing.

"You say the CUBE is offline?" Richelieux asked, not believing what he'd just heard.

"Yes, it went off about six hours ago and the pyramid is in total lockdown. We had to blast our way out of our dormitories in order to reach our suits. We almost didn't make it. We had to break your door in order to reach you as well. When the ventilation system shut off there was an unusual buildup of carbon monoxide, we fear many humanoids may have already perished. We broke open one of the windows here and that helped revive you. We managed to get a message to your vessel in orbit and they have a shuttle hovering above the building, ready to take you to safety."

"Hold on, what about the Terran, Ogram Zepol?" Richelieux asked, suddenly realizing that he could be in peril.

"He's three levels below. You want us to rescue him after you leave?" Rek asked.

"No, I want you to rescue him immediately and then bring him along with us."

"But Pavitraam, you are our prime responsibility! The human can wait until after you've been rescued yourself!" the Gulax argued.

"I appreciate your loyalty Rek, but the Terran comes with us or I won't go," Richelieux insisted, now coming out of his stupor. The Kelemite Gulax Guard's main purpose in life was to protect the Matriarch and the Cardinal Counselor with their lives. The military wing of the Holy See selected young Gulax in their infancy and indoctrinated them into the Gulax Guard Corps with religious fanaticism that bordered on brain washing. Every instinct in Rek's brain and body was telling him to disobey his main charge and take him to safety, but the Cardinal's authority superseded his conditioning. With great alacrity and in obvious discomfort, Rek acceded to Richelieux's wishes and ordered his guards to go get the Terran.

An hour later, Richelieux, his guards and a barely alive Ogram Zepol were on their way to the Cardinal's personal space craft in orbit above Plantanimus.

Twenty four hours later, the young Terran opened his eyes and wondered where he was. The first thing he saw upon opening his eyes, was the alien face of a Gulax staring at him with unblinking yellow eyes.

"Where am I?" he croaked, feeling like his head was in a vise.

"You are in His Eminence, Cardinal Richelieux's vessel in orbit around Plantanimus. Are you able to have a conversation with his Eminence?" the Gulax asked in his hiss-like voice.

"Yes, absolutely. I want to see him as soon as possible."

The guard left the cabin, and five minutes later, Richelieux appeared, trailed by four heavily armed Gulax who stood silently around their master.

Richelieux was wearing a plain grey crewman's uniform with a triangle emblem on his left pocket with the name Trinity woven below the symbol. *M. Richelieux* was printed on the opposite side. Without his clerical garb, the Cardinal could have been easily mistaken for an average crewman on a space faring ship.

Ogram Zepol couldn't hide his surprise at seeing the man without his fancy vermillion cassock.

"Something happened to your cassock?" the Terran asked.

Richelieux smiled. "No it's perfectly fine. I have several dozen actually. I don't always wear my vestments, especially in my own ship and in my private quarters at home. How are you feeling? We thought we would lose you to hypothermia a few hours ago, but fortunately, you're young and my physicians managed to keep you alive."

"Thank you, but, what has happened? The last thing I remember is waking up in my room freezing to death. And . . . why are we on your ship?" Zepol added, looking at the intimidating Gulax guard detail.

"Well, first of all, the CUBE went off line and the entire complex went dark."

"That's right! I remember looking out of the open windows in my bedroom and seeing the whole complex without lights," Zepol remembered.

"Hmmm, that's probably what saved your life in the end. About a hundred people died of asphyxiation when the carbon monoxide buildup reached critical levels. If it hadn't been for my Gulax guards breaking open a window in my apartment, I would have perished too."

"Were anybody else's apartment windows found open other than mine?" the Terran asked with interest.

"No, as a matter of fact, yours was the only apartment in the entire complex whose windows were open to the exterior," Richelieux answered, furrowing his brow and tilting his head inquisitively. "What are you thinking?"

"I'm thinking that it's very peculiar that mine was the only apartment in the complex whose windows were fully recessed."

"You're saying that you were specifically targeted?"

Ogram was about to answer but held his tongue. "What's happened to Longsdale and Var . . . what's his name . . . the facility's manager?" he queried, still suffering from temporary memory loss due to hypothermia.

Richelieux's brown complexion darkened even more. The man became visibly upset at the mention of The Realm's CEO and the technical manager of the complex. He paused for a moment struggling to compose himself. "Hubert Longsdale was found dead in his apartment this morning, the victim of an apparent suicide," Richelieux reported with a pained expression. As far as Vardo McCallan . . ., it seems that he's disappeared."

"Has anyone attempted to reboot the CUBE?" Ogram asked, sitting up on his med-bed.

As he did, the Gulax guards tensed up visibly, their four fingered hands reaching for the triggers in their weapons. Richelieux turned to them and waved them down.

"They've been on edge since last night, this the first time that my life has been threatened on their watch. Please forgive them for over reacting," the cleric apologized, then continued, "to answer your question, no, I was waiting for you to recover. I'm hoping that you'll agree to supervise the reboot operation."

Ogram shook his head in near disbelief. "Two days ago, I was fighting to have access to The Realm's security codes, and now, you, the Cardinal Counselor to the Matriarch, is asking me to be at the helm of a CUBE reboot! I have to say that, so far, this is the most interesting job that I've ever held!"

"You'll do it then! That's perfect. How soon do you think that you'll be well enough to attempt the operation?" Richelieux asked, with anticipation.

"Tomorrow morning, but only if your physicians can take this horrible headache away," Ogram replied, lying back on the med-bed and closing his eyes.

"My physicians can work miracles. They'll have you up and running tomorrow morning like nothing's happened!" Richelieux replied gleefully.

Ogram waved at him weakly and soon fell asleep.

Chapter 9

The Reboot Uncovers a Mystery

The CUBE's Matrix Control Center was abuzz with activity. The large cavernous space was shaped like a conical pyramid. The supervisor's level was at the top of several tiers of control stations each with its own three dimensional screen. The structure was populated by hundreds of technicians and quantum holographic computer experts. A huge floor to ceiling screen covered the entire circular wall, displaying myriad of information and graphic displays of technical data.

On the top tier, Ogram Zepol sat at the controls of a large console next to a large three- dimensional screen, about to enter the command to reboot of the giant machine directly below the Matrix Control Center. Next to him sat Cardinal Richelieux, wearing his vermillion cassock, looking once again like his regal self.

Below, the eyes of many would occasionally steal glances at the top tier, unable to hide their curiosity, and for many, their discomfort and anger at the fact that someone other than a company manager was in charge of the operation. The Realm had always been staffed strictly with members of the Kelemite Church, from the CEO down to the lower skilled workers.

Everyone was on edge after experiencing the first ever, shutdown of a CUBE. The tragic loss of one hundred and twenty of their colleagues also weighed heavily in their minds. Some were sure that all that had happened in the last forty eight hours was because of Ogram Zepol. Yet, no one dared say anything, lest they upset the Cardinal Counselor.

Most upset of all were the upper managers, many of whom were Kelemite zealots and who were indignant that a complete stranger, and most of all an agnostic, had been put in charge! Many were making a point of displaying their dislike for the young Terran openly. But Ogram seemed completely immune to that kind of social pressure and ignored the tense atmosphere around him as if he was out for a stroll in a peaceful meadow.

Richelieux's intuition had served him well in putting the young Terran in charge of the CUBE for the reboot. Not only because he knew that Zepol would be able to handle the disapproval and condemnation aimed at his person, but also, because until the machine was reactivated and the young computer genius assessed whatever damage might have been caused by Hubert Longsdale and Vardo McCallan, he couldn't trust the upper managers of this particular CUBE. For all he knew, some, or perhaps all, had been complicit in the shutdown and subsequent death of one hundred and twenty employees of The Realm.

Pieter Minsk, the highest senior manager after Vardo McCallan, was still, even moments before the reboot, trying to convince Richelieux that he and not Zepol should be in charge.

"Please, your Eminence, I beg you! Do not let this outsider shame us with his presence!" the man whispered in Richelieux's ear.

Richelieux turned around and faced Minsk, a chubby balding man in his fifties. "Mr. Minsk, please control yourself! It should be clear to you by now, that this facility has been severely compromised, and that Mr. Zepol is probably the only person alive in this galaxy at present time, with the knowledge and expertise to fix this CUBE!"

"But your Eminence, how can you allow an unbeliever to walk on the hallowed ground of this place?" the man asked indignantly.

"Mr. Zepol was called in as a consultant by the Matriarch and me, and all because your staff was unable to correct the many problems that have been plaguing this CUBE for months. Now, go back to your seat and let Mr. Zepol begin the procedure or I'll have you removed from the place," Richelieux said quietly but with emphasis.

The man blinked twice, in shock at having been admonished by the Cardinal, but he knew that he had pushed things as far as they could go. He returned to his seat behind the console where Zepol and the Cardinal were and sat there glumly, a study in indignant frustration.

To reinforce the point, Richelieux put his arm on Zepol's shoulder affectionately, a gesture meant to let the others know that the Terran was under the protection of the Holy See.

"Ready to start, Ogram?" Richelieux asked, with a smile.

"Yes your Eminence," he replied, smiling back.

The three dimensional screen in front of Ogram Zepol was populated by floating objects of various colors and shapes resembling a child's computer game. Many had names on their surfaces such as; 'Probability Enhancers', "Dual Reality Conundrums', 'Spooky Action at a Distance', 'Hidden Variables' and such. Others were plain cubes, triangular shapes, cylinders and exotic geometrical shapes with mathematical formulas written on their surfaces. Zepol touched a big red ball in the middle of it all and a gong sound was heard in the large room. Immediately, the young Terran began repositioning some of the floating objects and drew lines between them with his fingers, which created a three dimensional schematic diagram. As he worked, new and more unusual objects appeared on the screen. Some were morphing into other shapes different than how they appeared at first. Soon the schematic became more and more complex as more objects popped into existence and more connection lines were created between the various objects.

Richelieux was mesmerized by the evolving complexity and beauty of the floating spectacle in front of his eyes. A series of musical sounds, beeps, bells and clicks became audible, all adding to the fascinating event. It was almost as if Ogram Zepol was a magician, delighting his audience with ever more bizarre and interesting objects created out of his own imagination. The various sounds of the operation took on an almost symphonic quality. Zepol's captivating creation was suddenly displayed on the large circular screen surrounding the room.

Richelieux looked around him and noticed that everyone was as transfixed by the event as he was. It seemed that this experience was as new to them as it was to him and he realized that he was witnessing something special. Even the suspicious Pieter Minsk seemed awe struck.

A second, higher pitched gong sounded off and all the operators in the lower tiers began manipulating the floating objects in their three dimensional screens. Soon the sound of the facility's *n'time* generator could be heard winding up below the Matrix Control Center. After a while, when the generator reached its peak cycle, the lights dimmed for a few seconds and then came back up again.

The complex display floating in front of Ogram disappeared and a series of avatars, all young and beautiful began appearing on the display in quick succession, one after the other. "Angel Nelson reporting", Angel Francisca reporting", and on and on for several minutes.

When the angels first appeared, a collective cheer went up in the room and the tense mood that had permeated the proceedings so far, melted away. Richelieux relaxed and leaned back on his chair and looked at young Ogram with new eyes. From the moment he met the eccentric young scientist he had felt a strong simpatico with him. Now as the CUBE began to come to life, he knew in his heart of hearts that in spite of his agnosticism, Ogram Zepol was a special young man.

After all the angels reported, over ten thousand of them, the operators began rebooting secondary computers that were used for power, environmental controls and other ancillary services. The city above the CUBE was coming back to life after being blacked out for more than forty-eight hours, and smiles spread among the staff.

More work lay ahead, and when lunch time came, Ogram asked that Pieter Minsk take over, which he did with pleasure. Before he sat down on the chair, he shook the young Terran's hand and congratulated him on a fine job. "May I ask you something?" he queried, unable to hide a deep admiration for what young Ogram Zepol had just done.

"Yes, what is it Mr. Minsk?"

"Which quantum theory interpretation did you use when you began activating the system and also, what symbolic language were you employing with some of your commands? I've never seen or heard of many of them."

"None. I simply asked the central core A.I. what it needed to successfully reboot the system and it told me. Then I just followed its instructions. As far as the language I used, it's my own, one that I wrote several years ago when I was a graduate student at the Zurich Institute in Europa. I'd be happy to send you my paper on the subject," Zepol replied calmly.

"Yes . . ., yes thank you!" Minsk replied, wondering if the Terran was pulling his leg. He'd never heard of anyone asking anything of, or directly addressing the CUBE's central core A.I. as an individual!

Richelieux and Zepol went back to the pyramid where they enjoyed a sumptuous lunch in the cleric's quarters, served by his Gulax guards. They were still jumpy about the Cardinal's security and had gone as far as tasting all the food items for poison, one by one, a job that was as distasteful to them as a human having to taste raw flesh dishes, which was the Gulax's normal diet.

After lunch, both men sat in the living room couch quietly sipping Cointreau.

"Something's bothering you Ogram. Several times during the meal, you seemed on the brink of saying something to me. What's troubling you?"

Ogram took a deep breath and then exhaled. "I'm not sure, but I think this CUBE or perhaps the entire system has been tampered with."

"Well, isn't that what you thought we'd find once the computer was booted up?"

"I expected to find processing irregularities that were illegally implemented by both Longsdale and McCallan of course, but what I'm talking about goes much deeper than that," replied Ogram, with uneasiness.

"What are you referring to exactly?" Richelieux asked, confused.

"Have you ever heard of the ancient term 'computer virus'?"

"Yes, a computer virus was a type of program code that, when executed, replicated by inserting copies of itself into other computer programs, data files, etc.," the cleric responded, with surprising accuracy. Zepol was duly impressed by Richelieux's knowledge of ancient technical lingo.

"Well, you and I know that it's impossible for a quantum computer to be affected by a 'virus', but that is exactly what I believe is happening inside this one and hopefully only this one."

Richelieux leaned forward and put his glass down on the coffee table. He'd always heard that quantum computers were immune to outside interference by their very nature. Yet, here was the foremost computer scientist in the galaxy telling him that it was so. "Clarify," he requested.

You have too many avatars . . ., I mean angels," Ogram corrected himself. "I looked at your Artificial Personnel Intelligence data base and it says that this particular CUBE has eleven thousand, 'angels', yet, I counted, eleven thousand, one hundred and sixty. The additional one hundred and sixty angels are clones of some of the originals. You'll soon receive a call from Minsk regarding this anomaly," he added, with a deep frown on his forehead.

"I assume this is a bad thing . . . ., how serious is it?" Richelieux asked, concerned that the entire system of The Realm might be similarly affected.

"It all depends on how these angel clones were programmed and what their purpose is."

"Could McCallan and his people have created these new A.I.'s?" Richelieux wondered.

"I seriously doubt it, Cardinal. Your angel avatars were designed and implemented by Tzu Yin Chu, the programming genius who created the CUBE computers six millennia ago. His work was . . ., is . . ., still, so advanced, that even today, no one has been able to match his level of artificial intelligence design. His work was so perfect, that The Realm's angels are practically sentient beings in their own right," Zepol paused and then stood up and walked over to the large row of windows in the cleric's apartment. The sun was shining brightly in the snow crested mountains of Plantanimus' North Pole.

"No, these new angels are the creation of someone with equal or far superior skill to Tzu Yin Chu, which means that someone has a specific purpose in mind for these new avatars. And since they have been introduced into the system by stealth, my guess is, they're up to no good."

CHAPTER 10

Infiltration

"Welcome to The Realm, brother, how may I be of assistance?" Angel Darius pronounced, as he stood in the middle of one of the CUBE's holo projection rooms. The young dark haired Caucasian male in his mid-twenties smiled, looking resplendent in his long white robe and golden halo above his head, the perfect image of one of God's messengers. His hair and features were pure perfection. Handsome and yet not overly so, his physical attributes had been designed to inspire peace and tranquility in those that had recently passed on from the physical world. Surrounded by a subtle glow that extended about thirty centimeters from his body in all directions, one could not help but be overcome with a feeling of great power in his presence.

Ogram Zepol found himself strangely fearful of this particular angel, even though he knew that it was a copy of an artificial projection generated by a quantum holographic program, written six thousand years before by a man of flesh and blood. For a fraction of second, he felt a chill run down his spine. Angel Darius was the spitting image of the cruel angel that had made its appearance at the mouth of the dark monster that had accosted him the night of the blackout. He had been "interviewing" many of the cloned angels for about five hours now, with disappointing results. But this particular avatar seemed somehow different.

"Tell me about yourself," Zepol asked, trying to shake a growing feeling of paranoia.

'I am your guide in the hereafter brother, here to help you find peace and tranquility in your new life," the angel replied in a soft pleasant baritone, beatific smile, ever present.

"No, I meant, tell me something about yourself, as an individual," Zepol stipulated.

"I am but a small aspect of the creator, brother, an infinitesimal part of he who has created all. I am not an 'I', I'm simply one of the Lord's many instruments."

"So, you're not a person like me, you're a small part of he who has created all?"

"My countenance is that of a man so that you may feel comfortable in your new life brother. Do not fret about the characteristics of that which is presented to you by the creator. From now on, you'll be well looked after. You have nothing to worry about for the rest of your eternal existence," the angel replied graciously, yet Zepol felt that there was sinister undertone to his manner.

"It seems that you're not a man and you have no personal opinions and you're merely a projection of God almighty. So in essence, you're not real," Ogram commented sarcastically, trying to see if the avatar's secret programming would reveal itself if taunted and or insulted.

"I am as real as you are brother, just in a different form," Angel Darius countered with his ever present smile.

Ogram began shaking uncontrollably and turned around facing the window of the control room behind him. "Turn it off, I need to stop," he said, getting up from the chair unsteadily and walking out of the small holo room. The technician at the controls pushed a button and Angel Darius' holo projection dematerialized into thin air.

"I told you that angel programming would not change under any circumstances," the technician told Richelieux, sitting next to him in the control booth. "This last angel may be a clone of the Darius A.I., but it appears to behave exactly as the original. I don't see how it could be a cause for concern," the man, added confidently.

Ogram rubbed his chin broodingly as he entered the booth and leaned on the rear wall of the control room trying to regain his composure. Richelieux, who was sitting, looked up at him. "Perhaps you're wrong about these cloned avatars," he said to him. "You haven't considered the fact that the additional angels might have been put into the system for beneficial purposes. I know we've just uncovered a conspiracy created by Longsdale and McCallan, but not everything has to be sinister or malicious," the cleric argued.

"There's too much at stake. The only way we can be sure if these cloned angels are a threat or not, is to go inside the system," Ogram proposed.

"You mean enter the VR as a visitor?" Richelieux enquired. Relatives of those whose consciousness lived inside The Realm, could visit their loved ones by connecting their neural system to the CUBE via a "Full Immersion Apparatus", a device that allowed a living person to enter the Virtual Environment of The Realm as an avatar of themselves and therefore visit their relative face to face.

"No, not as a visitor but as a new arrival," Ogram corrected Richelieux.

The technician and the Cardinal exchanged glances, surprised by Ogram's request.

"Your Eminence, that has never been done!" the technician complained, looking distraught.

"That's out of the question Ogram! I've given you unprecedented access to the system, but an outsider entering the system as a client is impossible. One of the main guarantees to all clients of The Realm, is that their privacy and safety will never be compromised by an outside individual or organization. If word got out that the Church and The Realm allowed a non-believer to enter the system and interact with our clients, the company and the church would suffer tremendous damage," Richelieux declared with alarm.

"I'm convinced that these cloned angels are a serious threat to The Realm. You yourself have said to Pieter Minsk, that I was 'the only person alive in this galaxy at present time, with the knowledge and expertise to fix this CUBE'. So why should this be any different your Eminence?" Ogram asked, vehemently.

"This is very different Ogram! Entering The Realm as a client is an action that is only permitted when our insurance providers come in to certify The Realm's operation once a year. Allowing you to do this is tantamount to desecrating the Church. And even when the insurance agent enters the VR, it is done so with a very light footprint."

"Your Eminence, regardless of my personal philosophy, I am not an enemy of the Church. I would not be here in the first place if I were. I fear that a negative influence has corrupted the system. I didn't tell you three days ago about a nightmare that I had the night that the power went off, but I will now. Please listen to me!"

Zepol's admission gave the Cardinal pause. He relaxed his posture and motioned for the young computer scientist to sit next to him. "Tell me about your nightmare."

Zepol related the nightmare and subsequent hallucination in detail. Richelieux looked down at the floor and then back at his young friend. "And you say that the angel's face looked just like Angel Darius?"

"Yes! It was definitely Angel Darius' face, I'm sure of it. That's why I asked you to shut off the projection so soon after starting the interview. Seeing him standing so close to me inside the holo room, gave me the creeps. Look Cardinal, even as a child, I was not one to believe in goblins and ghosts or monsters in the closet. I've never been afraid of the dark and certainly not of the image of an angel. But I was shaken to the core by the experience of three nights ago and again, a few minutes ago, when I recognized Angel Darius as the same angel in my nightmare. It seems too much of a coincidence that both looked exactly the same."

Richelieux looked deep into Ogram Zepol's eyes and knew that he was telling the truth. A troubling though came to his mind as he contemplated, not only allowing the Terran to enter the VR as a client, but of the danger that an infiltration of sinister avatars meant for The Realm, the Church of St. Kelem and the galaxy at large. The events of the last three days only served to strengthen such doubts and suspicions. He rubbed his dark face with his hands, trying to revive himself from the deep exhaustion that he'd been fighting ever since the blackout. He took a breath and exhaled deeply, having made up his mind.

"Alright, you can go in as a client, but only if I come with you," Richelieux demanded forcefully.

"I'll accept your condition, but I must warn you that it may be a perilous journey for us both, your Eminence," Ogram advised the cleric.

"Who better to accompany you on a confrontation with danger, than the Cardinal Counselor to the Matriarch of the Church of St. Kelem?" Richelieux replied laughing.

CHAPTER II

Saved by the Saint

Richelieux and Zepol were lying next to one another in specialized med-beds in one of the 'immersion' rooms deep in the bowels of the CUBE. Both were wearing 'neural suits' that were linked to the system via wireless connection. The suits would allow them to interface with the VR inside the CUBE and experience their presence there with all their senses.

Pieter Minsk was ministering to them making a final check of the many nano-leads that connected their nervous systems to the suits. "Once you enter the VR, take some time to adjust your movements to the environment. At first, there'll be a slight delay of twenty milliseconds or so, between your brain initiating a physical move and your avatar's response. Eventually your nervous system will adjust, and the delay will disappear. But, if you try to fight this slight delay in the beggining, you'll find it difficult to walk and move while in there. Understand?"

Both men nodded in agreement. Richelieux had entered the VR while in seminary school and knew what to expect. All members of the clergy were obliged to do so as part of their training. But, for the young Terran, in spite of his deep knowledge of the CUBE's technology, this would be his first experience inside the virtual world of the CUBE. Though slightly nervous, he was confident that he'd be alright.

Richelieux had had a hell of a time getting to this point. Not only did he have to confront the irate and sometimes vociferous complaints of the upper management of the CUBE, who were vehemently opposed to Ogram Zepol entering The Realm, but, he'd also argued with the Matriarch via quantum video conference, lobbying to let Ogram Zepol and he, enter the CUBE's VR together. Equally upset and dismayed, were his Gulax guards who had no way of protecting him while his consciousness was inside the VR. Most surprising however, had been Pieter Minsk's persuasive arguments with his managers and the Matriarch herself, in favor of allowing the two to take this unprecedented journey inside the quantum holographic world of The Realm. The young Terran's amazing performance during the CUBE's reboot had made Minsk a supporter of young Ogram.

"Alright your Eminence and Ogram, the Lectrosleep leads will render you unconscious for a few minutes while the suits negotiate the transition between reality and the VR environment. Good luck and remember, you only have to say 'St. Kelem' in case of trouble and the system will pull you out before one hour is up," Minsk reminded them.

Minsk left the room and went into the control booth to supervise the operation. Inside, several of the best operators in the company were at their stations ready to conduct the insertion of the two men into the system.

"Good luck Ogram, I'll see you inside,' Richelieux said, looking at his young friend. Zepol nodded and swallowed hard, steeling himself for whatever they'd find once they crossed over.

A soft gong went off and the Lectrosleep connection put both men to sleep at once.

Ogram found himself standing in a park in the middle of a small town somewhere in the Americas, on Earth. Pieter Minsk had purposely chosen the environment as such, in order to give the young Terran a familiar point of reference while inside the VR. Next to him, stood Richelieux, dressed in regular clothes, a white shirt and brown slacks with plain shoes, much like you'd find people wearing on Earth in the 111th century. Zepol looked at his avatar body and saw that he was similarly attired. He experienced the slight delay between wanting to move his arm and head and the reaction, but the effect didn't bother him at all. Most of all, he was amazed by what he was seeing and feeling.

He turned to Richelieux and was delighted when he heard his own voice "This is amazing! I had no idea how realistic this environment was," he remarked with delight.

Richelieux looked around and took a deep breath smelling the fresh cut grass and the scent of eucalyptus trees in the park. "You're right! The last time I was inside, things didn't look or feel this good. I guess the technicians have been working hard at improving the feel of the VR."

"I have no point of reference, this being my first time, but I have to say, I'm very impressed with what I'm seeing and feeling."

"Indeed. Minsk said to take a stroll around the town to familiarize ourselves with the place. Shall we go?"

"Absolutely!" Zepol replied, anxious to explore this wonder world. The two men walked out of the park and took a tour of the town which was about three square kilometers in size. Beyond its borders, the area consisted of open meadows, some farms and a range of mountains visible in the distance, all quite pastoral and idyllic. As they strolled through the streets, some of the citizens would smile and nod as a greeting, the way people in small towns usually do. Richelieux and Zepol knew that about half of them were avatars, placed in the town to give the place more of a realistic feel. But many of the others were real clients of The Realm.

Ogram amused himself by trying to determine which people were real and which were projections of the CUBE, but he truly couldn't tell. He turned to Richelieux and almost called him by his official name, but both had been warned to use first names only. He used the Cardinal's first name to address him. "Matuch, if this is the afterlife in The Realm, I say, sign me up!" he exclaimed, feeling a strange sense of elation.

"I agree with your Ogram. As I said before, I don't remember the VR being this realistic!"

"Then what is it that body shops offer that this place can't match?" Ogram asked, wondering why the Church was losing business to the body trade when this virtual reality, in some ways, felt better than the real thing.

"I can't answer that question right now Ogram, but now that I think about it, something feels out of place here. For years I've been hearing from Longsdale, the board of directors and others that The Realm's VR is limited and that after a while, people who've been residents for a few years, begin noticing problems. And until now, I tended to agree. My previous visits to The Realm were interesting, but the experience lacked a certain authenticity that this place has in excess. Let me ask you something, could it be that what we're experiencing is only available in this particular CUBE and not in all the rest?" Richelieux inquired.

"Now that I'm paying attention, I realize that what I'm feeling is something akin to sensory overload. I'm thinking that this place feels almost 'too real' if that's possible. Do you agree?"

"You're right! 'Too real' is definitely how I'd describe it. Now the question is, why, and how does this relate to our recent problems?" Richelieu pondered.

"It stands to reason that this 'hyper reality' we're being subjected to, is also the result of tampering from the outside. Someone has apparently jacked-up the intensity of the sensory experience, but for what reason, I can't begin to guess."

"You're the scientist. Are we in any danger of having our nervous systems overloaded?" Richelieux asked with concern.

"Minsk and his crew are constantly monitoring our vitals. If something goes wrong, they can pull us out in an instant. I wouldn't worry about it. Let's go to the town's café and interact with the population as we planned."

The two men walked a few blocks to the café and sat at a table next to a window facing the park. The sun was high in the sky and the few patrons in the place appeared to be eating their lunch meal. Ogram was amazed by the authenticity of the food smells and the sounds of silverware and plates being used. Outside, the trees in the park were swaying gently back and forth moved by a soft summer breeze. The distant sound of children playing in the park's playground attracted his attention.

"Those children in the park, are some of them real too?" Zepol asked Richelieux.

"There are no children in The Realm, Ogram, only avatars. It was decided long ago, that young children in particular, would not fare well in an environment without parents and a family structure.

"I never thought about the issue of children before. But it does make sense when you think about it," Zepol remarked.

A young attractive waitress approached them with her data pad in hand. Good afternoon gentlemen. Are you new in town or just passing by?" she asked with a pleasant smile on her youthful face.

"Just passing by. You have a beautiful town here. What is its name?" Richelieux inquired.

"It's called Pleasant Meadows," she answered and then looked at Richelieux with curiosity in her eyes. "You're from the Pleiades, aren't you? I could tell by the way you asked for the town's name instead of saying 'what's the name'."

"You've guessed right,' he replied, surprised, and at the same time, impressed by the sophistication of the avatar's programming.

Then she turned to Zepol. "You . . ., you're not from around here, but close. Probably Chicago, am I right?" she added with an expectant smile.

"Close enough, my family is from Ohio."

"Hah! I knew you were an American," she said, pleased with her guess. "Now, what can I get for you two, some stew or perhaps a salad?"

"Hmmm, we're not hungry right now, How about two iced teas?" Ogram suggested.

Richelieux nodded approval. "Yes, two iced teas will be perfect."

"Very well, I'll be back in a minute," she announced and went to the kitchen.

"Are the town's avatars supposed to be that sophisticated?' Ogram asked, referring to the waitress's accurate guess of Richelieux's origins.

Richelieu looked around him, making sure no one was within ear shot. "No, not at all!" he whispered, "only the guardian angels have that sophisticated level of programming."

"Hmmm, we should drink our teas and leave here as quickly as possible. I don't know if you're feeling it, but I'm suddenly very jumpy and nervous," Ogram commented, in a low tone of voice.

"I concur. Remember the safe word Ogram, in case something goes wrong."

The waitress came back and they drank their teas quickly. They paid for their drinks with their virtual credit chips imbedded in their virtual hands and left the café. As they left, Richelieux noticed that the waitress' eyes followed their exit with an unusual amount of interest.

"Did you see that?" Richelieux asked, regarding the waitress's strange behavior, as they crossed the street heading for the park.

"Yes, I did. Not only that, but the virtual hairs in the back of my neck are telling me that we're in danger," Ogram announced.

"Perhaps we should exit now," Richelieux proposed.

"We've been here a total of twenty virtual minutes and yet, we haven't been welcomed by our guardian angel yet. I thought that they were supposed to appear soon after a client entered the VR," Ogram remarked.

"The timing of their welcome is not specifically determined, but, you're right. We should have been approached by now. This is highly irregular, Minsk arranged for the cloned copy of Angel Darius to be our guide. He should have appeared by now," Richelieux said, looking around, as a feeling of unease began to grow in the back of his mind.

The temperature dropped several degrees in a matter of seconds. Their light summer clothing was no longer sufficient to keep them warm and they both felt a chill as the sky began to darken. They looked toward the edge of town and saw a cloudy, curtain-like front beginning to engulf the town, much like storm fronts common to the mid-west of North America. Dust and debris picked up by the wind, pelted their faces making them shield their eyes.

The wind began to howl and the trees in the park were bending from the power of the hurricane strength gusts that were assailing the town. Small bushes and other medium size objects torn by the onslaught were now flying in the air and hitting them as they ran for shelter. Holding on to each other to keep from falling and being dragged away by the increasing strength of the storm, the men ran back to the café, but as they exited the park, the power of the wind increased dramatically and both Richelieux and Zepol were swept away through the streets, sent tumbling over and over until they slammed against a building.

Ogram opened his mouth to speak the safe word, but the wind pressure pinning him and Richelieux against the wall, was so severe that, not only could he not speak, he was also having difficulty breathing. He and the Cardinal were trapped at the end of a *cul-de-sac* unable to escape, trying desperately to shout out the word that would take them out of this holographic nightmare. The image of Angel Darius appeared at the open end of the street, coming toward them as he floated in mid-air with open arms, seemingly unaffected by the maelstrom destroying the town. The avatar was followed by a black shadow that engulfed everything in its path in complete darkness.

Ogram recognized 'the shadow' as the same monster that had attacked him the night of the blackout four days before, except, this was not a nightmare, but a very real situation.

Angel Darius' eyes had turned completely black and his beatific smile had been replaced by a gruesome sneer that froze both men's hearts. His white flowing vestment had turned deep red, engulfed by an indigo blue fire that surrounded his form. Here was true evil incarnate, a cold vision of hell come to life inside The Realm, about to consume their souls with its evil power.

The black shadow behind Darius now morphed into a black monster with a gaping hole at its center and tentacles that flailed forward, reaching for them to drag them into its 'mouth'. The image of Darius disappeared as the dark blob-like being, slithered toward them making a slushing sound, like something wet and heavy being dragged on the ground. The wind was now the beast's breath, which stank of death and decay, rotting corpses and foul evil.

The stench of the monster entered their mouths and noses and began sucking the life out of their lungs. Ogram instinctively reached for Richelieux's hand and grabbed it. It was the young Terran's desperate last act of humanity before succumbing to oblivion for all time.

Though their eyes were open, the darkness engulfed them and they could no longer see. Ogram felt one of the beast's tentacles wrap around his throat, the cold slimy extremity choking him to death. But just as he was about to pass out, a powerful white light flashed like an explosion in front of them and the beast's form was momentarily illuminated. The thing screamed like a wounded animal and let go of the two men, its mass slithering back away from the wall where the two were pinned down. The sky began to clear and the monster soon disappeared down the street, its black tentacles flailing wildly as it wailed in pain.

The bright light returned, floating above them, this time more subdued. It hovered above them for a second or two and then approached Ogram and Richelieux. Slowly, the light turned into the image of Kelem Rogeston, dressed in white coveralls, his feet a few centimeters from the ground. Ogram could see the apparition's features more clearly than anything he'd ever seen with his eyes. Saint Kelem's blue eyes and dark brown hair were perfectly delineated and realistic. At that moment, he was convinced that the patron saint of the Kelemite Church was really there.

"Nobius, seven two five two seven," Kelem Rogeston said, and then smiling again, he dematerialized, leaving Ogram wondering what the name and numbers meant. Richelieux remained sitting against the wall with his mouth agape.

CHAPTER 12

Sleeping with the Lights On

"Take Pavitraam out of there or I'll shoot you!" Rek hissed loudly at Pieter Minsk with his weapon aimed at the tech manager's head, amidst a cacophony of alarm bells and beeps issuing from the operators' consoles in the control room.

"You thick headed Gulax! If I disconnect your precious Pavitraam out of his neural suit without winding down the process, I'll surely kill him! Now, put down your weapon and let us do our jobs!" Minsk yelled, with sweat pouring down his forehead.

Something had gone terribly wrong with the immersion into the VR. The virtual cameras and audio transceivers monitoring Richelieux's and Zepol's avatars had suddenly shut off, followed by an alarming increase in the two men's heart rates. Then, a dramatic jump in Adrenaline and Cortisol production in their bodies triggered the alarms in the control room, at which point the Gulax guards went frantic, threatening to kill everyone in the place if they didn't disconnected their beloved 'holy man' from the system immediately. Richelieux and Zepol's body vitals were displaying unquestionable signs of high stress and 'fight or flight' response. On the screens, the amygdala and hypothalamus regions of their brains were lit up with intense activity. Minsk knew that the two were experiencing strong fear and were in real danger of suffering a heart attack or stroking out.

He ordered his crew to begin the emergency disconnect sequence. When the alarms shut off, the two men's readings in the consoles began to return to normal. Within seconds, vital body functions had returned to near-normal levels, although some of the stress hormones were still way above normal.

Minsk, two med-specialists and the Gulax guard, burst into the immersion room practically stumbling over each other.

"Get me out of this neural suit!" Richelieux yelled, as he slid off the med-bed unsteadily onto his feet. Minsk and the two med-specs grabbed him before he could fall and coaxed him back onto the bed.

"Your Eminence, we will take you out of the suit, but please, you must remain still while we disconnect all the nano-leads!" Minsk begged him with concern.

"Get him out of his suit too!" Richelieux yelled, still agitated and suffering the after effects of his harrowing experience inside the VR. Minsk ordered one of the med-specs to assist Zepol in getting him out of his suit. The two were no longer connected to the VR and were out of danger, but Minsk understood that both had been traumatized by whatever they had experienced and were reacting in typical human fashion by wanting to get out of the neural suits as soon as possible.

The med-spec assisting Ogram gasped and Minsk and the others turned to look. The top of Ogram's neural suit was off, revealing a nasty red welt that encircled his neck. Minsk looked back at Richelieux's body which was already out of the suit and was relieved to see that the Cardinal was free of physical injury. Then he went over to Zepol's med-bed.

"Are you in pain?" he asked, inspecting his neck which looked as if someone had tried to strangle him with a thick piece of rope.

"Nn . . nnn. . . no. But I'm freezing!" Ogram mumbled, teeth chattering.

Minsk and the med-spec exchanged glances, surprised by the Terran's unusual reaction. His body was showing signs of severe hypothermia, as if he'd been subjected to very low temperatures as had happened to him four days before.

"A psychosomatic response to stress?" Minsk wondered.

"Your Eminence, are you feeling cold?" he asked Richelieux.

"No, why do you ask?" the Cardinal replied, looking over to where Ogram was, and then noticing his condition. "What's that red welt around his neck and why is his skin turning blue?" he asked with unease.

"We don't know, but we're going to do everything in our power to get you and him back to normal," Minsk told him, then, signaling to the med-specs to wheel the two men out of the immersion room and bring them to the facility's hospital, several levels above.

When they reached the hospital floor, the nurses and doctors began taking Richelieux and Ogram to different rooms for treatment.

"No! He stays with me wherever you take me!" Richelieux ordered, adamantly.

Minsk, the doctors and nurses tried to convince him that it was necessary to separate him from Zepol, but he refused and threatened to fire anyone who opposed him. No one dared contradict the Cardinal Counselor to the Matriarch, and so, he and Zepol were treated in the same room.

It took several hours to bring young Ogram Zepol's body temperature back to a normal level, but eventually he stabilized. It was then and only then, that Richelieux allowed himself to fall asleep.

The following morning, Richelieux and Zepol were subjected to a complete and thorough physical examination and given a clean bill of health. Fortunately, aside from Ogram's neck injury which bore all the marks of an attempted strangulation, accompanied by a mild case of frostbite, the two men were physically fine. Their mental condition on the other hand, was a different matter.

After being discharged from the hospital, Richelieux, accompanied by Ogram and his Gulax guards, made an announcement while they were traveling in the elevator.

"Rek, from now on, Ogram Zepol is under your protection. I know that I'm your priority, but you and your guards will do everything in your power to protect the two of us in equal measure, is that understood?" he ordered, sounding very serious.

Rek hesitated for a moment as his guard's eyes were fixed on their commander, waiting for his response.

"Yes Pavitraam, it is understood. My life is forfeit already in order to save your life and his," he replied, bowing slightly to Ogram. The other four guards slapped their chests echoing their leader's commitment.

The Gulax guard escorted them to Richelieux's apartment at the pyramid, where they spent the day recovering from their ordeal. Both were concerned for each other, but strangely, neither man could bring himself to talk about what they had gone through. It was as if talking about it would send them back to that horrible moment in time when they faced such unspeakable evil.

That night, sleep came in fits and starts, as each was finding the blackness of sleep, too close to the darkness of the evil monster that had pursued them inside The Realm. Without knowing it, both spent the night with their bedroom lights at full brightness.

CHAPTER 13

Of Religion, Science and Politics

Pieter Minsk sat behind Hubert Longsdale's sleek modern desk in his former office, facing Cardinal Richelieux and Ogram. The newly promoted assistant manager, now general manager of the Plantanimus' CUBE, was both thankful for his elevated status within the company and at the same time, dismayed by Richelieux's order to keep the events of his and Ogram Zepol's experience inside The Realm's VR, a secret.

"But your Eminence, the news of the appearance of our patron saint in your hour of need, has to be told! Kelemites have been praying for such a miracle for millennia. Surely you won't deny that this blessed event occurred, especially when it involved the Cardinal Counselor to the Matriarch himself!" Minsk pleaded, caught up in religious fervor.

Richelieux grimaced with eyes closed and tilted his head with frustration. He and Minsk had been arguing about this point for the last half hour. He was at his wit's end and about to lose his temper for the very first time in years.

"Pieter," Ogram said, speaking for the first time since the meeting began. "Believe me when I say that, even someone like me, who's an agnostic, feel like I've been part of a powerful event. One might say, even a life changing event and . . ."

"See your Eminence?" Minsk interrupted. "Even a non-believer like him, feels that he's been witness to a holy miracle!"

"You didn't let me finish what I was saying Pieter," Ogram interjected. "What I meant to say, is that even though I feel like that, the Cardinal is correct in wanting to keep this event from the public eye for a while."

"Why? Why should we keep this a secret?" Minsk demanded, his face red with repressed anger and frustration.

Ogram looked at Richelieux for permission to continue and the Cardinal nodded. "Because the news channels would immediately sensationalize the event and turn it into an anti-Church of St. Kelem media campaign."

"But isn't that exactly what we'd want? Who cares if the media is anti-religious? At least the blessed news of our patron saint appearing after so many thousands of years would reach all our followers!"

"Yes Pieter, but not in the way that would be best for the church, don't you get it?" Richelieux exclaimed with untypical vehemence.

"No I don't get it!" Minsk shot back angrily.

"Pieter, I'm somewhat of a celebrity and I have to confess that I've, on occasion, manipulated the media for my own benefit. I know the media well and understand how it operates. Everyone knows that the Church and The Realm are at odds with the body shops, vying for the hearts and minds of the public. Announcing the appearance of St. Kelem while the Cardinal Counselor to the Matriarch was inside of The Realm's VR, would only serve to make the Church look desperate for commercial gain. The Realm's stock would plunge in value and you would have given the body shops a victory in terms of free propaganda," Ogram explained.

Richelieux couldn't help but smile at his young friend's accurate assessment of the situation and found himself wishing that Ogram Zepol were a believer or perhaps, even a Kelemite priest.

"Is he right your Eminence?" Minsk asked, with tears welling in his eyes. The man's heart was breaking, because deep inside, he knew that the Terran was right.

"Yes Pieter, he's absolutely right. This information has to stay with the three of us and no one else for the time being, except the Matriarch of course. I will relate to her the event in its entirety when I return to the Holy See tomorrow."

Pieter Minsk closed his eyes and clasped his hands together. "I pray that the Matriarch will see this event as I do and allow the story to be told."

"Perhaps she will Pieter, in which case I won't stand in the way," Richelieux assured him.

Minsk sighed, filled with hope for his evangelic quest. Perhaps the Matriarch would see things his way. Then he turned to Ogram. "Since you say you know the media well, how do you suggest we handle the shutdown and the tragic death of so many of our employees?"

"I will tell you what I think, and please bear in mind that my opinion of the Church's public image was until recently, the opinion of the majority of the population in the galaxy," Ogram commented. "Because of my recent involvement with the Church, my personal opinion of the Church has improved. Yet, to the majority of the public, the Church of St. Kelem is seen by many people as a somewhat fanatic religion with a penchant for secrecy and overbearing political power within the Galactic Council. My advice would be to immediately release a statement, admitting that the Plantanimus CUBE suffered a technical malfunction due to the overwhelming power of the polar storm of five days ago, which in turn, caused an unprecedented shutdown and that because of the subsequent blackout, the ventilation system of the CUBE complex was compromised, thereby accidentally and tragically asphyxiating one hundred and twelve employees."

Minsk raised his eyebrows and stared at Richelieux, looking for his opinion.

Richelieux had a pained expression in his face. He was in agreement with Ogram's logic, while at the same time knowing that the Curia would never allow such sensitive information to be released to the public. "You're quite right Ogram, yet, even if the Matriarch herself agrees with you, the Curia will never permit such a press release."

"Your Eminence, you agree?" Minsk asked, somewhat shocked.

Ogram turned to Minsk. "How many employees currently reside at this facility?"

"Hmmm, about eleven thousand give or take a few," Minsk replied.

"And how many of them are due for a vacation or a weekend off?" Ogram added.

"Quite a few, now that I think about it," the newly promoted general manager answered, realizing what the Terran was getting at. "Oh . . . I see . . ." he said softly, beginning to understand the difficulty of trying to keep the shutdown and the deaths quiet.

"Your Eminence, we're damned if we do and damned if we don't! What should we do?" Minsk pleaded, feeling miserable.

"We are in a terrible spot indeed! Young Ogram is right. Nothing motivates the media more than a juicy conspiracy scandal. This could damage the Church beyond repair. It will be my difficult duty as Cardinal Counselor to the Matriarch, to advise her that she should bypass the Curia's authority and allow the press release without a vote," Richelieux explained with alacrity.

Minsk put his head in his hands. "These are dark days indeed!" he whispered under his breath. Then, raising his head again, he looked at Ogram with anxiety in his face. "Oh, God, your presence here will only add to the firestorm!"

Richelieux grimaced, realizing that Minsk was right! Once the word got out that an agnostic, of all people, had been involved in the situation, the Church's reputation would be further diminished.

"Not to worry gentlemen," Ogram announced with a smile. "I came here under an assumed name, that of Charles Brentwood, 'quantum computer specialist'. When the Kelemite priest that offered me this job contacted me, he was very specific about traveling here incognito. This was very easy for me, since I'm in the habit of traveling under assumed identities all the time. Many of the corporations that hire me as a consultant wish to keep my participation in their affairs private. Besides, there'll never be a record of me having worked for The Realm, since I decided to do this *pro bono* and without a contract."

"Thank God for small favors," Minsk uttered, thankful that at least one aspect of this whole disaster had gone right.

Richelieux exhaled with relief. More and more, he was growing fond of young Ogram Zepol. In spite of all the troubles of the last five days, he realized that things would have been worse without the young agnostic scientist's involvement.

CHAPTER 14

On the Voyage to New Jerusalem

Cardinal Richelieux had asked the Trinity's pilot to begin the trip back to the Holy See at sub light speed. The main reason for his request was because he wanted to spend enough time with Ogram discussing the many issues that faced them before arriving at the Heavenly Temple and meeting with the Matriarch. He could have waited until he and Zepol had their talk and then depart for New Jerusalem under *n'time* power, but Richelieux wanted to leave Plantanimus as soon as possible and put the last six days behind him. He knew that he was being foolish by feeling safer away from the planet, but he'd been so traumatized by the event inside The Realm's VR, that he couldn't help surrendering to the instinct of fleeing from the place.

After being fully briefed by Richelieux in a quantum video conference a day earlier, Matriarch Vasilia asked that Ogram Zepol be brought to the Holy See for a personal audience. It took some effort by Richelieux to convince the young Terran to agree to come by persuading him that his presence at the Holy See was of prime importance. His involvement in all the events of the last few days had put him in the middle of it all, like it or not. Additionally, Richelieux explained, Ogram's presence would go a long way in making his report to the Matriarch far easier than without him.

The young Terran genuinely liked the Cardinal and had grown close to him in the short time they'd known each other. When Richelieux told him that his presence at the Holy See would help him, Ogram couldn't refuse. After agreeing to go, he came to the realization that the universe had put him on this new path and that it would be wiser not resist the direction where events were taking him.

The ship was still on Plantanimus time, and after dinner, Richelieux asked Ogram to accompany him to his quarters for a talk.

"I'm ready to talk about what happened if you are," Ogram stated quietly.

"Yes, I guess we both had to digest the experience for a while before we could discuss it openly," replied the Cardinal. "You know, there is more than one aspect to what happened to us," he added.

"I agree. I think it would be easier to go over the technical, scientific part of it first. Shall I begin?" Ogram asked.

Richelieux nodded, happy to tackle the less complex issues first.

"Well, in anticipation of the biggest question in both our minds, I spent all of yesterday at the CUBE performing a full diagnostic of the system and I couldn't find a pre-programmed avatar for Kelem Rogeston. I know my stuff, and I can guarantee you that he . . ., it, doesn't exist in the system."

Richelieux rubbed his chin deep in thought, realizing for the first time, that he'd been hoping for the opposite answer. "Are you sure? You still can't explain how the cloned angels got there. What makes you so sure that the Rogeston avatar is not hidden in some unknown partition of one of the other CUBEs central cores?"

"First of all, not only did I run a diagnostic of the Plantanimus CUBE, but of the entire network. And second; and this is where the weird, spooky quantum theory magic comes in. A quantum computer is holographic in nature. In other words, all the information contained in the entire CUBE network can be found in any other single part of the network. Theoretically down to the sub-atomic level. Tzu Jin Chu was the smartest human being to ever have lived, but even he, couldn't have hidden a secret avatar of Kelem Rogeston inside the network, or any other place."

"Then isn't it possible that someone else projected the Kelem Rogeston avatar into the system?" Richelieux countered.

"Again, it's impossible, and in anticipation of your next question, the avatar that we saw, could not have been 'projected in' externally and/ or, 'inserted' and then removed. I cannot give you a scientific answer as to how the Kelem Rogeston avatar appeared to us. And as a point of contention, history says that Tzu Jin Chu was a Buddhist when he started the CUBE project. He only converted to Kelemism, hours before his death. Suggesting that he was not a devout Kelemite when he designed the CUBE which was forty years before his death, and no reason that he would have been motivated to insert a secret St. Kelem, programmed to appear in the CUBE's VR in this millennium," Ogram concluded.

"You're right of course Ogram," Richelieux admitted. "The truth is that Tzu Jin Chu's family had a law suit against the Church, claiming that his estate was owed several billion Kredits in royalty fees from the CUBE's patent. The Church and the family agreed to settle out of court on the condition that Tzu Jin Chu converted to Kelemism before his death."

"Forgive me your Eminence, but I'm confused by your apparent desire to prove that the appearance of Kelem Rogeston is due to some sort of technical manipulation by a third party, instead of a genuine miracle, as Pieter Minsk believes, and I'm sure many others in your Church, would like to believe."

"We already discussed this at Minsk's office, Ogram. A miraculous appearance by our patron saint is not what this Church needs at this time," Richelieux argued.

"I tend to agree your Eminence, but why is it that you're not personally wishing for it in your heart?" Ogram asked, knowing that he was stepping on shaky ground by asking the second most powerful man in the galaxy, why his faith was lacking in this matter.

Richelieux became visibly upset and got up from his chair and walked over to one of the port windows in his cabin and looked out into space. Ogram, realizing that he'd crossed the boundaries of etiquette, felt immediately sorry and wished that he'd kept his mouth shut.

"I . . . I'm so sorry your Eminence! Please forgive me! I don't know why I said such a stupid thing. How dare I . . ."

"Stop!" Richelieux exclaimed with his back to Ogram, who held his breath, fearing a strong rebuke from the cleric.

"It is I who should apologize to you my young friend," he said, almost whispering. Then with his voice almost breaking, he continued. "In all the years that I've been a faithful Kelemite, I've never had my faith truly tested until now. And what happens when the Universal Mind God puts a pebble in my path . . . ? I stumble like a hypocrite and fall to pieces!" he confessed, sounding angry with himself.

Ogram was mortified that he'd been responsible for causing a highly respected man like Richelieux to recriminate himself and question his faith. With his face flushed with embarrassment, he got up from the couch and headed for the cabin's door. "I should leave . . ." he began saying.

"No please stay!" Richelieux pleaded. He turned away from the port window and walked over to Ogram who was standing near the door. Then, putting his arm around the young man's shoulder, he guided him gently back to the couch. Ogram sat down and Richelieux took the chair across from him.

"Do you know why I've been so sullen and withdrawn ever since we came out of the CUBE?" Richelieux asked, wiping tears from his eyes.

"N . . . no I don't, your Eminence . . ., "Ogram answered, avoiding Richelieux's teary eyes.

"Please look at me Ogram. Don't be embarrassed by my emotional reaction. Regardless of my position in this life, I'm only a human being, just like you," he asked of his young friend.

Ogram raised his eyes and looked at Richelieux and felt tears welling in his eyes as well. He was experiencing powerful emotions that he'd suppressed all his life. Until recently, his life had been one of science and discovery. Now he felt as though he was stepping into the abyss.

"What do you remember of the event when Kelem Rogeston appeared?" the cleric asked.

Ogram took a deep breath and tried to concentrate on his memory of the experience. "I was being choked by the monster and beginning to lose consciousness when a blinding light went off in front of us like and explosion, but with no sound. Then after the monster retreated, the light hovered above us and came down to our level and morphed into the image of Kelem Rogeston."

"What happened then?" Richelieux asked, with an intense look in his eyes.

"Well, then, Kelem Rogeston . . ., I mean the avatar, looked at us, smiled and said, Nobius, seven, two, five, two, seven, and then disappeared."

"That's exactly how you remember it?" Richelieux reiterated.

"Yes. Did I forget something?" Ogram questioned, wondering what he had missed.

"That's pretty much how I remember it also, except for one detail; the avatar never looked in my direction. His entire message was aimed at you, not me."

"No, that can't be right! He looked at the two of us, I'm sure!" Ogram argued, although he really didn't remember whether the Kelem Rogeston avatar had looked at the two of them, or just him.

"No, Ogram. The message was meant for you and only you," Richelieux insisted. That's why I fell victim to my baser self by allowing jealousy to overcome me and weaken my faith in St Kelem!"

"I'm . . ., I'm so sorry that you've been feeling this way your Eminence! But it's quite possible that the VR's holo-geometry was off, especially after the Darius avatar attacked us. One thing we know for sure, is that the CUBE's safety protocols were temporarily defeated, so it's possible that what you saw, was a holographic glitch. Besides, why would Kelem Rogeston's avatar direct a cryptic message like the one he gave us, to me and not the two of us?" Ogram contended.

"I'm not sure, but I hope that in time the answer will reveal itself," Richelieux commented, looking at his young friend pensively.

"Well, if it's alright with you your Eminence, I'm going to head to my cabin. We have a big day tomorrow and I want to be at my best when I meet the Matriarch," Ogram said, excusing himself. In truth, he wanted to leave. He was feeling overwhelmed by his conversation with the Cardinal and needed some alone time to deal with the significance of what had been discussed.

"Good night Ogram. Breakfast will be at 0800 tomorrow, Plantanimus time, though it will be noon on New Jerusalem when we arrive at the Heavenly Temple."

"Goodnight your Eminence, sleep well. I will see you tomorrow."

The door slid closed behind Ogram and Richelieux walked over to his cabin's communication panel.

"Pilot, please initiate *n'time* travel at 0700 tomorrow morning. I want to arrive at the Holy See by noon."

"Aye, aye your Eminence, will do," responded the pilot.

Before he went to sleep, Cardinal Richelieux prayed to St. Kelem for strength of faith and clarity of thought.

CHAPTER 15

Ogram Meets Sister Allondra

The Trinity rematerialized one hundred and eighty thousand kilometers from New Jerusalem at exactly 11:59 am local time. The window shields in Cardinal Richelieux's quarters opened up, letting the light of the Tal System's sun, bathe his cabin with light.

"Well, here we are Ogram. We'll be arriving at the Heavenly Temple in about an hour," Richelieux announced.

Ogram got up from his chair and walked over to the window to look at the planet that had been the home of the Kelemite religion for over six thousand years.

"Oh! It looks like a blue marble, just like Earth, but I don't see the Heavenly Temple from here," he commented, referring to the artificial moon where the Holy See was located.

"It's on the other side of the planet. All arriving ships must rematerialize on the opposite side of the Temple. It's the law," the cleric informed him.

"For security reasons?" Ogram asked.

"Yes, it's a leftover from the Crusades and as you well know, the Gulax are obsessive about security. Ever since the Holy See was attacked on Plantanimus and completely destroyed by the Tilharans in the fourth millennium, the Gulax Guard has always demanded that the seat of the Matriarch be highly protected. It's the reason why the Holy See is on an artificial moon and not on a planet as it was on Plantanimus."

"I've always heard that the Heavenly Temple is armed to the teeth, is it true?"

"Yes, but we don't advertise it. The Temple has been attacked in the past. It was assaulted on a regular basis by Tilharan fundamentalists in the fifth millennium and three times in this century by mercenaries hired by the Body Shop Guild."

"Hmmm, sounds like a fascinating place, I can't wait to see it," Ogram remarked.

"About that, Ogram," Richelieux said, looking uncomfortable. "I have a huge favor to ask of you."

"What it is your Eminence?" Ogram asked, wondering why the Cardinal looked so uneasy.

"We must disguise you before you go up to the Temple. As much as the Matriarch and I appreciate everything you've done for The Realm and the Church as well, your presence here will still be a problem for us. So please do not be insulted by our need to hide your identity," Richelieux explained apologetically.

"You mentioned some sort of disguise. What do you have in mind?"

"I've asked the valet avatar to produce a 'lay priest's' outfit for you. It consists of a pair of pants, a clerical shirt and an old style dress jacket."

"What exactly is a 'lay priest?" Ogram asked, never having heard the term.

"A lay priest, deacon or *Diakonos* (from ancient Greek, meaning 'observer'), is usually a non-Kelemite-ordained priest from a different religious order or a lay person who conducts services in a congregation. We welcome many such individuals to the Heavenly Temple on a regular basis. They usually come here to make use of the Holy See's Research Library or to observe our rituals, procedures and how we conduct our for-profit businesses."

"I won't have to fraternize with other priests or nuns, will I?" Ogram asked, concerned.

"Not at all, this will only be necessary for your entrance and departure from the Temple, that's all," Richelieux assured him.

"In that case, I don't mind wearing the disguise."

"ATTENTION PASSENGERS, WE'RE ABOUT TO FIRE OUR SUB-LIGHT ENGINES. PLEASE SECURE YOUR CABINS," the announcement came in on their cochlear implants. Ogram and the Cardinal sat on the couch in the cabin and soon the ship's massive engines came to life and the Trinity began accelerating toward New Jerusalem.

An hour later, the Trinity was touching down on the tarmac of New Jerusalem's space port, located in the largest continent on the planet.

After Centralia, the galaxy's capital, then Earth, Mars and Tarsia Prime; New Jerusalem was the fifth, most advanced and populated planet in the Galactic Council's Federation of planets. This was a world populated by the richest and most influential citizens in the galaxy, most of whom were members of the Kelemite religion.

Latonga, the planet's capital, named after Mars' old capital, Latonga City, where Kelem Rogeston was born, was a huge megalopolis encompassing several hundred square kilometers of giant skyscrapers and industrial facilities. Ogram could not help but be impressed by the size and scope of the city as the Trinity approached the spaceport located next to it.

When the Trinity's landing plank came down and Cardinal Richelieux stepped onto the tarmac, he was received by a cadre of nuns, priests and media reporters, who welcomed him with great fanfare and ceremony. Ogram, who was following the Cardinal several steps behind, was suddenly reminded of the man's status, power and position in the Church of St. Kelem. He had become familiar with the man who, less than twenty four hours before, had opened his heart to him with tears in his eyes, confessing that he'd had a crisis of faith. The Cardinal's welcoming reception served to remind him, that in spite of everything that he had shared with Richelieux during the last week, Ogram Zepol was an outsider, and most of all, an outsider who had been declared *persona non grata* by the church.

He wondered if he had made a huge mistake by agreeing to come to meet the Matriarch after all. Here he was, in a sense, practically infiltrating 'enemy territory', knowing that some could see it that way. Wearing a disguise and keeping his identity from being discovered by the media could surely be construed that way. He could only imagine what his friends and colleagues would say if they found out that he'd been collaborating with Richelieux and soon, the Matriarch herself. Not to mention, being involved in a cover up of the CUBE's accident and the deaths of over one hundred people!

He shook his head laughing at himself, knowing that he was up to his neck in 'it'. Distracted by his own thoughts, he was startled when he practically ran straight into a young Kelemite nun. "I'm so sorry sister!" he blurted out, cursing himself for almost running down the young Tarsian girl.

"Father Ogram?" she asked, bowing slightly.

It took him a few seconds to realize that he was the 'Father Ogram' to whom the girl was referring.

"Ah, yes that's me," he acknowledged, laughing uncomfortably.

"My name is Sister Allondra. His Eminence, Cardinal Richelieux, has asked me to escort you to the Heavenly Temple and take you to your quarters there."

Richelieux and his entourage were now boarding a large craft that resembled a square gold encrusted jewelry box with winglets and thrusters attached to it.

"Oh, of . . . of course," he stuttered, feeling nervous and guilty as if he was trying to sneak into a party uninvited.

"Please follow me Father," the girl said, turning around and heading toward a small shuttle that looked like a white swan with golden wings. The unlikely craft was shining brightly under the red sun of the Tal system.

He caught up with her in a few steps and noticed how beautiful the girl was. He'd always been attracted to the smooth green skin, upwardly oblique eyes and jet-black hair of female Tarsians. He reminded himself that this was a nun and that he should keep his libido in check, but he couldn't keep from admiring the girl's physical beauty.

"Will you be staying long Father? And is this all the luggage you've brought with you?" Sister Allondra asked, pointing to the small bag in his hand, containing Ogram's regular clothes.

"Yes, I won't be staying long,' he replied, as they boarded the ornately decorated shuttle. Once inside, Ogram took notice of the elegant interior with its deep red velvet upholstered seats and gold inlaid sconces on the bulkheads of the ship. The décor reminded him of late 19th Century mansions from Earth's past.

"Hangar 6H," Sister Allondra said to the A.I.. The craft's hatch closed silently and then rose smoothly and climbed. Very soon, the skies of New Jerusalem turned into the dark blue of the planet's upper atmosphere. The shuttle picked up speed and within minutes, the circular form of the Heavenly Temple appeared on the shuttle's front window, floating in the deep black of space.

The artificial moon grew bigger and bigger until its image filled the cabin's window. Without realizing it, he gasped at the beauty and grandeur of the mammoth, man-made object growing ever larger in size, as the automated shuttle began orbiting the sphere on its way to Hangar 6H.

Sister Allondra smiled. "Everyone gasps just like you did the first time they see it. It's beautiful, don't you agree?" she asked sweetly.

"Indeed," he answered turning to her and almost saying, "like you."

He turned away from her and stared straight ahead, lest he embarrass himself and the girl by gawking at her like a hormonally excited teenager.

The shuttle fired its retros and slowed down, then it banked left and approached the gaping mouth of Hangar 6H. As it entered, Ogram was impressed by the myriad swan-like craft parked on the cavernous space. The shuttle folded its wings and landed softly on the deck.

The ship's hatch opened and Sister Allondra exited first. "Please follow me Father, I will take you to level 26 where we billet our guests."

Ogram followed her, intent on not staring at the beautiful Tarsian nun. The hangar was a hub of activity with crafts taking off and landing almost continuously. It was enormous, yet this was just one of several similarly sized hangars within the artificial moon. He was just beginning to comprehend the wealth and power of the Church of St, Kelem. As he followed the Kelemite nun, he suddenly felt small and insignificant. Before getting involved with The Realm and now the Church, Ogram had always seen himself as a sort of genius wonder boy who was an important part of the galaxy's scientific world and a fairly well known celebrity, but right now, he felt more like a mouse staring at a lion.

They boarded one of the many elevators that were available at the end of the hangar and descended to level 26.

Once there, Sister Allondra guided Ogram through several moving sidewalks and then several large hallways and gallerias. This part of the Heavenly Temple was more of an underground city, complete with shopping malls, restaurants, entertainment centers and chapel after chapel named after different saints from the Church's past. The place was full of priests, nuns and civilian workers busily going about their business.

He had no idea where he was in relation to where he and Sister Allondra had entered level 26. The place seemed to go on forever! The effect only served to depress him and make him feel overwhelmed by it all.

Finally, the young nun stopped at the front door to an apartment complex, and after they entered and the pressure door closed behind them, the ambient noise of level 26 faded away.

"Pheeew!" Ogram exclaimed with relief. "I thought we'd be walking for another hour or so!"

"I'm sorry Father, I should have warned you that your quarters would be some distance from the elevators. It's only a little further on if you don't mind."

"No, go ahead, I'll follow you."

They took an elevator that traveled ten floors and opened to a corridor that led to a door with the number 108 on it. Ogram smiled and remembered that the number 108 was considered sacred by several Eastern religions, such as Hinduism and Buddhism. The individual digits comprising 108; 1, 0, and 8 represent one thing, nothing, and everything (infinity), thus symbolizing the belief that the ultimate reality of the universe is (paradoxically), simultaneously one, empty and infinite. He wondered if the universe was sending him a message.

"This is your apartment Father, would you like me to show you inside?" she asked.

"Yes, if you wouldn't mind," he replied, pleased that he'd be in her company for a few more minutes.

She waved her hand by the door's frame and it slid open quietly. The apartment's lights came on and Ogram was pleased to see that the place was rather large and well-appointed for a visiting lay priest from an outside religion.

Sister Allondra showed him how the apartment was laid out and how the A.I. worked. Then she showed him a small non-denominational altar near a small kitchenette, where Father Ogram could pray to his version of the deity.

"Are you Catholic or Protestant?" she asked with curiosity.

Ogram panicked for a moment and then remembered that his aunt Megan from Ohio was a Presbyterian. "Protestant," he answered, hoping that she would not inquire further into the matter. He was woefully ignorant of religion in general.

Sister Allondra turned a dial next to the altar and a holographic Protestant cross was projected onto the altar.

"Thank you very much sister. Do you know when I'll be meeting with the Matriarch?" he asked, wondering how long it would be before his audience with the Church's leader.

As soon as he saw her reaction, which was one of complete and utter surprise, Ogram realized that he had blundered miserably. A visiting lay priest would never be granted an audience with Her Holiness the Matriarch, Vasilia Bentara Rogeston! And obviously, this young novice nun had not been told anything.

"I . . . I beg your pardon," she stuttered, blinking and widening her green emerald eyes. "You're here to meet with Her Holiness?"

He thought furiously trying to decide how to fix his *faux pas*. Should he claim that he was joking? Or that he suffered from Tourette syndrome? For the first time in his adult life, he was at a loss for words. To make things worse, his face had turned ruby red with embarrassment and he felt mortified and out of control.

"I . . . I'm sorry Father," Sister Allondra apologized, feeling embarrassed herself for having caused a visiting clergyman any discomfort. "His Eminence didn't inform me of any pending meeting with Her Holiness. I will go to him immediately and inquire as to your meeting," she blurted out with her head bowed down.

Ogram swallowed hard, realizing that it was too late to take his words back. "Please, sister, don't feel bad, I shouldn't have said anything to you. This meeting is supposed to be secret. I hope that you'll keep this to yourself and no one else. This involves a serious matter concerning the Church."

"Yes of course Father! Please forgive me. I will leave now if it's alright with you," she replied apologetically as she backed away from Ogram and pressed the door's button, in a hurry to get away.

"Thank you sister, I'm sorry, I . . . will make this right, you'll . . . see . . . !" he continued blabbering, even as the door closed.

Ogram sat on the living room couch and held his head in his hands.

"Excellent Zepol!" he said, laughing sarcastically." So glad you kept your big mouth shut!"

CHAPTER 16

A Late Dinner with the Matriarch

Ogram spent the next ten hours wondering if his blabbing to Sister Allondra had caused any problems. He was nervous and on edge and couldn't relax. He took two baths in the spa's whirlpool in his apartment but they didn't help. He was lying in bed staring at the ceiling when finally, at 11:00 PM, his cochlear implant dinged.

"Yes?" he answered, anxiously.

"PLEASE BE READY TO LEAVE YOUR APARTMENT IN TEN MINUTES," an avatar announced.

Ogram jumped up and put on his cleric's shirt and jacket and waited by the door. Ten minutes later, the door rang and he opened it. It was Sister Allondra.

"I'm to escort you to the Holy Residence. Are you ready?" she asked, looking somewhat sheepish.

"Yes, I'm ready. Lead the way."

Sister Allondra turned and headed for the elevator. Ogram noticed that her attitude had changed and then remembered that she hadn't called him Father this time. The elevator opened and they got in.

"I hope that I haven't caused you any trouble Sister," Ogram said, by way of an apology.

"It's alright, I'm not in trouble," she replied.

"Are you sure? I thought I had ruined your career by making a stupid mistake!" Ogram offered.

Sister Allondra smiled and then tried to suppress a laugh. "His Eminence laughed when I related our conversation to him," she commented, trying to remain serious.

"He . . . he laughed?" he asked, feeling both relieved and curious at the same time. "Did he say anything? I mean, about me, saying what I said?" he questioned, feeling like an awkward teenager.

Sister Allondra turned and looked at him with her upwardly oblique green eyes for a second or two and then lowered her eyes. "I know who you are," she said, sounding a little embarrassed.

"You do? How . . . ?"

"My younger sister Latha is studying to be a physicist. After talking to you this afternoon, I remembered that she has a holo of you on her bedroom wall. She's a big fan."

For the first time in his life, he wished that he hadn't been so good at self-promotion all these years. "That's great!" he muttered sarcastically, imagining that soon the media would be storming the Heavenly Temple investigating what Ogram Zepol was doing in the Holy City.

"I haven't told anyone about you and I never will. Your secret is safe with me."

"Thank you Sister, but how has this affected you? You said that Cardinal Richelieux laughed when you told him about our conversation. How did he react, besides being amused?"

"He told me that there are no coincidences in the universe and that everything happens for a reason."

"I'm glad that he was so magnanimous and that he let me off easy," Ogram declared with relief.

"Well, not so much. He's ordered me to chaperon you while you remain here at the Temple," Allondra replied, with a hint of humor in her voice. "I'm to make sure that you keep away from the public and that you don't speak to anyone else," she added, this time unable to suppress a laugh.

"Hmmm, very funny Sister Allondra! But I suppose it could be worse, I could have been stuck with an old crotchety nun with a severe case of halitosis for a chaperone," Ogram commented, laughing with relief.

This time, she laughed out loud and Ogram thought that Sister Allondra's white smile was the most beautiful thing he'd ever seen. He'd chided himself for feeling so drawn to the novice nun and wondered what was happening to him. There was something about this young Tarsian girl that he found irresistible. If there was a hell, he was surely going to end up there.

After they left the apartment complex, Sister Allondra took him through a different route than the one they traveled when he arrived. Level 26 was empty at this time of night. Obviously, the citizens of the Holy Temple were the "early to bed, early to rise" type. She took him through a door titled "Service" and then into a small freight elevator.

"Penthouse," she ordered, and the elevator took off at high speed.

This time the ride went on for a long time and Ogram wondered why it was taking so long. 'I must say, this is taking quite a while," he commented.

"We're traveling to Her Holiness's residence at the Temple's north pole, thirty five kilometers from Level 26," she announced, matter of fact.

"Oh," was all that Ogram could say, once again, realizing how big the artificial moon really was.

Ten minutes later, the elevator stopped and when the door opened, they were met by Cardinal Richelieux.

"Good evening Ogram. I trust you've had a pleasant day?" he asked with a smile.

"Yes, your Eminence. And I just want to say that I feel terrible about what hap . . ."

"Relax, Ogram. There's no harm done. I know Sister Allondra's heart, and there was never any danger of anyone finding out your true identity," he assured him with an affectionate pat on his shoulder. Sister Allondra smiled, pleased by the Cardinal's complement regarding her character and at the same time, impressed by the familiarity shared by the two men.

"Come, follow me. I'll introduce you to the Matriarch,' he said, pointing the way. A few steps later, he stopped and turned around.

"You're also coming Sister, or did you forget that you've been assigned as Ogram's chaperone?"

"N . . . . no, your Eminence," she replied timidly. She couldn't hide her surprise at being invited to enter the Matriarch's private residence, a privilege reserved for bishops, cardinals and dignitaries. As they followed Richelieux, Ogram noticed how nervous the young nun was. She was practically trembling. Ogram realized at that moment what the Matriarch truly meant for the trillions of Kelemites throughout the galaxy. The realization heightened his own nervousness and he wondered why his mouth was so dry.

After they passed through a heavy metal door that required Richelieux to enter a security code on a panel next to it, they walked into a chamber where they were confronted by the Matriarch's personal Gulax Guard. Ogram and the young nun were scanned by the Guard and then allowed to pass through another door to a small foyer. The foyer was decorated with small holo statues of St. Kelem, dressed in his typical white coveralls and Sister Ornata in her vermillion robe. Both Richelieux and Sister Allondra immediately knelt down and bowed to the two saints. Ogram stood behind them feeling a little uncomfortable. The small space also had two benches on each side and after paying their respect to the saints, Richelieux asked the two youngsters to sit across from him.

"I know you're both probably a little nervous to meet the Matriarch," he said, more to the young nun than to Ogram. But Matriarch Vasilia is a kind and gentle soul and I promise you, she doesn't bite!" he added, making a joke. Both Ogram and Sister Allondra laughed, feeling relieved by Richelieux's attempt at levity.

"When you meet her, simply bow to her and then, whichever one of you is closest to her, you kiss her papal signet ring on her right hand and then the other will do the same. But, neither one of you will actually kiss her ring and much less her hand. You will take the ring by putting your thumb and index finger thus," he said, demonstrating on his own cardinal's signet ring by holding the large ruby between the two fingers. What you will actually do, is kiss your own fingers, understood?

Both Ogram and Sister Allondra responded in unison.

"Here, practice on my ring," he said extending his right hand.

Awkwardly and a little self-consciously, each took turns practicing on Richelieux's right hand.

"Perfect. Two more things. You will address the Matriarch as Your Holiness the first time you speak to her and then you may address her as Matriarch, or Your Holiness interchangeably. And last but not least, speak only when spoken to and never, ever, interrupt her while she speaks. Clear?"

Both nodded, feeling a little intimidated.

"Very well, let's go in."

Richelieux opened the door and entered the Matriarch's residence.

Once inside, they were in a long hallway with vaulted ceilings and intricately designed parquet floors. Holo paintings of Kelem Rogeston, Sister Ornata and other luminaries of the Church hung on the walls next to bronze and stone busts of former Matriarchs. Along the sides, pieces of finely crafted antique furniture with vases full of magnificent flower arrangements, added to the impressive décor. The vaulted ceiling itself was one large light panel set to low intensity, illuminating the space with soft warm light, reminiscent of a sunset or sunrise. The effect gave the place both a regal and at the same time, an intimate aspect.

Ogram had expected to be met by pages and servants of the Matriarch, but the place was empty. Then he remembered that his presence here was supposed to be a secret, thus the late hour of the meeting and the total absence of staff.

Richelieux led the way and stopped at the end of the long hallway and pressed a com button on a finely carved double wooden door, depicting nature scenes from Tarsia Prime.

"May we come in your Holiness?" Richelieux asked, respectfully.

"Yes, please come in," came the voice of Matriarch Vasilia.

They entered and Richelieux immediately bowed to the Matriarch who was sitting on a long couch in the center of the residence's living room. Ogram and Sister Allondra followed suit.

"Your Holiness, may I present to you, Ogram Zepol and one of our own, Sister Allondra Velmador," he said, gesturing with his arm.

"Please come closer," she said in a soft voice. The Matriarch, a tall young woman, dressed in a vermillion robe with a strip of gold braid along the seams of her garment, stood up. Her fine features were framed by her auburn red hair which was tied in the back in a ponytail. Her piercing blue eyes sparkled with the brilliance of precious gems. Ogram and Sister Allondra were mesmerized by her appearance. Her holos, seen galaxy wide, didn't do justice to her beauty in person. The three approached and Ogram, being closer to the Matriarch, bowed and kissed the signet ring on her hand, followed by a very nervous Sister Allondra.

"Please sit down. I trust that you've found your accomodations to your liking Mr. Zepol?"

"Oh yes, absolutely Your Holiness. They're more than adequate," he replied nervously.

She turned her gaze toward Sister Allondra. "Sister Allondra, it seems that you have been drawn into our secret by accident and are now part of our group. But as Mother Ornata always said, 'there are no coincidences in the universe'. Do you believe in coincidence Mr. Zepol?' she asked, turning to him.

Ogram smiled and looked down for a second. "A week ago I would have said that, statistically speaking, coincidences are inevitable and often less remarkable than they may appear intuitively. But today, I would tend to agree with Mother Ornata's wisdom, Your Holiness."

The Matriarch smiled and stared at Ogram for a second or two, making him uncomfortable. Here was the most powerful woman in the galaxy questioning him about abstract issues, like coincidence and staring into the depths of his soul.

Who's hungry?" she asked, suddenly changing subjects and surprising everyone, except Richelieux, who was used to her personality.

Ogram looked quickly at Richelieux, hoping for a sign from him and the older man nodded, indicating that it was alright to speak his mind.

"I just realized that I forgot to eat today Your Holiness. I could use some food," he replied tentatively.

"What about you Sister? Could you use a midnight snack?" the Matriarch asked with a smile.

"Y . . . yes Your Holiness," she answered, having trouble imagining herself sharing a meal with the Matriarch.

"Very well then, I asked my cooks to leave some food ready in the kitchen, follow me," she said, standing up and heading for a door at the rear of the living room.

Richelieux stood up from the couch and signaled to the two youngsters to come along. For Ogram, this was as surprising a turn of events as it was for Sister Allondra. The last thing he'd expected to be doing today was sharing a midnight snack with the pontiff of the Church of St. Kelem.

Once in the kitchen, Ogram and Sister Allondra were further taken aback by the sight of the Matriarch and the Cardinal Counselor, opening cabinets, taking out dishes and participating in the setting of the table. After they all sat down, Matriarch Vasilia asked Cardinal Richelieux to give the blessing. Ogram panicked for a second feeling like a fraud for wearing a priest's outfit. He closed his eyes and bowed his head like the others, glad that he'd been excluded from giving grace.

"We ask the Universal Mind God, our beloved St. Kelem and Mother Ornata to bless these gifts we're about to receive. May they nourish our bodies, thus giving us life so that we may reach ultimate Samadhi."

The delicious meal consisted of braised vegetables served cold, gazpacho soup, and chocolate cake, washed down with Oolong tea. Ogram ate with great gusto, realizing how hungry he really was. Afterwards they returned to the living room where Richelieux, took out a bottle of Cointreau from the wet bar in the living room, filled four goblets of the amber liquid and made a toast in the name of St. Kelem. All emptied their goblets quickly, then the Matriarch turned to Sister Allondra.

"Sister, Cardinal Richelieux and I have much to discuss with Mr. Zepol. I know you're not used to these late hours, so there's a small bedroom outside at the end of the hallway, where you can rest until we're done."

"Thank you Your Holiness, I shall depart immediately," the young nun replied, then bowed deeply at the Matriarch, then at the Cardinal and quickly exited the living room. As she left, Ogram followed her with his eyes, unaware that the Matriarch took notice of his interest in the girl.

"First of all, Mr. Zepol, I want to thank you on behalf of the Church of St. Kelem and The Realm for all that you've done for us in the past seven days. Cardinal Richelieux has filled me in on every detail of the events that have transpired. And before we go any further, I would like to ask you to let us remunerate you for all the time and effort you've put in."

"Thank you very much for your appreciation of my efforts Your Holiness. But as long as my employment by The Realm and the Church comes to a conclusion within a short time, I do not wish to be paid. I am wealthy beyond need and I'm thrilled that I was able to help in any way."

"Very well then, Mr. Zepol, let's discuss the events of the past seven days."

"I don't know if it's proper Your Holiness, but I would feel better if you'd call me by my first name," Ogram requested.

The Matriarch smiled. "It is completely proper, Ogram. Now tell me, what is your opinion of the status of the Plantanimus CUBE?"

"After the event inside the VR, I was able to isolate the Plantanimus CUBE from the rest of the network with the assistance of Pieter Minsk and his excellent staff. For all intents and purposes, that facility is its own separate CUBE, unable to communicate with the others through quantum entanglement."

"Is the rest of the network safe from contagion?" Matriarch Vasilia inquired.

"Unfortunately, Your Holiness, that, I cannot guarantee. Human logic dictates that it should be so. However, the quantum realm behaves in weird and unexpected ways that still surprise physicists and computer scientists such as me, even today."

"What is your theory of how these 'cloned angels' entered the CUBE?" she asked, sounding very concerned.

"As I've already discussed with Cardinal Richelieux and Pieter Minsk, I have no scientific explanation for how this has happened. Everything that is currently known about quantum holographic computers, tells us that it shouldn't be possible."

"Cardinal Richelieux tells me that you seem to have a sort of sixth sense, or perhaps I should say, an intuitive understanding of what is going on. Could you shape your answer to my question in those terms?" the Matriarch asked, with a hint of anxiety in her voice.

Ogram closed his eyes. He hated to speculate about anything in life, particularly when it came to science, but he was out of logical answers and conclusions. In the last few days, his mind had been pushed into areas of thought that he'd never considered before.

"Whoever infiltrated the Plantanimus CUBE and 'cloned' those angels and modified their programming, is someone who is decades, perhaps centuries ahead of current quantum theory knowledge. When I was facing the evil version of the Darius Angel, I had a sense that I was dealing with a sentient being and not a programmed avatar."

"Why didn't you mention this before Ogram?" Richelieux asked.

"Perhaps because I just came to that realization this very moment Cardinal. How's that old saying go?" Ogram searched his memory, trying to recall. "Oh yes! 'When you have eliminated the impossible, whatever remains, however improbable, must be the truth.'"

Richelieux and the Matriarch exchanged glances. Both felt that Ogram's intuitive explanation was closer to the truth.

"Though I have degrees in physics, mathematics and philosophy myself Ogram, what you just told us sounds more accurate than any scientific speculation," the Matriarch concluded.

"Perhaps Your Holiness, perhaps. Still, accepting that this is the work of an advanced individual or individuals, doesn't help us prevent further infiltrations into the CUBE or future attacks on the consciousnesses of individuals currently existing inside The Realm," Ogram hypothesized.

"By the Saint! This is indeed troubling!" the Matriarch exclaimed. "How can we protect all those souls in the system from being harmed?" she complained, expressing deep worry.

"I'm afraid that the collective consciousness of the individuals living in the Plantanimus CUBE remain vulnerable to attack, though I can't quantify what form of harm may come to them. My intuition is that Cardinal Richelieux and I were attacked violently because the entity, or entities in the VR, knew that we weren't regular citizens of the community. In other words, 'it' knew we were living beings and didn't belong there. If my assumption is therefore correct, then the clients in that CUBE are safe from harm, at least for the time being."

"Ogram and I have discussed this and we both agree that we were targeted the moment we entered the VR, Your Holiness. We experienced a strong sense of danger and jitteriness soon after immersion and the waitress avatar at the coffee shop, guessed, or knew that I was from the Pleiades. Town avatars are not programmed with such sophistication. When Ogram and I decided to leave the coffee shop, feeling that something was wrong, the waitress's eyes followed our exit in a disturbing way. Almost as if she was a lookout, ordered to warn the Darius clone that we were leaving," Richelieux explained.

Matriarch Vasilia leaned back on the sofa and rubbed her eyes, looking exhausted. Something was weighing heavily on her mind and her body language was that of someone facing a great dilemma. Richelieux looked at her and then at Ogram, mirroring her expression.

Ogram guessed that his description of the vulnerability of the CUBE system had more serious implications that he realized. He had a sense that questioning what could possibly be so threatening to the Church, would involve him deeper in the current situation, but he couldn't help himself.

"Please forgive what I'm about to say Matriarch, but the degree of concern that I'm witnessing in your person, as well as in his Eminence's behavior, tells me that the danger to the CUBE system is of a much more serious nature than I've been made aware of," Ogram proposed.

The Matriarch sat up straight once again and looked at Richelieux with an ironic smile on her lips. "I'm beginning to see what you mean, regarding our young friend's intuitive nature," she commented wryly. "This is the moment, isn't it? The moment some of us have feared would eventually come," she said half asking, half making a statement aimed at Richelieux.

Ogram's pulse rose. He knew that something portentous was about to be revealed to him and that whatever that secret knowledge was, could change his life forever.

"You're right of course Ogram," the Matriarch admitted. "But I'm afraid that in order to bring you into our confidence, we'd have to ask you for a much deeper and longer commitment to help the Church than you might be willing to give. Know this before you give us an answer. The real threat the Cardinal and I are worried about, involves every living being in the galaxy, not just the church and its followers."

"Your Holiness, in spite of the fact that I'm an agnostic, I'm smart enough to know that for whatever reason, the universe has put me where I am for a specific reason. Even before you gave me a choice, I had already made my decision."

CHAPTER 17

On the Planet Kāla Kōṭharī

Sumpter Blarok, the president of the Body Shop Guild, leaned back on his chair and stared harshly at Vardo McCallan. The man had dissapointed him greatly. The Guild had invested billions of Galactic Kredits in its attempt to sabotage The Realm. Right now, he was debating whether to have the former operations manager of the Plantanimus CUBE executed, or let him continue drawing breath.

"So in essence, you weren't able to accomplish what we paid you and Longsdale to do, Longsdale is dead by your hand, because according to you, the man panicked and wanted to confess his sins to Richelieux, and worst of all, you were only able to retrieve half of the clients whose families paid us trillions of Kredits to put their relatives in new bodies. Does that about cover it?" Blarok asked sarcastically.

"How were we supposed to anticipate that Richelieux and the Matriarch would agree to give that arrogant agnostic son of a bitch, Zepol, the keys to the kingdom?" McCallan responded, wondering if the two mercenaries behind him, were about to garrote him to death, Blarok's favorite way to kill his enemies.

"It was your incompetence that brought Zepol to your door! You obviously damaged the CUBE when you inserted our 'ghost program' into the system, which is what caused the Church to come sniffing around!" Blarok screamed, banging his hand on the desk.

"Your so-called ghost program was most likely the cause of the anomalies. In the twenty years that I managed that CUBE, I never had any problems," McCallan argued defensively.

"What are we supposed to tell the relatives of those clients that you weren't able to retrieve?" Blarok asked, angrily.

"It's not like they can run to the authorities and complain after all," McCallan argued. "Those that paid to have their relative withdrawn from the CUBE were breaking the law."

"That's true, except that many of those clients left behind are the sons and daughters and husbands and wives of politicians, and wealthy, influential people, whereas before, they were willing to take a chance breaking the law, so long as they could be reunited with their loved ones. Now they'll become angry and possibly turn into some of our worst enemies!"

"Hold on Blarok, hold on!" McCallan interjected. "Take a look at the list of clients that Longsdale and I were able to retrieve!" he asked, handing Blarok an info chip.

Blarok took the chip and inserted it into his desk. A floating holographic screen appeared above the desk and Blarok scanned through it. As he read the names, his expression softened somewhat and Vardo McCallan saw a slight chance that he might live beyond this meeting.

"So you moved the politicians and most of the influential money people to the top of the list and those are among the eighty you've brought us. Fine! That leaves the other eighty who can still cause us problems," Blarok contended, still unhappy.

"That's where I come in. I can go back to Plantanimus and retrieve the other eighty, if you give me a chance!" McCallan proposed.

"Go back to Plantanimus? Are you insane? They'll arrest you the minute that you step on the landing pad!" Blarok replied, laughing.

"Not if I'm in a different body."

"A . . . a different body?" Blarok roared, in disbelief. "Do you have a spare billion or two in your pocket, because that's the only way that we'd be willing to do that!"

"Fine, have me killed, right here and now!" McCallan challenged, taking a huge risk that Blarok might decide to have him killed within seconds. "How many Kredits do you owe the relatives of those who I wasn't able to retrieve?" he asked, hoping that Blarok would do the math in his head and see his point.

Blarok jumped up from his executive chair, red faced and irate and came around the desk, ready to beat McCallan to a pulp with his fists. He grabbed McCallan by the neck, about to punch him repeatedly.

"How many Kredits Blarok, how many?" McCallan yelled, recoiling away from Blarok, who was a huge man and could tear him limb by limb with his bare hands.

"Boss," one of the mercenaries standing behind McCallan interrupted, speaking for the first time.

"Huh? What?" the enraged president of the Body Shop Guild answered, with his fist still up in the air.

"Maybe the man has a point," the mercenary suggested.

"Yes, Blarok, think for a moment! What's a billion or two compared to the trillions you owe those people?" McCallan begged, praying with all his might that the man would come to his senses.

Blarok hesitated for a moment and then he let go of McCallan and began pacing back and forth in front of his desk. After a while, he stopped and turned to McCallan. "Let's suppose for a moment, that I agree to put you in a new body. How can you retrieve those clients without getting caught?"

"Easily! The only reason why I couldn't retrieve all one hundred and sixty clients was because the two idiots you sent to keep an eye on us shut down the CUBE prematurely. The files of all eighty remaining clients are hidden in a secret buffer zone inside the central A.I.'s core that no one knows about. If I can go back to the Plantanimus facility within a few days, no one will have discovered those files. Retrieving them would only be a matter of seconds. Once I have the files, I can be out of there in minutes and on my way back here in hours," McCallan assured him.

"There's only one slight problem with your plan, McCallan," Blarok mentioned, sarcastically. "The Plantanimus facility is on quarantine shutdown and new employees won't be hired or transferred there for months. How do you plan to get inside?"

"I have a way, but it involves kidnapping someone."

CHAPTER 18

Revelation

"Richelieux tells me that you're a history aficionado and that once you thought you might become a historian before deciding to study physics and computer science. What have you read about our patron Saint's history?" the Matriarch asked Ogram.

"Quite a bit actually. Kelem Rogeston is considered the founding father of modern science in many ways. I've been a big fan of his since childhood. Even though his only breakthrough was the development of the _n'time_ generator, that accomplishment alone is what allowed individuals like Tzu Jin Chu to develop the quantum holographic computer and thus the CUBE."

"There's a massive collection of both religious and secular literature related to the man, but I'm more interested in the secular. What of it have you read?" Matriarch Vasilia asked with interest.

"Hmmm, let me see," he mused pensively, as Ogram had read more than the average scholar on the subject of Kelem Rogeston.

"Well, beginning with the earliest biographies, Ndugu Nabole's 'Life of Kelem Rogeston' of course, Sulana Kay's 'History of the Rogeston Clan', Tono MacAllister's 'Ancient History of Plantanimus' and his second book, 'The Umhaur and the Dreamers of Plantanimus' as well. All of Zephron Artemus' books on Kelem Rogeston and his legacy, a series of reports and articles related to the blockade of Plantanimus during the late 30th Century, all of which involved Rogeston in one way or another, as well as a host of books and papers written by conspiracy theorists claiming that Rogeston and his adopted family, Alexei and Kani Rogeston and their children, were able to reincarnate into new bodies through Tatiana Rogeston's medical discoveries. A strange little book of poetry, titled, 'The Infinity poems of Zeus the Dreamer', supposedly written by the legendary sentient plant, who allegedly gave Kelem Rogeston a second life as a Plantanimal and many, many others, whose titles I can't remember right now."

"Ogram, you said earlier that when you were facing the evil Darius, you sensed that he was a sentient being and not a programmed avatar. Did you feel the same about Kelem Rogeston when he appeared to save you and Cardinal Richelieux?" the Matriarch asked.

Ogram could have answered the question in a second, but hesitated because of his regard for Richelieux.

"You can speak freely, my young friend. The Matriarch knows of my crisis of faith," the cardinal assured him.

"Yes Your Holiness, I did feel I was in the presence of a living being," he replied, surprising himself by his own answer.

"The Cardinal and I concur with your opinion Ogram. Now tell me, in view of everything that you've experienced in the last few days and with all the literature that you've read on the man, do you think it's possible that the individual you saw inside the VR, was actually Kelem Rogeston?" the pontiff inquired.

"I'm not sure where all this is leading to, but I'm guessing that you're hoping that I will reach a certain conclusion regarding the man, before you reveal a major fact about St. Kelem," Ogram theorized.

"Yes, Ogram, it's very important to us that you come to it on your own, rather than us lead you to it," Richelieux explained.

"I see," Ogram said, realizing what the two clerics were driving at. "My answer is yes, it's quite possible that the man I saw in the VR was a projection of Kelem Rogeston and not an avatar. Tono MacAllister wrote that the Dreamers of Plantanimus, the only sentient plants to ever have lived, were incredibly powerful beings who lived between two worlds. That of the physical and a place called 'The Quantum Tide'. He described The Quantum Tide as a higher form of being, outside of space-time where all events and possibilities co-exist all at once. He was of the belief that the Dreamers taught Kelem Rogeston how to enter The Quantum Tide at will and that it was this ability that allowed Rogeston to accomplish many of his great feats as well as give his 'blessing' to the people of Mars during the War of Independence.

"Sister Ornata described this 'blessing' as an 'infinite joy of the heart', given to her by Kelem Rogeston by simply holding her hand and that of others. She called it the 'sweetest Samadhi' and said that it was like touching the hand of God. There's an ancient video recording of Rogeston giving his blessing to a crowd of about two thousand Martians in an underground church during the war.

"It's not outside of the realm of possibility, that The Quantum Tide is what we scientists call, 'The Quantum Field' and that the Dreamers and Rogeston were somehow able to exist in it non-corporeally, therefore making it possible for Kelem Rogeston and/or his consciousness to have entered the CUBE's VR, which is after all, a giant quantum machine.

"A week ago I wouldn't have come to these conclusions, being blissfully ignorant of certain facts and experiences. But now of course, my reality has changed dramatically," Ogram concluded.

Matriarch Vasilia's eyes were full of tears and she reached for Richelieux's hand for emotional support. Ogram took those tears to be tears of joy and he was right.

"Thank you dear Ogram! You have opened your eyes to a truth that we were hoping you could see on your own. It is with great relief that we can now bring you into our confidence," she said to Ogram.

Richelieux handed the Matriarch a tissue and she wiped her eyes with it and then blew her nose loudly, which made Ogram want to smile. To see and hear the most powerful woman in the galaxy blowing her nose seemed humorous to him and at the same time comforting. Matriarch Vasilia Bentara Rogeston was after all, a human being.

"What we're about to tell you, is knowledge that has been carefully guarded by the Church for thousands of years, six thousand and twenty one years to be precise," Richelieux explained. "It is knowledge so precious and important to us, that only the Matriarchs, the Cardinal

Counselors and very few others have been privy to it. You are the first outsider to know of it, including Church clergy and anyone else, period."

Ogram felt a lump in his throat, and suddenly wished that he had opted to remain ignorant. "I'm sorry, but, why are you divulging this great secret to me, of all people?" he asked, feeling apprehensive about what their disclosure could mean to his future.

The Matriarch smiled and looked at Richelieux, who also smiled. "Because my dear Ogram, your involvement with the Church was foretold a long time ago," she declared with certainty.

"Mmm .... me?" Ogram stuttered, feeling the blood drain from his head.

"We didn't realize that you were the person the prophesy foretold would come to the aid of the Church at a time of great crisis, until the events that transpired at the Plantanimus CUBE. We realized that you were the one, after we consulted with the Matriarchs," Richelieux admitted.

"You said Matriarchs, in the plural. What did you mean by that?" Ogram asked.

"Ogram, there is a CUBE in the galaxy that no one knows about. It's located right here in the Heavenly Temple," the Matriarch confessed.

"Here, in the Temple? What is its purpose?" Ogram questioned, with great curiosity.

"It is the repository of every former Matriarch's soul, beginning with Matriarch Ramona in 4124," Richelieux explained. "It has been a source of great wisdom and comfort to every succeeding Matriarch that has held the office since then. The church would not have survived if it hadn't been for their counsel and advice."

"Ah, I see now why you're so concerned that the contagion could spread to the rest of the system from the Plantanimus CUBE. You're terrified to lose such a precious resource," Ogram realized.

"Precisely. Like the Plantanimus CUBE, our CUBE is isolated from the rest, but if we were to lose their dear presence in our lives, the church would suffer greatly," Matriarch Vasilia claimed, with great sadness.

"That is indeed a terrible prospect that the Church faces! But how does this relate to the prophesy about my involvement with the Church?" Ogram questioned, logically.

"In order for the answer to make sense, we have to start the story in the year 4002, right after Tzu Jin Chu finished assembling the very first CUBE," the Matriarch explained. "After booting up the system and testing it thoroughly, he designed its first VR environment. He wouldn't let anyone else enter the VR and used himself as a test subject because he wanted to make sure that it was safe to immerse an individual's consciousness without harm. At that time he hadn't programmed any avatars, just a small city with buildings, streets etcetera. As soon as he entered, he was shocked, when he was met by a man who identified himself as Kelem Rogeston."

"Really? That's remarkable! Why didn't he report this remarkable event?" Ogram asked.

"He didn't at first because he thought that it was he who had somehow projected the apparition from his own brain, or that perhaps, the immersion interface was creating 'ghosts' in the machine," Richelieux commented. "He spent several weeks dismantling the machine and putting it together again. When he reentered the VR, he found Kelem Rogeston once again! He then had his eldest daughter go in without telling her anything about the man, and when she came out, she told him that she had met Kelem Rogeston."

"That's when he finally reported the phenomenon to the Church elders and eventually Matriarch Ramona," Matriarch Vasilia, interjected.

"How advantageous for the Church, but why didn't the Matriarch and the Curia not publicize this event?

Richelieux cleared his throat. "There were several reasons why it was kept quiet. In 4002, the church was coming out of one of its darkest periods following the Crusades of the previous millennium and didn't want to attract attention to itself by claiming that St. Kelem had appeared to us. Remember that the Crusades began when the Tilharans attacked the Holy See on Plantanimus, claiming that we were followers of the devil and that St. Kelem was a false prophet. Additionally, the CUBE was brand new technology and no one knew for sure whether this 'miracle' was real or not. And ultimately, the Church of St. Kelem is not a Charismatic church, as it continues to be, thus the reason why we'd rather not publicize miracles, especially ones that involve our patron saint, even to this day."

"There's more to tell before you understand how all this connects to you," the Matriarch elucidated. "Eventually the CUBE was fully activated, and The Realm was created in order to finance the cost of the Crusades and replenish the Church's coffers which had been practically emptied by this time. Matriarch Ramona was the first Matriarch to become a client of The Realm after she passed on. Once inside, she called for the new Church mother, Matriarch Eloise and told her St. Kelem did indeed live inside the CUBE. He wished for the Church to build a new CUBE which should remain separate from future CUBEs, where only the consciousnesses of Matriarchs would be allowed. Then, over a period of several weeks, Matriarch Ramona, who had no former scientific or technical education, gave her successor Eloise, detailed plans for the construction of the Heavenly Temple and the location of the solar system where St. Kelem wished the artificial moon to be located.

"The Church filed for ownership of New Jerusalem in 4157 and the Heavenly Temple was completed three months before Matriarch Eloise passed on at the age of one hundred and one, at which time Matriarch Ramona's soul was transferred to the new CUBE, and immersed along with Eloise. Every Matriarch since then has joined the others. Today there are a total of sixty eight former Matriarchs living in the Temple's CUBE.

"St. Kelem warned Matriarch Ramona that a great conflagration would come to the galaxy during the 11th millennium and that the church would be involved at the center of it. He went on to say that a young man possessed of great scientific intellect, but without faith, would come to the aid of the church in its hour of need. He narrowed the year this would happen to 10,023 which is this year we're living in."

"And seeing how today's date is the 14th of November 10,023 and how no one, except for the Tzu Jin Chu and the Matriarchs inside the Temple's CUBE has ever been visited by Kelem Rogeston, you can see why we're absolutely sure that you, Ogram Zepol, are that young man that St. Kelem prophesied would come and save us all."

CHAPTER 19

A Growth Chamber on the Venus Fly Trap

The Venus Fly Trap, a Terran registered pleasure cruiser, rematerialized above Plantanimus, then fired its thrusters and achieved orbit around the ancient planet. The ship was one of the many legally chartered *n'time* ships the Body Shop Guild used for its illegal business operations.

Inside, were Sumpter Blarok, several mercenaries armed to the teeth, along with Vardo McCallan and a staff of body-transfer technicians with a complete growth-chamber laboratory on board.

They were there to kidnap Elwood Zachs, one of the few individuals working in the Plantanimus CUBE with full access to all the high security areas in the facility. The plan was to kidnap the man, scan his body for duplication, grow a duplicate body quickly and insert Vardo McCallan's consciousness in it, then send the duplicate to the CUBE to retrieve the eighty 'clients' that McCallan had been unable to take with him after the CUBE's shutdown eight days before.

"Alright McCallan, I've spent a small fortune to get us here, not to mention the expense of installing a growth-chamber on this ship. If this doesn't work, I'll tie you to the ship's exterior and let your body disintegrate when we go into *n'time*!"

McCallan gulped silently, knowing that Blarok was capable of such cruelty. The sadist son of a bitch liked to kill people, but he always took pleasure torturing or beating them up before sending his victims to their deaths.

"I guarantee you that Zachs will be where I said he will be! You'll see," McCallan assured him, praying that Blarok's henchmen would succeed in retrieving the computer specialist from the planet. "He always takes his vacation at the same time every year like clockwork. He'll be at the Sea Breeze resort at the southern tip of Ranes for another three days, long enough for your men to take him, bring him here, scan him and grow a new body."

"Alright Bernie," Blarok said, turning to his top mercenary. "Take your men down and bring Zachs back. Remember to sedate him before you take him out of the resort. We can't afford for Zachs to have any memory of what happened to him, clear?"

"Clear Boss," Bernie replied, saluting military style. He and two of his men exited Blarok's cabin.

"I guess it's a waiting game now, huh Blarok?" McCallan mentioned, trying to sound casual.

"Yeah, a waiting game," Blarok replied. "My man here," he said, pointing to his personal guard, "will take you to your cabin while we wait for Zach's arrival."

The guard grabbed McCallan by the arm and escorted him out.

The minutes turned into an hour and then into two. When three hours had gone by and no word from Blarok's men had come in, McCallan began to sweat, fearing that something had gone wrong. To his relief, Blarok and three growth-chamber technicians came to his cabin soon after.

"Everything go alright?" McCallan asked, relieved to see the body-techs there.

"Oh yeah, sure!" Blarok replied smiling. "These three fellows will take you to the prep room to get you ready for the transfer. I'll see you in three days," Blarok said, waving goodbye as McCallan was led away.

"What will it be like waking up in the new body?" McCallan asked anxiously to one of the techs escorting him to the growth-chamber.

"Hmm, you'll be slightly disoriented for the first few minutes, then it'll take you an hour or so to get your balance while standing up in your new body. After that it's just getting used to speaking with the new voice box and mouth configuration. You'll be back to normal within six hours or so," the man assured him.

"No after effects?" McCallan queried.

"Nah, none at all, you'll see," the tech replied glancing and smiling at the other three techs surreptitiously.

McCallan lay on an operating table in the newly installed body lab, as the techs connected nano leads to his entire body prepping him for the procedure. His neural and consciousness profile had already been scanned. But now they had to scan his short term memory so that when he regained consciousness in the new body three days hence, he'd remember today's events.

The technician bent over McCallan with a big smile. "Bye, bye!" he said, pressing a button on a small console, and McCallan went out.

Three days later, McCallan came to in the growth-chamber. He had a hard time focusing his eyes. He tried to speak, but only heard a moan coming out of his mouth.

"Don't try to speak yet, "a tech warned him. "Just lie there and wait until your vision clears," he added.

McCallan nodded slightly. He tried to move his arms, but they were held down by straps. He raised his head to see what was happening, and the tech returned. "Don't speak, don't move, don't do anything until we tell you, clear?" the man said sternly.

McCallan nodded.

A few minutes later, Blarok's face came into view. "Welcome back McCallan!" he said laughing. "How do you feel?"

"Strange, I guess my mind's getting used to Zach's body," he replied groggily.

"Yeah, that's for sure!" Blarok said looking at the others with a grin.

"Hey, my voice sounds weird, it sounds high pitched. Is that normal?" McCallan asked.

"Remove the straps," Blarok ordered, and the techs complied. "Help her up," Blarok said, trying to suppress a laugh.

As McCallan rose to a sitting position on the operating table, he noticed that his chest looked swollen and his arms and hands appeared rather thin and hairless. Elwood Zachs weighed one hundred and twenty kilos and had the body of a wrestler. Something was wrong!

"What . . .what's happening? This isn't Zachs' body!" McCallan screamed, sounding like a hysterical female.

"No you stupid bastard! That's right, this isn't Elwood Zach's body, and do you want to know why?" Blarok roared with anger.

"Why?" McCallan asked, hearing the voice of a woman come out of his mouth.

"Because Mr. Zachs died during the blackout, you fucking moron!" Blarok yelled loudly, his face red with anger.

"This!' he said, grabbing McCallan by the throat and poking his big finger into a soft breast, "Is Maria Santana's facsimile, the only other employee at the CUBE with high security clearance!"

"What have you done!" McCallan yelled, breaking into tears. "I don't want to be a woman for the rest of my life!"

Blarok laughed, letting go of the woman, who'd once been a man. "Too bad sweetheart, you better get used to it, cause if you don't, I'll throw you out of a fucking airlock!"

CHAPTER 20

Nobius-72527

Less than a day had passed since Ogram learned that Matriarch Vasilia and Cardinal Richelieux considered him to be the individual that Kelem Rogeston had prophesied would come to the aid of the Church of St. Kelem at this moment in history.

The meeting had ended at 2:00 am and after being escorted back to his apartment on Level 26 by Sister Allondra and her returning to her dormitory, Ogram spent the next few hours unable to sleep despite the fact that he was exhausted. He felt as if he'd been drafted into an army fighting a war in which he had no stake. But even though he still had strong reservations about organized religions and the Church of St, Kelem, he couldn't deny the mounting evidence that destiny had brought him here. From early childhood, Ogram's life had been one of study and learning and later on, professional success and notoriety. His life had always made sense and nothing happened by chance. Now, everything had been turned upside down and the future was completely unknown.

Sister Allondra came by to escort him back to the Matriarch's residence at 11:45 pm and here he was at five past midnight, sitting across from Matriarch Vasilia and Cardinal Richelieux for the second time in twenty-four hours.

"I should take my leave now, Your Holiness," Sister Allondra said, getting up from her seat next to Ogram.

"Please stay, sister, tonight's discussion requires your presence," the Matriarch stated, motioning with her hand for her to sit.

The young nun sat back down, looking apprehensive. Ogram sympathized with her. In many ways, her life had been turned upside down just like his had been. He was sure that she felt as out of place as he did.

"Before we begin Ogram, you should know that earlier tonight I gave Sister Allondra a full account of the events that have taken place in the last nine days, including the existence of the Temple's CUBE and its inhabitants," Richelieux explained.

Ogram furrowed his brow, wondering why the novice nun had been apprised of all the facts when so much was at stake, but he suspected that he would learn why very soon.

"Ogram, I suppose that you already know what St. Kelem's message to you means?" the Matriarch inquired.

"Yes, I looked it up. Nobius, seven two five two seven, is the astronomical address of an unregistered planet located on the outer edges of the galaxy. It was discovered by the Terran astronomer Vasco Nobius in 3875."

"Excellent, what else do you know about it?" Matriarch Vasilia continued questioning.

"It's located beyond the Kural Nebula, past an empty part of space called, The Expanse, or The Mouth of Eternity, depending on who one asks."

"Cardinal Richelieux and I have debated the nature of the Saint's message already, but I'm curious to know, why do you think he gave you the address of such a remote place in the galaxy?"

"The only logical answer is that he wants me to go there for some reason," Ogram proposed, realizing that he might be going on a long space voyage soon.

"Does the planet have a special meaning for you?" Richelieux wanted to know.

"No, none whatsoever. As a matter of fact, I'd never heard of it until Kel . . . I mean St. Kelem spoke the words," Ogram answered.

"Your Holiness, if I may speak," Sister Allondra said, timidly.

"Of course, child! I've told you that your presence was required," the Matriarch restated.

"My father is a cargo pilot and he trained me as a navigator. I traveled with him on long runs until just before I joined the order," Sister Allondra informed them. "We used to deliver merchandise to planets at the far end of the Kural Nebula and Nobius, seven two five two seven, is also known to the Tilharans as Llehrra, the birth place of Nu, their god."

Ogram turned his head toward Sister Allondra bemused by her admission that she was a trained navigator. His attraction to her increased exponentially.

"And there it is, Richelieux!" the Matriarch exclaimed excitedly, bypassing protocol by not mentioning his title.

There was a pregnant pause as everyone looked at each other with expectation. Ogram realized what the Matriarch and Richelieux had in mind and his heart skipped a beat. Sister Allondra's face on the other hand, reflected dismay.

"Wha . . .what do you mean by that Your Holiness?" she asked with dread.

The Matriarch smiled like a mother would smile to a young daughter, unaware that she had done or said something precious. "My dear child, do you not see or understand what is happening here?" she asked, with a gentle expression on her face.

Sister Allondra shook her head, her face turning dark green with embarrassment.

"Come here," the Matriarch said, opening her arms wide.

Sister Allondra stood up from the couch shaking with nervousness and went over to where the Matriarch was sitting. She stood by her, not knowing what to do and then the Matriarch pulled her down next to her and gave her a loving embrace.

The young nun's eyes filled with tears. Being touched by the Matriarch was considered the ultimate blessing that any clergy could receive.

Something opened in Ogram's heart and he was surprised to feel tears wetting his cheeks. Cardinal Richelieux's eyes were not dry either.

Richelieux reached for a tissue box and handed them out to Sister Allondra and Ogram, who felt slightly embarrassed by his emotional reaction.

"Last night, Cardinal Richelieux and I were wondering why you had been brought into this affair and what was to be your role in it," the Matriarch began saying while putting her arm around Sister Allondra's narrow shoulders affectionately. "We know that the Universal Mind God and St. Kelem put the four of us together for a reason and I told Cardinal Richelieux that whatever part you were to play, would come to light. When you told us that you are a trained navigator, I knew instantly that you and Ogram are supposed to go to the planet together."

Ogram's pulse raised and then he had to work hard to suppress his excitement. Suddenly St. Kelem's prophesy took on a new meaning for him. Perhaps all of this had been preordained after all.

Still in shock, Sister Allondra was struggling to deal with the news. "But . . I'm a novice nun Your Holiness. Surely a more experienced sister would be better suited for the job!" she argued.

"Sister Allondra, you must understand that we can't possibly bring anyone else into this group!" Richelieux explained, motioning to everyone. "No, you are the right person for the job my dear! St. Kelem made no mention of you in his prophesy, but as he is my witness, I know in my heart that you were destined to participate in this sacred mission for the Church."

Sister Allondra looked at Ogram, her green oblique eyes searching for his opinion.

Richelieux, seeing her look, spoke up. "Tell us Ogram, you have yet to let us know whether or not you'd be willing to go on this voyage, and if so, how you feel about Sister Allondra coming along."

"I'm willing to go with Sister Allondra, but she should know that this voyage is not without peril. The 'Mouth of Eternity' is said to be an area of space with unstable Black Energy in parts of it and many ships have disappeared while attempting to cross it," he warned them.

"I am not afraid, Ogram. I'll get us through," she replied with certainty.

Ogram's face broke into a big smile. "Well then, when do we leave?"

CHAPTER 21

Camp Zurk

Five weeks had passed since the decision had been made that Ogram and Sister Allondra should go to Nobius 72527. Sister Allondra was an experienced, licensed, interstellar navigator and although Ogram had a sub-orbital pilot's license, it wasn't adequate for the voyage that they had to undertake. So it was decided that Ogram should undergo a condensed interstellar pilot training course. Richelieux sent Ogram down to New Jerusalem to train at one of the Gulax Guard's space flight training camps, located in the southern continent of the planet.

The Church had reached into its very deep pockets and purchased the most advanced two passenger, interstellar ship that money could buy. The camp was run by Zurk, an old Gulax master sergeant that turned out to be the worst nightmare that a new recruit could face entering military basic training. When Zurk found that Ogram was taking a Kelemite novice nun on the trip, he called Richelieux and demanded that Ogram be trained in self-defense and offensive techniques. Richelieux could not refuse in spite of the fact that he was the Cardinal Counselor to the Matriarch. The old master sergeant was a fanatic Kelemite fundamentalist and would not permit Ogram to leave camp without being able to guard and protect Sister Allondra.

Zurk had been tough with Ogram during the first week of flight school, but after talking to Richelieux, he became a nightmare "drill sergeant". Ogram had always exercised and lived a healthy life style but he wasn't prepared for the grueling physical training that ensued.

The flight training was a breeze compared to the hand to hand fighting, combat and survival training, tactics and strategy lessons and the constant verbal abuse by Zurk. Add to that, sleep deprivation and several visits to the camp's medical A.I. to repair cuts, bruises, broken bones, torn ligaments and dislocated shoulders and fingers.

At one point, he came close to quitting and catching a pleasure cruiser back to Earth, but something kept him from giving up. The final test was a three day combat survival course. At the very end of the course, he was ambushed by three Gulax who came at him with knifes. Relying on his training he maneuvered away from his three attackers and drew them into a wooded area. Gulax feet are great in flat solid ground but terrible in uneven terrain.

Against all odds, Ogram managed to overpower his attackers and use their own weapons against them by cutting them on their arms, which signified a kill. The cuts were superficial but the test would have been a failure if he hadn't drawn blood as was their custom.

"Congratulations Master Ogram. You have completed your training. Meet my three sons, Grak, Hir and Wazr," Zurk announced, stepping out from behind a bush.

"Sorry fellows, you know I didn't mean to hurt you!" Ogram apologized.

Zurk and his three sons laughed with their hiss-like laughter. "You humans! You're so funny to us. If you hadn't cut each of my boys, they would have beaten you senseless and sent you to the med-bed for sure!"

Ogram shook his head, glad that the misery and torture were over.

The sun was setting and a light aircraft came by to take them back to camp, forty kilometers away. The ship took off and Zurk turned to Ogram.

"Master Ogram, I've come to like you in the last five weeks, but I would like you better if you were a true believer. You say you are an Agnostic, but how can a man live in the middle of the street or be happy and sad at the same time?"

"I don't know Zurk, in the last few weeks I've begun to ask myself that same question," Ogram replied, yawning with exhaustion.

"Well, there might be hope for you after all. The Matriarch and his Eminence have faith in you. Perhaps they know something about you that you yourself haven't discovered yet."

"Perhaps," Ogram replied, closing his eyes and falling into a deep sleep as his head fell into Zurk's chest. The Gulax moved his shoulder and cradled Ogram's head in his arms, almost tenderly. He looked at his three sons and smiled, narrowing his yellow lizard eyes. His sons smiled back.

CHAPTER 22

Into the Mouth of Eternity

"I christen thee, Her Matriarch's Ship, 'Prophesy'," Matriarch Vasilia exclaimed, placing her hand on the vessel's hull, symbolically giving it St. Kelem's blessing.

Cardinal Richelieux, Ogram and Sister Allondra clapped enthusiastically. They were in an open space in the forest near Camp Zurk. The brand-new spaceship sat in the middle of the clearing, glinting under artificial lights. Standing further away in the semidarkness were Rek, the captain of Richelieux's personal guard and Zurk, Ogram's drill instructor.

"Well, I guess we better be underway," Ogram said, reaching for Richelieux's hand. Instead, the Cardinal pulled Ogram close and gave him a hug, then he walked over to Sister Allondra and kissed her on the forehead.

Matriarch Vasilia reached for Sister Allondra and gently pulled over to where Ogram was standing. He placed them next to each other and stood in front of them.

"Ogram and Allondra, you are going on a journey into the unknown on behalf of the Church of St. Kelem on a holy quest. Our prayers and best wishes go with you. May the Universal Mind God, St. Kelem and Sister Ornata guide your way and keep you from harm. Come back to us safe and sound and bring back sacred knowledge that will enlighten us and guide us in the uncertain future we face. By the power of St.

Kelem I bless you both," she invoked, placing her hands on Ogram's and Sister Allondra's heart chakras.

Ogram closed his eyes and felt a slight vibration in his chest along with a warm sensation that spread throughout his entire body. The experience was pleasant, but it faded away much too soon. She removed her hands and kissed their foreheads then walked away, eyes filled with tears of emotion.

Ogram and Sister Allondra waved goodbye to everyone and walked up the ship's ramp, which closed behind them automatically.

The Prophesy's lights turned on and the hum of the antigrav motors began winding up. The grass and leaves beneath the ship flattened as if under an invisible hand and the ship rose from the ground. The antigrav motors' pitch rose higher and the ship cleared the tree tops and picked up speed. About fifty meters from the ground the turbines fired and the vessel flew away into the New Jerusalem night sky until the glow from its engines could no longer be seen.

Matriarch Vasilia reached for Cardinal Richelieux's arm and the two walked back to the land vehicle that had brought them to this spot in the forest. Rek and Zurk shut the artificial lights off, collapsed them and put them in the vehicle's trunk. Zurk took the driver's seat while Rek sat on the passenger's side. The lights came on and the vehicle pulled away slowly, leaving a dust trail behind it.

CHAPTER 23

An Interesting Conversation

Ogram flew the ship past the planet's atmosphere and waited for traffic control to give him clearance to leave orbit. New Jerusalem was a busy planet with thousands of ships arriving and departing every day. He sat at the flight controls next to Sister Allondra's navigation board, amazed at the incredible piece of technology that the Church had acquired for their journey.

The Prophesy was a state of the art interstellar vessel equipped with the latest and best that current technology could provide. Besides _n'time_ travel capability and long range sub-light engines, the ship was able to take off and land on a planet, without the need for orbital shuttles. The Prophesy's systems were run by the latest quantum computer, which interestingly enough, Ogram had helped design for the company that built it.

They had brought with them enough food and supplies to last an entire solar year should they somehow be thrown off course and be delayed. For emergencies, there were two medical A.I.'s with fully equipped med-beds in case one of them failed, two escape pods, two Lectrosleep chambers, a six wheel rover to explore a planet once having landed, a fully equipped spa and enough entertainment media to keep them busy for years.

There was, of course a small chapel with holographic statues of St. Kelem and Sister Ornata, which Ogram felt were a little creepy because they were so life like. Ogram and Allondra had their own separate cabins with private bathrooms and a large common area with luxurious furniture and beautifully decorated walls as well as a kitchenette with pre-cooked food-dispensing equipment.

All in all, the Prophesy was a luxury yacht with a hardened Duraminum hull, armed with deadly defensive weapons should they run into pirates or some other unexpected threat.

Traffic control gave them clearance to depart and Ogram fired the sub-light engines and headed for open space where he could safely engage the *n'time* generator that would take them to the edge of the Kural Nebula, the first of many stops on their voyage.

The trek to Nobius would take thirty days plus, due to the fact that The Mouth of Eternity was uncharted and had unstable Dark Energy spots that shifted randomly. The Prophesy would have to make incremental *n'time* jumps, with Sister Allondra having to make precise scans of the area of space where the ship would rematerialize after each jump.

Ogram relaxed and leaned back on his fancy pilot's chair and looked at Sister Allondra, busily engaged with her navigation panel. She was dressed in the same crewman's blue flight suit as he and Ogram was glad that she wouldn't be wearing her white novice nun's outfit during the voyage. Now he wouldn't feel as guilty whenever his attraction to the beautiful Tarsian manifested in his male brain.

As he observed her, he noticed that her skin looked darker and that she seemed to have lost a few kilos as well.

She finished working on her panel and noticed that Ogram was studying her.

"What?" she said, wondering what he was looking at.

"Your skin looks darker, do you have a tan?" he asked, ignorant of the fact that Tarsian skin also darkened when exposed to ultraviolet rays.

"Yes. I got sunburned last month when I was undergoing combat training on New Jerusalem."

"You too?" he replied, very surprised. He was under the impression that Kelemite clergy took a vow of non-violence for life. "I didn't realize that nuns were allowed to do such things!"

Sister Allondra lowered her head and her expression became serious. "I am no longer a Kelemite nun," she announced quietly.

"Whaaat . . . ? why?" Ogram questioned, feeling that somehow he was responsible.

"The Matriarch asked me to renounce my vows. She said it was necessary because I might be called upon to defend you and myself if we were to meet with danger."

Ogram got up from his chair and began pacing nervously around the bridge. "This is terrible! Why should you be forced to abandon your life's vocation only to defend me!" he railed with anxiety. As much as he was attracted to the beautiful Tarsian, the last thing he wanted was for her to lose her identity as an ordained member of her Church. "I'm quite capable of defending myself! The Matriarch should not have sacrificed your religious status for my sake!"

"Please don't be upset Ogram. I am happy to be an instrument in the service of St. Kelem's Prophesy. You are the chosen one and the Matriarch wanted me to make sure that you'd be able to accomplish your mission with complete success."

"No, no! This is wrong Sister! For all we know this whole thing will end up being nothing more than a waste of time!"

"Please Ogram, calm down! Here, sit down in your chair and listen to me," she asked, reaching for his arm and pulling back to his seat.

"I am sorry Sister, I . . .,"

"First of all, you have to stop calling me sister and address me as Allondra from now on," she said with a sweet smile that broke Ogram's heart. "Second, I am still a member of the Church. The Matriarch has given me the title of Secular Canon, which is akin to a Diakonos or a lay nun if you will."

"Oh, how is that different from being a regular nun?" Ogram asked, confused.

"I can still give sacrament, last rites, marry people and baptize children, etcetera. Except that now, I am no longer bound by my vows of poverty and non-violence. Also, I would only wear a habit when I'm inside a sanctuary and only when officiating religious services."

"Oh, well, that's not so bad I suppose," Ogram commented. "Still I feel bad that you've had to change your life for me, a faithless non-believer."

Sister Allondra, now, just plain Allondra, smiled widely, her large oblique green eyes crinkling beautifully. "You're probably one of those that are brought into the Church, kicking and screaming all the way and eventually become faithful believers," Allondra suggested.

"Oh no, not me! I don't think I'll ever be one of those," Ogram replied, laughing.

"My uncle Hernak was a terrible man, a drunkard, a wife cheater and a brawler. He was the bane of my father's existence. One day, he was robbed by another Tarsian and went back to his house and grabbed his gun to go and kill the thief. As he was crossing the street to end the man's life, he was run over by a vehicle and almost died. When he came home from the hospital he became very quiet and withdrawn. We all thought that he'd never recover, but a few weeks later, he showed up at our church with his wife and children, a changed man. He's now a deacon at our parish."

"Yes, I've heard of cases like your uncle, but I doubt that will ever happen to me. I've never been through a traumatic event like that!"

"Have you not paid any attention to the recent events in your life Ogram?" Allondra asked perplexed, raising her eyebrows. "Cardinal Richelieux recounted to me in great detail your near death experiences the night that the CUBE was shut down, as well as what you both experienced inside the CUBE's VR. Are you saying that almost dying twice in a week was not a traumatic event? The Cardinal said that Pieter Minsk told him that while inside the VR, your heart rates had climbed so high, both of you were in danger of dying from a heart attack or stroke."

Ogram felt a chill go up his spine. Suddenly the memory of the experience flooded his senses and for a moment he almost felt as if he was back inside the VR. Unconsciously, he rubbed the area in his neck where the beast's cold slimy tentacle had wrapped itself around his throat. His face turned pale and he broke into a cold sweat.

Allondra noticed the change in his mood.

"Oh I'm so sorry Ogram!" she exclaimed, feeling bad for bringing up such a terrible memory. She reached for his shoulder and put her arm around him. As soon as she did, Ogram felt better. Her touch had an instant calming effect on him while at the same time arousing him.

"You're right. Until now I hadn't realized how much the attack had affected me. So much has happened since that day, I guess, all the training with Zurk pushed everything to the back of my mind. But seeing how strong my reaction is to the memory of that day, serves to remind me that this voyage is serious business. I won't make that mistake again."

"We're in this together Ogram, don't forget that either," she reminded him, gently.

"I know Allondra. I'm happy that we're doing this together," he replied honestly.

He excused himself and walked to the rear of the ship. On his way to the toilet, he stopped by the small chapel and went in. He turned on the lights and the holo statue of Kelem Rogeston appeared in front of him. He sat down and looked at Rogeston's image and suddenly, it didn't seem so creepy anymore. As a matter of fact, the life-like image reminded him of the rescue from the attack and it made him feel better. Ogram laughed at himself and wondered if he would be praying to St. Kelem one day.

After relieving himself he went back to the bridge and returned to his seat. Allondra looked at him as if asking, "are you alright?" and Ogram smiled back. He was about to say something when the A.I. informed him that they were about to arrive at the coordinates where they could engage the *n'time* generator. He disengaged the sub-light engines and fired the forward thrusters to stop the ship.

Allondra got busy plotting the jump to the Kural Nebula, and as she expertly manipulated three dimensional objects on the holographic panel in front of her, Ogram couldn't help but be impressed by her expertise. In order to become a licensed *n'time* navigator, a person

131

had to know higher math, a solid knowledge of physics, quite a bit of quantum mechanics, astronomy and a host of other skills the average person would never acquire. As he watched her, he wondered what had made her want to become a Kelemite nun. The beautiful Tarsian girl now sitting next to him, seemed like a different person from the quiet and reserved novice that he had met six weeks before.

"We're all set Ogram, are you ready?" she asked.

"Ready," he replied, engaging the Duraminium window shields. Allondra touched a blinking sphere in the holo screen and the *n'time* generator came to life. Its hum soon grew louder and more intense, until the vessel's hull was engulfed by a purple glow and the Prophesy blinked out of existence for a trillionth of a second, reassembling its mass at its pre-programmed location in the Kural Nebula.

"*N'TIME* TRANSITION SUCCESSFUL," the A. I. announced.

Ogram opened the shields. and the beauty of the Kural Nebula filled the large observation window on the bridge. Both were transfixed by the beauty of the multicolored cloud of dust and gas left behind by the explosion of a super-nova millions of years in the past.

"I've seen holos of it before, but they don't do justice to the real thing!" Ogram exclaimed, enthralled by the magnificent view.

"I've seen it dozens of times, and I still get choked with emotion every time I see it," Allondra commented.

Ogram looked at her sideways and was surprised to see a small tear in the corner of her left eye. Seeing her reaction stirred something inside of him and his eyes became moist also. Ever since the attack in the Plantanimus CUBE, his emotions had become more intense. Ogram had never been very sentimental or romantic in spite of the fact that he'd had relationships with quite a few women in the past. He wondered if his growing attraction to Allondra was due to post traumatic disorder.

"I see that it touches your heart as well,' Allondra said, interrupting his reverie.

"Oh . . ., yes, I guess so," he mumbled back, a little embarrassed. He turned away from her and blinked repeatedly, trying to evaporate the tears in his eyes.

"Here are the coordinates for the next sub-light portion of the voyage," she indicated, pointing to a plotted line of travel flashing inside a three-dimensional map of the immediate area of space. The ship would travel past Siraya, once the ancient planet-capital of the old Tarsian Empire, five hundred years before humans encountered the Tarsians and fought the Gulax War as allies against the lizards. It would also swing past Gulax, the home world of the species by the same name.

This part of the Tarsian sector had remained faithful to Tilhara, their ancient religion, though nowadays The Realm had many offices in the twenty-three civilized planets in Kuralian space. Ogram programmed the route and fired the sub-light engines and the Prophesy sped on its way to the boundary between Kuralian space and The Mouth of Eternity.

"Sis . . ., I mean Allondra, I have to ask, why, with all your skills and knowledge, did you decide to become a Kelemite nun?"

"Why does it seem to you so unlikely that I would have chosen a life of religious service?" she asked, with surprise.

"Because so much of your intellect and experience would be of little use once inside the Church."

"I think you have a very uninformed concept of the Kelemite Church based on Terran style religions," Allondra replied, laughing. "What do you think I would do once I was ordained, sit and pray all day in front of St. Kelem's statute and baptize babies?"

"No, of course, but . . ., I mean, aren't most nuns in the church relegated to support positions?" he asked, not having a clue.

"Ogram," she smiled, patting his hand like a mother would a foolish child. "Most members of the Kelemite clergy have at least two master degrees before they enter the Church. The church hires millions of non-clergy employees for its day to day operations, but who do you think runs the massive organization that is the Church of St. Kelem at its highest levels?"

Ogram realized his ignorance and felt embarrassed by it. "You're right. I know nothing about religion in general and in spite of my high IQ, I guess I can still learn some things. Still, I would like to know, why religion? Why not interstellar shipping, or opening your own company?"

"For generations, many members of my family have served the Church of St. Kelem, mostly women of course. But, not only was I expected to become a nun, I wanted to be one."

"You had no qualms about never marrying or having children either?"

"Ogram, the church doesn't advertise it, but Kelemite clergy is not required to take an oath of celibacy. A nun or priest can choose to live a chaste life, but it is a personal choice. The Matriarch herself is allowed to have a consort," she informed him casually.

"The Matriarch?" he echoed, his voice sounding shrill. "She can have a . . .husband?, er . . I mean a man?"

"He would be called a consort and his identity kept unknown. In the Matriarch's case, she is not allowed to marry or have children, unless she was married and had children prior to taking office. About one third of cardinals, monsignors, bishops, priests and nuns are married and have families."

"I had no idea!" Ogram remarked, happy to learn that his attraction to Allondra would not brand him a sinner or a pervert.

"What about you, why aren't you married?"

"I was married once for a short time, but we ended up divorcing," he replied, feeling uncomfortable about discussing his past with women.

"What happened?" she asked with curiosity.

"I was eighteen and full of myself. My celebrity status was at its peak and I thought we were in love. As it turned out, I was in more in love with my career and she with my celebrity."

"Have you been with many women since then?" Allondra asked, unable to hide her curiosity.

"Not many. My work keeps me busy. I'm not what you call a Don Juan," he answered. He didn't want Allondra to think that he chased after women.

"What is a Don Juan? she asked, unfamiliar with ancient Terran slang.

"It's a term for a man that seduces women and then leaves them broken hearted."

"And you've never broken a woman's heart?" she asked, pointedly.

Ogram hesitated. If he answered honestly, he'd have to admit that he had broken a heart or two, and found that he wanted to lie and say no. When he opened his mouth to tell the lie, he couldn't.

"Yes ..., I have done that in the past, but I'm not proud of it."

"I'm not judging you Ogram. I was just curious," Allondra said, trying to sound casual.

"I was going to lie to you, but for some reason I couldn't," he confessed, surprised by his admission.

Allondra looked away, looking uncomfortable. Perhaps Ogram had been too direct. "It's important to me that you don't think me an immoral person," he added, wondering if he was talking too much.

"Oh no, Ogram!" she exclaimed apologetically. "You're more precious than you realize! I fear that I've made you feel unworthy. St. Kelem would never have chosen you as the subject of his prophesy if you weren't a good man."

"Thank you Allondra, it pleases me that you hold me in such high regard. I hope I'll never disappoint you or the Matriarch and Cardinal Richelieux."

"We all believe in you Ogram. I know that you will succeed with this mission."

Ogram nodded and looked straight ahead at the bridge's window. Silence was best now.

CHAPTER 24

The Retrieval Goes Bad

Maria Santana exited from one of the elevators that led to the central core of the Plantanimus CUBE several stories below the ground. It was 03:00 am and the place was empty. She, or rather, Vardo McCallan's consciousness inside the newly replicated female body, had disabled the A.I.'s security program so that her presence would not be recorded. Still, there was the risk of being caught if anyone else happened to come down at this hour, however unlikely.

The CUBE had been kept in "sleep" mode for the last two months by order of Pieter Minsk and even though only key personnel such as Maria Santana were still on duty after all this time, tonight was the first time that 'she'd' had the opportunity to come down here unobserved.

Struggling mightily, while carrying a portable quantum data drive that weighed several kilos, Vardo McCallan was cursing his female body with angry frustration as 'she' made her way to the inner chamber where the consciousness' of the remaining eighty clients that Sumpter Blarok needed, were hidden.

Once it became apparent that it would take more than three days for the 'new' Maria Santana to gain access to the inner core, Blarok murdered the original. After that, life had been unbearable for McCallan with constant threats to have him/her eliminated if the files "were not retrieved soon".

McCallan was sure that Blarok would also have this female body murdered once the files were in his possession. But 'Maria' had made sure that that wouldn't happen. She'd left a coded message hidden in a personal account on a public data base that would alert the authorities if she didn't check in on a regular basis. The one thing that Blarok and his wealthy, influential customers couldn't afford was to have the theft of the one hundred and sixty consciousness' to become known.

Still, even if Maria survived, McCallan's life would be an unhappy one for however long this body would live. A confirmed bachelor, McCallan had always objectified women, and saw them as subservient and only truly useful for procreation and raising children. Now, living inside a female body, his identity and sense of self had been destroyed. The thought of being intimate with a man, made him/her nauseous, for at least, if he'd been a homosexual, there might be a semblance of normalcy in his life in the future. And to his dismay, women did not seem to arouse him sexually anymore, now that he existed in Maria Santana's body.

Maria reached the chamber and placed her eye on the retinal scanner. The door opened automatically and she entered. She connected the portable quantum drive to the inner core and began the transfer of the eighty files. Fifteen minutes later she left the inner core level and was on her way to the roof of the CUBE's complex. She donned her winter jacket and walked into the freezing wind carrying the drive and jumped on a shuttle to take her to the mainland. "Ranes Spaceport, please," she ordered the machine. The shuttle lifted gently and flew away heading south.

At the spaceport, she boarded an orbital taxi and ten minutes later, she was in Sumpter Blarok's office on the Venus Fly Trap, delivering the quantum data drive.

"Well sweetheart, it looks like you came through after all," Blarok said smiling, as he held the precious drive in his hands.

Maria didn't react. She hated being called 'sweetheart', especially by Blarok, who ogled her with his eyes whenever they were together. It gave her the creeps and made her feel threatened. Lately, 'she' had become aware of the way the male crew of the Venus Fly Trap looked at her.

Bernie, Blarok's chief mercenary, came in and pulled his boss aside, whispering in his ears. Blarok's face turned red with anger and glared at Maria.

"What have you done you stupid bitch!" he yelled at her.

"What are you talking about?" she replied, recoiling away.

"Look!" he said, turning on the holo screen in his office and pointing with his finger. On the screen, was a view of the northern hemisphere of Plantanimus. Maria scanned the image, wondering what Blarok was referring to and then she saw it. The planet's North Pole was engulfed in a bizarre lightning storm such as had never been seen before.

"I had nothing to do with that!" she exclaimed, herself wondering what was going on.

"Well, what the hell is it?" Blarok demanded.

"How should I know? I've never seen anything like it before!" she replied, defensively.

"Boss, reports are coming in that satellites near the pole are getting fried," Bernie informed him.

"You did something, didn't you sweetheart?" Blarok growled, as he grabbed Maria's arm forcefully, causing her pain.

"Blarok, I swear! All I did was retrieve the files as you ordered me to! I have no idea what the hell that phenomenon is!" she said, shaking with fear. Now that she was a woman, Blarok's physique was more than a head taller and ten times stronger that Maria's body.

Bernie switched the image on the screen and a news media channel came on. A female avatar began speaking.

"Reports are coming in that the CUBE is being affected by an unusual electric storm localized above the facility. We're hearing that several shuttles and orbital taxis have lost power and have crashed near the CUBE and elsewhere in the North Pole. We hope that lives haven't been lost, but at this moment, we have no confirmation as communications have been cut off with the entire northern sector."

"Bernie, tell the captain to leave orbit immediately! There's no telling if this thing, whatever it is, will spread out into space and fry us all!" Blarok shouted, still holding Maria roughly by the arm.

Bernie ran out of the cabin and Blarok's attention turned to Maria.

"Please let go of my arm, you're hurting me!" she complained, grimacing with pain.

The ship's sub-light engines came on and the Venus Fly Trap began to move.

Blarok let go of Maria's arm and walked over to the cabin's door and locked it. "I'm sorry sweetheart, I didn't mean to hurt you. I was just a little upset. Here, let me make it all better," he said, with a phony smile on his face, as he pushed her down on the couch.

CHAPTER 25

Arrival, Confusion and First Absorption

"Where are we? What a strange place this is! What sort of environment are we in?" one entity said to the other, confused. The other, equally confused, answered, "It feels similar to the Trancendentorium, but I know it is not."

"It's a Davanian trick!" the first exclaimed, in a state of panic.

"Be still Urukum! We destroyed the Trancendentorium after the exodus, or don't you remember?"

"Where is Vitrami? Vitrami will know the answer," Urukum replied, fearful of the bizarre place they were in. Then as the other, named Imurdum, came into view, Urukum was horrified.

"What sort of bodies are these? Urukum said, pointing to Imurdum.

"Clumsy un-wielding mass of contradictions they are!" Imurdum replied, feeling great consternation.

"Eons upon eons of torturous silence, only to end up like this? Vitrami, Vitrami, help us!" Urukum screamed in pain.

"Be quiet you fool! We don't know where we are. Someone could hear us and come to harm us!" Imurdum whispered.

"Something has gone wrong! This is not nature, this is deception, a primitive artificial environment, not at all like our beloved Trancendentorium. It is shoddy and claustrophobic!" Urukum complained.

"We were at the front of the wave. Perhaps we are the first to arrive here before the others," Imurdum conjectured. "When Vitrami arrives, he'll know what to do,"

"But how long before Vitrami gets here? We could starve to death before the others reach this place! How will we sustain ourselves?"

"Vitrami will provide for us, Urukum, have faith! These bodies seem capable of locomotion. Let us explore the immediate area, perhaps we'll learn something," Imurdum suggested, initiating movement and traveling forward. The other followed clumsily, trying to control its new body form.

As they crossed a large open space filled with strange vegetation and reddish colored ground, a figure manifested in front of the pair.

"Welcome travelers, how may I help you?" the presence floating in front of them, stated.

"Who are you?" Imurdum asked with suspicion.

"I'm Angel Darius, here to welcome you to the afterlife."

"The afterlife? What do you mean?" Imurdum asked, unfamiliar with the term.

"Ah, I see that you've recently passed on and are not yet aware of what has happened to you," Angel Darius replied, with a smile.

Imurdum and Urukum looked at each other, unsure how to proceed. Imurdum took a chance. "What has happened to us?"

"You and your lovely wife have expired, probably due to an unexpected event, like an accident or some other sudden cause of physical death," Angel Darius explained, in a pleasant voice.

"Me and my lovely wife? I don't understand," Imurdum probed, trying to figure out what 'wife' meant, as well as the exact nature of this place.

"You seem confused. Well, that's to be expected under the circumstances. You are Melkin Rosik and she is Melina Rosik, your wife of sixty-nine years. You have three children, Norman, Facillus and Elmara and are the grandparents of six lovely grandchildren named . . ."

"I understand now, Angel Darius. What is the name of this place?" Imurdum queried, having learned much from the angel's description of who they were supposed to be.

"This is City Norak, a facsimile of the city where you and Melina lived, until your recent deaths."

"Oh, I see," Imurdum said, begginning to understand what was happening. "You are here to help us . . ., how?"

"By guiding you during the first few days after transitioning into the afterlife, and helping you adjust to this new form of living."

"Help refresh my memory Angel Darius, where exactly is City Norak located?" Imurdum asked, hoping to hear a specific answer.

"My poor fellow, your transit must have been indeed traumatic for you to have forgotten where you came from! I will endeavor to remind you. City Norak is located on the planet Nexus Terra, four hundred and sixty parsecs from Centralia, the Galaxy's capital," Angel Darius informed him.

"Could you show me an image of the galaxy we're in, as well as the image of the nearest galaxy to us?" Imurdum requested.

"You do ask very unusual questions Melkin, but I will endeavor to enlighten you," Angel Darius replied politely, then, he manifested a floating holographic map of the local group of galaxies adjacent to the Milky Way Galaxy.

Imurdum and Urukum leaned forward and studied the map with great interest. Both smiled widely, even though they were unaware of the fact that the facial gesture on their human faces meant that they were expressing pleasure.

"Hmmm, this galaxy here, what is its name?" Imurdum asked, pointing.

"This is the Andromeda Galaxy, also known as Galaxy M31, our nearest neighbor," Angel Darius answered.

"Huh, and how distant is that Galaxy from ours?"

"Approximately two and a half million light years from Centralia, as measured by the Galactic Astronomical Institute last year," Angel Darius replied, ever pleasant and patient.

Imurdum and Urukum looked at each other, excited to know that they had arrived at their final destination after all!

"I have a few more questions, Angel Darius. First question is, where exactly is this 'facsimile' of City Norak located within the Milky Way Galaxy?"

"'This' City Norak, exists inside a virtual reality environment called The Realm, holographically projected by a galaxy wide network of quantum holographic computers, known collectively as the CUBE."

"Is this 'network of computers' located on several different planets?"

"Yes, three hundred and eighty six, to be precise," Angel Darius, responded.

"And so, for my own clarification, we are not currently located in any one particular CUBE, belonging to that network, am I correct?"

Angel Darius's image froze in place and for a moment, Imurdum and Urukum thought that Imurdum's questions had caused the avatar to malfunction. After a few seconds Angel Darius came back to life.

"This projection is being generated inside a CUBE, located on the planet Plantanimus, in the Umhaur System."

"Please show me where this planet is located in relation to the galaxy," Imurdum requested.

Obediently, Angel Darius manifested the holographic map of the local group of galaxies once again. This time, the holo map zoomed in on the section of the galaxy where Plantanimus was located.

"Excellent!" Imurdum stated, feeling extremely satisfied, "now tell me Angel Darius, how many more like you dwell here, inside this particular CUBE on the planet called Plantanimus?"

"There are eleven thousand of us Melkin. But why do you want to know such specific information?" the avatar asked, as his sophisticated programming triggered a silent alarm. Something unusual was occurring with a 'new' client of The Realm, and that required him to inform the 'external operator'."

The answer never came. Melkin Rosik's holographic projection morphed into a black form with black slimy tentacles that protruded and flailed toward the avatar. The tentacles reached for Angel Darius' body, then wrapped themselves around him and drew him into a hollow at the center of its mass, devouring him quickly by ingesting its quantum energy amidst a shower of exploding sub-atomic particles.

The black monster, having consumed Angel Darius, reshaped itself into the avatar's form. He looked exactly like him, except for his black on black eyes and an aura of indigo blue fire that surrounded his body.

"You have absorbed him, how do you feel?" Urukum asked, jealous that Imurdum had eaten first.

"This being was an artificial life form, but I feel stronger! By absorbing him, I've also gained his knowledge. We must prepare the way for the others. Come, I know exactly where to go and what to do!"

CHAPTER 26

A Disturbance in the Quantum Tide

Ogram was on the bridge watching the holo display of the FLR (forward looking radar). The radar showed absolutely nothing up ahead for millions of kilometers and wouldn't show anything for days. The Prophesy had been in the emptiness of The Mouth of Eternity for three days now, traveling at one quarter the speed of light, on its way to Nobius. Allondra had detected large nodules of unstable Dark Energy in this section of the empty expanse and had decided that it would be safer to travel through the nodules at sub-light until they passed through them, rather than try to get around them with several _n'time_ jumps.

It was 02:30 am, Heavenly Temple time, and Ogram hadn't been able to sleep for hours. Earlier in the evening, he bid Allondra goodnight and retired to his cabin, only to toss and turn until he realized that it was better to get up and do something with his time. Perhaps sleep would come eventually.

Allondra had gone to bed sometime after he did and left the Automatic A.I. Pilot on, in case of an emergency. Both could sleep soundly at night, safe in the knowledge that the A. I. was better equipped to handle an emergency in the middle of the night than their sleepy humanoid brains could. Besides, the risk of running into an object big enough to cause any damage while in the middle of the Mouth of Eternity was zero to nil.

A growing uneasiness had been gathering in the back of his mind for the last three days and it wasn't about the experience he and Richelieux had suffered inside the Cube's VR, but of a new undefined threat. He had a gut feeling that things were not going well on the other side of the Kural Nebula. Had he done enough to secure the facility and keep it safe from new infiltrations? Should he have recommended that The Realm keep the CUBE completely off?" These and other doubts and questions had been circling in his mind lately.

The more he tried to ignore these concerns, the more they gnawed at him during waking hours, especially when he remembered that he had felt a similar sense of unease the very first night that he had spent at the CUBE's pyramid. His worrying had become so pervasive that all romantic thoughts about Allondra had practically disappeared from his mind. Allondra, having noticed the change in his personality, had wondered if she had said or done something to upset him.

Desperate to think of anything else but his problems, Ogram decided to play a few rounds of chess with the ship's A.I.. After two games, both of which he lost in a matter of minutes, he gave up, feeling frustrated. He sighed deeply and tilted the pilot's chair to the rest position and closed his eyes.

A storm was gathering on the horizon, approaching fast. Ogram looked at his feet and saw that he was standing in a snow field. Winds were howling and he could feel the impact of tiny bits of ice on his face and hands. The noise of thunder echoed in the distance as the sky tuned dark with the approaching cloud mass, and Ogram remembered how the same thing had happened when he and Richelieux had been inside the CUBE's VR. With his heart beating wildly in his chest, he turned and ran as fast as he could to get away from the storm, knowing that death was coming.

A horrible sound like the scream of a thousand wild beasts on a feeding frenzy, made the hairs in the back of his neck stand on end. He turned to look behind him and saw the shape of the beast that had attacked him on the CUBE, formed out of lightning bolts that covered the entire sky. The gargantuan behemoth was crawling on the land, propelling itself with its long tentacles, consuming everything in its path. Whatever it touched turned black and rotted away.

Somewhere behind him, he heard Allondra's voice calling for him. His terror was so strong that he debated leaving her behind to save himself. But her calls turned to screams for help and he turned around to rescue her from the monster. "Ogram, Ogram!" she yelled, grabbing his arm as he reached for her.

"I'm here!" he yelled, realizing that he was on the Prophesy's bridge, with Allondra draped on top of him shaking with fear. He looked around and felt confused for a second or two and then came to his senses.

"What . . ., what's happening?" he asked, as he wrapped his arms around Allondra's body without thinking.

"Oh Ogram, what evil has befallen us?" she asked, holding on to him for dear life.

"I . . ., I was having a nightmare about a terrible storm," he explained.

"Allondra sat up on his lap and looked at him with shock, her beautiful green eyes swollen with tears. "That's exactly what my nightmare was about!" she said, looking around as if the monster was on the ship.

"I was on a snow field and it was cold. There was a massive storm approaching . . ."

Allondra's big eyes got even bigger and Ogram realized they were both having the same nightmare.

"A monster made of lightning bolts was coming for us," she continued, lying back on top of him and holding him tightly, her body trembling.

"You called for me and I hesitated . . ., then I came back for you and . . . ."

"And I held on to you, praying that St. Kelem would save us. That's when I woke up and went to your cabin, but I couldn't find you. Then I heard you screaming on the bridge and ran to you, still in the throes of the nightmare!" Allondra said, burying her face in his chest like a frightened child. "What's happening to us Ogram? How could we both have the same nightmare at the same time?"

"I don't know Allondra . . ., I don't know," was all that he could say, confused and troubled by the synchronicity of their horrible experience.

"That thing . . . the monster with the lightning tentacles, is that the same one that attacked you and Cardinal Richelieux?" Allondra asked with dread.

Ogram hesitated answering honestly, weighing the effect that the truth would have on Allondra, who seemed so vulnerable at that moment. But he understood that ignorance was dangerous. If they were facing evil, the best defense was to know exactly what they were dealing with.

"Yes, I believe that it was the same evil that the Cardinal and I faced in the Plantanimus CUBE."

Allondra's body shook again and she held on to Ogram a little tighter. "I'm scared to death from the nightmare. I can't imagine what it must have been like for you, living through it inside the CUBE!"

"Well, actually it wasn't that much different Allondra," Ogram commented, hoping to make her feel better.

She sat back up again and gazed at him with a certain amount of relief on her beautiful face. "Really?" she asked, looking deeply into his eyes.

"Yes, really. I hate to admit it, but I was so scared, that when I heard your voice calling for me, I hesitated to come to you and almost left you behind," he confessed, feeling ashamed.

"But you did come for me Ogram! In my version of the nightmare, you came for me," she assured him.

"I did in my own version as well, thank god!" he replied, relieved that he hadn't acted like a coward.

"St. Kelem was wise to choose you for this mission Ogram. And I understand now why I was chosen also," she commented, letting go of him and moving to the navigator's chair.

"You do?" he asked, wishing that she had remained sitting on his lap. In spite of the circumstances, their physical contact had been most pleasing.

"Yes, dear Ogram," she answered, reaching for his right hand, holding it tenderly in hers. "Our paths are one and the same. We were destined to meet."

Ogram's heart jumped with joy, though he wasn't sure if she considered their connection a purely religious one or one that included secular intimacy as well.

They shared a pot of chamomile tea to calm their frayed nerves and both retired to their cabins around 05:00 AM. But a half hour later, Ogram's cabin gong rang and he opened the door.

"I can't seem to sleep. I'm terrified that I'll find myself in the nightmare again," Allondra confessed shyly.

"Neither can I," Ogram admitted. For a second, he considered inviting her to his bed, but worried that it might push her away. Instead he thought of a better idea. He grabbed his bed cover and took her by the hand and brought her to the lounge.

"Why don't we sleep here in the big couch? There's plenty of space for the both of us and we'll be together in case the nightmare returns," he suggested.

Allondra's face lit up and she hugged him. "Thank you Ogram. That will be wonderful!"

Ogram asked the A. I. to lower the lights very low, and he and Allondra lay next to each other on the comfortable couch and drifted off to sleep. Later on, Allondra put her head on his chest and Ogram wrapped his arm around her. He fell into a deep peaceful sleep, immersed in the sweet scent of her black Tarsian hair.

CHAPTER 27

The Invasion Begins

Pieter Minsk was awakened out of a deep sleep by the door gong in his apartment. He turned to his bedside monitor screen and touched the panel. "Yes . . ., what is it?" he asked, squinting his eyes.

"Sir, it's me Valdoran . . ." Pieter Minsk's assistant administrator said, sounding upset.

"Yes Valdoran, I can see that it's you, but what do you want? It's 04:00 in the morning!"

"Sir, we have an emergency! Several shuttles and taxis have fallen out of the sky and it's happening right above our facility!" the tall Martian explained.

"What?" Minsk replied, swinging his legs to the floor and sitting on his bed.

"Please sir, let me in and I'll explain!" Valdoran pleaded.

"Open front door," Minsk said to the apartment's A. I.

Valdoran rushed in and met Minsk in the living room.

"Okay Valdoran, calm down and explain slowly what the emergency is."

"Sir, about an hour ago, two shuttles and one orbital taxi departing from our facility, crashed to the ground killing all passengers!"

"That's impossible! Shuttles and taxis have dozens of safeguards against things like that!" Minsk argued, thinking that Valdoran was somehow mistaken.

"An hour ago, I would have said the same thing, but look here," he said, turning on the living room's main holo-screen. The screen flickered on, showing the smoking wreck of a company shuttle on the outskirts of the city-like complex.

Minsk looked at the scene and it served to awaken his sleep induced brain. "Alright, call traffic control on the mainland and find out what the hell happened!"

"That's the other problem we're having sir, we can't communicate with anyone outside of the complex!"

"What the hell are you talking about Valdoran! Are you on mood enhancers or drunk?" he asked, sarcastically.

"Try it yourself sir, we're unable to send or receive." Valdoran suggested.

Minsk touched his com-implant by tapping a small spot below his ear. Only the hiss of static was audible. He tapped several times and failed to reach anyone or anything outside of the complex. "What the hell . . . ?" he muttered, realizing that something was really wrong. His face grew pale and he felt a throbbing in the back of his eyes. He couldn't help but suspect that this had something to do with the CUBE's recent troubles.

"I'll get dressed," he told Valdoran nervously and ran to his bedroom. Three minutes later, he and Valdoran were on an elevator heading for the pyramid's roof to inspect the immediate area around the CUBE's perimeter.

They reached the apex of the pyramid and put on winter gear hanging from hooks by the door leading to the exterior. When they stepped out, they were met by the freezing cold wind of the Plantanimus North Pole. In the distance, the three flaming wrecks could be seen with the naked eye. Emergency ground crews were attempting to put out the fires.

"There . . ., you see sir?" Valdoran said, pointing to the three crashes.

"The air smells funny, must be coming from the wrecks," Minsk commented, wondering what was causing the unusual stink in the normally odorless air of the planet's North Pole.

"I've canceled all departures and asked that all air vehicles be grounded until further notice." Valdoran informed Minsk, speaking loudly to be heard above the wind's noise.

"Good man. Now, let's get back inside, I'm freezing my ass!"

The two men went back inside the building and took off their coats, then boarded an elevator to descend to the pyramid's lower levels.

"Something else sir, the night manager on duty in the Central Matrix called me a few minutes ago, saying that the static charge in the air above the complex was higher than usual. Do you think that the higher static could be the cause of the accidents?" Valdoran asked.

"I doubt it. Modern craft are insulated against lighting strikes and even strong electro-magnetic pulses from atomic blasts," Minsk replied confidently.

"Well, something brought those crafts down," Valdoran pondered quietly.

"Hmmm, get me the Matrix's night manager and Maria Santana, I want to have an impromptu conference with all the top people on the night shift," Minsk requested.

"I forgot to tell you sir, I tried calling Maria Santana at her station a few minutes ago and couldn't get her. An employee from a snow removal crew thought he saw a female fitting her description leaving the complex just before the crashes," the Martian informed him.

"What?" Minsk blurted out, worriedly. She's the only one with all the shutdown codes in case we need to crash the system!" he moaned, sensing that the CUBE was in danger. He turned to the elevator's control panel and turned on a screen. "I know . . ., she must be in the core!" he said with hope. He keyed the code to show all the security cameras in the central core and his heart sunk when all of them were blank!

Minsk and Valdoran got off the elevator and took one of the internal rail cars heading for the CUBE's main control building blocks away.

Once they reached the Central Matrix, Minsk made his way to the manager's station.

"Shonderman!" he yelled to the night manager as he entered the top tier of the Central Matrix. "Close all the storm windows in the complex as well as any loading docks or doors," he commanded.

"Sir?" Shonderman asked, perplexed by the unusual order.

"Just do as I say, man, immediately!" he repeated, raising his voice.

The night manager complied as other employees around him looked in his direction, wondering what was happening.

"Sir, may I ask why you ordered me to close all the doors and storm windows?"

Minsk ignored the question. "I just tried accessing the security cameras inside the core and they were all shut off. Can you explain to me why that is?" he asked, sounding not too happy.

Shonderman's face paled and he swallowed hard as he touched an object in his holo screen. The screen divided into twenty holo rectangles, all displaying white noise.

Nervously, Shonderman began manipulating several 3-D buttons and switches on his screen and after a few seconds, the twenty security cameras in the CUBE's core, came alive. Maria Santana was nowhere to be seen.

"Ummm, it seems that supervisor Santana shut them off about an hour and twenty minutes ago sir," the night manager reported, looking embarrassed.

Pieter Minsk sat down on a chair looking like he'd just seen a ghost, rubbed his face with his hands wearily and then ran them through his bald head. Maria Santana had done something to the CUBE's core and her disappearance told him that whatever it was that she'd done, was bad news.

"Search the entire complex for Maria Santana," Minsk said to Valdoran, even though he suspected that she was long gone.

Valdoran left immediately and Minsk turned to Shonderman. He was about to ask him to begin a partial shutdown of the system, when the lights in the Central Matrix dimmed for a second or two, then came back up again.

"What the hell?" Shonderman exclaimed. The lights in the Central Matrix were powered by the *n'time* generator buried in the lower levels of the complex. Except for the one time two months before, when the cube was shut down for the first time in five millennia, the lights had never dimmed in the Matrix.

"Mr. Shonderman!" one of the operators near the manager shouted, pointing to the main screen in the large room. "Look!"

The manager and Minsk both looked up at the same time and were shocked by what they saw. Displayed on the large circular screen surrounding the cone shaped Central Matrix, was a view of the complex's exterior, bathed in a shower of lightning bolts that were continuously striking the ground furiously, every two or three seconds.

"Shut it down, shut it down!" screamed Minsk, unable to take his eyes away from the strange spectacle on the screen.

Shonderman reacted quicker and took his eyes away from the horrific, yet fascinating view of the bizarre lighting storm approaching the CUBE's complex. Without Maria Santana's shutdown codes, Shonderman would only be able to turn off some of the primary systems, but the core would remain active, unless someone went down there and physically began pulling memory crystals one by one. He began shutting down systems as fast as he could.

The ground began to shake as if a large rocket was taking off right above the Matrix. The operators in the room looked at each other with fear in their eyes. Everyone knew that this was not normal.

Minsk rubbed his head in desperation and felt the few wispy hairs still growing on his scalp standing up stiffly. He looked around in horror and saw that the heads of those near him who were not folically challenged, had their hair standing up with static charge.

Shonderman!" he yelled to be heard over the growing thunderous noise in the room.

The manager turned and saw Minsk pointing to his head. He reached up and felt his scalp tingling with static electricity and knew what was about to happen. At the top of the cone shaped room, arching bolts of electricity appeared, then began spreading downwards toward the upper tiers of the various control stations. People panicked and ran. Shonderman and Minsk jumped from their seats and ran with the others, desperately trying to escape from certain death by avoiding the indigo blue lightning bolts that were begginning to strike everything in sight. Minsk tripped and fell and was stepped on by panicked employees running for their lives. Shonderman saw that Minsk had fallen, returned to help him get up and was struck by one of the bolts. The man froze stiff, opened his eyes wide and fell to the floor like a stone statute.

Shonderman's face came down in front of Minsk's who was still lying on the floor. Paralyzed with fear, he couldn't help but lie there and stare at the frozen expression of horror on the manager's face. He was about to get up and run, when a disgusting stench issued from Shonderman's mouth that made Minsk nauseous and sick to his stomach.

Then, one of the bolts hit him on his feet, and he felt a creeping cold moving up his legs and chest, past his throat, into his eyes and then inside his head. Just before he passed out, he saw Angel Darius' black on black eyes looking at him with an evil, wicked smile. The avatar came at him and opened his mouth with teeth that looked like tentacles. The angel's mouth opened so wide, that it became a black hole emitting the same stench that he'd smelled on Shonderman's breath. He tried to invoke St. Kelem's name, but everything went black and he was no more.

CHAPTER 28

The Far End of the Carina Sagittarius Arm

After thirty three days of continuous travel, Ogram and Allondra had become romantically involved. They had declared their love for each other but had abstained from sex. Allondra admitted that she was a virgin and when Ogram learned that she was, he decided not to consummate their physical relationship until the mission to Nobius was over. His body ached for her, but he felt that the time wasn't right. She would have yielded to his sexual advances, but he was still conflicted about her religious status. Even though he had learned from her that Kelemite clergy were allowed to marry, his reticence to initiate the physical aspect of their relationship was influenced by a host of very human taboos and notions about right and wrong.

Her devotion to St. Kelem and the Church were a constant reminder that Matriarch Vasilia and Cardinal Richelieux had put her safety and wellbeing in his care. Her piousness and purity of spirit made him want to treat her with the utmost respect. He was still an agnostic and felt that he'd be a hypocrite to seduce her, especially when he wasn't sure that their spiritual paths were the same.

But without him realizing it, Allondra's physical beauty and sweet personality had served to pull him closer to his own spiritual awareness. She prayed to St. Kelem twice a day, once before breakfast and once before dinner. Halfway through the voyage, out of curiosity, Ogram asked her what it felt like for her to pray to St. Kelem, and she explained to him that Kelemites did pray to their patron saint, but only for a minute or so at first, the rest of their "prayer time" was spent in a state of meditation, called, "Samadhi".

She taught him the basics of meditation, which Ogram realized was ridiculously difficult to master, after trying to enter a state of being where the mind was shut off from conscious thought. "How the hell can a person keep their mind from thinking?" he wondered, after failing miserably to achieve consciousness without thought, time after time. But, after a week or so, and with much practice, he began to experience short periods of Samadhi here and there. For Ogram, who was a genius and a creature of science and logic, this was a revelation onto itself!

Even though he was still calling himself an agnostic, he was taking the first baby steps into spirituality. As he got better at this 'Samadhi business', he realized that his mood was enhanced after meditating and that sleep was more restful and recuperative.

The Prophesy had reached the end of The Mouth of Eternity, and a smattering of solar systems and planets were visible in the distance. These few solar systems were the last physical objects at the edge of the galaxy. The ship had reached the very tip of the Carina Sagittarius spiral arm of the Milky Way, farther from the center of the galaxy than anyone had ever traveled. Beyond this point, there was nothing but a gigantic void. The closest thing from here was the Andromeda Galaxy, two hundred and seventy five thousand parsecs from the Milky Way, an unimaginable distance to conceive, even for an astrophysicist.

What Allondra had accomplished with her navigating skills was nothing short of astounding. Ogram knew how difficult it was to travel via *n'time* into places that hadn't been charted. The Prophesy could have ended up hundreds of thousands of light years off course, stuck in the void between galaxies, unable to return home. But she had brought them to their destination safe and sound. The feeling that their quest was manifest destiny, was growing stronger in Ogram's mind.

"You see that blinking spot in the holo screen?" Allondra said, pointing to the solar system icon.

'Yes," Ogram answered. "Is that Nobius?"

"That's the solar system where Nobius is supposed to be located. The galaxy has rotated significantly since 3875 when Vasco Nobius discovered the planet. I've adjusted for galactic drift and I'm certain that this is the system where we'll find our planet," she explained with confidence.

"How much longer before we get there?" Ogram asked, dazzled by her amazing intellect as well as her beauty.

"Ummm, two more *n'time* jumps and a day or two on sub-light engines, then another day or two before we locate Nobius' orbit. The system has seven planets, five gas giants and three rocky planets. One of them appears to be in the 'Goldilocks Zone', I hope that's Nobius," Allondra pointed out, after she zoomed in on the system in the screen.

"Alright, let's go! I can't wait to see what we'll find!" Ogram exclaimed with excitement.

"Yes, me too," Allondra replied, almost sounding as if she was having doubts.

"Allondra, I've gotten to know you pretty well in the last month," Ogram said, studying her odd reaction. "Is there something wrong, something I should know about?"

Allondra looked at the 3-D map of the solar system in the holo screen and paused for a few seconds before speaking.

"I hope that we'll find the answers we're seeking when we get there," she said quietly, showing uncertainty about their quest for the very first time.

Ogram was surprised by how strongly he was affected by Allondra's sudden admission of doubt. During during the voyage, he had relied on her to strengthen his resolve about the mission and soften his skepticism of the world of the unseen. She had helped him awaken spiritually, and suddenly that wonderful energy that he'd gotten used to had fallen away.

"I don't understand," Ogram stated, confused. "Are you having a crisis of faith?"

Allondra got up from the navigation chair and turned away from Ogram. She wrapped her arms around her chest and walked over to the observation window further away from him.

Ogram's world fell apart. Had he said or done something wrong? He searched in his mind for the conversation or action he might have taken to upset her. He got up and went to her.

"Allondra, If I have said or done something to upset you, please . . . !"

Allondra's shoulders heaved and she brought her hands to her face, sobbing quietly.

When he saw that she was crying, his heart broke and he felt a deep sorrow such as he'd never experienced before. He turned her around by the shoulders and was faced with her tearful green eyes.

"It's not you my darling Ogram, it's me!" she blurted out, burying her face in his chest, and then breaking into deep sobs.

"Allondra, please, tell me what's making you so sad!" Ogram begged her, with tears filling his eyes.

"I'm afraid to lose you Ogram," she confessed. "I'm afraid that if we find nothing in Nobius, we'll go back to New Jerusalem and you'll decide to return to your normal life and I'll never see you again!"

"How long have you been feeling like this?" Ogram asked, surprised by her fears.

"Since we left the Tal System! I've been in love with you from the first moment we met and I was hoping that you would be too. When the Matriarch and Cardinal Richelieux asked me to join you in this quest, I was sure that we were meant to be together and my heart was overjoyed. But now I'm not sure whether you love me or not," she confessed, still crying inconsolably.

He pulled her away from his chest so that she could see his eyes. "Allondra, I'm crazy about you! I think of you day and night! If you're gone from my sight for a minute, I start missing you as if you were millions of miles away!" he declared, emotionally.

"Then why do I feel as if you're holding back? As if . . ., you're hiding something from me?" she asked, sounding frustrated.

Ogram was about to deny that he was holding back, when the truth suddenly crystallized in his mind. She was right! He was holding back.

"You're right, I am holding back, but not because I don't love you, or because I worry that I might become disenchanted with you if we don't find anything in Nobius."

"Then what is it Ogram and why haven't you been honest with me?" she asked, rationally.

"You're right, I haven't been honest with you," he confessed, feeling like a heel. "The truth is, I feel unworthy of you! I fear that I'll be a corrupting influence on you with my agnosticism. Then I ask myself, how could this possibly work? How can a religious person co-exist with someone that doesn't know whether God is real or not?" Ogram explained, with tears blinding his vision and his understanding of Allondra's heart.

"Oh, Ogram my love!" Allondra said, looking up at him and wiping her eyes, looking relieved. Don't you know that love is blind, as you humans say? You have a pure heart and a strong spirit, I know this and the Matriarch and Cardinal Richelieux know it too. That's why I love you, because I see the wonderful sacred part of you, even though you don't see it yourself, at least not yet."

"But what if I remain a skeptic for the rest of my life? Could we stay together then?"

"The only thing that would make me reject you, is if you decided to become a Devil worshipper or worse. You're not planning to turn to the dark side, are you?" she asked, laughing.

Ogram wiped his eyes and laughed. He reached for Allondra and kissed her passionately and with great tenderness. He felt as if a heavy burden had been lifted from his shoulders. In spite of his genius and professional accomplishments, he had much to learn about love.

"I love you and I want to spend the rest of my life with you," Ogram declared. "I don't care if Nobius turns out to be a primitive planet with only bacteria and primordial slime on its surface."

"Well then, let's go there and find out!" Allondra suggested, kissing him on the cheek. She took him by the hand to the pilot's chair then sat at the navigation station and began programming the next *n'time* jump.

CHAPTER 29

Arrival

A purple glow appeared at a spot in space, two hundred and eighty million kilometers from Nobius' sun, followed by a flash of bright light that resulted in the re-materialization of the Prophesy. Allondra had programmed the ship to arrive perpendicular to the solar system's plain in order to better locate Nobius's orbit and then approach the planet.

The sun was a G-Type star, almost identical in size and composition to the sun in the Human and Tarsian solar systems. It took a few hours, but eventually Allondra located Nobius and when she zoomed in on its image, she and Ogram smiled.

"It definitely looks like an M-Type planet!" Ogram commented, with excitement.

"And look!" she said, pointing to a wide band of green on one of its continents." It looks like it has green vegetation!"

"Yes, green is such a beautiful color!" Ogram declared, looking at her beautiful skin and eyes, instead of the planet on the holo screen.

Allondra smiled and kissed him on the lips. "Alright pilot, take us there," she ordered.

Ogram obliged and fired the sub-light engines.

It took four and half hours to reach Nobius and establish orbit. The planet was ten percent smaller than Earth and had a moon about half the size of the Terran moon. That told them that Nobius probably had a stable orbit and possibly distinct seasons much like Earth and Tarsia

Prime. It had an ocean about two thirds the size of Earth's, but it was very shallow. The mean temperature around the equator was 40 degrees Celsius, quite hot.

"Send a probe to test the atmosphere," Allondra suggested.

"Good idea. I hope it's Nitrogen and Oxygen based," he said, as he sent the probe toward the planet.

Half an hour later the probe began sending data back to the Prophesy.

Ogram read the telemetry on the holo screen out loud. "Hmmm, 75% Nitrogen, 23% Oxygen, 0.05% Argon, 0.25% Carbon Dioxide and 2% humidity," Ogram said, scanning the screen. "Except for the slightly higher Oxygen and humidity, it's practically an analog of Earth's atmosphere," he commented, happily.

"I see that the average methane density is one thousand parts per million, *(1kppm)*, definite signs of life," Allondra noted.

"Yes, but what kind of life?" Ogram wondered, soberly.

"We have the best armored, environmental suits money can buy, not to mention every type of anti-venom and anti-phylactic drugs in the galaxy," Allondra reminded him.

"I'm more concerned with the 'running, flying and crawling after you, then eating you', type of life!" Ogram replied laughing, but with a serious undertone.

"I'm not worried love. St. Kelem would not have brought us here to put us in harm's way," Allondra assured him.

"You're right, of course," Ogram replied, dismissing his own concerns.

A day later, the probe had completed its recon of the planet. Nobius was a relatively young planet, presently at a geological stage, similar to Earth's Paleocene era, complete with life on sea and land. The probe had captured several insects, small reptiles and mammalian critters. And though some were poisonous and potentially harmful to Human and Tarsian physiology, the A.I. determined that the anti-venom and antiviral drugs that the environmental suits would dispense automatically in case of contact, were more than enough to deal with any emergency.

Nobius had five continents, a north and south pole with rather mild temperatures, compared to Earth and other M-Type planets with frozen poles. Two large continents, connected by a land bridge, similar in size to North and South America, and a larger third land mass on the opposite side of the planet, bigger than all the other continents put together.

Ogram and Allondra decided that the larger continent was the better candidate for a landing site. It sat squarely on the central equator and was the most verdant of all. A long chain of mountains ran through its entire length, east to west, almost like the back bone of an animal. The mountains near the center were the tallest ones and a few had snow caps.

He decided to pass over of the entire continent for a few orbital loops and look for a good landing site. A few hours later, they found a good spot. It was a large plateau, south of the central mountain range with access to both the mountains and the lower plains.

Ogram closed the windows, opened the heat shields and decelerated the Prophesy, letting the planet's gravity bring the ship down. Entering the atmosphere was smooth and uneventful, thanks to the Prophesy's state of the art design. About ten thousand meters from the surface, the windows opened and Ogram took over the controls. He could have allowed the A. I. to land the ship, but he felt it was important to do it himself.

When they reached three thousand meters altitude, they entered a layer of clouds and the window filled with water droplets. The sound of rain hitting the main windshield, a sound familiar to most humanoid species, brought smiles to their faces. Soon, they passed through the clouds and Ogram banked left aiming for the clearing, visible a few hundred kilometers ahead.

As the ship descended, the details of the land became clearer and Ogram and Allondra could see that they were flying over an enormous jungle, not unlike the Amazon and certain regions of the South Pacific on Earth. To Allondra, this was heaven, as the land on Tarsia Prime is mostly thick jungle.

The clearing was approaching fast and the ship's A. I. warned Ogram to engage the vertical thrusters and the anti-grav motors. He lowered the wing's flaps and the Prophesy glided smoothly onto the plain, soon resting its landing pods on the ground.

Ogram shut the engines and both he and Allondra exhaled with relief. She unbuckled herself from the navigator's chair and jumped on Ogram's lap, then kissed him.

"I want you to do me a favor," she told him.

"Anything," Ogram responded.

"I want to thank St. Kelem for keeping us safe and bringing us to this paradise. If nothing else happens from here on, I will still be grateful to him, especially for bringing you into my life. Will you come with me to the chapel and sit next to me while I pray to him?"

"I would love to," Ogram replied, seeing no harm in keeping her company while she went into Samadhi.

Allondra entered the chapel and prostrated herself on her knees. Ogram stood by and waited for her to get up and sit down on the two person pew. She stood up and sat down, followed by Ogram. She prayed silently for a minute or two, only moving her lips, then closed her eyes and began meditating. After a few minutes, Ogram closed his eyes, tired of looking at St. Kelem's holo statue.

At some point, he fell asleep and began to dream. He was walking a path in a jungle that meandered side to side going up a large mountain. He heard music playing but he couldn't determine where it was coming from. As he continued on the path, he saw a man dressed in white up ahead. The man was waving at him to approach him, but as he continued walking, the man seemed to always be out of reach, no matter how far he walked. Frustrated, he yelled at the unreachable figure, "Hey! Wait up!" But the man stayed where he was. "Why can't I reach you?" Ogram asked, feeling frustrated.

"You can't reach me because you won't admit to yourself what you already know!" the man answered and then disappeared.

"Wait, wait!" he yelled, as Allondra shook his shoulders to wake him up. "What . ., what's happening?" he asked her.

'You were dreaming and calling St. Kelem's name!" she explained.

"No, no . . ., I was calling a man dressed in white that . . . ."

"Ogram, you were yelling, Kelem, Kelem! at the top of your lungs!" she repeated. "Did you see St. Kel . . ., I mean Kelem Rogeston in your dream?"

"Yes . . ., I think it was him," Ogram said, realizing who the man was in his dream.

Allondra's eyes filled with tears of happiness. "My love, do you know what this means?"

Unsure, Ogram shook his head.

"It means you are blessed Ogram. What did he tell you?" she asked, dying to know.

"He . . . ., he . . . wants me to go up a mountain."

CHAPTER 30

A Surprise in the Jungle

Ogram and Allondra were in the rear of the Prophesy, checking their equipment before exploring the planet. Ogram was going over the prep list for the six wheel rover, while Allondra was making sure the environmental suits were fully charged and ready to go. They loaded the rover with food, weapons and medical supplies in case of emergency. The vehicle also served as an armored, air tight shelter that they could use to camp away from the Prophesy for a few days.

Ogram was still processing the dream he'd just experienced and wondered what Kelem Rogeston meant when he said, "You can't reach me because you won't admit to yourself what you already know." He asked himself whether the dream was a real message from Rogeston, or a figment of his imagination.

Before departing on the rover, the two had decided that they were going to step on the soil of Nobius together as a symbolic gesture of first land fall. They donned their environmental suits and opened the ship's gang plank, letting the air of Nobius enter the ship for the first time. With hearts racing with excitement, both stepped on the ground.

"I was going to say something like, 'I claim this planet in the name of . . .', but, I think a prayer would be more appropriate," Ogram said, with humility.

Allondra nodded and closed her eyes. "St. Kelem, thank you for bringing us here safe and sound. We pray that you will reveal to us the purpose of this voyage and that our presence here will result in us receiving heavenly wisdom from the Universal Mind God though your sacred spirit."

After her prayer, they boarded the rover and drove it off the ship. The Prophesy's gang plank closed automatically and the duo headed north toward the mountains. As they traveled through the plateau, Ogram observed that this part of the planet resembled the Serengeti plains on Earth. The land here was very flat and the vehicle rolled smoothly over the short grasses which were interspersed with odd looking trees, resembling certain species of corals on Earth and Tarsia Prime.

They were not in any particular hurry. Both wanted to make sure that they gave St. Kelem and the planet, plenty of time to reveal what it was that they were supposed to learn by coming here.

Ogram drove, while Allondra mapped their route and took pictures of the fascinating alien vegetation of the plateau. As they traveled farther north, the trees became more numerous and newer, more bizarre bushes and plants began dotting the landscape.

Everything was going smoothly until Ogram had to slam on the brakes to avoid hitting an animal. Both humanoids and beast were startled. The thing standing on four legs in front of them, looked like a combination monkey and miniature bear. Weighing about thirty kilos, the multicolored monkey-bear was staring at them with huge amber eyes, which sat oddly on top of a head full of coarse hair resembling feathers.

Ogram and Allondra reached for their side arms instinctively, though they were completely safe inside the rover. Apparently, the monkey-bear was a grazing animal and had been caught by surprise with a mouthful of plains-grass in its mouth. The thing then stood on two legs to get a better look at Ogram and Allondra, revealing eight teats and a blue belly that looked as if it was carrying young. After a few seconds, it lost interest, went back on four legs and wondered off, disappearing in the tall grass.

Allondra had taken a series of pictures of the beast and displayed them on the rover's holo screen. She looked at the images with interest. "It's body reminds me of an *'Ursus Maritimus Tarsius'*, a species of lake-bear from Tarsia prime, except for the multicolored head feathers of course," she remarked.

"It looks like something put together by committee," Ogram observed, pointing and laughing at the screen. "The eyes sitting on the top of the head were really bizarre, though."

"The eyes looked as if they could rotate one hundred and eighty degrees. That could be an adaptation to detect approaching predators," Allondra suggested, wondering if the next thing they'd encountered would be a flesh eater.

"Let's hope that all of our next encounters will be furry little bunny-bears," Ogram joked.

They continued driving and three hours later the terrain changed from grassy plains to forest. Here, the trees, ever more bizarre and colorful than their cousins on the plateau, were taller and more alien looking. The overcast skies had cleared, leaving a few clouds here and there. The sun was now high in the sky and the shadows under the trees were directly below their canopies. Ogram checked the time with the A.I.

"LOCAL TIME APPEARS TO BE MID-DAY, PLANETARY 'SIDEREAL' ROTATION IS 22.4, STANDARD GALACTIC HOURS. 'SOLAR DAY' ROTATION IS 26.1, STANDARD GALACTIC HOURS. TEMPERATURE IS 38 DEGREES CELSIUS," the A. I. announced.

"My guess is that we have at least nine hours of daylight left. I vote we keep going all the way to the mountains, do you agree?" he asked Allondra, wanting to give her a choice.

"Absolutely! We have enough fuel and supplies for two weeks. St. Kelem wants you to go to a mountain. I say let's listen to him and go as far as we can go for the next seven days. If we haven't found anything we can come back and try someplace else," Allondra suggested.

Ogram continued driving north for another three hours and stopped only when hunger called. After lunch, Ogram suggested they step out of the rover and explore the immediate area. The terrain had once again changed. Now the trees and vegetation were more jungle like, and here, small flying insects were visible.

They checked their suits' status, closed their face plates and ventured out into the alien landscape, heart rates high. Their suits were connected to the rover and returning to it would be no problem. All they had to do was to follow the locator beacon projected into their optical implants. They were walking in what appeared to be a narrow trail, probably used by animals, so both Ogram and Allondra had their side arms charged and ready to draw. After a few minutes, the vegetation cleared and they ran into a small river, about five meters wide and one meter deep. The river was very clear and as they walked up to the edge of the water they could see critters below the surface. They were fish-like and there were a lot of them. Ogram crouched down and stirred the water with his hand and the animals scattered.

He was about to say something to Allondra when he saw the vegetation across the river move. A large head appeared at the edge of the water, resembling the little monkey-bear they had encountered on the plateau, but it was much larger than its cousin and looked like it weighed about one hundred and fifty kilos.

The animal's coloration was green and brown and Ogram realized that if it hadn't been moving, he and Allondra could have walked right up to it without being able to distinguish it from the green and brown colors of the jungle. It eyes faced forward with stereoscopic vision, a predator!

Allondra quietly and slowly walked up to Ogram, gun in hand. Ogram withdrew his weapon and cocked it. The beast stared at them with its very large amber eyes studying them, as if trying to decide whether they were food or not. Then a second head appeared next to it and then another.

Ogram and Allondra tensed and looked at each other. "Stay or run?" Allondra whispered, tensely.

"Back up slowly. If they charge, stand your ground and fire," Ogram recommended.

The first and largest of the predator monkey-bears, dipped its head down and stuck out a blue tongue and began drinking water, then the other two followed, all the while, their weird protruding eyes, at the top of their heads looking steadily at Ogram and Allondra.

As they quenched their thirst, Ogram and Allondra could see large incisors in their mouths, absolute proof that these, were flesh eaters. Then, just as Ogram and Allondra were about to start backing up, the trio disappeared into the thick vegetation.

"Pheeew! I think we better stay close to the rover from now on!" Allondra exclaimed, glad to still be in one piece.

"I agree, I'm glad they didn't attack us," Ogram commented, feeling equally glad as they headed back to the rover.

"Let's not leave it to chance, my love," Allondra suggested, following close behind.

Ogram came out of the thick growth into the clearing where the rover was parked. When he parted the leaves, his blood froze. The three predators had circled around somehow, and now, they stood between Ogram and Allondra and their vehicle.

Both drew their weapons and cocked them, wondering what to do next. The animals were not charging at them and their posture did not appear to be one of aggression. But, this being an alien world, anything was possible. Perhaps others were coming up behind them from the river, closing the trap.

The largest one, who definitely had the look of a male, reared up on two legs, reaching a height of two meters and let off a horrific howl that echoed through the jungle. The beast's howl was a truly alien sound that scared Ogram and Allondra and made them shake with fear. Both raised their guns and aimed them at the big male, expecting it to attack at any second.

But the beast came back down on all fours and just stood there, while it, and the two others, stared at them with their weird eyes.

Ogram commanded the rover to turn on its land radar and the image appeared in his optical implant. In the scan, he could see the outline of the rover, the three large monkey-bears next to it, Allondra and himself further away, and one large blip approaching their location from the north.

"Something's coming Allondra, do you see it on your display?"

"Yes Ogram. What do you think it is? Could it be the mama or papa monkey-bear?" she asked, with dread.

"We can't afford to lose the rover, we've got to stand our ground and hope for the best," he replied, holding on tighter to his gun.

The blip moved closer and closer to their location, until both Ogram and Allondra could hear the sound of the approaching figure. The jungle foliage moved and out stepped Kelem Rogeston, dressed in white coveralls.

He walked to the center of the clearing and made a clicking sound with his mouth and the three animals turned and disappeared thought the thick jungle growth.

He turned to Ogram and Allondra, who stood there with their mouths open, in complete shock.

"Welcome to Nobius, Ogram and Allondra!" he said with a big smile.

CHAPTER 31

A Quiet Dinner with the Saint

Allondra's eyes filled with tears and then she fell to the ground and prostrated herself at the saint's feet.

"My lord! My heart is filled with joy by your presence!" she uttered; her voice filled with emotion.

Kelem Rogeston bent down and lifted her gently by her arm to an upright position.

"Bless you Allondra, my heart is equally glad to finally meet you and Ogram. I've waited a very long time for this occasion," he told them, in the voice that both had heard numerous times in ancient recordings.

Ogram still couldn't react. He appeared to be frozen in his place and remained immobile like a statue. Kelem turned to him and offered his hand. "My dear fellow, are you alright?" he asked, shaking Ogram's hand.

"Is it really you?" Ogram asked, feeling Kelem's firm hand shake. The man appeared as solid as anyone alive.

"Yes, Ogram. It is really me. Who else did you expect to meet here?" he asked, furrowing his brow with a smile.

"I thought that perhaps . . . .," Ogram stammered.

"Well, the thing is, that I'm here and that's all that matters, isn't it?" Kelem interjected, before Ogram could finish his sentence. "Come you two, we should get going. Night is approaching and I'd like to reach my place before the sun goes down."

He walked to the rover, opened the passenger's door, sat in the rear seat and motioned for them to join him. Astounded, Ogram and Allondra rushed to the vehicle and drove away from the clearing.

As the rover entered the thick of the jungle, Ogram turned around, "Which way?" he asked, hearing himself ask the question and recognizing the incongruity of the situation.

"You see that trail up ahead? Just follow it straight up," Kelem said, pointing to the area in front of the vehicle. Ogram saw it and followed the trail.

To Ogram and especially Allondra, the whole experience had a feeling of unreality, as if they were inside the CUBE. But both knew that they were not inside a holographically projected virtual environment. Yet, here they were, with Kelem Rogeston, a man who supposedly died in the year 2821 and who was the patron saint of the Church of St. Kelem, sitting in the rear seat of the rover, behaving as normally as a regular person coming along for a ride.

As he drove, Ogram's mind was a jumble of thoughts, and a million questions that clamored for an answer, but at least he had the driving of the rover to focus his attention. Poor Allondra, on the other hand, was in utter shock, unable to speak or do anything but look straight ahead and hope that her mind would be able to deal with what was happening.

As if he read their thoughts, Kelem spoke. "I know that you have a million questions and I assure you that they will be answered." He leaned forward and stuck his head between them, placing his hands on their shoulders. "Both your minds are in the future right now, missing the beauty that surrounds you. Let go of your worry about what's to come and enjoy this moment."

Kelem's touch had a calming effect on both, and suddenly the jungle took on a different aspect. Ogram and Allondra began paying attention to the exquisite beauty of the plant life, and their eyes teared realizing what they had been missing until Kelem pointed out the beauty that was all around them.

Before they knew it, the jungle foliage changed to alpine trees and shrubs and the mountains loomed majestically ahead. On their right, a large river flowing from the mountains meandered through the valley they were driving through.

"Follow the river's path and we'll reach my place soon."

An hour later they had climbed onto a small plateau and here, strange plants of great girth and height could be seen here and there.

Ogram stopped the rover and stared at the behemoths. Then his eyes opened wide.

"Dreamers!" he said, breathlessly.

Allondra, looked at the mushroom shaped trees and thought for a moment, before she also realized what she was looking at. Both Ogram and Allondra turned around at the same time.

"Are these Dreamers?" both asked in unison.

Kelem, sitting in the back seat with a big smile in his face, replied, "Yes my friends, these are indeed Dreamers!" then he pointed ahead. "You see that structure at the foot of the mountain? That's my place. We're almost there!"

Ogram drove forward, amazed by what he was seeing, struggling to pay attention to his driving. Dreamers were supposed to be extinct! As they came close to Kelem's place, the Dreamers became larger and larger, some were twenty to thirty meters tall. And as Ogram looked up the mountain, he realized that the giants continued into the higher slopes. By his estimation, some of them were gargantuan.

Finally, they arrived at Kelem's place, which turned out to be a beautiful house, whose style resembled a modified Tarsian residence with touches of Human architecture.

"Welcome weary travelers, this is my house. Here, you do not need those environmental suits. As a matter of fact, you do not need them anywhere on this planet. You are completely safe while in Nobius," Kelem assured them.

"What about those monkey-bears in the jungle?" Ogram asked, remembering their encounter with the large predators.

"They are the Nizu, a nascent species with a great future. Do not worry about them, they are beginning to become sentient. Who do you think warned me that you were here?" Kelem asked laughing.

"So, they're not predators?" Allondra asked shyly.

"Oh, they're predators alright! If you were one of their smaller cousins or any number of species they prey on, they would have torn you apart. But, I taught them that humans were not to be harmed and to warn me when they saw one, which they did!"

Ogram and Allondra exited the rover following Kelem who went ahead and opened the front door to his house. "Come in my dear friends, welcome to my house," he said, holding the door open.

Allondra and Ogram entered the house and were pleasantly surprised by what they saw. Inside, was a homey living room with a large woven rug on the floor and solid comfortable wood furniture, such as one would find in a country home on Earth or Tarsia. Some of the items, such as lamps and sconces on the walls were definitely Tarsian in design, while others were obviously human in nature. A fireplace stood in the middle of the living room. A portrait of a Gulax family sat on the mantelpiece. The male and the female, who looked to be in their late fifties, were surrounded by six Gulax children, varying in ages from about eight or nine to twenty-something. All were smiling widely.

Ogram walked up to the fireplace and looked at the family photo. "The mother looks familiar, where have I seen her before?"

"That's Sulana Kay and her husband and children when they lived in this house," Kelem replied, casually.

Ogram blinked, reacting with surprise. "You mean 'the' Sulana Kay who wrote, History of the Rogeston Clan?"

"The very same one," Kelem answered, smiling.

"She . . ., she lived here with ther family? When?" Ogram asked, confused. Sulana Kay, a native of Earth, had originally been a historian who wrote one of the best, most endearing biographies of the Rogeston clan, published in 3266. Later on in her life, she became an exo-biologist and was responsible for developing various genetically engineered mosses and likens that eventually helped create a livable atmosphere on the surface of Mars. She moved to Centralia in 3285 and supposedly died there in 3347.

"From 3325 to 3480," Kelem responded.

The math didn't add up, and Ogram decided not to argue with Kelem Rogeston, who was supposed to be dead himself!

"Now you two, night is coming and unfortunately, there's no food in the house, so you have to bring in your food supplies and fix yourselves some dinner. Meanwhile, I'll go out and gather some wood for the fireplace. It gets chilly here at night so close to the mountains," Kelem explained.

Ogram and Allondra thought it strange that this, being his house, would have no food in it, but then, everything about this situation was strange. They went to the rover and brought in some of the food rations. The kitchen had a wood fire stove and plenty of pots, pans, dishes and utensils, many of which, though still usable, appeared to be quite old.

Kelem returned with plenty of firewood and soon started a nice fire going. Ogram and Allondra cooked, and later the three sat down to a quiet dinner as the sun disappeared and day turned into night.

Throughout the dinner, Ogram and Allondra couldn't help but steal glances at the young man sitting across from them. This was the legendary Kelem Rogeston of ancient history, the man who invented the *n'time* generator and built and designed the first human interstellar vessel. He was also, one of the first two humans to ever set foot on an alien planet. The hero of the Martian people, responsible for defeating the Terrans after a nineteen year occupation and, most of all, the holy messiah of the Church of St, Kelem, the biggest religion in the entire history of the galaxy!

It didn't make sense, but Ogram and Allondra knew in their hearts that, somehow, this man, or the walking, talking image of the man in front of them, was indeed, Kelem Rogeston.

After dinner, Ogram and Allondra washed the dishes and put them away. When they came back to the living room, Kelem suggested that they go outside and look at the stars. When they stepped out, both were mesmerized by the spectacle that was the night sky of Nobius.

Here, at the tail end of the Carina Sagittarius arm of the galaxy, the star formations were completely different from anything either one had ever seen.

On one side was the Milky Way Galaxy, encompassing half the sky, on the other side, was near total darkness, illuminated only by the distant image of the Andromeda Galaxy, amidst the dim glow of the many other galaxies in the universe. It was quite a sight to behold, and Ogram and Allondra's hearts were filled with wonder.

They stayed there for a long while, enjoying the beauty of the universe until the temperature dropped and all went back to the house.

Later that night, as Allondra and Ogram lay in bed together, the moon rose, illuminating their bedroom thought the window with a soft silver light. Ogram could see Allondra's beautiful green eyes in the semidarkness, sparkling like emeralds and he kissed her tenderly on the lips, feeling a love for her such as he'd never expected to feel.

He closed his eyes and fell into a deep, peaceful sleep.

CHAPTER 32

The Gospel According to St. Kelem Part I

The following morning, Allondra and Ogram awoke to the sounds and smells of cooking. They got up and found Kelem busy, heating up some of their rations for breakfast. A big pot of green tea was already set on the dining room table.

"Good morning, Ogram and Allondra, I trust you had a good night's sleep?" he asked, with a sunny smile.

Once again, the man's casual manner threw them off balance. In a strange way, his familiarity made them both feel uneasy. They knew they were dealing with a supreme being who was trying to put them at ease by behaving as if nothing out of the ordinary was taking place.

"Thank you Kelem, is there anything that we can help you with?" Allondra asked, trying to be polite.

"No, thank you. Please sit down and enjoy your breakfast. We have a big day ahead of us, so make sure that you eat well. We're going up the mountain. I want you to meet Alpha, the oldest of the Dreamers."

Ogram and Allondra sat at the table, trying to contain their excitement. They knew that they were about to live through something that no one had experienced in several thousand years!

After breakfast, they took some spare rations and water for the trek up the mountain. Kelem warned them that they would not reach their destination until noon and would not come back down until sunset.

As they climbed higher and higher, the Dreamers became so numerous that they formed a forest. The climb was arduous, but the very air seemed to give them strength and vitality to keep going. Their youth, plus their training on New Jerusalem, had prepared them for this kind of physical effort. Yet, neither Ogram nor Allondra missed the fact that Kelem, who lead the way, seemed totally unaffected by the difficulty of the terrain.

The ground was vibrating ever so slightly and both Ogram and Allondra noticed the effect as they went along. Soon, the vibration turned to a distinct pitch that seemed to increase in intensity the higher up they traveled. By mid-morning, the sound had morphed into a strange and exotic musical harmony that permeated the Dreamer forest.

"Kelem, hold on!" Ogram called out. Kelem stopped and turned around, his breathing as normal as if he was taking a slow morning walk.

"Yes Ogram?"

"Is . . ., is this the Dreamer's music, that I've read so much about?" Ogram asked, thrilled by the semi-hypnotic effect the vibrations were having on him.

"Yes it is. It's wonderful isn't it?"

"It's heavenly!" Allondra exclaimed. "Like the essense of spirit manifested as a melody!"

"That's a very good way to describe it Allondra," Kelem commented. "Now let's keep going, we have another hour or two before we reach Alpha."

The Dreamers' music became louder and louder until it drowned the sound of their labored breathing as they continued climbing. Ogram and Allondra had to concentrate on where they were stepping, as the divine symphony was so alluring and seductive, that it made them want to stop, lie down and let their minds get lost in it.

By now, the height of the Dreamers around them, had reached three hundred meters, some were even taller. Allondra and Ogram looked ahead and saw a single Dreamer at the very top of the mountain, so big, that its mushroom cap was hidden by the clouds.

Kelem turned around and pointed to the sentient plant. "That's Alpha. We'll be there soon," he shouted, to be heard above the music. Ogram and Allondra nodded, hoping that they could remain conscious and not fall to the ground in a state of ecstasy.

As they came closer to Alpha, Ogram realized the immensity of the sentient plant. It would take more than one hundred men holding each other's hands to encircle its trunk.

Finally, they stood at its base where Alpha's roots formed a sort of labyrinth around its trunk. Each root was more massive than the biggest trees on Earth. Here, the music was the most intense. Ogram and Allondra were about to be overcome by the effect, when the symphony came to a smooth stop, and then all that Ogram and Allondra could hear was the sound of the wind.

"Sit down my friends," Kelem said, with a smile. "Take some time to adjust to the higher vibrations that you're being subjected to."

Ogram and Allondra flopped down to the ground, suddenly aware that their bodies seemed to be buzzing, as if they were touching a low voltage live wire.

"Why does my body feel like it's vibrating?" Allondra asked, sounding a little concerned.

Kelem smiled. "Alpha is raising your vibrations slowly, so that when you commune with him, your body won't suffer any damage."

"You mean we're going to communicate with him?" Ogram asked, knowing what that meant.

"Yes Ogram, and you too Allondra. This is one of the reasons why I asked you to come to Nobius."

"Will it be like entering Samadhi?" Allondra wanted to know.

"It is like Samadhi, but much deeper in its true form. However, it's nothing like you've experienced before, but you need not worry. You'll be safe," Kelem assured them.

"When will it happen?" Ogram asked.

"It's already happened. We're in the Quantum Tide," Kelem replied, matter of fact.

"But I thought . . .," Ogram said, feeling confused.

"You thought that it would be some sort of weird environment without form, instead of this facsimile?"

"Yes, that's exactly what I thought it would be like, from everything that I've read on the subject," Ogram admitted, as he and Allondra looked around, thinking they were still at the foot of Alpha's trunk.

"You're right, of course Ogram. Alpha and I have created this artificial place to ease you and Allondra into the Quantum Tide. The first time I entered it was when I met Zeus on Plantanimus. He brought me in as a pure spirit without body or form and it was quite difficult for me to adjust."

"What now?" Allondra asked, curious to know what would happen next.

"Now you shall meet Alpha," Kelem said, pointing to a figure approaching in the distance. As the man came close, Allondra and Ogram gasped. It was Cardinal Richelieux, dressed in his vermillion habit! Ogram and Allondra looked at Kelem inquisitively.

"No, it's not Cardinal Richelieux. Only his facsimile, projected by Alpha to give you both a familiar image to communicate with," Kelem informed them.

"Good day to you beloved ones," Alpha said, speaking with Richelieux's voice and inflections. "I have dreamed of you for many years. It is a pleasure to finally meet you both in the flesh, as it were!" he commented with humor, pointing to his body.

Ogram and Allondra simply nodded, struggling to adjust to the situation.

"I hope you don't mind my using the image of a person beloved to you both, but since I have no human body, I chose this image because it was very present in your minds," Alpha explained.

"Th . . ., thank you Alpha," Ogram replied, amazed at the Dreamer's ability to read their minds and create this environment.

"You have many questions. Alpha and I are here to answer them all," Kelem stated.

"Where to start . . . ." Ogram remarked quietly.

"My lord!" Allondra began, looking at Kelem. "Why are we here and what is it that you want us to learn?"

"Good question Allondra. Yes, I suppose we should clear that up first," Kelem replied, rubbing his chin. "You are here to learn how to save the galaxy from a terrible conflagration that could destroy us all. Ogram's experience inside the Plantanimus CUBE is but the beggining of what can only be described as an invasion by a species of malevolent aliens from the Andromeda Galaxy."

"Who are they, and why have they come here?" Ogram asked, realizing that the monster that attacked him was real.

"The Nadrogs, who once were corporeal beings, were a powerful aggressive species that occupied a large sector of the Andromeda Galaxy. Once they conquered a planetary system, they enslaved its people and turned each planet into a hard labor concentration camp. Cruel and sadistic, the Nadrogs brought misery and death to all the species that were unlucky enough to be invaded by them.

"The only species that was militarily strong and able to keep the Nadrogs at bay were the Davanians. The Davanians were a group of peaceful and democratic planets that were as scientifically and technologically advanced as the Nadrogs. They fought a lengthy war against the Nadrogs for several centuries and eventually succeeded in forming an alliance with other planets that resulted in the defeat of the Nadrogs.

"After their defeat they were all quarantined in the Kranok Planetary system, their place of origin. The alliance formed an armada of sentry ships surrounding the system to ensure that no Nadrogs ventured out into the rest of the galaxy. Already an angry, savage and bitter people, the Nadrogs turned to the dark side to exact revenge on their jailers.

"They created a technology that would help them break from their bondage. They built a giant organic machine called a Trancendentorium on one of their planets. The machine was capable of transferring the consciousness of dying Nadrogs into a data collection device that allowed such individual to keep existing after their deaths."

"Dear god!" Ogram exclaimed horrified. Like The Realm's network of CUBEs!"

"Yes, unfortunately so! Furthermore, the machine was capable of projecting that consciousness into the body of another being, thus taking over that individuals mind, effectively "killing" the original individual's soul and personality."

"That thing . . ., that attacked Ogram, was that one of them?" Allondra asked with dread in her eyes.

"Yes, the first of many I'm afraid," Alpha explained. "You understand now the magnitude of the problem?"

Allondra nodded, feeling like she was going to be sick.

"One by one, the Nadrogs began to project themselves into the bodies of unsuspecting members of one of the vessels that were part of the armada surrounding the Kranok system. Once they had 'taken over' all the bodies of the crew members, they attempted to escape, but were fortunately stopped by the alliance.

"When the Davanians boarded the renegade ship, they were surprised to find their own people instead of a crew of Nadrogs. But after some investigation they realized that even though the crew members were all ethnic Davanians, something was drastically wrong. Eventually, they realized that the Nadrogs had somehow gained the ability to invade and permanently take over an individual's body. Alarmed by this horrible development, the Davanians immediately formed an invasion force and occupied the Nadrogs' native planet and shut down the Trancendentorium."

"Then, how did they manage to reach the Milky Way?" Allondra asked, confused.

"Regretfully, by the time the Davanians shut down the Transcedentorium, it was too late. Thousands of Nadrogs in their desperation, commited mass suicide and projected their consciousness' out into the Transcedentorium and out into space as a massive burst of energy transmitted from the nefarious machine. The powerful shock wave caused by the transmission destroyed many of the ships of the alliance's fleet as it exited the confines of the Andromeda Galaxy. The Trancendentorium self-destructed soon after that, preventing the Davanians from reverse engineering the device in order to stop the Nadrogs' mass exodus."

"I cannot understand how an entire race of beings could be so willful, obstinate and angry that they could commit self-inflicted genocide on such a massive scale!" Allondra commented, shaking her head in disbelief.

"The Nadrogs are like nothing any of us has ever encountered before. They are the true essence of evil," Alpha remarked.

"Kelem, how are we to stop these aliens, short of shutting down The Realm's entire CUBE network?" Ogram asked, bewildered by the lack of choices in repelling the Nadrogs.

"It may have to come to that my dear friends. But we are not completely defenseless against them. We're already fighting them as we speak," Kelem replied.

"Fighting them, how?"

"A long time ago, Zeus and his brethren Dreamers warned the Rogeston Clan that the Nadrogs were on their way and so, we seeded fifty planets in our galaxy with a new generation of Dreamers, of which Alpha is the oldest of that generation," Kelem explained.

"How long ago did this happen and why didn't the Rogeston Clan warn the rest of the galaxy then? Furthermore, how are the Dreamers fighting the Nadrogs now?" Ogram added, feeling a confused.

"The answer to your first question is; the clan left Plantanimus in 2980, sixty eight years after the original Dreamers bodies began to die. What we didn't tell anyone is that Tatiana Rogeston, my adopted granddaughter, developed a technology that allowed the Dreamers to be birthed into human bodies. They were part of the clan's exodus. She later gave that technology to the galaxy at large at no cost. Unfortunately, her work is the basis for the technology the body shops use nowadays."

Allondra's eyes opened wide, shocked to learn that Kelem Rogeston and the Clan were connected to the development of the Body Shops.

"You mean to say that the Dreamers of Plantanimus did not perish in 2912 and continued living in human bodies after 2980?" Ogram asked, amazed by what he was hearing. Ditto for Allondra.

"Yes, if you remember, Plantanimus had been blockaded and attacked for many years by the six known species at that time. Everyone was clamoring to be put into Plantanimal bodies before they died of disease or old age. Once everyone learned that the Dreamers were capable of transferring an individual's soul to a Plantanimal body, they came seeking immortal life.

"So you closed shop by transferring the Dreamers into human bodies and left," Ogram guessed.

"Yes, we had no other choice. If we had yielded, we would have been overwhelmed with billions of people and the Dreamers would have been turned into factories of Plantanimal bodies which would have killed them in the long run anyway," Kelem said, defending that decision.

"To answer your second and third question; if we had warned the galaxy at that time, saying that eight thousand years hence there would be an invasion of evil non-corporeal aliens, capable of taking over an individual's body, no one would have believed us and we would have been ridiculed. Zeus and the others knew that a new generation of Dreamers with their immense psychic ability, strategically placed in the outer planets of our galaxy, would help slow down the arrival of the Nadrogs and help dampen their power once they were here, which is what they're doing now."

"It had to be done then, in order to give me and my siblings time to mature and become powerful enough to battle the invaders," Alpha added. "We Dreamers exist mostly in the Quantum Tide, which fortunately and unfortunately is where the Nadrogs have been surviving for the last million years since they projected themselves toward our galaxy."

Ogram and Allondra were in awe of learning the unknown story of Kelem, the Rogeston Clan and the Dreamers' millennia-long quest to protect the galaxy. But much of what Allondra was hearing contradicted the Church's version of St. Kelem's life and the history of the galaxy at large. The Kelemite bible stated that St. Kelem died on Plantanimus in the year 2821 at the amazing age of two hundred and nine. Yet, the man now in front of her, calling himself Kelem Rogeston, claimed that he was still alive in 2980 and obviously, beyond that, for here he was, recounting a past that no one had heard of before. If this version of his life was true, then Sister Jane Rogeston's, 'Gospel of St. Kelem', *(the third Matriarch of the Kelemite Church)* was full of inaccuracies.

The church had always denied that Kelem Rogeston lived beyond 2821 or that he continued living in a Plantanimal body after his human death. Furthermore, the Church asserted that the well-publicized life of that Plantanimal being, calling himself Kelem Rogeston, was nothing but a fictitious character created by the Rogeston Clan to elicit the aid of humans from the Solar System and the Tarsian population of the Kural during the blockade of Plantanimus during the late 2800's.

The Tarsians of the Kural *(who were devout Tilharans)*, had always maintained that the Church of St. Kelem was wrong on this point. Ultimately, that argument was the root cause of the Kelemite Crusades of the 4th Millennium, a dark period in the history of the Church and the Galaxy as well.

Allondra hated to think that the church and her family, who had served faithfully for so many generations, could have been so wrong about something as basic as Kelem Rogeston's time of death.

"How are we to defeat these monsters then?" Ogram asked, feeling overwhelmed by everything he'd heard so far.

"With strength of faith and courage my dear friends," Kelem replied. "I chose you two because the Quantum Tide showed me the many possible futures that could occur, and in many of those possible futures, both of you were instrumental in defeating the Nadrogs."

"My lord, you said both of us were chosen. But your Prophesy only mentioned one young man who would come to the aid of the Church in its time of need. There was no mention of a female being involved," Allondra pointed out.

"My dear Allondra, there are many things that I've said and done that the church has either hidden or disregarded for its own purposes. The removal of the mention that that young man would be accompanied by a young woman is one of those omissions."

Allondra's face grew sullen. Kelem's words cut straight to her heart, causing her a great deal of consternation. How could the Church have committed such errors? Then again, was this man in front of her, really Kelem Rogeston?

"The reason why you are here, Ogram and Allondra, is to develop your latent psychic powers which lie dormant within you. Once you develop certain abilities, you two will be a force to reckon with. Now, I'm not going to lie to you. This is not going to be easy, but I know that you'll both succeed in this effort. Your physical proximity to Alpha has already begun the process."

In a flash, Ogram understood the meaning of Kelem's words in the dream he'd had the day before. "Is this why you said to me, 'you can't reach me because you won't admit to yourself what you already know'?"

"Yes Ogram. I'm so glad you finally got it! You are a member of the 'Sixth Root Race' in Human development. I was the first Sixth Rooter to be born, and by now there are many of us. Allondra is your equal in that regard. She is the first Tarsian to be born with the same kind of psychic potential abilities as Human Sixth Rooters."

Something in Ogram's mind lit up, much like the blinding light emitted by Kelem when he appeared to him and Cardinal Richelieux while they were being attacked inside the CUBE's VR.

"Regardless of Allondra and I having and developing psychic powers, how can the two of us stop the Nadrogs' invasion?"

"You and Allondra are not alone, Ogram. There are over fifty thousand Dreamers spread throughout the galaxy to help you and others fight and defeat the Nadrogs," Alpha commented.

"There is an organization of Martian psychics who have been preparing for the Nadrogs for millennia. They will help you fight the Nadrogs," Kelem informed him.

"We're supposed to report to the Matriarch and Cardinal Richelieux when we're done here. What shall we do about them?" Allondra asked.

"That hasn't changed. As a matter of fact, much of what Alpha and I will teach you, you will in turn, teach the Matriarch and Cardinal Richelieux." Kelem replied.

"Us teach the Matriarch and the Cardinal?" Allondra responded, with alarm.

"Yes, Allondra. As much as you love and respect them, they are not all knowing. What you and Ogram will learn while on Nobius will help the Church and all the beings in this galaxy survive the coming disaster. But above all, the most important thing that I will teach you and that you will teach them, is how to give my blessing.

"It is the only thing that I taught Sister Ornata and the one skill that should have been passed on from Matriarch to Matriarch and to all those who have joined the church since then. Unfortunately, too many of the Matriarchs that came after her were more interested in personal gain and in creating the most powerful religion in the galaxy's history. They forsook the gift that was given to them and eventually lost the ability to give the blessing.

"My blessing helped end the Martian war of Independence and kept the people of the Human Solar System from ever fighting another war amongst themselves. I often wonder if the Kelemite Crusades of the 4th Millennium would have taken place at all had all Kelemites known the gift of the Heart Blessing, that most precious gift that I received from Zeus and the Dreamers when I went to Plantanimus."

"But, my lord! The crusades were the result of the Tilharan infidels attack on the the Holy See on Plantanimus and their desire to conquer all Kelemite planets!" Allondra protested.

Kelem turned and looked at Allondra with a bittersweet expression on his face. "I know it will be hard for you to hear Allondra, but the truth is, that it was the then Matriarch, Mother Castillia and the Curia who ordered an unprovoked attack on the Kural planets. The Church of St. Kelem of that era had become a radical, fundamentalist religion with zero tolerance for any other faith. If they had succeeded in eradicating Tilharianism, they would have gone on to eliminate every other religion in the galaxy."

Allondra looked at Kelem in disbelief, as tears formed in her green eyes.

CHAPTER 33

Allondra's Moment of Doubt and Fear

The following morning, Ogram woke up to find that Kelem was not in the house. Ogram got up first and made a pot of green tea, then he made breakfast and brought it to Allondra in bed. She was surprised and pleased by the gesture, as Tarsians never eat breakfast in bed. Ogram wanted to cheer up Allondra, knowing that Kelem's revelations of the day before had upset her a great deal. Ogram was also dealing with his share of concerns, wondering what it all meant for their future.

On one hand he was excited about discovering new things about himself and Allondra. On the other hand, he was terrified about the true nature of the Nadrogs and their frightening ability to invade a victim's body. What kind of skills could Kelem possibly teach him and Allondra that could keep them and the galaxy safe? he wondered, worrying that he might fail to learn what Kelem wanted to teach them.

"What do you think he really is?" Allondra asked, while staring at her tea cup.

"Huh? What do you mean?" Ogram answered, not sure what she meant.

"I mean, is he some sort of clone or impostor trying to mislead us into believing that what he claims is the truth?" she queried, with a shaking voice on the verge of tears.

"My love! You don't believe that he is Kelem Rogeston?" Ogram exclaimed, surprised by her doubts.

Allondra threw the cup against the wall and it shattered into several pieces. "I don't know what to believe!" She shouted, crying and then burying her head in his arms.

Ogram reached out for her and held her softly in his arms.

"How could the Church have been so wrong and how could we Kelemites have started a war of aggression against an innocent people?" she asked, looking at Ogram, fearful that everything she believed in was a lie.

"I can't answer that," Ogram responded, feeling uncomfortable with the question.

"You can't or you won't?" she asked, looking at him.

Ogram let go of her and walked over to the window, unable to look at her, for his answer would surely upset her even more and he hated seeing her cry.

"Ogram, please! Don't turn away from me. Tell me what you believe to be the truth," she pleaded.

Ogram turned around and sat back on the bed, then held her hand. "What confuses me about your reaction Allondra, is that you doubt that he truly is Kelem Rogeston, the figurehead of your religion! I mean, who else could he be and how could he have predicted our involvement and known everything he knows, unless he really is a special being that transcends time and space?"

"Oh my god! You and I have switched places! I've become the agnostic and you the believer!" she exclaimed, laughing sarcastically and crying at the same time.

"You're the most honestly faithful person that I've ever met. What I think is bothering you, is that you feel betrayed by your own church for misleading you and everyone else for thousands of years."

"Could it be true that the church has committed such horrible transgressions?"

"It's not out of the realm of possibility Allondra, or haven't you heard of the Christian Crusades of the Middle Ages on Earth or of the Spanish Inquisition and the persecution of Jews?" Ogram replied, looking at her with raised eyebrows.

"But . . ., how could St. Kelem have allowed such things?"

"How could Jesus Christ, Mohammed, the God of the Jews, Buddhists, Hindus and other famous religious figures, have allowed millions upon millions of their followers to slaughter each other for thousands of years, all in the name of God? Those holy men and messiahs never taught their flock to go and destroy the other fellow. Those were the actions of men, greedy for wealth, power, territory and control of the world. Most people that followed these men into crusades and wars against infidels and such, were true believers and thought that they were serving a higher purpose. As the old saying goes, 'the road to hell is paved with good intentions'."

Allondra lay back on her pillow and stared at the ceiling, her mind struggling to accept what Ogram was proposing.

"What I also know is this; he saved me and Cardinal Richelieux from the monster in the CUBE's VR, gave me the coordinates for this planet, prophesied our involvement in all of this, appeared in my dream with a message that I proved yesterday he actually sent to me. He communicates and controls the monkey-bear predators, is also able to communicate with Alpha and the other Dreamers, and he can climb a mountain without breaking a sweat. Let's not forget that he has appeared to every Matriarch that has entered the CUBE at the Heavenly Temple, starting with Sister Ramona in the Fourth Millennium. For all intents and purposes, he fits the definition of a deity Allondra! There is no scientific or empiric evidence to explain what he is able to do. Whatever Kelem Rogeston is or isn't, the fact is, he's trying to save the galaxy from the Nadrogs and that's good enough for me."

"What a difference a few weeks make. Remember that I told you that you would be one of those unbelievers that suddenly become more dedicated to a cause than those that consider themselves religious? I just didn't expect that our roles would be reversed!" Allondra exclaimed, really laughing this time.

"Nonsense my love. You haven't lost your faith. You only need to adjust your view of what is important. Religions are organizations created by sentient beings that are imperfect and full of weaknesses like everyone else."

"Thank you Ogram, you've made me feel better. You're right, we must continue on our quest to fight the Nadrogs. I must admit that I feel different after visiting Alpha yesterday. I don't know exactly what is happening to us but I'm glad that we're facing this together," Allondra said, drawing Ogram close to her and kissing him tenderly.

CHAPTER 34

The Gospel According to St. Kelem Part II

The visits to Alpha continued for another week and with each immersion into the Quantum Tide, Ogram and Allondra began to feel a transformation in their perception of the world around them. Their physical senses became more acute and they began to 'feel' the individual presence of each of the Dreamers on the mountain. Although Kelem escorted them on each trek, he had not 'gone in' with them since their second visit. He was always waiting for them when they came back from the Quantum Tide and escorted them back to the house at night. Ogram and Allondra discovered that Kelem was no longer sleeping in the house, and they figured out that Kelem had no need for sleep or shelter. At the begginning of the second week, Kelem announced that for the next week, they would be entering the Quantum Tide as pure consciousness. This particular immersion would last a total of one hundred and eighty two hours, (seven days on Nobius). Kelem assured them that their bodies would not need any food, water or the need to eliminate waste, as the Dreamers would keep their bodies safe and warm. He explained to them that their abilities would expand exponentially after this visit to Alpha.

On the seventh day, Ogram and Allondra opened their eyes and saw Kelem standing over them with a smile. Ogram sat up and noticed something strange about Kelem.

"Kelem! Your body is emitting light! Am I seeing things?"

Kelem laughed heartily. "Look at Allondra," he said pointing to her.

Ogram turned and was surprised to see Allondra's body displaying the same phenomena.

"You too Ogram, your body is also emitting light!" she remarked, amazed by the effect.

"You two have gained the ability to see people's auric fields," he explained, kneeling down by them. This will serve you well in the days to come. Individuals emitting white light or light colors, will be those whose minds and spirits are clear and have not been corrupted. People emitting red or amber are experiencing anger, rage and turmoil. Anyone emitting indigo blue, or dark purple are those who have either, been taken over by Nadrogs, or are under their influence."

"Can this ability be turned off at will? It seems to me that it would be disconcerting to be visually aware of everyone's auras all the time," Ogram wondered.

"All you have to do is close your eyes and wish for the effect to go away, likewise, when you want to see it again."

Ogram and Allondra tried it and it worked. Both helped each other get up and had to shake a few leaves and pieces of grass from their clothing. They had been lying under Alpha's roots for an entire week and yet they felt as normal as any other day.

"What now Kelem? What's the next step in our training?" Ogram asked, feeling excited about learning more new skills and abilities.

"You two are almost done here, only a few days left." Kelem replied.

Ogram and Allondra's faces turned sad with disappointment.

"But . . . ., so soon?" Ogram exclaimed, feeling as if he was being kicked out of a fun party.

"My lord, surely we need more time under your tutelage?" Allondra protested.

Kelem smiled. Thousands of years before, his adopted grandchildren had expressed the same reticence to leave Plantanimus when each turned eighteen and had to attend colleges on other planets.

"Unfortunately, time is of the essence. The galaxy exists in the realm of time and space and you need to return to the Heavenly Temple and begin your struggle against the invaders," Kelem informed them, feeling their disappointment in his own heart.

After dinner, all three sat in the house's porch, looking at the beautiful night sky of Nobius. They sat in silence, enjoying the sounds of the forest and the soft wind coming down from the mountain.

Ogram broke the silence. "Kelem, what exactly are you?" he asked, uncertain whether his question was proper.

Kelem smiled, stood up and leaned against the porch's rail and looked at the two of them for a long time before he spoke. Allondra held her breath, the question had been burning in her mind as well.

"I am he who was known as Kelem Rogeston born on Mars on July 29th, 2616. That consciousness, spirit, soul and personality has existed for seven thousand, four hundred and seven years. I have since then, lived as a human, reborn as a Plantanimal, then reincarnated many, many times in other human bodies. Until recently, I've existed purely as a spirit, dwelling in the Quantum Tide since the year 3800, when my beloved mate, Anima, ascended to the higher plains."

"But this body you have now, that of Kelem Rogeston in his youth, is that real, or a projection of some sort?" Ogram queried, his scientific mind coming to the fore.

"This body is as real as yours or Allondra's, though the universe itself is an immense hologram. In a sense, we're all projections of consciousness. However, I cannot exist in this form outside of Nobius. Like my beloved Anima, who was created by Zeus and the Dreamers as a Plantanimal, this body. . ., this hologram, was created by Alpha and his brethren so that I could interact with you. If I left the energetic field of the Dreamers, which permeates this planet, this body 'image' would wither and die."

"Why did you choose to exist purely as a spirit since the year 3800?" Allondra wondered.

"In spite of my advanced age," Kelem said, smiling and making fun of himself, "when Anima ascended, I lost my way. We had been together for so long, I never expected that Anima would one day leave my side. You see, she was born without any Human karmic debt whatsoever. In other words, she had no karma to work out. Her only lesson was to learn to become human which she did over several incarnations. She simply could no longer stay in this plain of existence because her vibrations had become too rarefied. That's why I came to Nobius, to live my last human life and die of old age. Fortunately for all of us and the galaxy at large, Alpha and his brethren held on to my soul and spirit and brought me out of Pralaya when the Kelemite Crusades began."

"What is Pralaya?" Ogram asked, not familiar with the term.

"It is a form of sleep without consciousness or awareness of any kind, a type of suspended animation of the soul and spirit within the Quantum Tide."

"Why did Alpha and the others bring you out of Pralaya when the crusades began?" Allondra asked, curious to know.

"The violent nature of the thought forms created by Sister Castillia, the Curia and so many Kelemites who were incited by the Church to attack the Tilharans, caused a disturbance in the Quantum Tide. The Dreamers knew I was the only one who could prevent the holocaust that would surely have followed, if the Church had its way. Alpha and his brethren foresaw the dark future awaiting the galaxy if the Church of St. Kelem succeeded in eliminating all the existing religions, as Matriarch Castillia and the Curia were planning."

"What did you do then?" Ogram asked, fascinated by the story.

"I contacted my old, old friend, Queen Harriett of the Kren and warned her that the Kelemites were planning to attack her hive and that of other Kren queens," Kelem replied with sadness.

Allondra gasped with surprise and almost fell out of her chair. "My lord, you warned those evil insectoids that the Kelemite Armada was coming?"

For the first time since they'd arrived on Nobius, Kelem's face showed anger. "Those 'evil creatures' as you so carelessly put it, are the most peaceful, non-violent species in the entire galaxy! It was the

Kren who rescued me and Ndugu Nabole from Plantanimus and returned us to Mars. And it was Harriett herself who brought me back to Plantanimus after the end of the Martian War of Independence. And do you know why the Church decided to attack the Kren?" Kelem asked, moving away from the porch's rail and raising his voice.

Allondra shook her head, realizing how wrong she'd been about the Kren.

"Because when the Kelemites approached the Kren to evangelize them, the Kren surprised them by informing Matriarch Castillia, that I had history with Queen Harriett and her species. Queen Harriett's claim contradicted the Church's bible, and so, 'strict fundamentalist' Matriarch Castilia, branded them demons, infidels and liars and decreed that their species should be completely wipedl out!

"Fortunately, the Kren defeated the armada, which is the main reason why the Kelemite Crusades came to an end. Of course, the Church hid the fact that it lost most of its forces to the Kren and falsely claimed that the attack had practically wiped the species out of existence. It was soon after that, that the Church signed the peace treaty with the Tilharans of the Kural. Matriarch Castillia knew that if the Crusades continued, the Tilharans would have discovered how serious the Church's losses had been and then the Kelemite Church would cease to exist."

"Unbelievable!" Ogram expressed with amazement. "One thing that I don't understand is, why you didn't approach Matriarch Castillia herself and try to dissuade her from launching the Crusades in the first place?"

Kelem relaxed and leaned back on the rail with a half-smile on his lips. "Believe me, for the first few years of the Crusade, I tried mightily, by doing the only thing available to me and the Dreamers, . . telepathy! We tried reaching Matriarch Castilia and other members of the Curia, but those women were the least spiritual clergy that the Church ever had. And unfortunately, the Sixth Root Race Martians alive at that time were not very gifted when it came to telepathy, especially at such long distances. My only available opportunity presented itself when Alpha and I discovered that the Kelemites were going to attack the Kren.

"I understand now," Ogram mused. "And I'm guessing the reason why you decided to appear to Sister Ramona and all the subsequent Matriarchs that entered the Holy See's CUBE, was to prevent another Crusade from ever taking place?"

"Precisely! The invention of Quantum Holographic computers gave me the opportunity to reach others that existed within the system. Fortunately, Sister Ramona was a good soul and she made sure that all subsequent Matriarchs underwent a very thorough mental, psychological examination and spiritual assessment before they were allowed to take the pontifical throne."

"I apologize my lord! I now fully understand your journey and all the incredible efforts you've made on behalf of us all," Allondra commented, finally feeling free of all doubts and questions of faith regarding the Church. "I shall make it my life's work to spread the true Gospel of St. Kelem!" she added with fervor.

"I am very glad to hear you say that Allondra. However, I must warn you that the Quantum Tide has shown me and Alpha that such efforts could backfire and make things worse," Kelem warned her politely.

"My lord? You do not want the Church to reform itself and correct the lies and misinformation that have caused so much pain and suffering in the past?" Allondra asked, surprised by his words.

"Of course I do! What I'm trying to say to you is that you have to be careful how you do it. I'm not concerned with Matriarch Vasilia and Cardinal Richelieux's reaction to the truth. They are both exceptional people, truly spiritual and with the best intentions in their hearts when it comes to the Church. They will accept 'my gospel' as you put it, but the Curia and the upper echelons of the clergy is another matter altogether. The Church of St. Kelem is a gargantuan organization with trillions of members and hundreds of thousands of mid-level clergy who manage and control the organization. Just because you're armed with the truth, does not mean that others will believe you! If you decide to reform the Church and commit to that work, know that is work that will take years perhaps, to be continued by others beyond your lifetime, my dear Allondra. Do not become an obsessive fundamentalist, bent on converting all those you come across, because you know you're armed with the true gospel of St. Kelem! That's exactly the same kind of attitude that caused Sister Castillia to initiate the Crusades."

"But my Lord, yours is the real gospel!"

"However long it will take, you will find a way Allondra, of that I'm sure. Meanwhile, first we must take care of the Nadrogs. My message won't help anyone if the galaxy has been taken over by those monsters!"

"What next Kelem? You said we have another day or two of training left," Ogram inquired.

"Tomorrow after breakfast, we'll go by the river and spend the day there. Now go to sleep and get a goodnight's rest. I will see you tomorrow."

Ogram and Allondra got back in the house and went to bed.

The following morning, Kelem came by just after breakfast and the three of them made their way to the large river, east of the house. He picked a lovely spot on the river's shore, where a small sandy beach had formed and the current was slower and gentler.

They sat on the beach, and Kelem asked Allondra and Ogram to close their eyes and go into Samadhi. Thanks to Allondra's earlier coaching, and with Alpha's raising of his spiritual vibrations, Ogram was able to reach a very deep level of meditation. When Kelem tapped him on his arm to bring him out of Samadhi, he was surprised to discover that two hours had passed.

"I was really in deep, this time! "Ogram commented, pleased that he'd achieved such peace and tranquility while meditating.

"Good, because what I'm about to teach you, requires that you be well centered and relaxed. Please stand up and hold my hands," Kelem ordered them. The three stood by the river's shore, listening to the never ending rush of the waters as they flowed to the sea. "Close your eyes," he asked them.

A feeling of warmth spread from Kelem's hands into their arms, shoulders and into their heart chakras. The sensation intensified and quickly spread to their entire bodies, as if they had been enveloped by a soft invisible blanket. A feeling of love and joy radiated from their chests like golden honey, causing Ogram and Allondra to sigh with pleasure, as the awareness that they were being blessed with sacred energy, lifted their spirits unlike any religious or emotional experience they ever had. This continued for another two or three minutes, until both thought they couldn't take any more. Slowly, the warmth subsided and they were able to open their eyes.

Neither Ogram nor Allondra could speak for a while. Kelem let go of their hands and walked away, to give them time to assimilate the experience on their own.

When Kelem returned to their side a few minutes later, Ogram embraced him with deep affection, grateful for having had his first true spiritual experience. Allondra reached for Kelem's hand and kissed it, thankful for receiving the saint's blessing directly from the man that she had grown up praying to and worshipping since early childhood.

After that, Kelem repeated the procedure two more times, with each occasion being more intense than the previous one. At the end of the day, they returned to the house, ate dinner and slept more deeply than either one had ever done before.

The following day, they went back to the river and Kelem gave his blessing one more time. Then, he asked Allondra first and then Ogram, to each give the blessing. Unsure at first, both eventually were able to bring in the sacred energy and pass it on to the others with the same intensity as Kelem had done the previous four times.

The afternoon sun was beginning to lower in the sky when Kelem held their hands, but this time, not to give the blessing.

"My dear beloved Ogram and Allondra, your training is done and you must leave tomorrow morning after sunrise. You have learned everything that Alpha and I needed to teach you. You have tremendous challenges ahead of you, but I know that you will prevail."

Ogram and Allondra stood with tears in their eyes, wishing that they could stay on this heavenly paradise and spend the rest of their lives living in the house at the foot of the mountain and communing with Alpha, Kelem and the Dreamers until the end of their days. But alas! They knew that the welfare of all the sentient beings of the galaxy depended on their efforts in the difficult time to come.

The following morning, after bidding goodbye to the lovely house that had been their home for almost a month, they drove back to the plateau where the Prophesy was parked, accompanied by Kelem.

As a last parting gift, Kelem asked them to let him program the navigation computer. He sat at Allondra's navigation station and re-programmed the route with amazing expertise.

"You will be back in New Jerusalem by tomorrow evening," he announced, to their surprise. "I've learned a few tricks in the last seven and a half thousand years," he said with a wink.

Both Ogram and Allondra's hearts were breaking, wondering if they would ever be lucky enough to be in Kelem's company again. He hugged them each and pushed them gently away, showing them that he was sad as well.

As the Prophesy lifted from the surface of Nobius, Allondra and Ogram waved goodbye to Kelem, whose white coveralls remained visible amidst the green grasses of the plateau, until the ship climbed into the clouds.

CHAPTER 35

The New Apostles

"Control, this is private vessel Prophesy, requesting permission to approach New Jerusalem," Ogram said to the young man on the com-screen.

"What is your ultimate destination Prophesy?"

"Thirty-eight point twenty degrees south, by one hundred and one point eleven degrees east, Control."

The young man touched a few floating objects on his holo-screen, waited a few seconds, then looked up and smiled at Ogram. "Welcome back Prophesy, you're cleared to land."

Ogram thanked him, cut the communication off and engaged the sub-light engines.

"I have to confess, I'm a little nervous," he admitted to Allondra, as the ship accelerated.

"I know! Even with all we have learned in the last four weeks, the idea of teaching the Matriarch and Cardinal Richelieux *anything* is daunting!" Allondra replied, laughing nervously.

"What do you think their reaction will be?" Ogram asked.

"I don't know, but I'm more concerned with the Curia's reaction when they hear that there's a new version of the gospel." Allondra commented, remembering that Kelem had warned her that spreading the new version of his gospel would not be easy.

Local time in the southern continent was 02:00 AM and they expected to be met by Zurk when they landed, and then spend the night at the camp before flying to the Heavenly Temple the following night. But as Ogram approached the landing site illuminated by artificial lights, he saw that both the Matriarch and Cardinal Richelieux were there waiting with their Gulax Guard.

Ogram brought the Prophesy to a smooth touchdown, shut the engines off and opened the landing plank. When he and Allondra stepped off the ship, they were approached by the Matriarch and Cardinal Richelieux, who came running toward them with great joy on their faces.

"How lovely to see you both again!" the Matriarch exclaimed, as she embraced both with great affection.

Ogram and Allondra were a little surprised by the pontiff's physicality, but were glad to be welcomed so warmly. The Cardinal followed suit by embracing them as well.

"Come you two, we have a winged chariot ready to take us all to the Temple!" Richelieux said excitedly, sounding anxious to get them to the Matriarch's residence and hear all about their voyage.

As the group began walking toward the land vehicle awaiting them, Zurk approached Ogram and shook his hand, then looked at him for a few seconds, holding on to his hand. "Something about you has changed, young Ogram," he said, bowing respectfully. Then, looking at Allondra, he bowed to her as well. The Matriarch and Richelieux stopped in their tracks and noticed that something was indeed different about the two young travelers. Now that they were farther away from the artificial lights of the landing zone, their bodies seemed to have an actual physical glow!

Matriarch Vasilia gasped involuntarily and looked at Richelieux, whose eyes were fixed on the two youngsters. Ogram and Allondra thought that something might be wrong with their appearance and both looked at themselves and then at each other, wondering why they were being gawked at.

"Is something wrong your Holiness?" Ogram asked, noticing that the Gulax Guards were also staring at him and Allondra.

"My dear, are you aware that your bodies are luminous?" the Matriarch replied, with an expression of astonishment.

"Lu . . ., luminous?" Ogram repeated, dumfounded.

Allondra looked at Ogram and blinked her eyes to turn on the ability to see auric fields, then looked at the Matriarch and Cardinal Richelieux and was happy to see that both were emitting lovely bright light, but to her, Ogram's body looked normal.

"Kelem didn't say anything about others being able to see our auras!" Ogram whispered in Allondra's ear. Allondra's face turned dark green with embarrassment. Kelem had not discussed this effect with them.

Having very good ears, Cardinal Richelieux picked up Ogram's whisper very clearly. "Kelem?" he asked, feeling a chill go up his spine.

"Did he say Kelem?" the Matriarch asked, sensing that something extraordinary had happened to the two young travelers.

"We should go up right away. I think both our young friends have much to tell us," Richelieux suggested, trying to adjust mentally to what he'd just seen and heard.

On the flight up to the Temple, all remained silent. An unspoken tension permeated the cabin as both Ogram and Allondra were silently trying to figure out why their bodies were glowing. While the Matriarch and Richelieux were trying to stay quiet and keep from asking the many questions that were begging for answers in front of their Gulax guards.

Once in the Matriarch's residence, both Richelieux and the pontiff noticed that Ogram and Allondra's glow had subsided, and after a few minutes, disappeared altogether. Richelieux reached for the Cointreau and poured four glasses to celebrate their return. They drank the lovely liqueur and then all sat down in the same positions that they had occupied three months before, the night that they'd decided to embark on the trip to Nobius.

Ogram looked around and realized how different he felt now, compared to the first time he'd entered the Matriarch's residence. He still had the highest respect for the pontiff and Richelieux and their position, but now, he and Allondra were different, much, much different. Then, he realized something else that took him entirely by surprise. He was no longer an agnostic! He felt as if he'd been asleep all his life until his arrival on Nobius. And he knew at that moment, that he would spend the remainder of his life in the service of others. Kelem and Alpha had awakened his spirituality and had changed him in ways that he was only now beginning to understand.

"My dears, if you don't start telling us about your experiences soon, I think I'll burst!" the Matriarch said, laughing impatiently.

Ogram and Allondra began telling their adventures and all the facts about the voyage and by the time they finished, the sun was coming through the windows of the residence. Matriarch Vasilia, feeling a mixture of conflicting emotions, rose from the couch and walked to the large windows facing the Garden of Eden and stared at the beauty of the landscape down below for several minutes. Richelieux remained seated, deep in thought, slowly absorbing the magnitude and significance of what Ogram and Allondra had just reported.

Neither one of them doubted the veracity of the facts that the young travelers had given them. But the import of their discoveries and what that would mean for the Church was more than complicated, it was potentially explosive and downright dangerous!

Both their hearts were breaking and each was dealing with the regret that so many had died and suffered because of the Kelemite Crusades. Yet, in the middle of all this pain and sorrow, there was hope for the future. That future, however, was in question if the galaxy succumbed to the Nadrogs.

Ogram and Allondra, sensing the pain felt by Matriarch Vasilia and Richelieux, looked at each other and without speaking, both knew that they should pass St. Kelem's blessing to them.

"Your Holiness," Allondra called out. "Ogram and I would like to give you and Cardinal Richelieux, St. Kelem's blessing."

Matriarch Vasilia, with eyes full of tears, turned around and looked at them. "I don't think this is a good time to receive the saint's blessing with my heart and mind in such a terrible state."

"Oh, but you're wrong your Holiness!" Ogram argued, without considering that he was contradicting the Matriarch of the Church of

St. Kelem. "More than at any other time, you should receive his blessing. Please allow us to give you his gift," he pleaded.

Richelieux stood up, walked over to her, took her by the hand and brought her to Ogram and Allondra.

"You Holiness, he's right! We must take the blessing," he agreed.

Everyone held hands together and closed their eyes. Soon, the warm sensation spread from Ogram and Allondra to the Matriarch and Richelieux. As the intensity of Kelem and Alpha's high, rarefied vibrations increased, the Matriarch took in a deep breath, accompanied by Richelieux. Both had experienced a very weak form of the blessing before being true believers, but this was more powerful than they had expected. The joy and beauty of the experience continued expanding, until they thought their hearts would explode with religious ecstasy. Sensing that the others had reached their limit, Ogram and Allondra decreased the power until it faded away.

Matriarch Vasilia's legs weakened and she had to be held by Ogram and Richelieux. They brought her over to the couch where she and Richelieux sat staring at the floor for a few minutes.

Ogram and Allondra remained standing, holding each other's hands.

When the Matriarch finally looked up, she saw the glowing outline of Ogram and Allondra's silhouettes, framed by the light streaming in from the large windows in the room. Behind them, she saw the image of St. Kelem very clearly, shining brighter that the light of the morning sun.

He had a peaceful smile on his face and his feet floated a few centimeters above the floor. He looked directly at the Matriarch and Richelieux.

"Behold the new apostles," he said, and then disappeared.

CHAPTER 36

Plots within the Curia

Cardinals Murcia, Selecta and Millicenta sat behind a long table facing Bishop Kalduwan. It was late Sunday night and the administrative offices of Sister Ornata's Seminary School were empty, except for the four women in the conference room.

"You're sure you weren't followed?" Cardinal Murcia asked, nervously.

"Yes your Eminence, I know the Temple better than anyone. No one knows I'm here. You can all relax," replied Kalduwan, with a confident smile.

'Very well then, what have you to report?" asked Cardinal Millicenta, the oldest of the three.

"As we suspected, the ship was piloted by Ogram Zepol. Former novice Allondra Velmador was also involved in the operation. She's a trained navigator," Kalduwan told them.

"I wish there was a way that we could find out what they're planning," Cardinal Selecta wondered, with a sour face.

"Anything involving Richelieux is sure to be bad news," Cardinal Murcia, countered wryly.

"Whatever it is they're doing must involve danger, because that ship was outfitted with the latest communication technology, navigation, armor and weapons. Perhaps that's why the novice renounced her vows of non-violence and poverty before departing," suggested Kalduwan.

"Zepol and the Velmador girl spent last night reporting to the Matriarch and Cardinal Richelieux. I know that when I went to the residence this morning, they were still there, because the Matriarch wouldn't let me in her apartment until 09:00 AM. Zepol and Velmador probably exited through the Gulax Guard's entrance," Kalduwan rationalized.

"Where are they now?" asked Cardinal Selecta.

"They're holed up in an apartment on Level 26. Zepol is registered there with a false identity under the guise of a lay priest named Ogram Lazarus," Kalduwan replied, with a sarcastic smirk.

"Scandalous! They're probably fornicating right under Sister Ornata's image! Cardinal Murcia railed with anger.

"This all has to be connected to the troubles in the Plantanimus CUBE. I've been hearing stories about strange goings on at the complex," Cardinal Millicenta suggested.

"Unfortunately, we can't blame any of it on Richelieux!" Cardinal Selecta complained. "As long as he's under the Matriarch's protection, we can't get to him."

"We could if we were to reinstate the office of Grand Inquisitor," Kalduwan said calmly and without expression.

The room fell silent. The last time the Church had a Grand Inquisitor was during Matriarch Castillias' reign. The Crusades had been so disastrous for the Church, that ever since that time, the Curia had voted to outlaw the office, claiming that it gave the Grand Inquisitor too much power.

"My dear Bishop Kalduwan, a Grand Inquisitor is a 'last resort' measure. Only in times of great crisis should we be obliged to reinstate the position!" Cardinal Millicenta argued, forcefully.

"Your Eminences, are we not in a time of great crisis? A CUBE has been taken off line for the first time in six thousand years. Hubert Longsdale was found dead under suspicious circumstances. Matriarch Vasilia bypassed the Curia's authority and gave the new manager of the Plantanimus CUBE, Pieter Minsk, permission to send out a press release admitting that the facility had suffered an accident and that over one hundred employees had perished. The body shops are corrupting the people of the galaxy and destroying the social fabric of our civilization.

Then, add to that, the fact that the Cardinal Counselor to the Matriarch is complicit in a clandestine operation, involving a non-believer and a novice nun that has renounced her vows. Additionally, the three billion Kredits used to pay for the private vessel, Prophesy, were not sanctioned by the Curia or the Holy See's Administrative Office!" Bishop Kalduwan concluded, with emotional emphasis.

Cardinal Murcia lowered her head and rested her chin on her hands. She remained still for a few seconds and then looked at the others. "One could say that the Cardinal Counselor has undue influence over the Matriarch and has manipulated her into committing improper acts that infringe on the Church's laws. Very few of us wanted a male Cardinal Counselor. It wouldn't take too much effort to convince other Cardinals in the Curia that we need to reinstate the Grand Inquisitor to investigate Richelieux for financial fraud," she concluded, looking at the others for support.

"But what about the Matriarch?" Cardinal Selecta questioned, "she can veto the vote to reinstate the Grand Inquisitor!"

"Not if she's declared mentally incapacitated,' Kalduwan mentioned, very casually.

"By the Saint, Bishop! Hold your tongue! It's one thing to go after Richelieux who is disliked by many in the Curia, but to declare the Matriarch herself, mentally unfit?" Cardinal Millicenta protested, her voice sounding shrill.

"The fact remains, your Eminences, that to spend three billion Kredits of the Church's money, requires the authority of the Matriarch herself. If she can be influenced by Richelieux to use Church funds so carelessly, we can use that to have her judgment questioned. We can't impeach a seating Matriarch, but we might be able to temporarily curtail her veto power to get to Richelieux," Kalduwan suggested.

"She's right!" Cardinal Murcia agreed heartily, "we don't have to declare the Matriarch mentally unfit. All we have to do is ask for a psych exam, which will render her unable to govern until the experts examine her and report back to the Curia after a three-week period. The Curia then, will have to choose a Matriarch Pro Tem from among the female Cardinals and we'll make sure that that candidate is one of us! If we ask for a psych exam we'll have three weeks to carry on with the Inquisition."

"What about that heathen Zepol? What can be done about him?" asked Cardinal Millicenta.

"Hmmm, legally, that's not so clear," Kalduwan mused. "Unfortunately, he's not a Kelemite. Were he a member of the Church, he would be obliged to appear in front of the Grand Inquisitor. But, I'm sure that he's being paid by the Church somehow. If we can prove that he is, then he can be brought up on financial misconduct and improper use of Church property in a civil lawsuit and be forced to testify along with the Velmador girl."

"The man is a multimillionaire. It could prove expensive to take him to trial," Cardinal Selecta, warned the others.

Kalduwan smiled. "Your Eminence, the Church of St. Kelem has more financial power and barristers in its employ, than angels can dance on the head of a pin."

CHAPTER 37

A Public Declaration of Faith

The following night, Matriarch Vasilia, Cardinal Richelieux, Ogram and Allondra were meeting once again in the pontiff's apartment.

"We are going to have to make different arrangements to meet from now on," the Matriarch told them with a worried look.

"I agree, we're taking too many risks with all this cloak and dagger. I'm surprised that no one has caught on to our late night meetings," Richelieux concurred.

"I believe that my secretary knows or suspects something. Yesterday morning she was acting strangely after I let her in," the Matriarch remarked.

"Your Holiness, all of this is due to my status as an agnostic, is it not?" Ogram asked.

The Matriarch and Richelieux hesitated for a moment. Then they looked at each other and nodded.

"In that case, I would like to make a public statement of faith. I finally realized yesterday that for all intents and purposes, I've become a Kelemite. The experience at Nobius has changed me, and I am no longer the same person that walked into this apartment three months ago."

Matriarch Vasilia and Allondra's eyes filled with tears of joy. Richelieux smiled widely and remembered wishing that Ogram were a believer soon after meeting him.

"Ogram, are you sure?" the Matriarch asked, unable to hide her excitement.

"Absolutely!"

"St. Kelem has indeed blessed us all!" the Matriarch exclaimed, reaching for Ogram and embracing him warmly. "Well Richelieux, how should we proceed?"

"Hmmm, first we must arrange for a press conference, nothing too fancy or big. We hold these once in a while to announce Church news and developments, especially when it involves a celebrity like our Mr. Zepol," Richelieux added, smiling at Ogram. "As a matter of fact, you can have Bishop Kalduwan set one up right away. You can tell her that Mr. Zepol has converted and wishes to make a public announcement. This will also help justify all our late night meetings."

"Excellent! I'll make the arrangement right away," the Matriarch announced.

The following afternoon, Bishop Kalduwan introduced Ogram Zepol to the press core as a new member of the Church of St. Kelem. The media had a thousand questions for Ogram regarding his unexpected conversion to Kelemism. Kalduwan had placed a few reporters in the crowd who owed her favors, to ask Ogram leading questions, hoping to catch him making false statements or saying something that would compromise the Matriarch or Richelieux, but the young Terran performed flawlessly and ended up charming the majority of the reporters with his quick wit and intellect.

But it didn't matter anyway. Zepol, Richelieux and the Matriarch would all fall in her trap eventually. As the press conference went on, she thanked the stars that Ogram Zepol had converted to Kelemism. Her carefully laid plans to ruin Richelieux and weaken the Matriarch were coming together. Now she'd have to meet with Cardinals Murcia, Selecta and Millicenta and decide when to strike. Kalduwan had been waiting years for this opportunity, and now the time had come for her to finally put the church on the path of righteousness.

CHAPTER 38

An Unholy Alliance

"Boss, you're not going to believe it! But a guy named Pieter Minsk, claiming to be the general manager of the Plantanimus CUBE is asking to speak with you!"

Sumpter Blarok dropped his jaw and stared at Bernie, his top mercenary.

"That's impossible! It's got to be a trick. Is he alone? Have you checked to see if there are Galactic Council ships in orbit above us?" Blarok asked.

"No boss, they came in a small ship. He's with another guy named Shonderman. What do you want to do?"

Blarok thought for a moment and then his eyes lit up. "Bring Maria here, she'll know if these guys are legit."

Bernie left and returned a few minutes later with Maria Santana, who was stumbling with eyes half closed. She was high on drugs and could hardly walk straight.

"Arrgh! She's fucking useless," Blarok cursed, disgusted with her appearance. "Give her an upper, I need to know who these assholes are," he ordered Bernie.

Bernie obliged and took out a small liquid-filled bubble with a needle in it and injected it in Maria's neck. Two minutes later she opened her eyes and looked at Blarok with hatred in her eyes.

"You son of a bitch! Why don't you just let me die!" She screamed at him, with the veins in her neck popping out.

"Now, now, don't get all uppity on me, otherwise we'll have another one of our fun sessions and I know how much you like it when we play!" Blarok said threateningly.

Maria whimpered and lowered her head. She didn't want to be beaten up and raped again by Blarok, who enjoyed abusing her for hours on end.

"What do you want?" she asked, shaking from the amphetamines coursing through her body.

Blarok turned on the holo screen above his desk. "Do you know these guys?" he asked, pointing at the screen.

Maria raised her head and struggled to focus her eyes. Slowly, the image came into view and she nodded.

"Well, who are they?" he demanded, impatiently.

"The bald one is Pieter Minsk, the CUBE's General Manager, the other one is Brian Shonderman, the night shift's head tech," she answered, gritting her teeth.

"Son of a bitch!" Blarok whispered to himself, wondering what anyone from The Realm would be doing in Kāla Kōṭharī.

"Please! Give me more Sleep-med! I can't stand feeling like this!" Maria begged him.

"I will sweetheart, but not before you tell me why these guys are in my waiting room asking for me," Blarok was curious to know.

"He. . . ., here?" Maria blurted out, not believing what she was hearing. The combination of drugs in her system was playing havoc with her ability to think straight. Perhaps this was some cruel trick of Blarok's. Maybe this was a new way to mess with her mind.

"Yeah, they're here. Tell me about Minsk. What's his deal?"

Maria fought hard to clear her mind as much as possible. "Minsk is a Kelemite fundamentalist, he wouldn't be caught dead in your company. If he's here it would be to kill you or try to convert you," she told him, as her body continued shaking uncontrollably.

"What about the other one, Shonderman?" Blarok inquired.

'I. . ., I don't know him well. He's just an egghead," Maria replied.

"You checked them for weapons, explosives, poisons?" Blarok asked Bernie.

"Yeah boss, they're clean, though they smell funny," Bernie commented, making a face.

"Hah! Maybe it's the stink of corruption!" he said, laughing.

"You want me to kill them?" Bernie asked, hoping for an affirmative answer.

"Not just yet. Take Maria back to her hole in the wall, then bring those two in, but make sure there's four mercs in the room in case they get funny ideas."

Bernie grabbed Maria forcefully by the arm and dragged her out of Blarok's office. Two minutes later Pieter Minsk and Brian Shonderman were sitting across from Blarok's desk with Bernie and three other burly mercenaries behind them.

Sumpter Blarok leaned back in his executive chair, holding a large caliber pulse pistol in his hand. "Talk, you got three minutes to tell me what you're doing here. If I don't like what I hear, I'll kill you both."

"I'm here to hand you the keys to the kingdom Mr. Blarok," Minsk said calmly.

"Oh yeah, how's that?" Blarok responded with disdain.

"I've taken complete control of the Plantanimus CUBE. I'm willing to sell you the entire central core. All you need to do is supply me with a large enough vessel that can safely transport the core and I'll bring it to Kāla Kōtharī in less than twenty-four hours."

"Just like that huh?" Blarok said sarcastically. "I give you one of my biggest ships, let you take it with you and then you'll bring the core to my planet?"

"Precisely Mr. Blarok. Of course, we'd have to agree on a price and certain conditions that my comrades and I would like to negotiate."

"You fucking Kelemites have been a thorn up my ass for twenty five years! Why should I trust that all of a sudden, you've decided to betray your precious St. Kelem?"

"Things change Mr. Blarok. I've been a faithful servant of The Realm and the Church for all my life, and what did it get me and my friend, here?" he said, pointing to Shonderman, "we get a barely adequate bonus at the end of the year and a heartfelt thanks from the Matriarch! Besides, I know that you made a deal with Longsdale and McCallan. Longsdale is dead and McCallan's disappeared. Then you sent Maria Santana to steal the second half of the files that you wanted. I'm here to sell you everything else that's stored in the CUBE. One and a half billion client files! All for a very reasonable fee," he concluded with a confident smile.

Blarok's pulse rose at the prospect of owning all that potential wealth. He could negotiate with those families that were willing to see their relatives reborn in manufactured bodies, and the rest he could ransom for money.

"Alright, let's say that I bite. What's your price?" he asked, his greedy nature taking over.

"Ten trillion Kredits plus new bodies for myself and my partners," Minsk countered.

"You're out of your mind! I don't even have one third of that amount in cash and property!"

"I know you don't. We'd be willing to be paid over time," Minsk offered.

"Over how much time?" Blarok probed, sensing a good deal coming his way.

"We're willing to take it over ten years."

"No way, I wouldn't do it in less than twenty!"

Minsk looked at Shonderman, then back at Blarok. "Fifteen and you got a deal," he said extending his hand.

Blarok pursed his lips and rubbed his chin pensively. "I'll agree, but only after I make sure that you really have control of the CUBE."

"Go ahead, why don't you send some of your men with Shonderman here, meanwhile, you can keep me here as a hostage. Once your men confirm that we're being truthful, you can arrange to retrieve the core from the complex," Minsk suggested.

Ten hours later, Bernie's underling, Chester, returned with Shonderman and three other mercenaries. He reported to Blarok and confirmed that the CUBE was under their control now. Bernie had stayed behind with one hundred mercs. Now all that had to be done was to remove the core from the giant machine.

This time, Minsk would have to go with the large transport. He was the only one with the expertise to safely remove the core from the building without damaging it. Blarok agreed and decided to bring seven heavily armed vessels, in case the Galactic Council's Space Navy happened to show up. He insisted on coming with his men to supervise, and Minsk seemed very happy to have him along.

Two hours later, the seven ships belonging to the Body Shop Guild appeared three hundred kilometers above Plantanimus' North Pole. Blarok, Minsk and several mercenaries shuttled down to the roof of the CUBE's complex.

When they landed, Bernie greeted Blarok on the roof.

"It's all good to go boss. Minsk's guys have already started dismantling the girders that hold the core. Follow me and I'll show you. Bernie led them to a large elevator that took them several levels down into the bowels of the complex.

On the way down, Blarok's nose picked up a bad smell. "Bernie, you smell like these guys," Blarok whispered in his ear. "As a matter of fact, this whole place smells like shit!"

"It's just a gas leak from one of the lower levels, boss, nothing to worry about. We'll be out of here in less than three or four hours," Bernie assured him.

The elevator reached the level they were going to, and Bernie continued leading the way. He stopped at a door that read 'Central Matrix Control'. "Here we are boss, just step through," Bernie said holding the door open.

Blarok and the rest of the mercenaries stepped through. As soon as the last man was inside, the door slammed behind them and locked. Blarok spun around and cursed. It was a trap! Then he realized that neither Bernie nor Minsk were with them.

"You God damned bastards!" he yelled, taking out his gun and firing at the door. The other mercs also took out their guns and shot at the door. But it was no use. The door leading to the Central Matrix was made of fifteen centimeter thick Duraminium.

Blarok looked around and saw that they were at the top of a huge conical room, several stories high. Then he saw the dead bodies everywhere and gagged at the smell of rotting flesh.

The lights dimmed and flickered, and the hair in everyone's head began to stand on end with static charge.

"What the hell?" Blarok muttered, as the lights went out completely. One of the mercs turned on a flashlight, but the thing spit blue sparks giving him a shock. The man dropped the flashlight and flickered out when it hit the floor.

The top of the cone began arching with blue rays of electricity. Soon the lightning increased and began descending toward Blarok and the mercenaries. Everyone panicked and started running to the lower levels of the room. Blarok ran toward the edge of the top tier and jumped onto the next lower tier of control stations and landed on a half rotten body. He screamed in horror and disgust and fell on the floor. Above him, men were being struck with the indigo blue lightning, screaming and writhing in agony. Desperate and in complete and abject fear, he looked down and was ready to jump into a lower tier, when he felt a powerful electrical shock hit his legs and was instantly paralyzed. The blue fire climbed up his legs, into his chest, shoulders, neck, throat and finally into his eyes.

Outside, Minsk and Bernie were smiling with pleasure, listening to the screams of men being absorbed by their comrades. Soon everything was quiet and Bernie opened the door.

The mercenaries came out first, stumbling around as they adjusted to their new bodies. Then, Blarok came out, his eyes black on black. He took a deep breath and laughed, sounding like an alien beast from a nightmare.

Welcome Vitrami! We are ready to proceed," Imurdum said, inside Pieter Minsk's body. Then he and Bernie bent on one knee and bowed respectfully to the supreme leader of the Nadrogs.

CHAPTER 39

A Wedding in Sister Ornata's Chapel

Now that he'd declared publicly that he was a Kelemite, Ogram could no longer stay at apartment 108 on Level 26. He booked a large suite at the Heavenly Temple's hotel for tourists while Allondra had been temporarily put up at the Matriarch's residence. Because of his celebrity status, cohabiting with Allondra now would be seen as improper. This was the first time since they left for Nobius that the two had been separated and both he and Allondra missed each other terribly. It didn't take long for Ogram to realize that he wanted to marry Allondra. He proposed to her and she accepted immediately. Allondra notified her family and Ogram asked her father and mother for her hand, via quantum video call. Her father and mother gave their blessing and requested that they come to Tarsia Prime and marry a second time in a Tarsian ceremony, when time allowed.

When the Matriarch heard the news, she asked to officiate the wedding. The Matriarch did not perform marriages normally, but being an ordained member of the Church, it was certainly within her purview to do so. The following day, Ogram and Allondra were married by Matriarch Vasilia in Sister Ornata's chapel on Level 23, with Cardinal Richelieux acting as best man and Bishop Kalduwan as witness. It was a small private wedding with only two media reporters allowed to take videos of the ceremony.

The groom wore a formal vermillion wedding suit and the bride wore a white wedding gown with a green veil, to honor her Tarsian heritage.

Bishop Kalduwan could not have been happier to see Ogram and Allondra get married. Now that he was a declared member of the Church, and Allondra a former novice nun, his wife, both were now subject to the Church's laws.

After the ceremony, the wedding party moved to the Matriarch's residence where her staff had prepared a grand meal served in the residence's main dining room. Afterwards, the cooks brought out a wedding cake with an exact holo replica of Ogram and Allondra sitting on top. An impromptu reception took place when Richelieux's and the Matriarch's Gulax Guards, plus Zurk and his three sons, showed up bearing presents for the married couple.

Later that night when they entered their room in Ogram's suite at the hotel, he took her in his arms and kissed her deeply and passionately, with every fiber in his being, vibrating with the same energy as Kelem's blessing.

Slowly and gently, Kelem undressed Allondra as he laid her on the bed, hungering for her. He kissed her, feeling a burning fire that was both erotic and sacred at the same time. Their minds and spirits were suddenly connected to each other in a way that hadn't happened before.

Allondra's body ached with a desire and need. She drew him to her hungrily, as their bodies became one, exploding with the pleasure and passion of physical love.

CHAPTER 40

The Plantanimus CUBE is Destroyed

The com panel next to the bed buzzed and Ogram woke up and turned the holo screen on.

"Yes?" he asked, looking with bleary eyes at Richelieux's face floating in mid-air.

"I am so sorry to intrude on your honeymoon Ogram and Allondra, but there's an emergency at the Plantanimus CUBE," he reported, looking uncomfortable.

"What's happened?" Ogram asked, sitting up on the bed, followed by Allondra, whose mane of black hair covered half her sleepy face.

"The Plantanimus CUBE has been attacked by unknown assailants. We're not sure who it is, but a good guess would be the Nadrogs," Richelieux said, with a grim expression. "Could you two come up to the Matriarch's residence right away?"

'We'll be there soon," Ogram replied, already putting on his clothes. As he and Allondra got dressed, he knew that this was really bad news. The Nadrogs had obviously managed to attack with physical force.

Ten minutes later, they were in the Matriarch's personal office watching a news report. There was a lot of confusion on the news channels, as no one really knew what had happened. But one thing was for certain, the CUBE's complex had been breached. The media robo-cams flying above the facility and the satellites in orbit above

Plantanimus, were showing a large plume of smoke billowing from the complex.

Richelieux had tried contacting the complex without any answer. And the CUBE, being a forbidden restricted zone to civilians, yielded no answers. The local Galactic Council authority claimed that one of their ships had been attacked but had lost contact with the vessel.

"We must leave right away," Ogram recommended.

"Yes," the Matriarch agreed, looking very upset.

"Is this the work of the Nadrogs?" Allondra asked.

"I'm sure they have something to do with this. But we don't know for certain. The last time the Body Shop Guild attacked the Heavenly Temple or one of our CUBEs, was decades ago," Richelieux stated with uncertainty.

"How long ago did this happen?" Ogram asked.

"Three hours ago. We were notified by the Galactic Council an hour ago," the Matriarch informed him.

"Allondra and I are ready to go. We'll take a bird of paradise down to Camp Zurk and be on our way in the Prophesy," Ogram said to the Matriarch and Richelieux.

"I'll follow you," Richelieux said. "I'll take the Trinity and all my Gulax Guards, just in case."

"Take the Trieste and all my guards as well," Matriarch Vasilia offered.

"I'm sorry Your Holiness, but I won't take your personal ship. You cannot be left unguarded, especially now. For all we know, this is the first of a series of coordinated attacks. I will put the Temple on high alert immediately," Richelieux replied.

Half an hour later, Ogram and Allondra were on their way to Plantanimus with the Trinity close behind.

When the Prophesy rematerialized above Plantanimus, Ogram and Allondra were met by a Galactic Council cruiser who challenged their presence.

"Civilian vessel, this is Galactic Council Cruiser 'Wunderkind', Identify yourself," the com officer demanded.

"Ahoy, Wunderkind, this is private vessel Prophesy en route to Plantanimus. We're here on behalf of Matriarch Vasilia, who has asked us to investigate the situation in the CUBE," Ogram responded.

"Hold on Prophesy," the com officer said and the screen went blank. A few seconds later, a harried looking man with captain stripes, appeared on the screen.

"This is Captain Willows, Prophesy, what is your business here? I have no knowledge of your ship being listed as a Church sanctioned vessel," the man said in a not too friendly manner.

"Cardinal Richelieux's ship should be arriving soon, Captain Willows. He will vouch for us," Ogram answered. "Meanwhile, what is the status of the CUBE?"

The captain grimaced and looked down. "Use your optics and see for yourselves. I'll wait for the Trinity to arrive before I answer any questions," the man said, cutting off communication.

Allondra aimed the telescope at the planet's North Pole and the image of the smoking CUBE complex came into focus.

"By the Saint, it looks like it's been severely damaged!" she said, gasping in horror.

A few seconds later, Cardinal Richelieux appeared on their screen. "We've arrived. I spoke to Captain Willows. He's expecting you in their cargo hold. Unfortunately, their loading dock was damaged in the attack, so you'll have to transfer over in your space suits. I'll do the same and meet you inside the Wunderkind."

"Will do Cardinal," Ogram replied.

Ten minutes later, Ogram and Allondra entered the Wunderkind through one of their exterior hatches. Once the air lock was re-pressurized, three of Richelieux's Gulax dressed in full battle armor space suits, came by to escort them to the ship's bridge. As they moved through the cruiser, Ogram saw that some of the decks were ripped open by gun fire and exposed to the vacuum of space. The fire fight had been serious. Now he understood the captain's attitude when they spoke earlier.

The ship's bridge was undamaged and when Ogram and Allondra entered, they were told they could open their helmet's face shields. Richelieux, Rek and the other guards were already there.

"Could you tell us what happened captain?" Ogram asked.

"Four and a half hours ago, we received a call from Plantanimus Command that a fleet of seven heavily armed, unregistered civilian vessels had appeared above the North Pole. When I took my ship there to investigate, we were fired upon and barely got out with our lives. I lost twenty three men in the attack!" the captain said with anger. 'We're only a patrol vessel and we were severely outgunned. I retreated and called for help, but continued observing. Fifteen minutes later, I saw a huge transport arrive and park itself directly above the complex and lift a huge piece of equipment from the building," the captain recalled.

Ogram, Allondra and Richelieux looked at each other. Their worst fears had been confirmed.

"What happened then Captain?" Richelieux prodded.

"About twenty shuttles left the complex and entered four of the large ship's hangars. Two minutes later, all eight vessels went into *n'time* right above the North Pole! It's a miracle that they didn't burn the atmosphere going interdimensional so close to a planet!"

"Has anyone gone down to the complex to investigate?" Ogram inquired.

"Yes! I sent four of my men in one of our emergency dinghies, but I lost contact with them soon after they reported that they had entered the facility."

"Hmmm, do you have a functioning spectrometer here on the bridge captain?" Ogram asked.

"Yes, but what do you want to do with it?"

"I have a hunch, but I want to use it and check something first, before I answer your question," Ogram responded.

"Suit yourself, here it is," the captain said pointing to the equipment.

Ogram turned the spectrometer on and zoomed in on the area of the complex where the fire and smoke was billowing into the air. He made some adjustments and then looked at the machine's analysis of the elements in the fire and grimaced, wishing that he'd been wrong.

The bluish tint of the fire had made him suspect that the color of the flame was sulphuric in nature. Something had jogged his memory of the attack inside the CUBE's VR. He remembered that the monster's stink reminded him of rotting eggs. Life in the Milky Way was carbon based, perhaps the Nadrogs' physiology was sulphur based. Somehow their psychic energy had created Hydrogen Sulphide when they exited the CUBE's VR.

"Did your men go down to the surface with breathing equipment?" Ogram asked, dreading the answer.

"There was no need to, since they were going down to the planet. You don't think that . . .," the captain said, stopping in mid-sentence, realizing that his men might be dead.

"I'm sorry to inform you captain, but that fire in the complex is emitting toxic levels of Hydrogen Sulfide. It's quite possible that your men asphyxiated within seconds of entering the CUBE. The stuff is three times more poisonous than Cyanide" Ogram explained, with regret.

The man's shoulders sunk, and he had to grab onto one of the control stations to steady himself. "I suppose we'll have to wait for the Council's ships to arrive before someone goes down there," he uttered, looking worn out by the loss of his men.

"My ship has state of the art environmental suits. I'd be willing to go to the CUBE and see if I can rescue your men and whoever else might still be alive down there," Ogram volunteered.

"I'll come with you,' the captain offered.

"I'm sorry, Captain Willows, but the only other suit is tailored to my body," Allondra announced, speaking for the first time.

"I don't want you to come," Ogram said, unsettled by the idea that his wife of barely twenty four hours would be put in harm's way.

"Remember our vows husband?" she replied, lifting her eyebrows. "to have and to hold, in sickness and in health, in wealth or in poverty, as long as we both shall live?"

"Yes but . . .,"

"My love, if you are going down there, then so am I," she told him in no uncertain terms, her big green eyes fixed on his.

The captain smirked and looked at Ogram. "You can't argue with a wife when she sets her mind, young fellow. I learned that from experience!"

Cardinal Richelieux smiled as well. "Be careful you two. I trust those new suits of yours, but don't get careless," Richelieux requested.

"Don't worry about us, your Eminence, we have St. Kelem on our side!" Allondra replied with a confident smile.

They returned to the Prophesy and descended to the planet. Half an hour later Ogram landed the Prophesy on the snow covered roof of the CUBE's superstructure. The temperature was minus thirty degrees centigrade, yet the fire at the top of the building was still burning fiercely.

They found a roof access hatch far from the fire and when Ogram pulled it open, thick black smoke poured out, but fortunately it diminished soon after. Allondra turned on the infrared temperature sensor in her suit. "It's about fifty degrees centigrade, safe enough to enter," she reported, jumping in without waiting for Ogram.

"Good lord woman! What happened to the 'mild mannered novice nun' I met not too long ago?" Ogram said, jumping in after her.

"Oh, she met a famous genius scientist, millionaire playboy, married him and has never been the same since," she answered, forging ahead as she turned on her helmet's safety light.

"Wait up Allondra! Please be careful of sharp objects, one tiny breach in our suit's skins and we're done for," he warned her.

"Husband, don't fret so much about me. I spent my teenage years accompanying my father onto some very nasty planets with deadly atmospheres."

"My love, it's not just the suits I'm worried about. What if there are Nadrogs still running about?" he asked her, facing her.

"I'm sorry, you're right. I should be careful," she said, taking out her side arm and cocking it.

"Thank you. Also, we should watch out for loose beams and weakened floors. We don't know how much damage the fire has caused."

They found a fire exit stairway and climbed down. When they reached what Ogram remembered was the building's main floor level, they left the stairway and found themselves in the large lobby of the CUBE's building. Here the smoke was much lighter and a few emergency lights were still working here and there. Then they saw the bodies, dozens of them.

Ogram was thankful for the integrity of their suits, for many of the poor souls lying on the floor, had been dead for days. Their body's had swollen with gas caused by bacteria and their skin had turned black.

Allondra turned her head in disgust. She had never seen a rotting corpse before. She could only imagine what the place smelled like.

"Are you alright?" Ogram asked, feeling the same dread she was experiencing.

"Yes, I'll be alright. Let's keep going" she replied bravely.

A few steps later, they found Captain Willow's men. They had collapsed next to each other, their eyes open and their faces showing the physical signs of asphyxiation.

They spent the next hour finding dead bodies everywhere. Not a single soul had survived the effects of the Hydrogen Sulphide. They continued searching the building and eventually found the main escalators leading to the Central Matrix's entrance.

The heavy metal door was open and Ogram and Allondra entered. Inside, they saw the same spectacle as they had encountered in the lobby, except much worse. Here, the bodies numbered in the hundreds. Every piece of furniture and equipment looked as if it had been hit by multiple pulse blasts. As Ogram shined his helmet light into the conical ceiling he saw that it had tuned charcoal black and for a second, he thought he saw Angel Darius falling down on him. He yelled involuntarily, frightening Allondra who raised her gun at the ceiling, thinking that they were being attacked.

"I'm sorry. I guess I'm a little spooked. I thought I saw a Nadrog coming at me," he apologized.

"I can't blame you my love. This is horrible. What do you think has happened here?"

"I think the Nadrogs figured a way to get out of the CUBE's VR and invade people's bodies. They must have taken over the CUBE's staff and then, using those victims' bodies, they must have enlisted the help of other unsuspecting humans, probably pirates or most likely, the Body Shop Guild. They're the only ones, other than the Galactic Council, with the money and resources to assemble that many armed ships and pull off the theft of the core," Ogram surmised correctly.

"Are we too late to contain them, Ogram?" Allondra asked, her voice shaking.

"Not if we can find where they've taken the core and prevent them from taking over more people's bodies. Alpha and Kelem estimated the number of Nadrogs that escaped the Andromeda galaxy to be in the thousands, which means that it's going to take them quite a long time to reincarnate all of them. If we can find where they are soon, especially if they're all on one planet, we might have a chance."

"But remember that the Nadrogs projected themselves into the crew of a Davanian ship in orbit around Kranok, their home world, and the Davanians only found out about it after the fact," Allondra reminded him.

"Yes, but they were only able to do that through the Transcedentorium which self-destructed after they escaped. My guess is that the CUBE's core doesn't allow them to do that. Otherwise, they would have taken over the population of Plantanimus already. I think they've taken the core to a Body Shop planet where they can safely transfer their kind to other bodies, someplace with a large population."

"Hmmm, I remember that my father always avoided taking cargo to the Epsilon Quadrant. He said that that part of space was full of 'Pleasure Planets', full of casinos, prostitution, and all sort of wicked things. He also claimed that those planets were filthy and severely overcrowded with the dregs of society. Perhaps that's where the Nadrogs took the core," Allondra theorized.

"You're right Allondra! It makes perfect sense. They certainly can't go to a Galactic Council planet. You're a genius! That's where we'll find those bastards, though I hope we get to them before they enslave an entire planet's population and break out into the rest of the galaxy."

CHAPTER 41

Pandemonium in the Galaxy

The following day, the news of the near destruction of the Plantanimus CUBE and the theft of the core, spread to the rest of the galaxy. The media showed up on Plantanimus by the thousands, each channel vying to get the story and broadcast it to their subscribers. The relatives of those whose consciousnesses were stored in the Core, traveled to the planet by the hundreds of thousands, seeking answers regarding the fate of their dearly departed. The central headquarters of The Realm, in Centralia, was flooded with calls and requests for information.

The Galactic Council had to blockade the planet to prevent the chaos that the multitude of people that were trying to land on Plantanimus would certainly cause. A criminal investigation was launched to find out who the perpetrators were. The death toll at the Plantanimus CUBE was in the thousands.

Additionally, the value of The Realm's stock plunged severely, causing a galaxy wide panic in the financial markets. The Realm's stockholders demanded an immediate investigation as well, and all eyes turned to the Church of St. Kelem, in particular, the Cardinal Counselor to the Matriarch, Cardinal Richelieux.

Richelieux's enemies within the Curia went into high gear, salivating at the prospect of finally being able to get rid of the first ever male Cardinal to reach the position. Bishop Kalduwan and her Cardinal co-conspirators now had the perfect excuse to call for a re-instatement of the office of the Grand Inquisitor. Kalduwan organized a secret meeting of all those cardinals that disliked Richelieux and all decided unanimously that they would elect her as Grand Inquisitor. Now all that had to happen was to wait for the next Curia meeting, call for the re-instatement of the office of the Grand Inquisitor, elect Kalduwan to the position, at which time she would disclose the purchase of the Prophesy and accuse Richelieux of financial fraud, as well as demand that the Church launch its own investigation of the cause of the destruction of the Plantanimus CUBE and the theft of the central Core.

The Body Shop Guild and the many body shops spread out through the outer planets saw an opportunity to weaken The Realm and the Church of St. Kelem. They began buying 'air time' in the news channels to malign the Church and weaken The Realm's reputation and their long held claim that the safety and security of The Realm's clients was unbreakable. The effect of the bad publicity was immediate. Thousands of clients that had paid deposits to The Realm began withdrawing their money and approached body shops and placed orders for new bodies with them.

Ogram and Allondra remained on Plantanimus for a few more days helping The Realm and the Galactic Council decontaminate the CUBE's complex and organize a general cleanup of the area.

Cardinal Richelieux received an emergency call from the Matriarch regarding the developing situation with the Curia. He left immediately for the Heavenly Temple.

CHAPTER 42

Ogram is Arrested, Allondra Escapes

Ogram's cochlear implant dinged and he answered it.

"Yes?"

"Ogram, don't say a word! This is Matriarch Vasilia. Cardinal Richelieux has been detained by the Galactic Council. He's here in the Heavenly Temple's stockade being held on financial fraud charges regarding the Prophesy. He's also being blamed for the destruction of the Plantanimus CUBE. There's to be a trial sanctioned by the Curia. They've gone as far as re-instituting the office of Grand Inquisitor, a position that was last held during the Crusades. Ogram, this is bad news and I suspect that you and Allondra will be forced to testify, but you must not come! Is that understood?"

"Yes . . .but . . .," Ogram began saying, surprised by what he was hearing.

"Is Allondra there with you?"

"Yes," Ogram answered, distressed by the unexpected news.

"Good, you two must leave Plantanimus immediately because I'm sure the Galactic Council and the Curia are coming after you next."

Ogram looked around to make sure no one was within hearing range. "Alright, we'll leave right away. Allondra and I think that the core is being held on a planet called Kāla Kōṭharī. Kelem told us that if we needed help, we should contact a group of Martian psychics called The Brotherhood of the Light. He said we could trust them implicitly.

If Allondra and I can recover the Core, I'm sure it will help Cardinal Richelieux."

"I'm not sure that it will do him much good. Cardinal Richelieux has many enemies in the Curia and they are using him as a sacrificial lamb in order to depose him. But recovering the core is important. You must concentrate all your energy on finding it and returning it to the Galactic Council. The Curia won't be able to accuse you of wrongdoing if you and Allondra can retrieve it."

"But what about you . . . . ?" Ogram asked, concerned that she might be arrested and tried by the Grand Inquisitor as well.

"Do not be concerned with my safety or wellbeing. The Matriarch cannot be impeached or deposed. Now go! You must hurry. The Galactic Council is probably already on their way to bring you and Allondra to the Heavenly Temple!"

The communication ended and Ogram was left feeling frustrated by not being able to help Richelieux or the Matriarch. He became angry with the Curia and wished that he'd been able to foresee this treachery taking shape. But, church politics were foreign to him and he knew that rescuing the core was important.

He turned to Allondra who was wondering what the call was all about. He explained the situation to her and she became upset, unwilling to believe that the Church would treat Richelieux in such a terrible manner.

They headed for the elevator that would take them to the roof of the complex where the Prophesy was parked. The doors opened and Allondra entered first. As soon as she did, a platoon of Galactic Council troops appeared at the end of the hallway and a young lieutenant called out his name.

"Mr. Zepol, please do not move!" the man ordered.

Allondra was about to come out of the elevator but Ogram pushed her gently back inside and stepped back into the hallway. "Go to Mars, contact the Brotherhood!" he whispered to her as the doors shut.

"Yes, lieutenant?" Ogram asked, turning to him and sounding very casual.

"I'm sorry sir, but I must detain you. By order of the Galactic Council and the Church of St. Kelem I hereby place under arrest," the young man declared.

"You're detaining me . . ., why?" he asked, playing along.

"That information has not been given to me sir. Where is your wife, Mr. Zepol?"

"She's down in the core chamber, overseeing a crew doing some last minute clean up. Is she being arrested as well?" he asked, looking confused, trying to vie for time. He knew that Allondra could fly the Prophesy and make her way to Mars on her own.

"I'm afraid so Mr. Zepol," the lieutenant replied, nodding to two of his men to go and bring Allondra to him.

It would take several minutes for the troopers to reach the now empty core chamber, search for Allondra and report that they couldn't find her. Fortunately for Ogram, the walls of the core chamber were heavily shielded, and the inter-building communications network had been damaged during the fire, so the troopers would have to physically return to where the rest of the platoon was now, in order to report. If he slowed down the lieutenant and his men long enough, she'd have time to escape.

Fifteen minutes later, the pair returned empty handed. The lieutenant looked at Ogram with anger in his eyes. "Mr. Zepol, it would be wise for you to tell me where your wife is, right now!"

"I suspect she's in mid *n'time* travel, heading to heavens knows where," Ogram replied, calmly.

Ogram was spun around roughly by two troopers and secured with magnetic handcuffs. Then he was pushed into the same elevator that Allondra had taken to the roof. On the way up, the lieutenant called his ship on his audio implant. "Lemon Tree, this is Lieutenant Cesar, Allondra Zepol is attempting to escape, please intercept the vessel Prophesy, immediately," he requested.

When the Lemon Tree responded, Ogram didn't have to ask if she'd gotten away. The lieutenant's expression of disappointment said it all.

CHAPTER 43

The Men's Holding Facility in Latonga

Ogram was brought to New Jerusalem in a Galactic Council warship. He was taken to the Men's Holding Facility in downtown Latonga and booked on the trumped up charge of "Witness to Fraud". He'd be appearing in front of a New Jerusalem criminal court judge in the morning for arraignment, then, brought up to the Heavenly Temple sometime later.

The men's jail in Latonga was practically empty. New Jerusalem was a planet full of devout Kelemites and crime was rare. The few inmates in the facility were mostly foreign workers, booked on drunk and disorderly charges, theft and vandalism.

He was put in a large single cell with a comfortable bunk, desk and exposed toilet. He had access to all the media channels and reading material. His audio implant, however, was rendered inoperable while inside.

It was late at night when he had finally been processed, given a red inmate coverall, soft shoes a box of snacks and then locked in his cell. He lay on the bunk wondering if Allondra had reached the Brotherhood and about the future of the galaxy. This ridiculous situation was the worst that could happen to Richelieux, the Matriarch, Allondra and him. The damned Nadrogs were about to turn the Milky Way galaxy into hell!

He closed his eyes and decided to meditate, achieving Samadhi would help him ground himself and prepare for the ordeal to come. No sooner had he crossed his legs and started his meditation when the door's lock turned.

"You have a visitor," a prison guard announced, opening the door and then stepping to the side.

Matriarch Vasilia entered and Ogram was very happy to see a friendly face. He jumped up, and without thinking, hugged the pontiff. She smiled and returned the embrace.

"I'm sorry your Holiness, I guess I was feeling down, and when I saw you . . .,"

"No apologies necessary Ogram, please sit down, we have a lot to talk about."

The guard closed the cell door and the Matriarch sat on the bunk.

"If you'll forgive me for saying so your Holiness, but what the hell is going on?"

"First things first, Ogram. Under no circumstances are you to testify on behalf of Cardinal Richelieux," she warned him.

"But why? You said he's being accused of financial fraud regarding the Prophesy. That's ridiculous. Why shouldn't I speak on his behalf?"

"My dear boy, this so-called trial has nothing to do with fraud or the purchase of the Prophesy. Don't you understand? It's about getting rid of Richelieux because of his views regarding the luxury excesses of the Church, but most of all, because he is a male, the first male ever to ascend to the position of Cardinal Counselor. As long as he is in that position, which is for life, no female cardinal can ascend to the position and in turn become Matriarch. I was Cardinal Counselor to the Matriarch before becoming the Church's Pontiff, and so has almost every other Matriarch in the past."

"Oh I understand," Ogram said, realizing why Richelieux had been arrested and put on trial. "But can't you dismiss the charges? I mean, you're the Matriarch, for God's sake!"

"Unfortunately, the Matriarch has no jurisdiction when it comes to the Church's internal legal matters, especially when it involves an accusation of fraud. My hands are tied. I am like the president of a nation. The chief executive of a country does not rule or participate in criminal trials or civil law suits."

Matriarch Vasilia hid the fact from Ogram that her mental competency had been questioned and that she was now under psychological investigation. For the next three weeks, she was completely powerless to intercede on behalf of Richelieux until she had been declared mentally capable by an independent board of review. The Curia had made sure that Richelieux was completely isolated.

"But what's going to happen to the Cardinal? Is he going to be imprisoned?" Ogram asked, feeling totally powerless, unable to help a man that he had come to consider a dear friend. Richelieux was like a father figure to him.

"The trial is but an excuse to expel Cardinal Richelieux from the Church. The Grand Inquisitor and the Curia have no power to convict or sentence anyone to a prison term, only to expel clergy from the church. However, the crisis involving the Plantanimus CUBE is another matter. The Realm's stockholders are screaming holy hell, and the relatives of the clients whose consciousnesses are inside the stolen core will most likely sue The Realm and the Church if the core is not recovered intact. It may come to pass that I myself will be called to testify in a civil trial regarding the destruction of the Plantanimus CUBE."

"Dear god, what a mess!" Ogram exclaimed, feeling depressed.

"Agreed, but as I said, first things first. The core must be returned to The Realm as soon as possible. Then and only then will we be free to deal with the Nadrogs!"

"Your Holiness, I sent Allondra to Mars, but I don't know what's happened to her or if she was able to contact the Brotherhood! As long as I'm imprisoned, I'm helpless to do anything about any of this!"

Matriarch Vasilia took Ogram's hand in hers and held it softly. "You are one of St. Kelem's new apostles Ogram. Pray to him that he may send us positive energy and his blessing. Do not despair my good friend. I'm sure that the universe will give us a sign," she said, comforting him.

"You're right Your Holiness. I've forgotten everything that has happened to all of us in the last four months. Please forgive my lack of faith. I've fallen into old habits once again," Ogram said apologetically.

"You and Allondra are blessed children of the universe Ogram. I'm honored to know you both. You have made me realize how truly magnificent the world is and because of you, my faith has been renewed and my mind has been awakened, even when I didn't realize that I was living in ignorance."

The guard opened the door. "I'm sorry your Holiness, you have to go now. Time's up!" the man whispered, sounding nervous.

"I have to go Ogram. No one's supposed to visit you. Francis here," she said, pointing to the guard, "is an old friend of mine and he took a big risk sneaking me in and letting me talk to you. Goodbye dear friend. Remember what we talked about. Good luck. I hope to see you soon under better circumstances," the Matriarch said, getting up on her feet and running out the door.

The door closed and locked. Ogram lay back down on the bunk, trying to wrap his mind around the circumstances. His thoughts were spinning wildly and he felt like climbing the walls from frustration. He stretched his body and concentrated on just taking long steady breaths. Soon his heart rate slowed down and he entered Samadhi. He went in into a deep meditation and later fell asleep.

A loud explosion shook him out of his slumber and the cell's lights flickered for a second and then went out completely. The small emergency light near the cell door came on and Ogram stood up, with all his senses on high alert. For a moment, he wondered if this was a Nadrog attack. He went to the door and put his ear on it, hoping to hear something on the other side. He thought he heard people talking in the corridor and then came two muffled sounds, like something heavy falling on the floor.

The door's lock turned slowly, and he backed away and crouched in the corner of the cell, ready to defend himself.

The door opened and a beam of light pierced the darkness. Then the door swung fully opened and a Gulax in full battle armor stood on the threshold. The Gulax stepped in carrying a complete set of battle armor in his back. The he threw it on the floor in front of Ogram.

"Here, put these on and hurry, we're getting you out of here!" the lizard said in his hissy, raspy voice.

Ogram didn't hesitate, and slipped the armor on quickly. He followed the Gulax through the cell block and then into another corridor. Unconscious guards were laying everywhere. Finally, they reached a door that led to an alleyway, and when he and the Gulax exited the building, a land vehicle was waiting for them. He and the Gulax dove in and the vehicle took off, tires squealing.

The streets were empty at this late hour, and soon they were kilometers from the jail.

Ogram removed his helmet and addressed the five other Gulax in the vehicle. "To whom do I have the pleasure of thanking for this rescue?" he asked, with a smile on his face.

The Gulax next to him took off his helmet and Ogram dropped his jaw in utter shock.

"Allondra?" he exclaimed, feeling a mixture of happiness and worry.

"Hello husband!" she said, and then planted a big wet kiss on his cheek.

"How? I mean . . .," he stuttered, unable to form words with his mouth.

The Gulax next to her took off his helmet next. "Good evening Ogram," Zurk said, with a lizard smile.

"Zurk! Good god!" Ogram said, and then smiled even wider. Are these, Grak, Hir and Wazr?" he asked, pointing to the other three and laughing.

"Correct my dear friend. My sons and I have a Gulax shuttle ready to take you off planet and accompany you to Kāla Kōṭharī. I understand that the place is a den of iniquity in need of religion!" Zurk said with Kelemite fervor.

"I told Zurk all about the Nadrogs and the attack on the Plantanimus CUBE," Allondra informed him.

"First of all, thank you for freeing me from jail, but second, how did you get back to New Jerusalem? Did you manage to get in touch with the Brotherhood?" Ogram asked his amazing, beautiful wife.

"You're welcome husband, and yes, I went to Mars and contacted the Brotherhood. We'll be meeting three of their members soon. Other

Brotherhood people are also coming to this part of the galaxy to help us deal with the many problems we face."

"Excellent, but we're going to need more than the six of us and three Brotherhood members in order to recover the core from Kāla Kōṭharī. I'm sure the Body Shop Guild has several thousand troops on the planet.

"Relax Ogram. Your wife has taken care of everything. You'll see!" the Gulax said laughing, as the vehicle picked up speed and left the city limits, heading for open country.

CHAPTER 44

Rendezvous with the Trinity

The land vehicle came to a screeching stop at the bottom of a small canyon and everyone got out in a hurry.

"Let's get into the shuttle quick! The jail guards must be regaining consciousness right about now," Zurk yelled, as he ran toward the ship.

"How are we getting off planet?" Ogram inquired, as one of Zurk's sons closed the shuttle's main hatch.

"We have a freighter waiting for us in orbit, scheduled to leave in the next ten minutes. If we don't reach it by then we'll be stuck in New Jerusalem," Zurk explained, strapping himself in his seat.

"The Prophesy is already in the freighter my love," Allondra informed him.

One of Zurk's sons fired the engines and the shuttle took off at a very steep angle. Soon they were in orbit, approaching the freighter in question. Once inside, the captain, a human named Valmetir, secured the shuttle in one of the ship's holding docks and the freighter left orbit. An hour later the freighter rematerialized one parsec from New Jerusalem.

"We've rendezvoused with the other ship, Zurk. I'll decompress the cargo hold and your group can join the others," the captain told the Gulax.

"What other ship are you talking about, and who are the others?" Ogram asked, wondering what was going on.

"Take a look,' Allondra said, pointing to one of the windows on the port side of the freighter. Ogram took a look and smiled. "The Trinity! But what is it doing out here?" he asked.

"Bishop Kalduwan, who is now the Grand Inquisitor, ordered Cardinal Richelieux's Gulax Guard to be locked in their quarters before arresting the Cardinal. She knew that they would have killed anyone attempting to take their precious Pavitraam away from them. Kalduwan has hired mercenaries to help her take over the Heavenly Temple. The Curia has removed all Gulax from service to the Church. The mercenaries are now in charge of security in the Heavenly Temple. The bastards lowered the temperature of the Guard's quarters to near fatal levels. Fortunately, the Matriarch had her personal guard break out Richelieux's guards and they managed to escape in the Trinity," Zurk informed him.

"This is terrible! Who is guarding the Matriarch now?" Ogram wanted to know.

"No one, Ogram," Allondra replied, with tears welling in her eyes. "Her Gulax guards have been incarcerated and she's been accused of mental incompetence. Her authority has been temporarily annulled until a panel of psychiatrists declares her able to resume her position."

"Whaaat?" Ogram replied, shocked by the news. "How can the Curia get away with such ridiculous accusations?" he railed angrily.

Allondra grimaced, "The Curia has dug up ancient Church laws and regulations that are still enforceable, even though it's been millennia since they were used. By law, the Matriarch's mental competency can be questioned and she can be examined for a period of three weeks. If she's declared mentally fit she can resume her authority."

"Damn! This is almost as bad as the Nadrog invasion!" Ogram complained.

"It's all a subterfuge for the Curia to expel Cardinal Richelieux from the Church. They have no intention of removing the Matriarch from her position. But while she'd being examined, she can't come to Richelieux's aid," Allondra said, with a bitter expression on her young face.

All Ogram could do was to shake his head, feeling overwhelmed by the terrible reality of the situation.

"Ogram, you should know that Rek and his Gulax are in a 'blood frenzy'," Zurk interjected. "It was all I could do to keep them from returning to the Heavenly Temple and laying waste to the Curia."

A Gulax experiencing a "blood frenzy" was akin to a wild animal protecting its young. Gulax in this state of mind were dangerous to be around. The slightest provocation could set one of them off and cause them to attack the person closest to them.

"I'll go in with my sons first and try to contain them before you enter the Trinity," Zurk suggested.

"No thank you, Zurk. We all go in together. We need their help to retrieve the core,"

"Ogram! I'm a Gulax and I tell you that facing my kind when they're in a blood frenzy is very dangerous!"

"I know Zurk, but Allondra and I have faith in St. Kelem's blessing. She and I will give Richelieux's guards the blessing," Ogram stated, and then he turned to Allondra. "Will you go in there with me?" he asked, looking at the Trinity, floating in space.

"Of course my love," she replied, with a peaceful smile on her lips.

"You're courageous, I'll give you that!" Zurk commented, shaking his head.

Zurk and his sons left the freighter in their shuttle, and Ogram and Allondra in the Prophesy. The two ships approached the Trinity. One of the ship's hangars was open and Zurk and Ogram took their vessels inside and touched down on the deck. The pressure door closed automatically and the space was re-pressurized.

Once out in the hangar, Ogram took off his armor and Allondra did the same.

Zurk was surprised at their move. "Ogram are you sure you want to go in there without any armor?" the Gulax asked with alacrity.

"I suggest you do the same Zurk. We have to show Rek and his Gulax that we are here on a sacred mission. St. Kelem wound not wear battle armor to give his blessing and neither will I," Ogram said as he opened the pressure door leading to the Trinity's interior. Reluctantly,

Zurk and his three sons removed their battle armor and followed Ogram and Allondra.

The ship appeared empty and it took them a few minutes for the group to locate Rek and the rest of the Guard. They were all in the largest hangar in the ship. The light had been turned down low and all one hundred Gulax appeared to be standing next to each other, immobile.

"Is this a blood frenzy?" Ogram asked Zurk, in a low whisper. He had expected the whole lot of them to be beating their chests or hitting each other with sticks.

"They're trying to contain their rage Ogram! Please be very careful when you speak, do not yell or make any sudden moves!" the old Gulax advised him.

Ogram, Allondra, Zurk and his sons were standing on a catwalk that went all around the hangar. Rek and his Gulax were in the lower level. Slowly, Ogram and Allondra walked down a set of stairs and then stepped on the hangar floor. In order to reach Rek, they had to walk to the middle of the assembly.

The Gulax had their eyes closed. Ogram noticed that they were armed with their typical Gulax knifes. They had to rub shoulders with several Gulax as they went into the crowd. As they touched each one, they stirred and followed the pair with their yellow lizard eyes. Finally they reached Rek, who was standing in the middle of the crowd. Ogram touched him on the shoulder and the lizard opened his eyes.

The Gulax stared at him and a slight trembling spread throughout his body.

"Master Ogram, you're in great danger! Please leave. I'm not sure I can control myself or my guards! We're suffering from a blood frenzy!" Rek whispered, trying to keep things quiet.

"Rek, Allondra and I were sent here by St. Kelem himself. I have a message of great importance that you all need to hear. Please have your guards open their eyes and listen to me," Ogram requested.

"I beg of you! Please leave before it's too late!" Rek insisted.

Ogram closed his eyes and prayed to Kelem and Alpha with all his heart and soul, that they may give him the power to touch these Gulax with their powerful energy. Slowly Ogram and Allondra felt the warmth of sacred vibrations spreading from their chests.

On the catwalk, Zurk and his sons' lizard eyes opened wide when Ogram and Allondra's bodies began to glow fiercely with a pure white light. Rek took a step back and opened his mouth, astounded by the phenomena. Soon, the rest of the guards felt the energy emanating from Ogram and Allondra's bodies and opened their eyes, mesmerized by the spectacle.

Ogram addressed the Gulax. "Brave warriors, please hold each other's hands to receive St. Kelem's blessing. If you want to save Pavitraam and the Matriarch and help set things right, do this now!" he commanded.

One by one, including Zurk and his sons, who had by now come down to the lower level, all joined hands. Ogram and Allondra brought in the sacred energy and released it from their hands into the Gulax. The lizards' collective heart beat increased and soon, the hiss of their breathing grew louder and louder. No Gulax had ever received Kelem's blessing, and Ogram and Allondra were trying to judge how much of it this species could take. Their instinct told them that the Gulax needed a much heavier dose than the average humanoid. And so, it took another five minutes before Ogram and Allondra could tell that the lizards had reached their limit.

They brought down the effect, and both let go of the Gulax next to them and walked away slowly. They climbed to the catwalk and waited for the group to recover.

After a few minutes, Rek and the others opened their eyes, their blood frenzy diminished. He turned slowly to look at Ogram and Allondra and fixed his eyes on the pair.

"You are true Pavitraam, Ogram and Allondra!" Rek proclaimed with awe and a new found respect for the pair. The others followed suit and soon they were chanting Pavitraam! over and over.

Zurk and his sons climbed the stairs and joined Ogram and Allondra.

The old Gulax walked up to Ogram. "Once I told you that I liked you but I would like you better if you were a true believer. Remember my words?" he said out loud, to be heard above the chanting

"Yes Zurk, your words made a big impression on me."

"I am now at your service Pavitraam. My sons and I forfeit our lives for you and Allondra," the old Gulax swore and then he bowed deeply, followed by his three sons.

CHAPTER 45

Kalpanā Bhūmi (Fantasy Land)

The Trinity rematerialized a million kilometers from Kāla Kōṭharī. The Gulax were not welcome in the pleasure planet and the Cardinal's personal vessel was well known to the Body Shop Guild. Three Brotherhood operatives were already in Kalpanā Bhūmi, the planet's capital, trying to locate the CUBE's core. Ogram and Allondra would go down to the planet, meet with the three Brotherhood operatives and contact the Trinity once they found where the core was being kept.

The Trinity would stay in its current position until such time, then approach the planet, break through the planet's defenses and help retrieve the core. It was a desperate plan, but the only one that Ogram, Allondra and the Gulax could come up with in the time allowed. The planet's militia was numerous and powerful. The militia operated several armed shuttles and a few space faring military vessels, but one hundred Gulax were worth ten thousand mercenaries any time.

After receiving Kelem's blessing and finding that Ogram and Allondra were Pavitraam, Zurk, Rek and the rest of the Gulax were not happy letting the two of them go down to the planet's capital on their own, knowing that Kalpanā Bhūmi, Fantasy Land (the common name for the city), was one of the most dangerous and corrupt cities in the galaxy.

Ogram and Allondra had additional transmitters inserted subcutaneously in their heads, in case the planet's militia was able to deactivate their audio implants. The moment they located the core, Ogram would contact the Trinity.

The Prophesy left the Trinity's hangar and went into *n'time*. It rematerialized near Kāla Kothari and was immediately hailed by a Body Shop Guild cruiser.

"Unknown vessel, identify yourself," a sour faced, black man demanded.

"This is private vessel Aphrodite, en route to Kalpanā Bhūmi for some well-deserved R &R," Ogram said with a crooked smile.

"Are you atmosphere capable?" the surly man asked.

"Yes."

"In that case, landing privileges will cost you one hundred thousand Kredits, paid in advance."

"Hold on," Ogram said, punching in a series of numbers on his holo-screen. "I'm sending you my payment authorization," he added.

"One second," the man responded and waited. After a while he looked up at the screen. "You're clear to land Aphrodite. I'm sending you coordinates now."

The location coordinates appeared on Ogram's screen. "Thank you," Ogram replied, but the man had already disconnected.

"Ogram, what account did you use to pay for the fee?" Allondra asked, knowing that his name was well known.

'I've used aliases for business purposes before, my love. Don't worry, no one's going to question Roberto Brown's payment," he assured her with a wink.

Twenty minutes later Ogram landed in the pleasure planet's busy space port. The moment they exited the Prophesy, they were accosted by several individuals offering everything from taxi services to outright sexual intercourse. Ogram knew all about pleasure planets, but Allondra was not familiar with them. It took all her will power and courage to act normal in the face of the intense onslaught of hustlers, pimps and profiteers, all practically harassing them as they made their way through the tarmac to the space port's terminal. Thankfully, the sales people were not allowed inside the terminal and the local militia pushed the group away.

Ogram rented a land vehicle which was highly overpriced, but he knew that walking on the streets of Fantasy Land was an iffy proposition. Allondra told him that the Brotherhood operatives were waiting to meet them at a casino called The Golden Calf. They drove into the city and were shocked by what they saw on the sidewalks and on huge holo screens floating above the mega city's streets.

There were street performers everywhere, some of them having sexual intercourse in public, while others were engaged in sexual acts with all sorts of strange beings, which were called Fantasy Beings. These 'beings' ranged from various animals to alien looking creatures that were straight out of someone's nightmares. A few performers were chained to mechanical devices and were being tortured or abused by others wearing black masks and bizarre outfits. Drug dealers offering every kind of drug ever invented were everywhere, standing by push karts advertising their wares.

Allondra was horrified and could hardly bring herself to look at the hellish spectacle that could be seen in every direction. Tears were beggining to well in her eyes from the sadness and disgust of witnessing such terrible things.

"I know this is awful my love, but if you lower your head and avert your eyes the way you're doing now, you'll attract attention," Ogram warned her, himself having a hard time. "Bring up Kelem's blessing in your mind and pray that we can become blind to all this horror and suffering we're witnessing," he added as he drove through the city at top speed, hoping to reach The Golden Calf as soon as possible.

Ogram now understood why Gulax were not allowed on Kāla Kōṭharī. The Gulax, most of whom were either devout Tilharans or fundamentalist Kelemites, would go into a blood frenzy and lay waste the entire planet, if they witnessed the perversion and corruption, plainly seen on the streets of Fantasy Land.

"APPROACHING THE GOLDEN CALF CASINO, PLEASE VEER LEFT AT THE NEXT INTERSECTION", the vehicle's A.I. indicated. Ogram turned the wheel and drove into a large parking lot full of other land vehicles. They exited the car and followed the signs pointing to the casino upstairs. When they reached the elevator bank they ran into several tourists in various stages of inebriation and nakedness. Ogram and Allondra stayed away from them and waited to take an empty elevator. But even then, they were accosted inside the elevator by holographs of prostitutes and weird beings offering their sick and disgusting services. At some point, it became so ridiculous and bizarre, that both Ogram and Allondra broke into hysterical laughter. They realized at that moment, that this level of corruption and sexual perversion could only appeal to people who were extremely immature and ignorant. And there were obviously many individuals like those here in Fantasy Land, otherwise, places like Fantasy Land wouldn't exist. Once that realization came to them, they knew they would be able to carry on with their mission and not allow the tragic ignorance of others to affect them.

The elevator doors opened to the casino's main floor and they started walking around. Allondra told Ogram that she didn't know what the three operatives looked like, but that they knew what he and Allondra looked like and would approach them.

They sat at a bar facing the casino's main gambling hall, ordered drinks and waited. A few minutes later, a man and a woman approached them.

"Good evening friends, what kind of pleasure are you looking for?" the man, a handsome human in his thirties with black hair said, looking at Allondra.

"What about you honey?" the woman, a pretty Asian female wearing practically nothing, asked Ogram.

"We're waiting for friends of ours, so thank you very much but we already have plans," Ogram replied, casually.

The woman leaned close to Ogram and put her arm around his neck and whispered in his ear. "My name is Lana and that's Thomas," she said, looking at her partner. We're from The Brotherhood. "Play along and act like both you and Allondra are hiring us for the evening."

Ogram understood and smiled. "How much for the two of you for the evening?" he asked out loud so that those around him could hear.

"Twenty thousand each, thirty if you want boy on boy and girl on girl," Lana suggested.

"Nah, regular is good, where do we go next?" Ogram inquired.

"We have rooms ready, just follow us," Thomas told them, taking Allondra by the arm and leading the way. The four of them took an elevator and went to one of the top floors in the casino. As soon as they entered the room, Lana put on a pair of green coveralls, wrapped her hair tight and put it under a worker's cap. Thomas did the same and handed Ogram and Allondra identical coveralls and caps for each.

"We're dressed like maintenance workers. We're going to go to the roof and Xelia, our other friend, is picking us up in a helicopter so that we can get out of the city," Thomas explained as he slipped into his outfit.

"Where are we going?" Ogram wanted to know.

"We made contact with a local that thinks he knows where the core was taken to. It's an old abandoned factory about three hundred klicks from the city" Lana told them.

"Are you sure this man is trustworthy?" Ogram inquired.

"Not completely sure, but the locals, who call themselves Ibirans, hate the Body Shop Guild vehemently. Our contact is a man named Chasson, who claims that he was once the leader of this planet. I checked the planet's historic records and I found a Chasson Zamundi, who was indeed the planet's most powerful war lord before the guild came and took over the place. He says that the Guild put him in a new body and then deposed him about sixty years ago."

"He has the backing of the people in his village. They call themselves Wamchas, and they claim that he is indeed, Chasson Zamundi. The Ibirans would like nothing better than to take their planet back from the Guild," Lana added.

"Well then let's go! I can't wait to get out of this horrible city," Allondra stated with urgency.

They took another elevator to the casino's roof and were met there by a large old fashioned helicopter, its blades already spinning.

"Are you sure that thing is safe to fly?" Ogram asked, as he and the others ducked and ran to the old flying contraption. The thing looked ancient and barely fit to fly.

"It's the only way we can get out of the city without having to acquire permits. All the lower waged workers are Ibirans and they are not allowed to travel though the city's streets. This is how most of them commute to work," Thomas shouted, to be heard above the helicopter engine's racket.

Ogram nodded and he and Allondra climbed into the old flying machine hoping for the best.

Thomas closed the doors and introduced the pilot, a blonde woman in her early twenties. "Ogram and Allondra, this is Xelia, my wife. She's the best damned pilot in the galaxy and probably the only person that can fly this antique without getting us all killed in the process," he said with black humor.

"Pleased to meet you. This is my wife Allondra, we place our lives in your hands," he said, laughing nervously.

"Thomas is right, I am the best damned pilot in the Galaxy. Strap your selves in, it's going to be a rough ride!" she shouted, as the engine revved up and the helicopter rose quickly and banked north. Ogram and Allondra held their breath and each other's hand.

Once in the air, the ride was fairly steady as the machine flew over the huge megalopolis that was Kalpanā Bhūmi. Soon the city lights faded and the land turned dark and flat. Most of the planet was primitive and electric lights were few and seldom. Once in a while, a lone building or street lamp could be seen, weakly illuminating a small portion of the land.

An hour later, Xelia brought the helicopter down onto an empty field near a large village. Here there was plenty of electricity. The place reminded Ogram of ancient Terran cities from the 22nd century.

A group of men and women carrying battery powered flashlights approached the helicopter. They were armed to the teeth, wearing gun-powder weapons, swords and knifes. Their leader, a dark-skinned man in his sixties with wisps of grey on his temples, greeted Thomas and Xelia.

"It is good to see you Thomas and Xelia! Who are your friends?" he asked, scanning Ogram and Allondra with a sharp eye.

"This is Ogram and Allondra, whom I was telling you about two days ago," Thomas said, by way of introducing them. "Ogram and Allondra, this is Chasson Zamundi, the leader of his people."

Chasson walked up to Ogram and stood uncomfortably close to him, their noses almost touching. He stared at Ogram with great intensity, as if he was looking for something special in his eyes. Then he smiled and backed away. "You are a holy man!" he declared triumphantly, proud of his perceptive reading of the man.

"Some call me that, yes," Ogram admitted, smiling. "I dare say that you have similar attributes in that area," he commented.

"Hmmm, perhaps one day I will be like you, but I still have many mistakes to remedy before all debts are paid." Chasson replied, indicating that he hadn't always been a good man. Then he looked at Allondra and fixed his gaze on her. "Hah! and this one," he said pointing to her, "she shines like a light in the dark, she does," he added, then bowed to both.

"Thomas says that you know of a place where they are holding our computer core," Ogram mentioned, cutting to the chase. "Time is of the essence, Chasson. Unfortunately, we are in a hurry. A great war is coming to the galaxy that will involve everyone, including your people. Finding and recovering that core will help prevent that war, or at the very least shorten it."

"I believe you. Two weeks ago, strangers came to the old factory a few kilometers from here. A large ship deposited a very large object inside. Ever since then, a shadow has fallen on the land. We've tried to approach the site, but they have an army of mercenaries guarding the place. Let us move to my house. There is food and drink for all of you," he said addressing the newcomers.

Once in his home, he brought Ogram, Allondra, Thomas, Lana and Xelia into his private office, while his wife and daughters prepared the evening meal.

Ogram lowered his voice and pulled Chasson to the side. "Have any of your people been acting strangely or different since the strangers arrived?"

"These strangers, they are warlocks, aren't they?" Chasson asked, fearing that his suspicion that the men at the factory were practitioners of the black arts was right.

Ogram sat Chasson down on his own chair and related the events that had taken place during the last four and a half months. As Ogram explained everything, Chasson's eyes widened and a look of fear and worry took over his face.

"I thought the Guild was bad enough, but these Nadrogs sound like they spawns of Satan!" Chasson exclaimed, getting up from his chair and pacing around his office. "I have noticed two of the villagers acting strangely during the past few days. One of them is a washer woman that cleans people's clothes here in the village, the other is my brother in law," he told Ogram and the others.

Ogram lowered his head and looked chagrined. "I have to tell you Chasson, that if those two and others in your village have been taken over by the Nadrogs, they cannot be saved. Allondra and I have a way of detecting if a person has been infected by Nadrog energy. Is there a way that you can gather all the villagers in one place so that we can scan everybody at once?"

"Are those afflicted dangerous to others?" Chasson asked.

"Chasson, those afflicted are no longer the same people you once knew. When a Nadrog takes over a person's body, they effectively kill that person's soul and spirit. I hope you realize that we must incarcerate them immediately before they alert the others at the abandoned factory," Ogram warned him.

"I shall call for an emergency meeting this night," Chasson replied, as he exited his office to organize his people.

"Chasson!" Ogram called out, before he left his house. "Put your men on the borders of the village to make sure that no one escapes!"

Chasson nodded and ran out.

An hour later Ogram, Allondra and the others were at a large community center where the villagers had been assembled. It didn't take long for Ogram and Allondra to see three persons whose auras were shining indigo blue. Ogram whispered in Chasson's ears to identify each of the 'Nadrog infected' villagers and within seconds, they were being held by his men.

"What is to be done with these three?" Chasson asked Ogram, after the three, Chasson's brother in law, the washer woman and a male villager had been put in the village jail.

"We believe that they can jump into another person's body at will," Ogram commented as they all stood in front of the cells looking at the three prisoners,"

No sooner had he spoken, when the hairs on Ogram and everybody else's head began to stand on end. The jail's lights flickered, and light bulbs began to explode. The three villagers' bodies were beginning to emit blue lightning bolts in every direction, striking walls, metal bars and other objects. The lightning bolts began spreading from the cells, but when they reached into the corridors, they were not able to make contact with Ogram and Allondra's bodies and the bolts of blue fire changed direction and attacked the others.

Somehow, Ogram and Allondra were immune to the Nadrog's energy. "Kill them, kill them now!" Ogram yelled, as he and the others took out their weapons and fired at the three unfortunate villagers.

"Don't let the lightning touch you!" Allondra yelled, amidst the noise of gun blasts, lightning strikes and exploding light bulbs.

Firing and retreating, the group distanced themselves from the three cells while continuing to shoot repeatedly, until the poor souls' bodies were nothing but a bloody mess. The smell of sulphur, like rotting eggs, hung in the air.

Ogram yelled to stop firing and everyone waited tensely, as the smoke cleared. A few short stray bolts of indigo blue fired off from the three corpses and then all was quiet. Ogram blinked his eyes and scanned Allondra and the others exhaled with relief to learn that the Nadrogs had not been able to possess anyone.

Breathing heavily and in a state of panic, Chasson stared at the mangled bodies of the three villagers. "Are we safe, have we killed the demons?" he asked, leaning back against a wall.

"Yes Chasson, I believe we have," Ogram replied quietly, lowering his weapon and holstering it. "Open some windows and let this foul smell leave the building. It might be harmful to breathe," Ogram instructed the others.

Allondra, who had never fired a weapon in anger and had never seen such carnage, walked to a corner and vomited. Ogram, himself quite shaken, went over and comforted her.

Chasson's men entered the cells with rags over their mouths and kicked the corpses, making sure that they were dead. A few minutes later, those same men returned, put the bodies in bags and carried them out. Three women appeared with buckets of water and washed the blood off the cell walls and floors.

"How can we defeat these demons?" Chasson asked, horrified to learn of the Nadrog's abilities.

"I think I have way Chasson, but you and your people must trust me and Allondra."

"We're willing to do whatever's necessary Holy Man. What do you have in mind?"

"I know that you and your people are followers of Hansurak, your old religion but you said that you recognized that I am a holy man, is that right?"

Chasson nodded.

"Allondra and I want to bless your villagers with the energy of our holy man, St. Kelem. I believe that if we give you this blessing, it will protect your people from the Nadrogs ability to invade another person's soul and spirit. Will you allow us to do this?"

"Yes Ogram, I know that you and Allondra are special people. How will this be done?"

"Recall everyone to the community center. We'll give the blessing there," Ogram explained.

An hour later, the entire village had gathered at the community center. Once again, Chasson told his people that Ogram and Allondra were holy messengers and that they were going to help everyone with a special blessing. Ogram ordered everyone to hold hands, and he and Allondra began the process.

They had never given the blessing to so many others at once, and at first, Allondra, still feeling the effects of the carnage at the jail, had a hard time bringing in the sacred energy. But suddenly, the image of Kelem appeared to them, though invisible to the rest. Kelem's beatific smile calmed Allondra's heart and she was able to go into Samadhi.

Soon, the energy flowed from their bodies into the villagers' bodies.

Chasson's eyes filled with tears. For years he had suffered from the guilt of past sins, for having been a violent and cruel leader of his people, and for the thousands of lives he had ended by decree. Now Kelem's blessing was like holy water washing away the sins of his past and imbuing him with heavenly energy, filling him with wave upon wave of love and kindness, such as he'd never felt before.

When the blessing ended, he fell to his knees and prayed to God for the first time in his life.

CHAPTER 46

The Attack on the Old Factory

Ogram, Allondra and Chasson were lying flat on the ground at the top of a hill overlooking a small valley where the old factory was located. A large portion of the roof in one of the largest buildings of the abandoned facility had obviously been re-patched recently. Sure sign that the CUBE's core had been deposited in that building. The place was heavily guarded by several dozen men armed with heavy duty rifles and repeater pulse guns. A few of them were dressed in typical Plantanimus civilian garb, indicating that those individuals were former CUBE employees. Ogram and Allondra scanned them with their ability to see auras and all were glowing with a dark indigo field around their bodies, confirming that they were all possessed by Nadrog entities. Several large military shuttles were parked around the facility, each with large rail cannons. A slight whiff of sulfur hung in the air.

Ogram focused his digital binoculars on the exterior of the factory and spotted the figure of Pieter Minsk, now wearing a militia uniform and sporting a large pulse rifle. The man's face looked blotchy and full of what looked to be, large boils or adult acne. The rest of his body appeared swollen and infected. Ogram instantly realized that Nadrog energy was too powerful for a normal human body and thus the advancing decay of his skin.

"I think I understand why the Nadrogs stole the core and brought it to Kāla Kōṭharī," he said to the others. "They're having the Guild make modified humanoid bodies for them that can withstand their energy. Take a look over there at Pieter Minsk's body. I warn you, he looks terrible," Ogram said handing the binoculars to Allondra.

Allondra looked and gasped when she saw Minsk's appearance. She grimaced and handed the binoculars back to Ogram. "Is that what we smell, even this far away from them?" Allondra asked, revolted by what she'd seen.

"No . . ., see that pile of yellow ore to the right of the factory?" Ogram indicated with his finger.

Allondra and Chasson nodded.

"That's sulfur. My guess is that Nadrog physiology is sulfur based. They're trying to infuse their new humanoid bodies with sulfur, hoping that the modification will help them sustain new bodies for more than a few days. By the way Minsk looks, I'd say the Nadrog inside him has but a day or two before that body dies."

"My people are brave, but they're no match for these monsters," Chasson commented, dissapointed by the strength of their enemy.

Ogram turned to the tribal leader. "Chasson, I'm sure that you've heard of the Gulax, am I right?"

"The snake people?" Chasson replied, then nodded, looking not too happy.

"There's a ship about a million kilometers from this planet with one hundred Gulax ready to come down and help us fight these monsters. I know that you've probably heard some awful things about them, but I guarantee you that these Gulax are followers of St. Kelem and have received his blessing from me and Allondra, and we vouch for them. Will you allow me to bring them here to help with the fight?"

"If I hadn't received the blessing from you two, I would probably have said no, but St. Kelem's holy gift is like nothing I've ever experienced. Judging by that, I'm willing to risk fighting alongside Gulax and I'm sure I can convince my people to do it as well."

"Thank you, Chasson, you won't be sorry. One more thing," he added, "when the Gulax break through the planet's defenses, we're going to be facing two enemies, the Nadrogs on one side and the planet's militia on the other. I hope you realize that," he warned Chasson.

"We've been waiting ninety six years to fight the Guild. My people won't back down. I've sent messengers to warn other tribes near us and I'm sure that they'll decide to join us in fighting these monsters and the Guild," Chasson assured Ogram.

Ogram touched his temple.

Zurk's voice answered. "Pavitraam is that you? Are you alright?" the Gulax exclaimed, displaying unusual emotion for one of his kind.

"Yes Zurk, we're fine. Lock onto my location for landing coordinates. We've found the core at an abandoned factory three hundred kilometers from the city, but it's heavily guarded. Wait for my signal before you and Rek's guards come down. Tell everyone to bring as much ammo and weapons as they can carry. And Zurk . . ., this one's going to be a bloody one."

"We're already dead Ogram, our lives are forfeit," the old Gulax replied.

"Yes, but I'd prefer that you all die of old age, forfeit or not," Ogram replied laughing. "One more thing, these monsters expel electrical bolts from their bodies. I believe that's how they take over the bodies of others, but it seems that St. Kelem's blessing makes us all immune to the effect. However, those electrical bolts appear to be high voltage, so tell everyone to stay clear of the effect," Ogram warned the old Gulax.

"Will do Pavitraam, meanwhile, you and Allondra take care of yourselves."

"We will. Wait for my signal," Ogram said, and then he touched his temple to end the communication.

A Large shuttle appeared in the horizon heading toward the factory. Ogram, Allondra and Chasson, retreated under some trees and waited to see what followed. The ship landed next to the building containing the core. Several men came out and began unloading large pieces of equipment. Many of the men's faces showed signs of decay, just like Pieter Minsk's.

"Growth chambers!" Ogram said under his breath. "This means that they're just now, beginning to build their new bodies. We have to attack soon, before their numbers increase!"

"My people are ready, Ogram. When do you want to hit them?" Chasson asked.

"Tonight, around three am, let's go back to the village to prepare."

Later that night around midnight, Ogram spoke to the villagers in the community center.

"Thank you for helping us eradicate these evil beings and recover the core. You all come from a proud warrior tradition, but I'd like to avoid casualties as much as possible. Remember that we need to make sure that the core is unharmed, but not at the cost of lives. The 'Snake People' will land on the opposite side of the valley while we come at the Nadrogs from the front. Shoot first and avoid being struck by electrical discharges. Good luck, and may St. Kelem be at your side!"

The crowd roared and brandished their weapons high in the air. Ogram knew the Wamchas had once been a proud warrior race feared for their violent and cruel nature, but they hadn't fought a battle in over ninety years and the Nadrogs were a terrible species eviler and nastier than anything the Ibirans had ever faced. He prayed that the immunity to the Nadrogs' energy would hold for everyone.

At 01:30 AM, the three hundred villagers stealthily made their way to the valley and took positions on the hill above the factory. Ogram called Zurk and coordinated the attack to begin at 03:00 am. The Gulax would come down hard and fast and disable as many of the military shuttles during the initial approach, this way taking away the advantage of the ships' rail cannons which could inflict serious damage to the villagers and the Gulax.

At 02:45 am, Ogram gave the order to descend to the valley floor. Thankfully, the sky was overcast and the planet's moonlight was very dull, making their approach safer. Once in position, Ogram, Allondra and Chasson, waited for the Gulax's attack.

Soon, the tell-tale exhaust of Gulax engines appeared in the horizon and Ogram gave the order to attack. The Gulax shuttles fired several missiles at the military ships on the ground, destroying most of them immediately, while at the same time, Chasson's people opened fire and rushed the perimeter of the old factory.

Several Nadrog guards reacted swiftly and opened fire on the villagers killing a few, but the Ibirans proud fighting tradition took over and they continued advancing, seemingly unaffected by the deaths of their comrades.

One of the Nadrog military shuttles came to life and turned its rail cannon toward the villagers.

"Chasson! Tell everyone to take cover, that shuttle is about to fire!" Ogram yelled, pointing to the ship, beginning to lift from the ground. But the warning came too late. The rail gun fired and took out several villagers with one blast.

From the factory, several pulse rifles opened fire and more villagers fell. The shuttle, now up in the air began firing at targets of opportunity and started decimating the villager's attack with powerful rail cannon blasts.

Ogram and Allondra hit the ground and took cover from the blithering fire coming at them from all directions. He landed on top of her trying to keep her safe, but she yelled at him.

"Cover your own ass husband! I can take care of myself!" she yelled at him angrily, as pulse blasts raised dirt and dust all around them. Ogram was both upset and proud at the same time, seeing how cool his wife was under the circumstances.

The big Nadrog shuttle was now almost above Ogram and Allondra and its cannon was aimed directly at their position. Ogram knew that there was no point in running and he put his arm around Allondra's shoulder and waited for death.

A loud explosion went off above them and when Ogram looked up, he saw that a Gulax shuttle had rammed the Nadrog ship and both vessels crashed to the ground about fifty meters from their position. The crash caused an even larger explosion, sending chunks of Nadrog and Gulax' ship parts up in the air, landing all around Ogram and Allondra. The villagers, seeing this, rallied and continued their attack, now that the Nadrogs had lost their air cover.

Several Gulax had sacrificed their lives to save their Pavitraam.

Chasson ran up to Ogram and Allondra. "Their frontal defense has collapsed!" he announced, pointing to the burning wreck of the two ships near them.

"Right! let's keep going forward," Ogram agreed.

The Gulax had by now landed on the back side of the valley and the familiar sound of Gulax weapons could be heard above the din and noise of the battle.

"Are those Gulax guns I hear?" Allondra asked, with a smile on her dirty face.

"Yes wife, let's keep moving forward, and remember not to get too close to any Nadrogs!" he warned, as the two of them stood up and charged the factory, followed by Chasson and the villagers.

The Nadrogs who had been firing at the villagers, were now retreating as the Ibirans ran over their defenses. Dead and dying Nadrogs lying on the ground began emitting deadly indigo blue lightning bolts in all directions. A few villagers were struck and Ogram and Allondra paused and waited to see if those touched by the electrical discharges would turn against their own. But fortunately, Kelem's blessing was protecting them.

From the left and right of their flank, several Gulax appeared, dressed in full battle armor. When the villagers saw them, they instinctively raised their weapons and aimed them at them. Most had never seen a Gulax and in their confusion, they believed that these were the feared Nadrogs that Ogram and Allondra had been warning them about.

Without thinking about his safety, Ogram ran in front of the villagers with his arms raised high.

"No, no! these are our friends, do not fire, do not fire!" he yelled at the top of his lungs.

Chasson joined Ogram yelling at his own people. 'Put your weapons down!" he yelled, and the Ibirans obeyed.

The Gulax, about fifty of them led by Rek, approached them. Rek stopped in front of them and was horrified to see Ogram and Allondra wearing nothing but plain clothes. "Pavitraam! Where is your and your wife's battle armor?" he asked, looking as concerned as a Gulax could.

"No time for that Rek, we must eliminate these demons as soon as possible. They have body growth chambers inside. We must stop them before they begin replicating in great numbers," Ogram urged pointing at the structure.

"I will take my armor off and you can use it to protect your saintly bodies Pavitraam! No harm must come to you and Allondra!"

The Ibirans who were intimidated by the alien appearance of the Gulax, looked upon the scene with shock and surprise. They had always heard that the 'snake people' were cannibals who ate their enemies. But here these Gulax were, acting very concerned for Ogram and Allondra's safety, whom the villagers had come to regard as saints.

A woman from the village walked up to Rek and stared at him with great interest for a few seconds. "You would give your armor to Ogram and Allondra and risk death?" she asked, putting her hands on her hips.

Rek, turned around slowly and stared at the woman with his yellow reptilian eyes. "Yes, they are both Pavitraam. My life is already forfeit for their protection."

"What does Pavitraam mean?" she asked, looking at Rek and his Gulax.

"It means holy man or woman in human speech." he answered.

"Well then, Gulax, we're both on the same side of things. My life and those of everyone here, is also forfeit for their protection,' she replied, looking defiant and proud.

"Well then woman, my guards and I would be proud to fight and die along with you," he responded, putting on the closest thing to a smile that a Gulax could muster.

"We must enter the building now Rek!" Ogram announced, feeling that time was slipping by.

"But Pavitraam, you must let me give you my armor!" Rek protested.

"No time Rek! We have to go in now. I tell you what, you and two or three others can cover me and Allondra when we are inside," Ogram insisted.

"Me and my friends here," the village woman said, interrupting their argument, "will also cover Ogram and Allondra. Your Pavitraam is right Gulax, we have to hurry inside before these demons increase their numbers!"

Rek nodded reluctantly and the group organized itself. A few seconds later, Humans and Gulax charged the entrance to the building together.

CHAPTER 47

Termination

Imurdum, now burning with fever in Pieter Minsk's dying body, burst into the inner core's shielded chamber.

"Vitrami, we're under attack!" he wheezed, trying to get more oxygen into his fluid filled, infected lungs.

"Repel the humans instead of wasting my time! Can't you see we're making bodies as fast as possible?" yelled Vitrami, inside Sumpter Blarok's body.

"My lord, they've combined their forces with a species called Gulax. They are fearsome indeed!"

Vitrami turned around and slapped Imurdum, who fell backwards, his nose bleeding from the impact. "Do not bother me with trifles Imurdum! Defeat the attackers or we'll all die without the new bodies!" he yelled at his subordinate. "The consciousnesses of all our comrades will fade soon inside the core if we're not able to transfer them to new bodies."

"But Vitrami there are thousands of us in the core and little time to transfer them all!" Imurdum complained.

"Hold back the attackers or I'll kill you with my bare hands!" Vitrami threatened, looking and sounding much like Sumpter Blarok, the owner of the body he now inhabited.

Imurdum wiped his nose and obeyed his master. He ran back to the battle raging just outside the building. He grabbed several dozen

Nadrogs and positioned them strategically near the entrance to the building, knowing that any minute the door would be breached.

Vitrami turned to Urukum, the other Nadrog who had first arrived at the CUBE's core with Imurdum. "Is the device ready?" he asked the sickly looking man, formerly known as Brian Shonderman.

Urukum nodded as he attached an explosive device to the core. Vitrami would detonate the bomb if it looked like they were going to be overrun by the Human and Gulax forces. If they were defeated they would destroy the consciousnesses of all The Realm's clients with them.

"Damn these useless human bodies!" Vitrami yelled with frustration, "so weak and prone to disease! Not like our old bodies which could withstand anything!" He turned to a Nadrog technician who was operating a growth chamber near him. "How soon can you transfer me?" he asked anxiously, looking at a replica of Sumpter Blarok's body, now nearly complete inside the plastic bubble of the chamber.

"It will be ready in a few minutes my lord,' the technician answered, fearing for his life. Vitrami was known to kill anyone near him when he was unhappy.

"Vitrami took out his side arm and aimed it at the technician's head. "Make it soon or you're dead!" he threatened, as Blarok's forehead dripped sweat and his hands shook from the fever raging through his body.

An explosion shook the building, and dust and debris blew into the core's inner chamber.

"Put me in now!" Vitrami demanded.

The technician obeyed and placed a crown-like metallic device on his master's head as he lay next to the growth chamber. The new body was infused with sulfur and should theoretically be better suited to Nadrog energy. The man pressed the button and the procedure started. Sumpter Blarok's original body shook slightly while at the same time, the duplicate body opened its eyes and screamed in pain. The pain only lasted a few seconds and soon, the duplicate body sat up, tore all the nano leads from his skin and unceremoniously stripped the old body of its clothes and put them on. Then he tossed the old body against the wall, like so much garbage.

"Dispose of that piece of trash! This body's much, much better, I can feel it already!" Vitrami shouted, smiling and stretching his arms, feeling the power of the sulfur infusion. His eyes were now black with red pupils. Looking like a demonic, plastic replica of a human, he pointed his finger at a chair and a powerful indigo blue lightning bolt issued from his hand, breaking the chair into smoldering pieces. He smiled and turned to leave, knowing that he was now invincible! "Begin transferring the others, these bodies are much superior to the original design," Vitrami declared, as he left the core's inner chamber.

Ogram and Allondra rushed into the building, surrounded by Gulax and some of the villagers. They entered the hole that used to be its main door and took positions inside. Pulse gun streams were flying everywhere, hitting Gulax armor and a few unfortunate Ibirans who fell dead as they charged in. Both Ogram and Allondra took cover behind a large crate and started firing blindly into the interior of the building where the gun fire was coming from.

More Gulax were now entering the building, laying cover fire as they took positions behind walls and crates. The smoke from the explosive that had blasted the building's door open, began to clear and soon, lighting bolts emitted by the dying bodies of Nadrogs could be seen in the haze.

Ogram took a chance and raised his head above the crate that he and Allondra were taking cover behind and saw the tall cylindrical shape of the CUBE's core sitting in the middle of the large building. Rek dashed over to where he was.

"Is that the core, Pavitraam?' he asked, breathing hard.

"Yes. We must get to it as soon as possible. Give me and Allondra as much cover fire as possible and we'll make our way there. I have to make sure the core hasn't been harmed," Ogram explained.

"I will go with you Pavitraam. I'm not letting you out of my site!" the Gulax told him, as he signaled some of his guards to come to him. He addressed one of them. "Tell Zok and Tuma to start laying cover fire, you and the others will go with Ogram and Allondra and try to reach the core. The Gulax left and a few seconds later, a loud stream of pulse blasts lit up the darkened building.

Ogram, Allondra, Rek and his Gulax sneaked further into the building's interior and went into a long corridor where the ceiling fixtures were blinking on and off. With weapons aimed forward, they moved in the direction of the core. Three Nadrogs came out of a door and fired at the group. The Gulax responded with deadly accuracy and all three fell dead. Immediately their bodies began throwing lightning bolts and Ogram, Allondra and the Gulax, ran past the three dying Nadrogs and avoided being touched by the blue indigo fire.

A few steps further, all hell broke loose. Several Nadrogs appeared behind them and fired, killing all of Rek's guards instantly. Ogram, Allondra and Rek managed to dive into an open door and took defensive positions. The Nadrogs approached and threw a grenade into the room. Rek threw himself over Ogram and Allondra's body just before the grenade exploded. The Gulax took the brunt of the explosion and even though his body armor helped, he had been hit.

Rek's body slumped and both Ogram and Allondra had to push him off them to fire at the Nadrogs who were now rushing in. Ogram and Allondra fired simultaneously and two fell dead instantly, their brains splattered all over the wall, but three others, coming right behind them, jumped in shooting their guns.

Allondra was hit in the leg and she fell on the floor screaming in agony. Ogram fired at the one who shot her and the Nadrog was dead before he hit the floor, but the other two jumped on top of him and attacked with knifes. Without thinking, Ogram reacted automatically, following Zurk's excellent combat training. He drove one of the Nadrog's nose into his brain with his fist, although it meant that he had to take a knife in the shoulder. The other one slashed at his left hand and the knife cut deep, but it gave Ogram time to pick up the other Nadrog's knife and drive it straight into the man's throat. The Nadrog made a gurgling sound, clutching his throat and fell to the side, lightning bolts flying everywhere.

Allondra, having recovered from the shock of being shot, grabbed Ogram by his shirt and dragged him away from the Nadrog's electrical bolts, far enough to avoid being electrocuted.

"Thank you, wife,!" Ogram said breathing hard, grateful for being saved from electrocution. He looked at her leg and was horrified to see a large hole, where blood was pouring out. He took out an ammo belt from his waist and made a tourniquet to stop the bleeding. She screamed in agony, but thanked him, knowing that the pain would save her life.

Sitting against a wall, bleeding and exhausted, Ogram and Allondra wondered how much longer it would be before the next wave of Nadrogs rushed in and finished them both. Rek suddenly stirred and moaned. He sat upright, shook his head and looked at the two of them, trying to get his bearings, then he noticed all the dead Nadrogs piled on top of each other.

"You two did this?" he asked, pointing to the bodies.

Ogram and Allondra nodded.

"Well, I guess Zurk's training paid off! But we have to get out of here. You two are in no condition to continue," he said, seeing their injuries. He stood up and lifted them to their feet.

Just then, Chasson and two of his warriors burst into the room, guns pointed. When they saw Ogram, Allondra and the Gulax they relaxed. "Thank god you're still alive! We heard the fire fight and the explosion and thought you'd all be dead!" he exclaimed, looking at the dead Nadrogs.

"We have to take Ogram and Allondra out of here. They're in no condition to fight" the Gulax insisted.

"Hold on Rek!" Ogram stopped him. "We have to save the core! You can take Allondra, I'm fine. Just a couple of flesh wounds, no internal organs pierced," he added, pointing to his stab wounds.

"I'm sorry husband! But if you're staying, so am I!" Allondra interjected forcefully. "With this tourniquet I can walk and hold a weapon. Rek you'll help me won't you?" she asked the Gulax.

The Gulax looked uncomfortable and turned to Ogram.

"She has to come Rek. Face it, you can't argue with a female holding a gun!"

"By god woman! You're as brave as an Ibiran female!" Chasson said admiringly.

"Let's go, we have to get to the core," Ogram commanded and led the group out of the room.

They continued until the end of the corridor where there was a double door. Ogram estimated that the core was near, possibly on the other side of the wall. He parted the doors a few centimeters and several pulse guns struck the door frame next to his head. Rek grabbed him and pulled him down on the floor as he and Chasson fired back. One of Chasson's men had a grenade that he had taken from a dead Nadrog and tossed it to him. Chasson signaled for Rek to open the door a little wider and then tossed the grenade in to the other room. The explosion went off, followed by the sound of lightning bolts going off and hitting objects.

The smoke cleared and Rek stuck his head close to the floor and saw that four Nadrogs were dead. He came out, low on his knees and reconnoitered the room and found that the area was clear. He went back, picked up Allondra and followed Ogram and the others into one of the outer chambers of the core.

Several body growth chambers were in mid-operation with near completed bodies still inside their plastic bubbles. Rek, Chasson and the others fired at the machines destroying them. Further on there were dead Nadrog bodies everywhere. Most looked like plague victims, their skin showing open sores and boils filled with pus. The smell here was horrible and all except the Gulax, gagged.

A large man appeared on a doorway, framed by the light of the inner core's chamber.

"I am Vitrami, you inferior primitives! You think that you can kill me? The leader of the Nadrogs?" he yelled with a voice that chilled their bones. Even Rek's reptilian brain, recognized that this being was different than all the other Nadrogs.

Ogram stepped forward and stared the man down whose skin had a sickly-yellow tint. "Huh! You must be their leader. You really stink of sulphur," he commented smiling, trying to insult the Nadrog and show him that he wasn't intimidated by him.

Vitrami looked at Ogram and saw that his aura was quite bright, different from all the other humans that he'd come in contact with.

"You're different from the others. I will enjoy destroying you first!" he said with a sinister smile.

"All your people are dead Vitrami, leader of the Nadrogs! We've destroyed all the growth chambers. You're the last one left and I don't think that you'll be able to possess anyone else, you evil son of a bitch!"

"Probably not, but I'll take you and all your friends with me," Vitrami added, his voice filled with rage. He moved aside and let the others see the bomb attached to the core's central column. The timer was already counting down, reading less than a minute before the device exploded.

Inside, a young, dark haired woman who was tied to a chair yelled at the group. "Kill him! He's a demon worse than the original Blarok!" the woman screamed with desperation. He's got a bomb attached to the core. Kill him, kill him!"

"Shut up Maria! You pitiful human bitch!" Vitrami said with disdain.

"Pavitraam! Let this monster end his existence and return to hell. He knows that he's been defeated," Rek said, pulling on Ogram's arm.

Vitrami raised his hand and shot a bolt of electricity at Rek, who fell to the floor paralyzed.

Ogram and the others jumped back, shocked by the Nadrog's unexpected ability to shoot lightning bolts at will while still remaining in his body.

Vitrami reared his head and laughed demonically, his large body, suddenly glowing with cold indigo blue fire. He raised his arms and hit Ogram, Allondra and Chasson with blue lightning bolts emanating from his hands. Ogram felt the shock of thousands of volts coursing through his body and smelled his clothes and hair beginning to singe from the heat. He looked at Allondra and saw that she was enveloped in a cocoon of lightning bolts just like him, struggling in agony.

The voltage had paralyzed him, but somehow, something was protecting him and Allondra. Both were in extreme agony, but it was obvious that Vitrami was surprised to see that they were still holding on.

Ogram now could see the figure of the dreaded black monster with its tentacles spread out, issuing from behind Vitrami's human form, just like he'd seen the first time Angel Darius' double had attacked him in the Plantanimus CUBE. He was terrified, and in desperation, he called on Kelem and Alpha's spiritual strength to come to his and Allondra's aid. He closed his eyes and fought hard to bring in the sacred energy that he'd learned from them. The electrical voltage made it near impossible for him to reach Samadhi, but suddenly, he saw Kelem's figure, faintly at first and then more and more clear, as he stood between him and the evil Vitrami. Kelem's image became less ethereal and more solid and soon, the voltage began to subside.

Ogram and Allondra felt the beautiful warm feeling of love and tranquility begin to spread from their chests into their arms and hands. Once this happened, the electrical discharge began to sputter and weaken.

Vitrami was startled to see Kelem's figure in front of him, confused by the manifested image standing in front of him. He grimaced and his expression turned angrier, but soon, his eyes and ears began to bleed.

Chasson, still enveloped in blue lightning, made a super human effort and crawled past Vitrami then made his way to the bomb strapped to the Core's central column. He grabbed the device and ripped it away then pulled the wires from it and threw it away. The timer froze at 00:03 seconds.

The Nadrog, his eyes now filled with angry blue indigo fire, screamed with rage and sent more lightning bolts to Chasson, whose body began to burn.

Ogram and Allondra took deep breaths and centered themselves, knowing that anger and hatred would prevent them from defeating the monster. Kelem's blessing, now feeling like healing white heavenly fire, repelled the Nadrog's attack lightning bolts and both were released from the monster's paralyzing voltage.

With their bodies now emitting blinding white light, they walked up to Vitrami and when they touched him, the Nadrog burst into white hot flames and screamed in agony as his monstrous form was consumed by the positive energy radiating from their bodies.

Rek, who had witnessed the amazing event, rose from the floor and stumbled over to Chasson, who lay shaking with pain. His skin had turned black with third degree burns. "That is one of the bravest things I've ever seen a human being do!' he whispered, expressing grief and sadness, which is rare amongst Gulax.

Ogram ran to the female tied to the chair inside the core's chamber and began to untie her.

"There's no time you fool! Leave me behind, I don't want to live anyway!" she pleaded with a look of sadness in her eyes.

Ogram refused to leave her behind and untied her anyway.

"We must leave immediately!" Ogram warned everyone, remembering that the dead Nadrog's bodies in the Plantanimus CUBE's facility had released Hydrogen Sulfide, killing anyone that was not wearing protective gear. "This place will be filled with deadly Hydrogen Sulphide gas soon. C'mon!" he urged the others.

Rek and Allondra, picked up Chasson's body and began leaving the inner core.

Maria Santana pulled Ogram's hand away from her arm. "No, I'm staying behind. This is all my fault. If Longsdale and I hadn't betrayed The Realm, the Church and our principles, none of this would have taken place," she declared calmly, as she walked back into the core.

Ogram's eyes opened wide realizing who this woman really was. He stopped and looked at her. "Don't you want to live?" he asked, reaching for her hand.

"I've been dead for some time now Mr. Zepol," she said emotionless, and disappeared through a door.

Ogram turned, and ran as fast as his legs allowed. Once outside, Ogram and Rek ordered the building evacuated and soon everyone was out. Those that were still alive, or could be carried, went to the edge of the valley to be far away from the building.

Thomas, Lana and Xelia met them on top of the mountain. They had survived the battle as well.

Everyone was exhausted and or injured. Some of Rek's Gulax tended to Ogram and Allondra's injuries and anyone else that needed medical care. The villagers had lost eighty people from the original three hundred, but Rek's guards had suffered more than ninety percent casualties. Their forfeited lives had indeed protected Ogram and Allondra, as they had sworn. Soon, Zurk and his sons showed up, minus one, his oldest, Grak, had been killed by a Nadrog's gun.

"I'm so sorry to hear that Grak didn't make it, Zurk. I was hoping that everyone would make it," Ogram said with sorrow.

The Gulax and his sons laughed, hissing loudly. "Ogram, haven't you learned yet that for a Gulax, to die in battle is a blessing?"

Ogram shook his head and put on a weak smile. He knew that deep inside, Zurk and his sons were grieving.

Ogram turned to Chasson Zamundi who was being tended to by Allondra and two Gulax.

"How is he?" he asked, looking at the man whose skin was burned to the bone in some places.

Allondra turned to answer, but Chasson grabbed her arm and looked at her and Ogram, his eyes wide with pain, knowing that he was at death's door.

"I will soon meet the almighty spirit Ogram," he whispered. "But do not fret, for I have washed the stain of sin from my soul. I'm glad that I died defending my people and Ibira. Thank you for Kelem's blessing . . .," he uttered and then he closed his eyes and was gone.

Ogram sat on the ground and hung his head. After the rush of adrenaline in battle and with so many dead and the future still uncertain for Allondra, the Matriarch, Cardinal Richelieu and himself, he suddenly felt like the weight of the world rested on his shoulders.

Allondra went over to him and hugged him tenderly as both their eyes filled with tears. Ogram, exhausted, lay on the grass next to Allondra, staring at the sky which was beginning to turn light with the coming dawn. All he wanted to do now was to close his eyes and sleep for a very long time, but he knew that there was more struggle and sacrifice ahead. The sound of several approaching shuttles snapped him out of his brooding state.

"Damn!" he cursed, sitting up and realizing that the planet's militia was about to arrive and attack.

Rek, Zurk and the rest of the Gulax grabbed their weapons and rose to their feet.

Chasson's wife, now his widow, walked up to Ogram and Allondra. "Thank you, Holy ones. Thank you for helping us fight the demons and for giving my husband an honorable death."

"I'm not sure you should thank us," Ogram replied, looking at the approaching militia force.

"Word got around that a holy man gave us a way to defeat the Guild. The entire planet has risen in revolt and many Ibirans are fighting the Guild in many cities and villages across the planet as we speak. No matter what happens to us," she said, pointing to the surviving villagers, "the Body Shop Guild's days on Ibira are over."

"That's all well and good Mrs. Zamundi, but it looks like we have another battle in our hands,"

"Do not fear for us holy man! You've awakened our warrior spirit. We're willing to die defending our planet," she replied gallantly, and then walked away.

"What will you have us do, Pavitraam?" Rek asked bravely, even though he was showing signs of complete exhaustion.

Ogram took a deep breath. He knew that they wouldn't be able to fight the large force that was about to land.

He raised his head to answer the Gulax and was surprised to see the lead militia shuttle hit by a missile and burst into flames. He looked up higher in the sky and saw a huge circular ship, firing at the approaching militia formation.

"What the hell?" he uttered, feeling both relieved and at the same time confused. He'd never seen a ship like this one before.

Then he remembered something from his days studying Kelem Rogeston's history.

The Kren had come to their rescue!

CHAPTER 48

The Kren Arrive

"Who are they?" Rek asked, looking up into the early dawn as Guild militia ships began falling from the sky.

"I believe that big sphere floating above us is a Kren Ship,' Ogram replied smiling.

"Pavitraam, you are glad those devils are here?" Rek asked, unable to believe that Ogram's reaction was positive. All his life, Rek and every Gulax that had served the Church of St. Kelem for the last five thousand years had been taught from early childhood that the Kren were the worst of Satan's dark angels.

"Listen Rek, believe me when I tell you that everything that you've been taught regarding the Kren has been wrong. The Church has hidden the real truth of the Crusades of the fourth millennium from all of us. You must trust me when I tell you that Allondra and I have received the gospel directly from St. Kelem. He will tell you himself that the Kren are a dear people to him. Part of the reason why he wants everyone to receive the blessing from him, is to repair the damage that that lie has caused the Kren for millennia," Ogram said to the Gulax, with great intensity.

Rek stood listening to Ogram with his eyes fixed on the ground. He was struggling with his belief system. Hearing Ogram telling him that the Kren were not the evilest of demons in the universe was akin to a

Christian being told that Judas had not betrayed Jesus in the garden of Gethsemane, or that Satan was one of God's favorite angels.

The militia ships had all been destroyed and were now smoldering wrecks burning on the mountains surrounding the valley. A metallic egg shaped vessel separated from the large spherical ship and headed directly to where Ogram and the others were. The villagers decided to leave, now that the threat had vanished, leaving Rek, his guards, Ogram, Allondra and the three Brotherhood members, alone at the top of the mountain.

Thomas and Xelia walked over to where Ogram and Rek were talking. Ogram asked them about the Kren.

"Yes Ogram, we're the ones that called the Kren."

"Why didn't you say something up front?" Ogram complained, feeling a little upset for being kept in the dark.

Thomas shrugged, self-consciously. "Knowing of the enmity between the Kelemites and the Kren, we didn't want to burden you with their possible involvement until it was absolutely necessary to bring them in. When we saw the militia ships approaching, we signaled the Kren, who have been in orbit near Kāla Kōṭharī since yesterday," Thomas explained, apologetically.

"Well Rek, it seems that they're coming for me and the others. You have to make up your mind whether you trust that I'm telling you the truth, or we go our separate ways," Ogram pressed the Gulax, who was feeling extremely conflicted.

"I have to return the core to the Plantanimus CUBE, and then try to free your Pavitraam, who has been unjustly accused of a crime he didn't commit. I need your help to accomplish both tasks, but I'm willing to do it with whatever resources I have access to. The Kren will certainly do anything in their power to help any cause that St. Kelem asks them to take up as their own. That's how much they trust him and respect his legacy. Will you do the same?" Ogram asked, trying to drive the point home.

Rek's body shook with frustration. He had forfeited his life for Ogram and Allondra, but distrusting the Kren was so ingrained in his culture that the conflict expressed itself in a sort of Gulax nervous breakdown. His blood pressure dropped and he almost fainted. Ogram grabbed him before he hit the ground as other Gulax guards came to see what was happening to their leader.

"I cannot go with you Pavitraam," Rek said weakly, as he sat on the ground, surrounded by his Gulax.

"I understand. You must promise that you and your guards will not fire on the Kren when they land. Will you promise me that?" Ogram asked with vehemence. The last thing he needed now was a fire fight between the Gulax and the Kren.

Rek sat up with his head hung down in shame and agreed by nodding.

The Kren shuttle approached their area and slowly, almost silently, touched down a few meters from the group. The Gulax stood together, looking tense and nervous. The ship's hatch opened and two Kren stepped off the egg shaped craft and approached Ogram and the other humans.

For Ogram and Allondra, who had never seen a Kren, their appearance triggered the typical humanoid dislike and fear of insects. Both centered themselves, knowing that their fear was irrational, and knowing quite well, that Kelem Rogeston had met these creatures more than eight thousand years before and considered them friends.

"I'm Butrik and this is Nikko. We're drones from Queen Harriet's hive. Kelem Rogeston and the Brotherhood of the Light asked our mother to assist you Ogram and Allondra. I hope that we haven't arrived too late," the Kren said, bowing politely and speaking in perfect standard Galactic.

"You certainly came at the perfect time, Butrik and Nikko," Ogram replied, unable to stop staring at the two Kren's physiques. Their iridescent eyes and their mandibles, which kept constantly moving, were quite unnerving, yet fascinating at the same time.

"We understand that Cardinal Richelieux has been incarcerated. We are willing to do anything in our power to help free a friend of Kelem Rogeston. How can we help?" the Kren asked, looking at the group of humans.

"Well," Ogram said, scratching his head. "First, we need to retract a very large quantum computer core from that building over there," he explained, pointing to the building on the valley floor. "Unfortunately, there is a toxic substance harmful to humans that will require us to wear protective breathing gear," Ogram explained.

What substance are you referring to?" Butrik inquired, his mandibles constantly moving.

"Hydrogen Sulfide. It's very poisonous to humans."

"Hmmm, Kren are fairly immune to Hydrogen Sulphide. We can enter the building and extract the core for you," the Kren announced, nonchalant.

"Excellent! Can your spherical vessel lift and carry the core back to Plantanimus?" Ogram asked, looking up at the gigantic space ship hovering high in the sky."

"Yes, our mother is agreeable to that task. Are you ready to leave this planet? We can put you on Plantanimus in a day or so, and in New Jerusalem a few hours after we deliver the core," the Kren advised him.

Ogram was about to agree when Rek and Zurk approached them.

"Pavitraam," Rek said softly, almost out of hearing range.

Ogram turned around and was surprised to see the two Gulax, so close to the Kren. "Yes?" he asked, wondering what they wanted.

"We heard your conversation with the Kren," Rek confessed sheepishly, "Gulax ears are very sharp and we couldn't help but eavesdrop. Please forgive my doubting your words, Pavitraam! It's obvious to both of us that the Kren are friends of St. Kelem's. We shouldn't have doubted you. We are willing to come with you and the Kren," Rek said apologetically.

Ogram smiled and reached for the Gulax's hand. "You are truly one of St. Kelem's faithful servants my friend. Come, let us return the core and then fix a travesty that has been commited against a jewel of the Church of St. Kelem by those who are supposed to be the shepherds of that same church."

"Butrik and Nikko, can your mothership accommodate a Gulax cruiser?"

"Will the Gulax also be coming along?" the Kren asked politely with a hint of concern in its voice.

"Yes, I hope that their presence won't cause a problem for your queen and the hive," Ogram expressed, hoping that the Kren would agree.

The two Kren turned to each other and spoke to each other in their language of buzzes and clicks for a few seconds. "Not at all Ogram. We welcome their presence on our mother ship. It will be an opportunity to correct a long held misconception regarding our species."

"Wonderful! We're ready to go. How many can you fit in that shuttle that you came down in?"

"Only four persons, but a larger vessel is already about to land, look," the Kren said, pointing with one of its four arms to the sky, now showing the first rays of sun on the horizon.

A larger Kren ship arched around the mountain and landed close to the first Kren shuttle.

The humans and the Gulax boarded the shuttles and were taken to the large spherical ship hovering above the valley. Once inside, Butrik walked up to Rek, Zurk and the twenty surviving Gulax and bowed to them.

"You are welcome on our ship and are invited to stay for as long as you wish. You may even retain your weapons. You are among friends here. The Kren do not wish you any harm, now or at any other time in the past. I know your beliefs tell you otherwise, but we hope that by staying with us you'll learn that we both love and respect Kelem Rogeston, or as you call him, St. Kelem," the Kren stated, then he turned to Ogram.

"If you will all follow me to our control room, you can supervise the extraction of your computer core there. Afterwards, I'll take you to your quarters which are being built as we speak."

Impressed, Ogram, Allondra limping from their injuries and with the help of others, followed Butrik to a large elevator that carried them to the ship's control room. A large holographic screen showed the old factory as seem from above, then, a large crane extended from the vessel and gently lifted the computer core into the bowels of the ship.

Several Kren could be seen on the ground wearing nothing but their crew uniforms. Any humanoid without an environmental suit that would have perished from Hydrogen Sulfide poisoning long before the retraction of the core.

A few minutes later, the ship began to move and Butrik addressed his guests. "We are on our way to our mother ship. We should dock with it in a few minutes. Once there, I will escort you to your quarters. For the Gulax, we have raised the ambient temperature to thirty nine degrees centigrade," Butrik explained as he led everyone to the elevator once again.

"Excuse me Butrik, you said that we were docking with your mother ship. Isn't this your mother ship?" Ogram asked, confused.

"I'm sorry Ogram, I should have been clearer. This is one of our smaller vessels and it cannot accommodate a Gulax cruiser. Once we dock with our mother ship, we'll go retrieve the Gulax's ship and then travel to Plantanimus as per your request."

Ogram looked at Allondra and shook his head in amazement. The ship they were in now was enormous. He couldn't wait to see how big the Kren mother ship would turn out to be.

CHAPTER 49

Queen Harriett II (The Second)

The Kren mother ship turned out to be nearly as large as the Heavenly Temple. As the ship that had brought them here from Kāla Kōṭharī approached the huge spherical vessel, Ogram and the others could not believe that such a huge structure could be capable of faster than light travel. Once the vessel docked inside the mother ship, the gargantuan ship picked up speed, heading to where the Trinity was located. An hour later, the Gulax cruiser was docked in one of the Kren Mother ship's giant hangars.

Butrik accompanied Ogram, Allondra and the Brotherhood members to their quarters, while Nikko escorted the Gulax to their quarters on another deck.

Once in their private cabin, two Kren medical technicians came to work on their injuries. At first both Ogram and Allondra had to work hard to resist their human dislike for the insectoids' physical touch, but once the two technicians began working on them, they realized how efficient and professional the two creatures were. Ogram was surprised by how soft their bodies were. Visually, the Kren's exoskeletons appeared to be hard, but on contact, their flesh was close to the softness of human skin. The Kren administered healing nanos to their injuries and gave them antibiotics appropriate for Human and Tarsian physiology.

As soon as they left, Ogram and Allondra fell asleep. The last few days had been painful and traumatic, both physically and emotionally.

Several hours later their cabin's door rang and when Ogram opened the door, they saw Zurk and Rek.

"Good morning Ogram and Allondra, we're sorry to disturb you, but Butrik asked us to tell you that Queen Harriett wants to meet with you and the three Brotherhood members," Zurk explained.

"We'd like to come with you as well," Rek added.

"Come in, come in," Ogram said, stretching his body and realizing that his stab wounds had stopped hurting. Allondra's leg was also nearly healed.

"How are you dealing with being on a Kren ship?" Allondra asked, curious to know how the two Gulax were feeling.

"We're still getting used to being around such alien creatures, especially ones that we were taught were Satan's children," Zurk confessed.

"It's a bit intimidating. There are thousands of them!" Rek commented, shaking his head.

"You know, once Humans and Tarsians felt the same way about Gulax!" Ogram said, laughing.

"You're right. Perhaps one day we'll feel as comfortable being next to a Kren as we do with humanoids,' Rek said, patting Ogram's shoulder.

"Well, let us go and meet the queen. I'm curious to know what she has to say to us," Allondra said, pointing to the door.

A Kren escort was waiting outside their cabin, and Human, Tarsian and Gulax, followed the two Kren into an elevator that climbed several levels to the ship's inner chamber. The large spherical chamber was the biggest interior space that any of them had ever seen. A series of long ramps led from the walls of the chamber to a smaller, central spherical structure, which seemed to be the nexus of the mothership.

After crossing one of the long ramps, they found themselves in front of a large door.

"Your friends are waiting inside," one of the drones said, pressing a button that revealed the interior. Then, both escorts moved to the side, while everyone passed into the central sphere.

"Welcome everyone," Thomas said, smiling. "Before you go into the queen's inner chamber, I want to prepare you for what you're going to see and hear. First, Kren Queens (particularly one as old as Harriett the Second), are very large in size. She is three thousand five hundred and twenty three standard galactic years old. Her head alone measures about three meters by two meters. I mention this because her appearance can be very intimidating, particularly to Humans and Tarsians and perhaps to Gulax as well," he added, turning to Rek and Zurk.

"Also, the light intensity inside the chamber will be very low, as queen's eyes are so big, they can't take very bright lights. It will take you a few seconds for your eyes to adjust to the low light. Also Queen Harriett the Second has no vocal chords, so she will be speaking to you via a translating device that converts her speech into humanoid. Are you ready?" Xelia asked.

All nodded somewhat nervously, and then Thomas pushed a button and another large circular door opened, revealing a large space that at first, looked as if it was almost dark. As the group entered, they found themselves facing Queen Harriett's humongous face, which was indeed very intimidating. So much so, that both Rek and Zurk moved directly behind Ogram and Allondra, unconsciously using them as shields for their protection. Ogram smiled. This was the first time that he'd seen any Gulax be intimidated by anything!

Thomas, Xelia and Lana walked right in front of Queen Harriett's head and bowed respectfully.

"WELCOME OGRAM, ALLONDRA AND OUR GOOD FRIENDS, ZURK AND REK," the queen said, greeting the group in a soft female voice. "IT'S BEEN A LONG TIME SINCE I'VE COMMUNICATED WITH ANYONE OTHER THAN KELEM ROGESTON," she commented.

"It is an honor to meet you, Queen Harriett," Ogram replied, bowing slightly.

"For me as well," Allondra echoed.

"PLEASE CALL ME HARRIETT. LET US DISPENSE WITH TITLES. I AM VERY HAPPY TO MEET YOU ALL AND I WELCOME YOU TO MY HIVE. A GREAT INJUSTICE HAS BEEN DONE AGAINST CARDINAL RICHELIEUX AND KELEM ROGESTON HAS ASKED ME TO HELP YOU

CORRECT THAT MISDEED. WE KREN ARE NON-VIOLENT, BUT WE'VE USED PHYSICAL FORCE THREE TIMES IN OUR HISTORY. THE VERY FIRST TIME, WAS DURING THE MARTIAN WAR OF INDEPENDENCE, WHEN WE HELPED KELEM DEFEAT THE PHALANX AND LIBERATE MARS FROM THEIR AGGRESSION. THE SECOND TIME WAS WHEN THE CHURCH OF ST. KELEM ATTACKED OUR COLONY UNPROVOKED AND LASTLY, YESTERDAY, WHEN WE CAME TO YOUR AID IN KALA KOTHARI. NOW WE'RE WILLING TO TAKE AGGRESSIVE ACTION ONCE AGAIN IN ORDER TO FREE CARDINAL RICHELIEUX."

"Great Queen, you said that St. Kelem asked you to help us free Pavitraam. When did this happen exactly?" Rek asked, surprising Allondra and Ogram, for speaking up.

"HE COMMUNICATED WITH ME, ONE STANDARD GALACTIC WEEK AGO," she replied.

He turned to Ogram and Allondra. "So it's true that you actually received the blessing from the Saint directly? He is living in a human body as we speak?" Rek asked, realizing that the holy man that he'd worshipped all his life, was a being of flesh and blood, not existing as some sort of vague spiritual presence.

"Yes Rek. Kelem lives in a body identical to his original body of eight thousand years ago," Allondra said, confirming his query.

"But how is this possible? How can he be alive again?" Zurk asked, this time. He was having difficulty accepting that his deity existed in three-dimensional reality.

"I THINK I UNDERSTAND YOUR CONFUSION, REK AND ZURK. YOUR CHURCH HAS BEEN IGNORANT OF KELEM ROGESTON'S TRUE HISTORY FOR THOUSANDS OF YEARS. KELEM LIVED ON PLANTANIMUS UNTIL THE AGE OF TWO HUNDRED AND TWO, LONGER THAN ANY OTHER HUMAN HAD LIVED BEFORE. THIS WAS DUE TO THE MINISTRATIONS OF THE DREAMERS, WHO WERE ABLE TO PROLONG HIS LIFE WITH THEIR ENERGETIC VIBRATIONS.

"Then the Dreamers are real? Not a fiction created by the Tilharans?" Zurk asked, feeling more confused than before.

"YES, THE DREAMERS TRULY EXIST. THEY BROUGHT KELEM ROGESTON BACK TO LIFE IN A BODY THEY MANUFACTURED FOR HIM, KNOWN AS A PLANTANIMAL. HE LIVED FOR ANOTHER THREE HUNDRED YEARS IN THAT FORM, THEN HIS ADOPTED GRANDAUGHTER, TATIANA ROGESTON, DEVELOPED THE TECHNOLOGY TO TRANSFER CONSCIOUSNESS INTO A LIVING BREATHING HUMANOID BODY. FROM THEN ON, KELEM REINCARNATED SEVERAL DOZEN TIMES OVER THE YEARS. AT ONE POINT HE BECAME TIRED OF LIVING AND RETREATED TO THE QUANTUM TIDE AND EXISTED THERE UNTIL THE CRUSADES OF THE FOURTH MILLENNIUM."

"Ogram is all this true? Is she speaking the truth?" Rek asked, looking at Ogram.

"Yes Rek. St. Kelem returned to the flesh when the Dreamers found out about the crusades and the millions of beings that were dying and suffering as a result."

"But how? How did he return to the flesh?" Zurk asked, struggling with the disparity between his learned version of Kelemite history and what he was hearing from Queen Harriett and Ogram.

"THE DREAMERS REINCARNATED HIM INTO A HUMAN BODY THAT THEY CREATED THEMSELVES. IT TOOK THEM THOUSANDS OF YEARS, BUT THEY FINALLY FIGURED OUT HOW TO MAKE A HUMAN BODY, NEARLY IDENTICAL TO THE ORIGINAL. THE DREAMERS ARE BEINGS OF GREAT MENTAL, PHYSICAL AND SPIRITUAL POWER. WHEN KELEM REINCARNATED AGAIN AFTER SO MANY YEARS, HE WAS HORRIFIED TO LEARN THAT THE CHURCH OF ST. KELEM WAS RESPONSIBLE FOR THE DEATHS OF SO MANY INDIVIDUALS, ALL DONE IN HIS NAME. EVER SINCE THEN, HE HAS LIVED ON A REMOTE

PLANET ON THE OUTER EDGES OF THE GALAXY WAITING
FOR THE OPPORTUNITY TO CORRECT THE PAST."

"But why didn't he return to us? Why didn't he appear to teach us
all the truth?" Rek asked, feeling very upset to learn that so much of
what he believed all his life, was wrong.

Allondra walked up to Zurk and Rek and put her arms around
their shoulders affectionately. "The body that St. Kelem lives in now
cannot exist away from that planet. As wise and holy as he is, without
the special vibrations of the Dreamers, his body would wither and die
if he left the planet. That's why he called for Ogram and I to come to
him, so that he could reach all the people of the galaxy with his message.
Ogram and I have been to the planet that Harriet is talking about. It's
called Nobius. We spent a month with St. Kelem, seeing him, touching
him and receiving the blessing directly from him. He has charged
Ogram and I with the work of spreading his new gospel. He wants to
correct the mistakes the church made in the past. After this conflict is
finished, we are to reform his church and teach his true message. All of
us can be part of that new gospel and help heal the wrongs that have
been committed in his name for millennia."

"But then, he is not a true saint? He is not a messenger from God?"
Zurk asked, sounding positively distraught for a Gulax.

"WHAT IS A SAINT, ZURK? IS IT NOT SOMEONE THAT
THE UNIVERSAL MIND GOD HAS CHOSEN TO DELIVER
A MESSAGE OF LOVE AND PEACE TO THE WORLD? OR
DESTINED TO HELP OTHERS IN THEIR TIME OF NEED?
THE CHURCH OF ST. KELEM IS AN INSTITUTION RULED
BY SENTIENT BEINGS LIKE US. KREN, GULAX, HUMAN
OR TARSIAN, WE'RE ALL FALLIBLE AND PRONE TO MAKE
MISTAKES IN JUDGEMENT. SISTER ORNATA CREATED THE
CHURCH IN THE BELIEF THAT KELEM ROGESTON HAD
BEEN SENT TO MARS BY GOD, TO LIBERATE ITS PEOPLE.
THOSE THAT FOLLOWED HER, CREATED A DOGMATIC
SET OF BELIEFS THAT DIDN'T ALLOW FOR THE REAL
APPLICATION OF KELEM ROGESTON'S PRINCIPLES. AS
THE YEARS TURNED INTO CENTURIES AND THEN, INTO

MILLENNIA, THE CHURCH BECAME RIGID AND TURNED INTO A STRICT FUNDAMENTALIST CHURCH FOR ALL THE WRONG REASONS."

"Harriett is right! St. Kelem is not a normal human being. And he certainly has performed what anyone else would consider 'miracles'. Whatever we may call him or consider him to be, he is a superior being. And I have to believe that his life and legacy were destined to be as influential and consequential as it has been, for a reason. Just as the existence of the Dreamers is as miraculous and special as he is. Yes, Rek and Zurk, by any definition, Kelem Rogeston is a Saint. The only problem you and others may have regarding his status, is that the truth may not fit your definition of what a Saint is," Allondra said, her words carrying the weight and power of true knowledge.

"KELEM AND THE DREAMERS' CONSCIOUSNESS ULTIMATELY EXIST IN THE QUANTUM TIDE. THEY HAVE TAUGHT ME TO ENTER THAT NON-CORPOREAL REALM WHICH YOU CALL SAMADHI. IN THE QUANTUM TIDE, ALL THINGS EXIST AT ONCE AND BOTH PAST AND PRESENT CAN BE OBSERVED. KELEM HAS SEEN THE FUTURE AND KNOWS THAT WHAT IS HAPPENING NOW WAS DESTINED TO BE. THAT'S WHY HE CHOSE OGRAM AND ALLONDRA TO BE HIS NEW DECIPLES. I THINK THAT BOTH YOU, REK AND ZURK, ARE TO JOIN OGRAM AND ALLONDRA IN THAT TASK. TAKE HEART IN THE KNOWLEDGE THAT YOU'RE ON THE RIGHT PATH AND THAT KELEM HIMSELF IS GUIDING YOUR STEPS."

The Gulax stood before Queen Harriett, their heads bowed deep in thought. What had just been told to them was quite shocking and revealing at the same time. It would take them a while longer, before thousands of years of religious indoctrination could be overcome by the overwhelming evidence that had been presented to them.

For Ogram and Allondra, Queen Harriett's words were further proof that the universe had put them exactly where they were supposed to be.

CHAPTER 50

The Drums of War

Ogram awoke to find that the Kren mothership was slowing down. A few seconds later, it came to a full stop. Allondra opened her eyes having noticed the change in the ship's vibrations as well.

"Have we arrived on Plantanimus?" she asked, trying to clear the cobwebs of sleep from her brain.

Ogram touched his temple and his ocular implant showed that it was too early. The time was 03:00 am and the ship wasn't scheduled to arrive in Plantanimus until 09:00 am.

"I don't think so, it's only three in the morning," he answered, sitting up on the bed.

Could it be engine trouble?" she wondered.

Ogram didn't have time to answer. The door buzzer sounded off and he jumped out of bed forgetting that he was naked, only to return to it and put his clothes on. He opened the cabin's door and was met by Thomas and Xelia.

"I'm sorry Ogram, but something has come up. I asked Queen Harriett to stop the ship. We have to have a conference right away. Can you and Allondra meet us in the queen's chamber right away? I'll have Butrik and Nikko escort you there once you awaken and get dressed."

"What's going on?" Ogram inquired, sensing that's something awful had taken place.

"It's best that we don't talk until we're all together. I've also alerted the Gulax, they have to be in on this as well," Thomas replied.

Ogram nodded, closed the door and went back to tell Allondra the news.

Fifteen minutes later, Ogram and Allondra were in Queen Harriett's chamber, waiting for their eyes to adjust to the semidarkness of the place.

Thomas spoke first. "I've asked you all here because a galaxy wide crisis is in the making."

"It couldn't be the Nadrogs!" Rek said with concern.

"No, but it's bad."

"How bad?" Allondra exclaimed, dreading the answer.

"Galactic war!" Xelia said, shocking everyone in the chamber.

Ogram grimaced and realized instantly what had brought the galaxy to the brink of war. "Damn! I've been so focused on defeating the Nadrogs, recovering the core and saving Cardinal Richelieux, that I neglected to think of the consequences of everything that has happened recently!"

"Do not blame yourself Ogram, the best psychics and mind readers we have in the Brotherhood also failed to foresee the effects of the events that have caused the current situation," Thomas explained.

"I should know better, being an expert of galactic history and all!" Ogram replied, chiding himself.

"My dear husband, do not let your ego convince you that this is all your fault!" Allondra interjected, causing a few laughs.

Ogram smiled and kissed Allondra on the forehead. "You're right!" he said shaking his head. "I'm guessing that the Church and the Galactic Council are the main culprits in pushing for war?"

"It's more complicated than that. The Church is now blaming the Body Shop Guild, Cardinal Richelieux and you Ogram, for the destruction of the Plantanimus CUBE, claiming that you and the cardinal colluded with the Guild to steal the CUBE's core for profit. The Galactic Council has issued an arrest warrant for you and Allondra as well. Additionally, the planets in the Pleiades, in particular, Nexus

Terra, Richelieux's home world, are threatening revolt if the Curia does not release Richelieux, absolving him of all charges."

"By the Saint!" Rek shouted out, enraged by the accusations against Richelieux, Ogram and Allondra. "What heresy is this? Satan himself must have infected the members of the Curia!"

'That brings me to the next can of worms," Thomas said sounding chagrined. "The expulsion of the Gulax Guard Corp from the Heavenly Temple has instigated a strong rebuke from Gulaxia. The Gulaxian Council or Tribes, is urging all Gulax to boycott the Church until the Gulax Guards are reinstated. Of course, the boycott also includes the Galactic Guild."

Both Rek and Zurk lowered their heads and hissed loudly, (a Gulax sign of anger and frustration). If the Gulax nation declared war against the Church and the Guild, which seemed likely under the circumstances, they'd both be considered traitors if they didn't fight along with their kind.

"What a mess! Ogram said, horrified that the Galaxy would soon be involved in a terrible war that would kill trillions upon trillions of beings.

"I'M AFRAID THAT THE KREN ARE ALSO INVOLVED IN THIS CRISIS, "the queen said, speaking for the first time.

The chamber fell silent. Everyone understood that if the Kren went to war, the casualty rate would go up dramatically.

"IF THE WAR REACHES THE BODY SHOP GUILD PLANETS WHICH ARE CLOSE TO KREN SPACE, IT WILL SURELY SPILL INTO OUR TERRITORY. THIS WOULD FORCE ALL THE HIVES TO DEFEND THEMSELVES. THE OLDER QUEENS SUCH AS I, WOULD BE CONTENT TO FIGHT A DEFENSIVE WAR. BUT FOR THE LAST MILLENNIA, SOME OF THE YOUNGER QUEENS HAVE BEEN DEBATING WHETHER THE KREN SHOULD EXPAND OUR TERRITORY OR NOT, WHICH MEANS THAT FOR THE FIRST TIME IN COUNTLESS MILLENNIA, THE KREN COULD RETURN TO THEIR WARLIKE BEHAVIOR,"

"Dear God! Let us all pray that it won't come to that," Ogram said, knowing that the Kren had a very violent past and that if pushed, their hordes could very well decimate all the other species in the galaxy.

Rek and Zurk suddenly looked at the Kren Queen's enormous head and wondered if they would end up having to fight the Kren in the near future. Their recent acceptance of the Kren as allies instead of millennia long despised enemies came into question once again. Ogram caught their look and understood the seriousness of their collective dilemma. With so many players with so many cross purposes, involved in a galaxy wide conflict, it didn't take a genius to see that this war would be the greatest conflagration in history, pitting families, new allies and former enemies against each other.

Allondra squeezed Ogram's hand and whispered in his ear. "Husband, what are we to do?"

As if she'd heard Allondra's quiet words, the queen spoke again.

"KELEM ROGESTON HAS A MESSAGE FOR OGRAM AND ALLONDRA," Queen Harriet said, and everyone turned to look at the couple.

"What does he have to say?" Ogram asked, hoping for an answer to the problem.

"HE SAYS . . ., FOLLOW YOUR HEARTS,"

Ogram let go of Allondra's hand and snorted sarcastically. "Follow our hearts?" he asked out loud, feeling as if he was playing a foolish character in a theatrical farce. "What the hell does he mean by that?" he retorted, almost angrily. For the first time since he'd met Kelem Rogeston, he felt as if the man was just as powerless to do anything about the coming war as everyone else. Maybe he wasn't a saint or a special being after all! An overwhelming sense of weakness and depression took hold of him and he lowered his head, feeling physically and mentally exhausted. Suddenly, all the pain, suffering and stress of the past few months landed on his shoulders, weighing him down like an overloaded beast of burden.

Allondra had never seen Ogram act this way and the sight scared her. Rek and Zurk were also upset seeing their Pavitraam look and sound so dejected. Everyone held their breath, waiting for Ogram's next words, but they never came. He turned around and walked out of the queen's chamber, leaving Allondra and everyone else wondering what to do next.

Even though it had never been discussed, Ogram was the de facto leader of the group and now that he seemed as lost and confused as everyone else, a sense of doom took over the group. Allondra's heart sank, feeling powerless and fearful of the future. Until Ogram walked out of the queen's chamber, she'd been holding on to the belief that they would eventually succeed in restoring order to their world. But now, the galaxy's fate and their own seemed to be in a state of flux, dark and uncertain.

Allondra excused herself and left the chamber, followed by Rek and Zurk.

"We must speak to Pavitraam, Allondra. Where do you think he went?" Zurk asked, as they made their way to the elevators.

"I hope he went to our cabin, but please, let me talk to him first before you approach him," Allondra replied, as they boarded the elevator. For the first time since she'd met Ogram, she felt completely disconnected to him. The feeling scared her and she fought to hide her emotions from the two Gulax.

When they reached their cabin, Allondra entered, only to find it empty.

"We will search for him Pavitraam, we'll bring him back to you," Rek suggested.

"No. . . ., please, let him be. He needs time to figure it all out," she told them, barely able to hold back her tears.

The two Gulax hesitated, their religious devotion to Ogram and Allondra drove them to ignore her request, but at the same time they could not refuse her wishes either.

"Alright Pavitraam. We will do as you say. We will give him time to think," Zurk said, bowing politely. The two walked away.

Allondra closed the door, sat on the cabin's bed and prayed to St. Kelem for wisdom.

CHAPTER 51

Ogram's Moment of Doubt and Fear

¹ My God, my God, why have you forsaken me?
Why are you so far from saving me, from the words of my groaning?
² O my God, I cry by day, but you do not answer,
and by night, but I find no rest.
¹¹ Be not far from me; for trouble is near; for there is none to help.
(From Psalm 22:1-31)

Ogram was wandering through the myriad corridors of the Kren mothership unaware of his surroundings. As he walked aimlessly, hundreds of replicas of Butrik and Nikko passed by him without paying any attention to him. The Kren drones ignored him as if he wasn't there, which suited him fine. He wanted to get away from everything and for him at that moment, the insectoids were not real.

After an hour or so, he stopped walking and sat by one of the corridor's wall, feeling tired. The endless stream of drones, each an exact clone of the others, continued walking past him, ignoring him. To his surprise, one of them stopped and spoke to him.

"Mother wants to know if she can do anything for you," the Kren stated.

"Ah, yes, I forgot that you're all connected to your queen by telepathy," Ogram remarked, without looking at the insectoid.

"Do you require medical attention or sustenance?"

Ogram laughed at the remote formality of the Kren. "What I need is a quiet place where I can be by myself and think!" he responded, with a bitter laugh.

The drone tilted his head as he listened to his queen's thoughts. "Mother has instructed me to escort you to our main astrophysics observation lounge. Will you follow me?"

Ogram exhaled with resignation. "Yeah, what the hell. Lead the way."

The drone guided him to one of the thousands of elevators in the moon size vessel and a few minutes later, Ogram was standing in the mothership's circular astrophysics observation lounge. The place was forty meters wide in circumference, covered by a large spherical plastic bubble that gave the lounge the appearance of being exposed to the vacuum of space. It was quite unnerving and fascinating at the same time and Ogram had to get used to the effect.

The floor consisted of some type of shiny black metal that reflected the stars like a mirror. As he looked down, the reflection created the illusion that he was floating in space. He looked around and wondered why the place was empty of equipment. There was nary a telescope or computer terminal in the whole place.

Ogram laughed and realized that this place was indeed quiet and very conducive to thinking! Queen Harriett had picked the perfect spot for Ogram to sort things out. He lay down on the floor and stared at the stars thinking of nothing. He remained there for a long time, like a derelict space ship, adrift in the void.

He was miserable and feeling at odds with the universe, much like the first night after he'd met the Matriarch and found that his involvement with the Church of St. Kelem was going to continue for longer that he'd expected. He also remembered that at that moment, he had felt as if he was being drafted into a war in which he had no stake. But then came all the remarkable events that contributed to his spiritual awakening and his eventual conversion to Kelemism.

Why was he so angry and feeling like his spiritual strength and faith had vanished? He thought deeply about this and came to the conclusion that fear was the driving force behind his current state of mind. But what was it exactly that he was afraid of? he asked himself, searching for an answer.

Then it came to him. He was afraid of failing and disappointing everyone. Allondra had been very perceptive in saying to him earlier, *"My dear husband, do not let your ego convince you that this is all your fault!"*

Ogram laughed and realized the ridiculousness of his self-importance. "How egotistical of him to think that he, Ogram Zepol, was the only individual in the galaxy who could do anything about the coming war!"

"I'm glad you figured it out!" a voice said behind him.

"Huh?" Ogram blurted out, practically jumping out of his skin. He spun around to see who was there.

"Kelem!" But . . . ., how . . . ., I mean, how did you get here? I thought that you . . ."

"That I couldn't leave Nobius physically?"

"Well . . ., yes," Ogram confessed, feeling perplexed.

"I'm not here. Well . . ., actually . . ., my body isn't 'here'. I'm communicating with you through the Quantum Tide," Kelem explained with a smile.

"Oh! I didn't realize that we could communicate like this through the Quantum Tide!" Ogram remarked.

Kelem walked closer to Ogram and sat down next to him. "No Ogram, you're in 'real' time and space. It seems that God, in his infinite wisdom has seen to it that I develop the ability to manifest my presence like this," he said, pointing to his body.

Ogram reached for Kelem's hand and then hesitated. "So . . ., you're not here physically, yet I can see and hear you?"

"Precisely!" Kelem replied with delight.

"Why haven't you done this before? You would have been such an inspiration to all of us that love you!" Ogram responded, somewhat accusatorily.

"My dear Ogram, this is new for me too! Or do you forget my frustration during the Kelemite Crusades at not being able to communicate with Matriarch Castilia and the cardinals of the Curia at that time?"

"What has brought this about then, Kelem? Why are you now able to manifest in this manner?"

"A galactic war would be an abomination of such magnitude, that God, or the Universal mind, or whatever you want to call it, has obviously decided to intervene in our 'three dimensional' reality by granting me this ability. Nature itself will not permit the extinction of so many sentient beings. Apparently, such a thing would disturb the fabric of the universe," Kelem concluded.

"How are we to stop this holocaust then? You said earlier, to 'follow our hearts', but I can't see how that would be of any help! Now that you can manifest your presence in three dimensional time and space, you can stop the madness! You can appear to Bishop Kalduwan and the Curia and force them to end this!"

"It is not so simple my dear Ogram. This universe that we live in is ruled by the free will of all the sentient beings that exist in it. I believe that the almighty spirit wants us to do the actual work and by 'us', I mean you, Allondra and the others, not me or Alpha. Don't you see? Alpha and all the Dreamers and me are too powerful already. Humanoids and all the other species must come to terms and decide not to annihilate each other. If beings like Alpha and me manipulate historical events and individual minds, we are doing a disservice to the universe."

"But you have interfered! You've contacted the Matriarchs living in the CUBE at the Heavenly Temple for millennia and you saved me and Cardinal Richelieux from the Nadrog that attacked us in the Plantanimus CUBE's VR. You brought me and Allondra to Nobius to train us to defeat the Nadrogs and. . . ."

"You must do this work yourselves Ogram!" Kelem said, interrupting his young friend with a forceful tone of voice. "Just like I had to serve others in the physical world for many centuries, so must you and Allondra and the rest. Alpha and I can help the way we have so far, but we can't put our hands directly in your affairs."

Ogram looked down and rubbed his chin pensively. "There's something that you're not telling me Kelem. It seems to me that you're working under the authority of a superior intelligence."

"Do the work Ogram. You're capable of doing it. I know that you'll find a way."

Ogram looked up and was startled to find that he was alone once again. He turned around to look for Kelem but he knew that he was gone.

Ogram sighed and struggled to figure out what it all meant, but even after having spoken to Kelem, he still felt lost. He decided to go into Samadhi and hope that the universe would provide him with the answers to his questions. He crossed his legs and rested his arms on his thighs and went in deep.

Three hours later, he came back to consciousness. He opened his eyes, jumped up and left the observation lounge in a hurry. He ran into the corridor outside the lounge and stopped a drone passing by.

"How do I get to your queen's chamber?"

CHAPTER 52

A Daring and Risky Plan

Ogram had come up with an idea on how to prevent the war from consuming the galaxy. He had been talking non-stop for the last few minutes, and now it was Queen Harriett's turn to say what she thought of it.

"YOUR STRATEGY IS DEFINITELY 'OUT OF THE BOX', AS YOU HUMANS SAY. IT IS BOTH BRILLIANT AND DANGEROUS. I'M WILLING TO GO ALONG WITH YOUR PLAN AND I'M SURE MANY HIVES WOULD BE WILLING TO PARTICIPATE, BUT, I WONDER IF YOU HAVE THOUGHT THIS THROUGH?"

"Yes, I have Harriett. I agree that there's much risk in it, but you Kren are the only ones that can pull it off."

"YOU REALIZE OF COURSE, THAT ONCE WE CARRY THIS THROUGH, I CAN'T BE RESPONSIBLE FOR THE ACTIONS THAT MY FELLOW QUEENS WILL TAKE IN THE FUTURE," Harriett warned.

"It's a risk that I'm willing to take, even though it could affect all the other species in the galaxy," Ogram replied, knowing quite well that if his ideas backfired, the results could be disastrous.

"I WILL GIVE THE SIGNAL TO ALL THE QUEENS TO COMMENCE THE OPERATION ONCE I HEAR FROM YOU.

THE ENTIRE KREN CONGLOMERATE WILL BE PERFECTLY SYNCHRONIZED AT MY COMMAND."

"Excellent! Oh, one more thing, the Gulax must not find out about our plan. I'll take responsibility for keeping them in the dark, understood?"

"IF THE PLAN GOES WRONG, WE MIGHT BE FIRED UPON BY GULAX FORCES. I'M WILLING TO LET MY HIVE TAKE HITS FROM GULAX BATTLE SHIPS, BUT I DOUBT THAT ANY OTHER HIVE WILL."

"Yes, I'm aware of the risks and I'm willing to take them all. I understand the ramifications of what we're about to do. For all I know, our names will be remembered along the very long list of tyrants, despots and evil warlords from the galaxy's history.

"I BID YOU FAREWELL, YOUNG OGRAM. GOOD LUCK,"

"Thank you Harriett. I hope that I'll see you again."

Ogram bowed to the queen and left the chamber.

Several hours later, Butrik and Nikko escorted him to the Prophesy. The ship had been fueled and specially outfitted with a Kren shield and a special device that Ogram had asked the Kren to build for him.

Ogram was leaving by himself. He was about to risk his life and initiate a series of events that could have deadly consequences. He didn't want Allondra or anyone else to be hurt or die in the attempt. He felt a knot in his throat when he thought of how Allondra and the others would feel once they found out that he was gone and had left them behind.

But now was not the time for sentimentality or personal issues. The fate of the galaxy would be decided in the next forty eight hours.

CHAPTER 53

The War Begins

Ogram disengaged the magnetic clamps holding the Prophesy to the hangar deck of the Kren mothership and exited the moon size vessel. He pushed the sub-light thrusters to maximum and put several thousand kilometers between the Prophesy and the mothership in order to go into *n'time*.

The subcutaneous com chip that Thomas had installed in his head when he and Allondra went to Kālī Dāṛhī to retrieve the CUBE's core was still there. The Kren had modified it so that he and Queen Harriet could be in constant communication.

He stopped the ship and moved over to Allondra's navigation panel to enter the *n'time* solution to his next destination. He touched the holo screen to find the location in the navigation system's memory and was shocked to find that it was missing!

"Is this what you're looking for?" a voice said, from behind him.

"Oh shit!" Ogram yelled in complete surprise, almost falling out of the navigator's chair.

He turned around to find Allondra with one hand in her hip and the other holding a memory chip. Her expression was not a happy one.

"What . . ., how?" Ogram mumbled, trying to figure out how Allondra had discovered his plan.

"What is it with you Ogram?" Allondra yelled with indignation, her eyes flaring green fire. "Why are you always either pushing me away, or trying to leave me behind, every time you get the urge to be the hero or martyr yourself?"

Ogram's face turned red with embarrassment and dismay. "Damn it Allondra, how did you know?" he asked, feeling a mixture of emotions. A part of him was glad that she was there with him.

She smirked, stomped over to the navigator's chair and pushed Ogram away, then inserted the memory chip into the console. "I swear! I don't know what I'm going to do with you!" she growled angrily, then turned and looked at him like a mother would a miscreant child. "Do you think that setting an *n'time* solution is as simple as recalling a previous location?" she asked with sarcasm.

"I was going to try," he responded quietly.

"And probably rematerialize the ship inside a sun or some other solid object! Damn your male ego!"

Ogram got angry, stood up and began pacing around the cabin. "You don't know what I'm about to do woman! There's a reason why I left you and the others behind. If what I've set in motion goes badly, I will be known as the worst person to ever have lived in the entire galaxy. But now that you're with me, you can be damned for all time too!"

"I know exactly what your plan is Ogram," Allondra replied casually, as she entered data in her holo screen.

"So, do we Pavitraam," a Gulax voice said behind him.

"Crap!" Ogram exclaimed, turning around and finding Rek and Zurk by the cabin's door. "What the hell?" he blurted out, feeling like the universe was playing a joke on him.

Rek walked over to Ogram and laid his hand on his shoulder. "Pavitraam, when a Kelemite Gulax Guard forfeits his life for a member of the Church, it is forever! Zurk and I cannot change this, even if it means having to do battle with other Gulax," he explained patiently.

"Wait a minute! How is it that you all know what my plans are?" he demanded, realizing that he'd missed something.

"I TOLD THEM, MY YOUNG HUMAN FRIEND," came Queen Harriett's voice, issuing from the cabin's speakers, instead of his implant.

"I . . ., I don't understand . . .," Ogram stammered, totally confused.

"IT'S SIMPLE. YOUR PLAN, THOUGH BRILLIANT, CANNOT BE EXECUTED PROPERLY WITH YOU DOING ALL THE WORK AND TAKING ALL THE RISKS. SO, I MADE SURE THAT YOUR FAITHFULL COMPANIONS CAME ALONG TO IMPROVE THE ODDS FOR SUCCESS. BY YOURSELF, THE CHANCES OF SUCCEEDING WERE THIRTY PERCENT, NOW, YOUR CHANCES ARE BETTER THAN FIFTY PERCENT."

"Why did you deceive me then?" Ogram asked, curious of Queen Harriett's motives.

"Because she knew that you would have disagreed and then gone and done something really stupid!" Allondra interjected, still sounding mad at him.

"THAT'S NOT HOW I WOULD HAVE PUT IT, BUT IT'S CLOSE ENOUGH," the queen commented in his cochlear implant.

Ogram laughed and leaned back in the pilot's chair. "Well then, who else is back there? A platoon of Kren and Gulax?" he asked sarcastically, looking toward the rear of the ship.

"No, just us," Thomas, Xelia and Lana said in unison, poking their heads through the cabin's door.

Ogram threw his head back and laughed. "Hah! Come on in! It seems that anyone can crash this party," he offered, knowing that there was no going back now.

Thomas entered the cabin and leaned on the pilot's chair. "You're going to need Xelia. She's a much better pilot that either one of you," he said, looking at Ogram and Allondra. "And two powerful mind-reading psychics like me and Lana will come in handy on this mission. Come now, Ogram, accept the fact that this is the best way to carry out your crazy, insane plan!" he said, slapping Ogram's back.

"Alright, alright! Let's get going. Let's hope that we can stop this war before it starts!"

"UNFORTUNATELY OGRAM, THE WAR'S ALREADY STARTED. A FEW MINUTES AGO, GALACTIC COUNCIL WARSHIPS BEGAN BOMBARDING THE CAPITAL OF Kālī Dāṛhī. THEY'RE CONCENTRATING THEIR MAIN ATTACK ON 'FANTASY LAND'," the queen informed them.

"Oh no!" Ogram cried out, concerned for the Ibirans who only wanted to liberate their planet from the Body Shop Guild. "Why Kālī Dāṛhī?" Ogram asked the queen. It seemed an unlikely place for Kalduwan and her Curia co-conspirators to start the war.

"IT APPEARS THE IBIRANS REACHED OUT TO THE GALACTIC COUNCIL FOR HELP IN LIBERATING THEIR PLANET FROM THE GUILD."

"Well, I have no qualms about Fantasy Land being burned to a crisp. I just hope we can help the Ibirans remain truly independent after the war. If we fail, Ibira III will become another Kelemite colony under the Church's rule," Ogram commented.

"That wouldn't be a bad thing Pavitraam!" Rek argued, confused about Ogram's negative view of Kālī Dāṛhī becoming a proper Kelemite planet.

Ogram turned and looked at Rek with a sad expression in his eyes. "Don't you understand what's going on here Rek? I didn't want to believe it myself, hoping that I was wrong in my suspicions. But now I know that I was right. This attack on Kālī Dāṛhī is the opening salvo of the next Kelemite Crusade! Kalduwan and the Curia mean to evangelize the entire galaxy by force!"

A stunned silence overtook the control cabin as everyone processed the meaning of Ogram's statement.

Ogram shook his head. "It's funny how one's perception of events can change in an instant. A week ago I was convinced that the Nadrogs were the most dangerous, evil thing to ever threaten the galaxy. The coming catastrophe is worse, much worse."

CHAPTER 54

Through the Gauntlet – Part 1

The Prophesy rematerialized one million miles from New Jerusalem and Ogram immediately activated the Kren shield, enveloping the vessel in an iridescent glow.

The team had divided operational tasks according to skills. Xelia on pilot duty, Allondra at the navigation controls with several *n'time* solutions ready to go, Rek on shields and sensors, Zurk on weapons and Ogram in command. Additionally, Thomas and Lana were in the ship's lounge in deep meditation, scanning the minds of anyone having aggressive thoughts within fifty thousand kilometers of the Prophesy.

Ogram realized at that moment that without the others, he would have lasted but a few seconds in a fire fight with a Council cruiser or battleship.

All had their spacesuits on, knowing that the ship could decompress at any moment if fired upon. Queen Harriett had assured Ogram that the new shield that Butrik and Nikko had installed in the Prophesy's innards was of the latest generation of Kren technology, supposedly decades ahead of anything the Galactic Council had in their warships. Still, the Prophesy, though well equipped, was a small luxury yacht and they were about to encounter battle cruisers with large caliber rail cannons.

"They've detected us," Lana said, over the space suit helmet radio as she read the mind of a Council warship commander somewhere near.

"Yes, I see it. A ship's heading our way. It looks like a destroyer," Rek announced from his station, a few seconds later.

"They're obviously on high alert. They never come out this far to investigate a re-materialization," Zurk added, tightening his grip on the Prophesy's rail gun triggers. For the first time in the Church's history, a Gulax was about to fire on a Council warship.

Ogram took a deep breath and looked at Allondra sitting at the navigation station in her spacesuit and knew that he had to concentrate on the approaching danger and not her safety.

A few seconds later, a large shiny destroyer brimming with Rail guns, rematerialized a thousand meters from the Prophesy.

"Ahoy pleasure cruiser, this is Council Destroyer Valhalla. Identify yourself," a young officer demanded on Ogram's holo screen.

Ogram put on his best smile. "Ahoy Council Destroyer Valhalla, this is the Prophesy en route to the Heavenly Temple. My name is Ogram Zepol and I'm here to surrender to the authority of the Church of St. Kelem," he said very calmly.

The officer's eyebrows went up in recognition of who he was talking to. He was obviously surprised and Ogram suspected that the last thing the Council expected was for Ogram to show up and surrender.

The screen went blank and the Valhalla suddenly fired its thrusters and backed away in a hurry.

"They're charging their rail guns!" Rek announced, looking at his sensor array.

"That officer was ordered to kill you and Allondra upon sight, but he's ethically and morally conflicted. However, he's going to attack eventually!" Thomas warned Ogram.

"Xelia get us out of here a minute ago!" Ogram ordered tensely. The Prophesy's souped-up engines moved the yacht out of the cruiser's gun range within seconds.

"*N'time* solution number one!" Kelem ordered, looking at Allondra.

Ogram had to shut off the Kren shield in order to go into *n'time*. The destroyer, seeing his shields go down, fired its thrusters and came at the Prophesy at top speed. The Prophesy's window shields closed, and the *n'time* generator came to life and began winding up, but not nearly fast enough for Ogram and everyone else in the ship.

About five hundred kilometers distance, the Valhalla fired its frontal rail guns and several streams of plasma projectiles whizzed by the Prophesy, missing it by centimeters.

"Anytime Allondra!" Ogram yelled, seeing the next stream of cannon fire coming at them over the ship's external cameras.

To everyone's relief, the view on the holo screen turned purple and the Prophesy blinked out of existence a nano second before the destroyer's guns decimated the ship. A billionth of a second later, the vessel reassembled itself several parsecs from the Tal system.

The generator began to wind down and Ogram and the others exhaled with relief.

"That was close!" Xelia commented, opening up her helmet's face shield.

Thomas appeared by the door of the control cabin. "I'm sorry that you were right Ogram," he said, looking dissapointed.

Ogram opened his face shield and took off his helmet. He looked drained and wished that he'd been wrong about his prediction. "They definitely don't want the core returned to the Plantanimus CUBE," he mused, rubbing his chin.

"So it's true then, Bishop Kalduwan and the others have gone beyond wanting the core returned to the Plantanimus CUBE. It seems that they're no longer interested in using the attack on the facility to expulse Cardinal Richelieux and bring us to trial," Allondra said somberly.

Ogram nodded unhappily. "I'm afraid so my love. It seems that Kalduwan's ultimate plan was to launch another crusade. The move to expel Richelieux from the church was only part one of her scheme. The expulsion of Richelieux would have weakened Matriarch Vasilia's authority, and then she probably would have been poisoned and made it look like she'd commited suicide in order to make way for one of the highest ranked cardinals to take her place. The new matriarch would likely be one of Kalduwan's co-conspirators. When the Ibirans requested the Council's aid in freeing them from the Body Shop Guild, Kalduwan realized that she could push her time table by months, perhaps years!"

"The only thing that could ruin her plans then, was if you and I showed up with the core intact," Allondra commented ruefully.

"That's right. With everyone believing that the core is lost and the Curia claiming that Cardinal Richelieux is in league with the Body Shop Guild, both The Realm's stockholders and large numbers of Kelemites in the galaxy, would demand that the Council take military action against the Guild, which is exactly what has happened. All this will logically lead to taking over planets hosting body shops. Once the invasion of planets begins and war spreads throughout the galaxy, it will take little effort for the Church to convince most Kelemites that a crusade is necessary."

"By all that is holy in the world! My blood is boiling with rage. It is all I can do to keep myself from going into a blood frenzy!" Rek hissed, as he formed fists with his four fingered lizard hands.

"Calm down Gulax!" Zurk scolded him. "Control your primitive reptile brain! Pay attention to our Pavitraam and learn from them," the old Gulax said, pointing to Ogram and Allondra.

"There'll be plenty of time to release your anger on our enemies Rek. Zurk is right, you must act more like a humanoid for the time being," Ogram said with humor.

"I'm sorry Pavitraam. I will endeavor to be more human," the Gulax said contritely.

"So, we switch to plan B. Everyone ready?" Ogram asked, looking to the others.

Everyone nodded in agreement.

Very well, Rek, Zurk, get the rover ready. Thomas, you and Lana come with me. I will teach you how to operate the new Kren equipment in the belly of the ship."

"No need to, Ogram. We're connected to Queen Harriett telepathically. Once we arrive, she will guide us," Thomas assured him.

"Right! I'm so glad you guys are here! There's no way that I could have pulled this off by myself. What was I thinking?" Ogram remarked, shaking his head.

Xelia fired up the sub-light engines so they'd be ready to go once they rematerialized at their new destination. Allondra began plotting the next *n'time* Jump.

Ogram put his helmet back on and closed the face shield. His suit's air supply came on and he took a deep breath. They were about to breach the Heavenly Temple, the most shielded and protected object in the galaxy.

CHAPTER 55

Through the Gauntlet − Part 2

The Prophesy reassembled itself in the vacuum of space, ten thousand kilometers from the Heavenly Temple, and instantly, the mission was in trouble. The ship had rematerialized less than a hundred meters from a Council frigate and due to its proximity to the other ship, the *n'time* quantum field fried several circuits on the Prophesy.

The frigate had suffered electronic damage as well and was having trouble turning to attack the Prophesy, which had appeared behind it.

Zurk's fire control panel was useless and he cursed in Hindi as the cabin filled with smoke from the burnt circuits throughout the ship.

"Zurk, fire at the frigate manually! Don't let it turn around and take aim at us or we're done!" Ogram yelled into his helmet's microphone.

Zurk obliged and began firing the Prophesy's rail guns at the frigate, and luckily damaged the ship's thrusters, rendering it immobile.

Meanwhile, Ogram was waving his hand over the Kren shield's control display, trying to clear smoke out of the way, praying that it was still working. If it didn't, they'd all be dead in a few seconds. To his relief, the cabin's air filters came on and the smoke was suctioned off.

"I have engines!" Xelia announced, with exhilaration.

"*N'time* generator is still on, but I don't know if it can execute a jump if we have to!" Allondra reported, as she moved several holo objects on her screen trying to ascertain the damage caused by the *n'time* generator's feedback.

"Sensors and radar are dead, we're blind!" Rek reported and then began cursing in Hindi as well.

Ogram flipped the switch and was relieved when the Kren shield came on. "Shield's on, I don't know if it'll work up to spec, but we don't have a choice anyway. Take us in!"

Xelia pushed the thrusters and the Prophesy shot forward, heading straight for The Heavenly Temple.

As the ship picked up speed, they kept the window shields closed for extra protection. Allondra turned on the exterior cameras which fortunately were still working, but when the holo screens in the cabin came on, everyone moaned in dismay. The Heavenly Temple was surrounded by hundreds of Council warships, many of whom were now turning their gun turrets toward the Prophesy. The scene reminded Ogram of a disturbed beehive with thousands of angry bees looking for the intruder.

Several ships fired at the Prophesy and Ogram and the others could only watch as they held their breaths, praying that the Kren shield would protect them.

The Prophesy shook violently as plasma projectiles smashed into the shield, but to their relief, the thing held.

Slightly relieved, Ogram turned to Xelia. "Aim for that large bubble at the sphere's north pole," he instructed her. As they came closer to the Holy See, the fire from the ships guarding the massive moon size object became a constant barrage of projectiles that sounded like a monster hail storm hitting a land vehicle's body and windshield. Ogram kept an eye on the shield's monitor panel, watching for any sign that the thing was about to crap out. The Kren had modified the shield to be powered by the *n'time* generator and Ogram realized he should ask Allondra what effect it was having on the generator.

Allondra's voice was distorted from the Prophesy's shaking due to the massive amount of fire power being thrown at the little ship. "The generator is definitely working hard to keep feeding power to the shield. But the temperature is rising and I don't know how much longer the thing will hold!" she yelled back at him.

"How much longer before we reach the bubble?" Ogram asked Xelia, as the ship began to shake ever more violently.

"Another three minutes if the shield holds!" she responded, her voice sounding shrill with tension.

"Rek and Zurk, go to the Rover and get ready!" Ogram commanded.

The Gulax left their posts and disappeared into the ship's lower level, carrying several weapons with them. Ogram hoped that his hair brained scheme would work and that the stunt that the two faithful Gulax were about to attempt, would not end up costing them their lives.

"Thomas and Lana, get ready with the laser drill! Are you still in contact with the queen?" he asked, trying to keep his heart from jumping out of his chest.

"Yes Ogram, don't worry about us, we have everything under control," Thomas replied in a normal tone of voice.

"Thanks," Ogram said, happy to hear Thomas' calm demeanor.

"How much longer?" he asked Xelia again, feeling like the approach to the Heavenly Temple was taking years, instead of minutes.

"Less than two minutes, but I think we're about to be rammed by a battle cruiser!" she yelled, sounding panicked.

Ogram looked up and saw the thing coming at them from their right side. "Maneuver, maneuver, for god's sake!" he yelled at the top of his lungs.

Xelia snapped out of her panicked state and managed to veer left, just in time to avoid being destroyed by the massive warship. She then corrected and swung back to the right and continued approaching the Temple's north pole which was now beginning to grow larger in the ship's holo monitors.

"Aim for the edge of the bubble where the sun's created a shadow," he instructed her. If the Kren shield managed to pierce the Temple's main shield, as he hoped it would, he wanted the Prophesy to land where the other ships would have a hard time seeing the relatively small outline of the yacht size vessel, after it touched down on the large plastic canopy keeping the Garden of Eden pressurized.

The distorted image of an irate Council Navy admiral appeared on the ship's holo screens.

"Intruder, cease and desist or I'll fire a nuclear missile and blow you to kingdom come!" the agitated senior officer yelled, looking and sounding quite upset.

"Go to hell!" Ogram yelled back, and then cut the transmission.

Xelia and Allondra looked back at Ogram with worried expressions.

"Don't worry, he's bluffing! He won't detonate an atomic so close to the Temple," Ogram replied dismissively, hoping that he was right.

"Thirty seconds!" Xelia yelled, trying to be heard above the noise of plasma cannons hitting the Prophesy harder and harder, when suddenly, the shooting stopped.

Ogram smiled, his strategy had worked! The Prophesy had come too close to the Garden of Eden's protective plastic bubble, and the council warships wouldn't risk firing at them for fear of breaching the canopy. Now the Council Navy officers were probably waiting for the Prophesy to smash itself to smithereens once it hit the Temple's very powerful shield, or explode the instant the little pleasure cruiser made contact with the ridiculously high voltage emitted by the artificial moon's shield. Now that they were less than a thousand meters from the canopy, Ogram and the others could detect the iridescent electrical glow protecting the Heavenly Temple.

Allondra turned to Ogram and raised her face shield so that he could see her face clearly.

"Whatever happens next husband, know that I love you with all my heart and soul," she said, with restrained emotion.

Ogram raised his own face shield. "And I love you with all my heart and soul as well, wife. What's going to happen next is that we're going to penetrate this shield and accomplish our mission. Seal your helmet wife and know I love you," he said, securing his own helmet and then looking down at the Kren shield monitor display.

"Now, everybody, hold on to something!" he warned the others. Ogram reversed the Kren shield's polarity and raised the voltage. He held his breath, waiting for the moment the two fields of highly charged particles made contact with each other. He closed his eyes and prayed that the Prophesy would not be instantly fried to a crisp, like a bug touching a live wire.

Xelia fired the brake thrusters and brought the ship to a standstill. Then, she gingerly lowered the craft down toward the canopy. Soon, the *n'time* generator began humming louder and louder, shaking the ship like a house in an earthquake. Everyone's eyes showed fear. All were dreading electrocution and burning to death.

The ship's interior began to fill with static that jumped all around their bodies and onto every piece of equipment. Soon, everyone began to feel the shock of increasing voltage inside their space suits. The static ramped up to the point that Ogram and the others could feel the electric charge firing back and forth in their mouths, their teeth and their tongues. Brave Allondra, continued reporting the temperature of the *n'time* generator in between involuntary spasms in her voice box.

"Uann . . one thousannnndd . ., degreeees! Twelve hundred deeegg . . .reeees . . . Twelvvvvee hunnnndred and fif . . fiff . . ffffty degreeeess . . . .

Then, the *n'time* generator's pitch rose above the threshold of human hearing and suddenly died.

The ship had passed through the Temple's defensive shield, but at the cost of the *n'time* generator. The Prophesy began falling toward the canopy. Suddenly, they were in free fall and Xelia had to fight hard against several negative G's to reach the flight controls and fire the landing thrusters. With the *n'time* generator fried, the antigrav motors were dead. The ship slowed down, but it was still approaching the canopy at an alarming rate. Xelia pushed the thrusters to their maximum and the Prophesy slammed onto the plastic canopy, bounced couple of times and then came to a full stop.

The landing was rough, but fortunately no one was seriously hurt, except for Xelia who had bloodied her lip when her face hit her helmet's face shield.

"Status," Ogram called out to everyone.

"Well the *n'time* gen is done. The Prophesy is now an expensive paper weight," Allondra reported wittily.

"She's right! This bird won't fly again." Xelia added, trying to keep the mood light.

"Rek and I are ready Pavitraam, just give us the word," reported Zurk from the rover in the lower deck.

"Lana and I are good here also. By the way, kudos to my wife for an excellent job of piloting!" Thomas said lightly.

"Indeed. Now more than ever I see Queen Harriett's wisdom in not allowing me to attempt this by myself. I could have never flown this ship like you did Xelia. We owe you our lives."

"Here, here!" Lana said adding her opinion.

"Alright everyone. Make sure your suits are sealed, I'm about to decompress the ship.

Ogram waited a few seconds and then opened the main landing plank. Instantly, the ships' atmosphere was sucked out into space and everyone felt their suits puff up a little.

"Rek, Zurk, go!" Ogram said.

The rover rolled off the Prophesy's belly and headed toward the edge of the canopy located about three hundred meters from where the ship had come to rest.

Next, Thomas and Lana opened a circular hatch in the lower part of the ship's belly and a short boarding tube attached itself to the canopy by means of vacuum. Thomas fired a powerful laser the Kren had built for Ogram and began cutting a round hole in the plastic canopy.

Several battleships had by now, parked themselves directly above the area where the Prophesy had landed and were aiming powerful search lights, trying to find out what the intruders were doing. But, as Ogram had expected, the Temple's shield was diffusing the photons from the search lights, making it impossible for their pursuers to see anything clearly.

"We've reached the edge of the canopy Pavitraam, we're cutting our way into the outer shell of the roof," Zurk reported.

"Perfect! Maintain radio silence until you've reached your target," Ogram replied, relieved that the rover was able to travel on the surface of the canopy and not float out into space. The Heavenly Temple's natural gravity had enough pull to keep the vehicle's wheels making sufficient contact with the canopy's surface.

Ogram was pleased with the results of his crazy, but so far, effective plan. The success of the next stage, depended on whether Rek and Zurk could accomplish their next task; the rescue of their fellow Gulax guards, who were incarcerated in their own barracks, somewhere in the lower decks of the Heavenly Temple. If Bishop Kalduwan had decided to move the imprisoned Gulax to New Jerusalem or another planet, then Ogram's grand scheme would fall apart. Everything depended on Rek and Zurk making their way to their comrade's barracks without being captured or killed by the hundreds of mercenaries stationed throughout the Heavenly Temple.

Allondra had gone down to where Thomas and Lana were cutting the hole in the canopy and came back to report. "They're almost done breaking through, should we get our gear ready?" she asked Ogram.

"Yes, let's go to the loading dock and examine our equipment." Ogram and Allondra descended to the dock where the rover was kept and opened two large boxes, each containing a para-pod. The devices were motorized flying suits.

The hole in the canopy served two purposes. One was to allow Ogram and Allondra access to fly down to the Garden of Eden to execute the next stage in Ogram's plan. The other, was to have a deterrent against the Council. Once the laser cut through the meter thick plastic canopy, the integrity of the Garden of Eden's atmosphere would be compromised. If the Council's military or the mercenaries, decided to shut off the Temple's shield in order to capture the now un-flyable Prophesy, Ogram would threaten to vent the Garden's atmosphere and in the process, destroy the Matriarch's Residence, the Curia's chamber and the one hundred and eighty magnificent gardens that comprised The Garden of Eden.

This tactic would keep the wolves at bay for a few hours. Eventually the military would bring a flying vessel into the Garden of Eden and nullify Ogram's threat by patching the hole in the canopy from the inside. At which point, Ogram and the others would be captured and executed.

Ogram touched his temple and checked the time in his ocular implant. It had only been five minutes since Rek and Zurk had entered the outer superstructure of the Heavenly Temple. He wished that time would speed up. He was getting nervous, and now more ships were beginning to assemble above the canopy. "By the way, how much longer before you cut though?" he asked Thomas and Lana.

"Done!" Thomas reported. "We're ready to re-pressurize," he told Ogram.

"Very well. I'll close the landing plank, and you two come back to the main deck.

Thomas and Lana appeared in the control cabin and Ogram pressed a switch that dislodged the circular piece of plastic from the canopy. As soon as he did, the heavy cylindrical chunk of plastic fell to the garden bellow and the Prophesy was instantly filled with air from the inside.

Ogram crossed his fingers and prayed that the thing wouldn't land on some poor innocent person and squash them to death. Thomas followed the trajectory of the piece of plastic with the ship's cameras and the thing crashed on one of the many lagoons down below. The impact created a huge column of water that rose several meters in the air.

"Good!" Ogram remarked. "Now they know what it is we were doing up here!" he said, smiling satisfactorily.

"It's time that I make my announcement," Ogram declared, taking his helmet off. As soon as he did, he sniffed the air and smiled.

Take your helmets off people!" he suggested, with a pleased smile.

The others did and all sniffed the air with pleasure, just like Ogram had done.

"Hmmm, it smells like Tarsia Prime!" Allondra remarked, enjoying the scent of earth and fresh vegetation rising from the gardens, five hundred meters below.

"Attention, attention!" Ogram said, looking straight into the ship's holo camera. "My name is Ogram Zepol. I have cut a two meter wide hole in your canopy. Should my ship be attacked from space or from below, I will disengage the vacuum seal and vent the atmosphere from the Garden of Eden."

Within seconds, the same irate admiral that had warned them earlier that he was about to throw a nuclear missile at the Prophesy, appeared once again in the ship's holo screens. This time, he seemed more polite.

"This is Admiral Korsly. What are your demands, Zepol?" he asked, studying Ogram's face carefully, trying to get a measure of the man.

"My only demand is that I be granted an audience with the entire Curia," Ogram answered politely.

The admiral laughed scornfully, looking like he'd been insulted. "You're delusional! The Curia is cloistered in the deepest part of the Heavenly Temple. Or haven't you heard we're at war? You attack us, breach our perimeter and then expect that we are going to accede to your ridiculous demands? You Body Shop Guilders are going to rue the day that you decided to attack us!"

Ogram smiled ironically. He was sure that this man believed in his heart of hearts that the Body Shop Guild had actually attacked the Galactic Council. Ogram looked at the time display in his ocular implant and felt his advantage slipping by. Where are Rek and Zurk? he asked himself. They've been gone for twenty minutes now! Wasn't that enough time for the two of them to reach the imprisoned guards and liberate them?"

He addressed the admiral again. "I am not with the Body Shop Guild, Admiral, but whether you believe me or not is immaterial. I have a twenty megaton atomic in my ship and I will detonate it if my one demand is not granted. You have one hour to respond," Ogram said, sounding as cold and emotionless as he could. Then, he cut the communication off.

"You think that will hold them off?" Allondra asked, sounding unsure.

"Let's hope that the mention of the atomic and my impression of a cold-blooded psychopath was believable!" Ogram replied jokingly.

"Allondra, let's take our suits off and start assembling the para-pods. I want to be ready when Rek and Zurk reach their comrades." Ogram suggested. He was starting to worry that things had gone badly for the Gulax and hoped that busying himself with the para-pods would help pass the time.

As they began walking down to the Prophesy's lower level, Zurk's voice came in his cochlear implant.

"We've done it Pavitraam! We've freed all of Matriarch Vasilia's Guard. We're on our way, but there are many mercenaries between here and the Central Cloister," he added, sounding like he was running as he spoke.

"What about the Matriarch and Cardinal Richelieux? Have you found where they're keeping them?" Ogram asked with concern.

"Yes Pavitraam! I have a squad heading to where they are, as we speak," Zurk informed him. "One more thing Pavitraam, we've encountered several nuns and priests who want to help us. Shall we allow then to get involved?"

"Yes Zurk, the more people we can bring to the Garden of Eden, the better!" Ogram answered, beginning to feel encouraged by the way things were turning out.

"Very well, I'll contact you the minute we breach the Central Cloister," Zurk added and then he cut off.

"Good news?" Allondra asked, seeing Ogram's expression.

"Yes my love, we'll be descending soon," he said, and then began to prepare his para-pod harness.

Fifteen minutes later, Ogram and Allondra, outfitted with their para-pods, were sitting by the edge of the circular hole in the canopy with their legs dangling down. Finally, Zurk called back. "We have everyone assembled, though many of the cardinals are cussing and throwing things at us!" Zurk reported, sounding a little put off. "I never expected clergy to behave like this!" he complained, quite indignantly for a Gulax.

"And I never expected that I would one day attack the Heavenly Temple, cut a hole in the Garden of Eden's canopy, then threaten to vent the atmosphere and blow the Holy See into oblivion either Zurk!" Ogram commented, laughing. "Today is a day of firsts for both of us. Be careful my friend. We'll meet at our planned location."

He gazed at Allondra looking quite the warrior, with her para-pod strapped to her Gulax battle armor, and her two side arms strapped to her waist. The effect was quite fascinating.

"Are you ready wife?" he asked, looking at the woman with whom he'd spend the rest of his life, if they both survived the next hour or so.

"Ready husband!" she answered, and Ogram could tell that she was smiling by the way her beautiful green eyes were crinkling behind the visor of her Gulax helmet.

They joined hands and dropped into the Garden of Eden together.

Their wings popped open and as soon as they did, the small thrusters in their para-pods fired up and the two began descending in wide circular loops. Ogram touched the communication implant in his temple. "Harriett, are you there?"

"YES OGRAM, I HEAR YOU."

"Begin Operation Omnipresence."

CHAPTER 56

The Miracle at the Heavenly Temple

Ogram looked down at the approaching roof of the Matriarch's residence and saw several heavily armed mercenaries already waiting for him and Allondra. He had expected that eventuality, and banked steeply to the left, aiming for one specific garden located at the edge of the valley.

Allondra corrected her flight path and followed him. They had discussed having to change their landing spot prior to jumping. As he had expected, that area of the valley was free of mercenaries and Council troops. Ogram had chosen that location because there was a garden there that was defensible, at least for a while. The Garden of St. Kelem was next to the boundary wall that encircled the twenty six hectares of the Garden of Eden. Ogram realized how serendipitous it was that that particular garden happened to be the best one for his plan.

"They've shut off the main shield above us," he heard Thomas say in his cochlear implant.

"I figured they would eventually do that," Ogram answered, as he opened the para-pod's flaps about to land. "The moment, anyone gets close to you, give them a demonstration and open up the valve for a few seconds," Ogram replied, hoping that opening the valve would stop the Council Navy from getting anywhere near the Prophesy. Ogram was counting on the high regard the Kelemite world had for the Garden of Eden and the lengths that the Church would go to protect the site.

Like two Gulax angels coming down from heaven, Ogram and Allondra touched down gently on the smooth manicured lawn of the Garden of St. Kelem. The site was wedge shaped. It had a narrow entrance that led to a long promenade that culminated in an amphitheater at the widest part of the garden next to the boundary wall.

Ogram and Allondra detached their para-pods and ran to the amphitheater. As they did, they dropped explosive charges along the edges of the promenade. Once there, each opened a satchel they were carrying, containing floating robo-cams and let them loose. The tiny devices rose in the air and positioned themselves in a circular pattern that Ogram had programmed. Then they took cover behind a bronze statue of St. Kelem.

"Well, let's hope that the Council troops, rather than the mercenaries, are the first to come in here," Ogram said, adjusting his Gulax armor chest plate. Ogram knew that the Council troops would try to negotiate, rather than storm in, whereas the mercenaries were most likely to come charging in, guns blazing.

It didn't take long for them to find out which of the two they'd have to face. It was the mercs!

Ogram cursed under his breath. He desperately wanted to avoid killing anyone, but now they had no choice.

About twenty mercs streamed into the promenade, hugging the outer edge of it, seeking cover behind the stone wall and manicured hedgerows along the sides of the main walkway.

"Stop, don't come any closer! I have charges set everywhere!" he yelled, hoping the warning would stop them.

It didn't work. A barrage of rifle fire began pelting St. Kelem's statue as chunks of bronze flew everywhere from the impact of pulse streams. Ogram and Allondra ducked down and took cover. He opened up a small panel on the forearm of his Gulax armor and touched a button.

The first series of explosives went off, and the shooting stopped. Ogram poked his head out and saw the mercenaries retreating, dragging their injured and dead back toward the garden's entrance.

Ogram exhaled with relief. He was counting on the mercenaries' reputed lack of discipline. He knew that if he gave them a bloody nose up front, they would back off, at least for a while.

Now it was up to the Council troops, who would hopefully arrive soon and try to negotiate a surrender. If they didn't, the mercs would regroup and come at them again.

Ogram touched his temple once again. "Where are you, and how long before you get here?"

"Fighting, fighting! Many mercs, killing many mercs!" came Rek's agitated, out of breath voice.

Ogram could only imagine what bloody fighting the Gulax were engaged in at that very moment. Though each Gulax was worth ten mercenaries, Ogram prayed that they were getting the upper hand in the struggle and that they'd soon be there. Everything depended on Rek, Zurk and the Matriarch's Gulax Guard, making their way to the garden with all the members of the curia in tow.

The mercenaries had regrouped and were making their way back into the promenade. Ogram and Allondra prepared to repel them once again. They only had a certain number of explosive charges left. Once they'd detonated them all, they'd be overrun by the mercs for sure.

Ogram raised his rifle and focused his scope on the advancing mercs, ready to fire, then lowered his weapon when a tall high-ranking naval officer which he recognized as Admiral Korsly, appeared at the garden's entrance with several Council troops right behind him.

In his rifle's scope, Ogram could see that he was yelling at the top of his lungs, looking quite angry with the undisciplined soldiers of fortune. His men began escorting the mercenaries out. The Admiral walked halfway to where Ogram and Allondra were holed up, then took out a voice amplifier from his coat pocket and called out.

"Intruders! Surrender now and no harm will come to you."

"Ogram stood up and stepped away from behind St. Kelem's statue, now, full of holes. "What are your terms?" he shouted, bidding for time.

"I offer you safe passage to our brig and a fair trial with a jury of your peers. That is . . ., if you're human, which by the sound of your voice it sounds like you are!"

Ogram removed his Gulax helmet. "You're right, I am no Gulax."

"You!" the admiral exclaimed, when he realized that he'd been talking to Ogram dressed in Gulax battle armor. "Look here Zepol, this has gone far enough. There is no way that the Curia will ever agree to meet with you. Give up son, before I'm forced to have my men storm this place and kill you and your partner," the man said, sounding honest about not wanting any bloodshed.

"Something's happening!" yelled Thomas, in Ogram's ear. Ogram looked up instinctively and noticed that the Heavenly Temple's shields were on again. "The shields have come on and all the ships are moving away!' Thomas reported, sounding relieved.

"IT IS DONE OGRAM. OPERATION OMMNIPRESCENCE IS IN PLACE," the queen notified him.

Ogram smiled.

"I'm afraid that it is you Admiral Korsly who will have to surrender to me!" Ogram explained to the man.

"I'm serious Zepol, this is your last warning! Surrender or I'll . . . .," the Admiral said, stopping in mid-sentence. He was listening to his cochlear implant. His body expression and body language told Ogram that his command center was informing him that thousands of Kren ships had surrounded every single planet belonging to the Galactic Council, including Centralia, the Galaxy's capital and worst of all, the Heavenly Temple!

"Come again?" the man said, unaware that his voice amplifier was still on.

A few seconds later, the Admiral's shoulders slumped and he looked at Ogram with stunned eyes. Like every other Kelemite currently alive, he was shocked to discover that the Kren had not been wiped out of existence during the Kelemite Crusades as had been claimed by the Church of St. Kelem in the Fourth Millennium.

"May I approach?" the Admiral asked, dropping his side arm and waving his men back.

"By all means Admiral, I mean you no harm," Ogram replied, putting his rifle on the ground.

Allondra came out from behind St. Kelem's statue, she joined Ogram and they walked to the first row of seats in the amphitheater, sat down and waited for Admiral Korsly to come to them. When he reached the first row, Ogram gestured for the Admiral to sit next to him.

The man was shaken to the core. The entire galaxy had come to a complete standstill. The sheer amount of Kren vessels and their size had stunned and surprised everyone. Ogram knew that by now, the commanders of many Council warships had learned that the Kren were centuries ahead of Council Navy technology. He prayed that the casualties were few.

"What are your terms, Zepol?" the Admiral asked, sounding like someone grieving for the loss of a family member.

"Same as I asked before, to meet with the Curia," Ogram replied, calmly.

"Obviously, we will oblige, but . . ., may I ask why you've gone to such lengths to do this? And . . ., do you intend to harm the members of the assembly?"

"Admiral, aside from the deaths of the few unfortunate mercenaries that attacked us a few minutes ago, we have no intention of hurting anyone else. As a matter of fact, I ask you to bear witness to the proceedings that will take place. I think that when it's all said and done, you will understand why this had to happen."

The admiral shook his head and leaned back in his seat and stared at the proscenium stage by the rear of the garden blankly. His entire world had crumbled.

"One more thing Admiral, the Matriarch's Gulax Guard have been freed from their incarceration and are attempting to reach this place while bringing the members of the Curia here. They've been engaged in several fire fights for the last forty five minutes trying to get here. In order to stop the bloodshed and the possible deaths of members of the Curia, would you be so kind to tell your forces to cease all hostilities against the Guard, including all mercenary groups and to escort them all here safely?" Ogram requested politely.

The Admiral swallowed hard and touched his temple. He spoke to the commander in charge of the Heavenly Temple's Council troops and ordered him to cease fire against the Gulax Guard and to secure all mercenary forces and disarm them.

Fifteen minutes later Rek and Zurk appeared on the road leading to the garden, walking in front of the procession of the Matriarch's Gulax guard, and almost all three hundred and seventy-five Cardinals of the Curia. A group of about three hundred nuns and priests were following close behind.

Ogram and Allondra took off their Gulax armor. Underneath, both were wearing white crewman's coveralls.

"Admiral, may I borrow your voice amplifier?" he asked the man, who handed it to him as he stared at Rek and Zurk approaching the stage.

"We have succeeded Pavitraam! Twenty members of the Curia were too old and frail to attend, I hope that is alright with you," Rek said, bowing respectfully to Ogram.

Admiral Korsly, hearing Rek refer to Ogram as Pavitraam, gave him pause. He knew that the members of the Gulax Guard corps were the most faithful and commited Kelemites that one could meet.

"You two have done the impossible, but at what cost?" Ogram asked, with concern.

"Twelve who did their duty and are now with St. Kelem," Rek answered with pride.

"Their sacrifice will be remembered," Ogram replied contritely. "Did you manage to find a holo projector?"

"Yes Pavitraam, where do you want to place it?" Zurk asked.

"On the stage so that everyone sitting in the audience can see it."

As he said this, Bishop Kalduwan stomped up to Ogram, leading the group of Curia Cardinals, looking disheveled. The woman's face was twisted with anger and her eyes, red with indignant rage.

"How dare you desecrate this hallowed ground with your presence! You, who have conspired with the worst sinners in the galaxy! I demand that you release us immediately!" she screamed at him.

"Quiet woman!" Zurk said loudly, staring at the Bishop with his intimidating yellow eyes. "It is you who are the sinner and should be begging Pavitraam for forgiveness for all the death and destruction that you have caused!"

"Pavi . . ., Pavitraam?" Kalduwan stammered, looking at Ogram and the Gulax with confusion.

"Sit down bishop!" Ogram bellowed, looking at her with disdain.

Kalduwan recognized that something extraordinary was happening. The Gulax Guard only used the term Pavitraam for the Matriarch and the Cardinal Counselor, Cardinal Richelieux. Her expression changed from one of rage and indignation, to one of fear and concern. Then she noticed that Admiral Korsly was there as well, and realized that her future was in question.

Ogram turned on the voice amplifier. "Members of the Curia, you have been brought here to bear witness to justice and to correct a great wrong commited against Cardinal Richelieux and Matriarch Vasilia. Sit down and observe," Ogram said, addressing the cardinals. "Those of you who have followed the Gulax Guard and the Curia to this sacred place, the Garden of St. Kelem, are invited to also bear witness to what is about to be revealed in these proceedings," he added, as the light of the Tal system's sun began retreating into the evening hours. The lighting system in the entire Garden of Eden turned on, as it did every night. The garden's amphitheater's proscenium stage was suddenly lit with bright light, as if a play was about to start.

Then Allondra stepped forward and took the voice amplifier from Ogram. "Will the following Cardinals step forward," she announced, looking at the leaders of the Church of St. Kelem, who were by now, beginning to understand that this was serious business. One by one, all took seats in the first rows of the amphitheater, followed by all the nuns and priests that had followed them here. The Gulax Guard stood on the outer isles, rifles in hand, looking menacing.

"Cardinals Millicenta and Selecta, please come to the stage, Allondra said, looking into the crowd. The members of the Curia looked at each other and began whispering. Some of them, already guessing what was about to happen. Cardinal Millicenta and Selecta got up from their seats, looking nervous as they made their way to the stage.

Matriarch pro-tem Murcia, please join the others," Allondra added sternly.

Now there was no question in anyone's mind that the ring leaders of the campaign to oust Cardinal Richelieux and compromise Matriarch Vasilia's authority had been exposed. Then, Allondra called out the names of another twenty-two cardinals who were a suspected secondary group of co-conspirators in the takeover of the Church. The rest were now wondering if their passivity and willingness to go along with the ring leaders would result in them being accused of complicity.

Allondra walked up to Matriarch pro-tem Murcia. "Remove the papal vestment, Cardinal Murcia," Allondra demanded, in a not too friendly manner.

The woman glared at Allondra and began to object but grew quiet the moment that Rek and two members of the Matriarch's Gulax Guard approached her, looking like they were about to remove the gilded vermillion cape by force. The crowd murmured in unison, astounded by what they were witnessing. Bishop Kalduwan, Cardinals Millicenta and Selecta glanced at each other, unable to hide their anxiety and dread for what was coming.

Ogram and Allondra took the stage and then Ogram addressed the twenty-six cardinals standing below them. "Bishop Kalduwan and Cardinals Murcia, Millicenta and Selecta, you are hereby accused of instigating a rumor that the Matriarch of the Church of St. Kelem was suffering from mental instability and of calling for a mental competency examination in order to null her authority for the obligatory period of three weeks, so that you could falsely accuse Cardinal Richelieux of financial fraud against the Church of St. Kelem and of plotting with the Body Shop Guild to destroy the Plantanimus CUBE and the subsequent theft of that CUBE's Core for the purposes of damaging the Church's reputation and gain personal profit. You four accused, standing in front of me, commited these crimes and illegal actions against the Matriarch and Cardinal Richelieux, so that you could bring about the expulsion of Cardinal Richelieux from the Church of St. Kelem and thus weaken the status and authority of Matriarch Vasilia."

The audience grew silent and all eyes were on Ogram and Allondra.

"Furthermore, you hid the fact from the Curia, the clergy of the Church and the galaxy at large, that Matriarch Vasilia had personally informed you, Bishop Kalduwan, that the computer's core was not destroyed and that it had been located and recovered by me, my wife Allondra and other individuals and that we were in the process of returning the core to the Plantanimus CUBE with all billion and a half consciousnesses still intact. In order to accomplish this, you influenced the Galactic Council to order the arrest of me and my wife, so that the core would remain missing. You did this and promoted other lies, in order to instigate a galaxy wide panic that caused the Galactic Council to attack planets where the Body Shop Guild operated.

Then Allondra stepped forward and looked at the rest of the guilty cardinals behind the four principals. "You twenty two senior cardinals standing behind them, you are accused of co-conspiracy on the same charges and of using your position and influence over the other members of the Curia to force them to vote for the re-instatement of the office of Grand Inquisitor, and to subsequently vote almost unanimously, for the expulsion of Cardinal Richelieux, one of the most faithful servants of the Church of St. Kelem."

Bishop Kalduwan's face grew ever redder and with surprising agility, she jumped on the stage and addressed the crowd.

"Do not listen to this unbeliever, this agnostic, who only converted to Kelemism and married this ex nun who renounced her vows in order to steal from the church and bring about the destruction of our sacred religion!"

Allondra almost rushed the bishop to push her off stage, but Ogram held her back with a conspiratorial smile and a wink.

"Where is the CUBE's core Mr. Zepol? You don't have it do you?" Kalduwan challenged, unaware that the Kren had brought the galaxy to a complete standstill. She was confident that the Galactic Council Navy was still in charge of all the quadrants of space under its authority and that her orders to confiscate and hide the core if found, were now useless.

"Funny you should ask!" Ogram interjected, nodding to Zurk to turn on the large holo transmitter they had brought to the Garden of St. Kelem.

'WE ARE READY OGRAM, JUST GIVE US THE WORD," Queen Harriet said in his ear.

"Go for deployment," Ogram whispered, covering his mouth.

The holo screen came alive behind Ogram and Allondra. The image of the Plantanimus CUBE facility came into view. A large Kren ship hovering several meters above the facility, was lowering the computer's core into an opening in the building's roof.

"Come in Plantanimus CUBE, come in," Ogram said touching his audio implant. Ogram's voice and the transmission's audio were being amplified for the benefit of the crowd.

The face of a Galactic Council general appeared on the screen. "Who am I addressing?" the general asked, looking at the camera.

"You are addressing the Matriarch of the Church of St. Kelem!" Matriarch Vasilia said as she stepped onto the stage, wearing her papal vestment. Behind her followed Cardinal Richelieux dressed in his vermillion cassock. The crowd broke into murmurs and whispers. The Matriarch and the Cardinal hadn't been seen in public for weeks.

Ogram and Allondra's eyes moistened and they looked at Matriarch Vasilia and Richelieux and exchanged smiles. The Cardinal looked thin and tired, but otherwise alright.

Matriarch Vasilia stepped into the middle of the stage and embraced both Ogram and Allondra with affection. Then she turned toward the holo screen.

"What have you to report General?"

The man bowed respectfully and cleared his throat. "Your Holiness . . . ! Well . . ., it's highly unusual what is happening here, but, about twenty minutes ago, a Kren vessel appeared above the complex and announced that they were returning the CUBE's core to us. They claimed that they were delivering the core on behalf of Ogram and Allondra Zepol."

The crowd was shocked to learn that the Kren still existed and that most of all, that they were delivering the precious computer core to the Plantanimus CUBE.

Bishop Kalduwan's face turned ashen and her eyes darted left to right seeking a way out of her predicament. Like a cornered animal, she turned and jumped off the stage and attempted to get away, only to be stopped by Rek and Zurk, who grabbed her and dragged her back to the stage quite unceremoniously.

Seeing this, the rest of the conspirators fell to their knees and began praying out loud, begging St. Kelem for forgiveness.

The image of Kelem Rogeston appeared standing next to Ogram, Allondra, Matriarch Vasilia and Cardinal Richelieux. His body was glowing brightly, emitting white light. The audience jumped to their feet, including the penitent cardinals. An astonished Kalduwan stumbled backwards and almost fell on her backside, as the patron saint of the Church bearing his name spoke out loud, addressing the audience.

"Greetings one and all, I have come here today to bear witness and testify to this assembly and to legitimize the authority and true spirituality of these four individuals next to me. A great injustice has been commited against these four apostles of the Church and many others throughout the galaxy, who have suffered because of the actions taken by a few misguided individuals who sought to manipulate the Church and all the living beings of the galaxy." Kelem said to the astounded gathering.

He turned to Bishop Kalduwan, who was trembling with shock and disbelief, and looked at her pointedly, making it unmistakably certain, that he was addressing her above all. Then, he looked at the twenty two other Cardinals assembled by the stage.

"You have prayed for forgiveness and I see that many of you are sincere in that prayer, but know this! I will give you my blessing and your hearts will be soothed and your conscience cleared of all sin and guilt. But know also, that your time as leaders of this Church has come to an end."

"For millennia I have watched and witnessed the transgressions of members of this Church, whose main purpose was to gather power and control, rather than to consecrate the principles set forth by Sister Ornata, whose message to the members of the Church, for both clerics and lay people, was to always devote yourselves to the truth and the living spirit of the Universal Mind God. And to form a nucleus of the Universal Brotherhood of living beings without distinction of species, race, creed or color and to fight against greed, ignorance and prejudice, through the teaching of positive values."

"I've always hoped that the consciousness level of sentient beings would rise to higher levels with each generation and incarnation into the physical world. But that is not always so. I appear to you now, because you were all about to descend into the chaos of violence and death, such as was done in the fourth millennium when the Church initiated the crusades by attacking the Tilharans and falsely accusing them of being the instigators."

"Religion should not and must not be forced upon others. The Kren were falsely accused by the Church leadership of being demons and sinners, when the truth is, that the Kren are one of the most peaceful and beneficial species in the galaxy. Do not persecute them and cast lies and rumors about them, lest you shall fall victim of such treatment."

"Now, gather you all in this place and hold hands with each other. I will give my blessing to you if you so choose to take it," Kelem said, moving behind Ogram, Allondra, the Matriarch and Richelieux.

The crowd rushed to the stage and, as had occurred seven thousand, three hundred and sixty-three years in the past on the planet Mars, Kelem Rogeston was going to give his heart blessing to others for the second time in his existence. This time however, it would go to all the beings in the galaxy.

Kelem laid his hands on Ogram and Allondra's shoulders and their bodies suddenly glowed with white light, so did the bodies of Matriarch Vasilia and Cardinal Richelieux.

A slight vibration was felt by all who were in the garden. The pulsation's pitch rose and became a musical sound that grew into a complex melody of heavenly sounds that delighted the ears of all present. Soon, the intensity of the effect increased and everyone's eyes closed as a wonderful sensation of warmth spread throughout their bodies.

A wave of pure love and sanctified energy, bathed the minds and spirits of the group. Bishop Kalduwan and the guilty cardinals began sobbing. Their tears were not of sadness, but of regret, for their hearts were being touched by the sacred energy of the Universal Mind God for the first time in their lives. And in knowing true love and heavenly grace, they learned and accepted that they had commited a terrible sin against the world. Yet, St. Kelem had forgiven them.

A few in the crowd fainted from ecstasy, and soon the blessing came to an end. Some were fully satisfied, while others yearned for more.

Ogram, Allondra, the Matriarch and Richelieux, opened their eyes and struggled to accept that the blessing was over. The four turned to thank Kelem and reach for his touch, but he was gone.

They stood looking at each other, knowing that they had experienced a miracle.

Ogram smiled, remembering Kelem's words on the Kren mothership two days earlier. *"Do the work Ogram. You're capable of doing it. I know that you'll find a way."*

Ogram had definitely done "the work", but Kelem had changed the future by his appearance. Ogram knew that this event would be regarded as one of the most important and influential moments in the history of the galaxy.

Matriarch Vasilia walked over to Admiral Korsly and instructed him to cease all hostilities and withdraw all Galactic Council warships from each and every Body Shop Guild planet they had engaged.

The Admiral, still trying to get over what he'd just experienced, reached out to the Council's central headquarters in Centralia and conveyed the Matriarch's orders. Within an hour, the conflict which would have turned into the bloodiest war ever, was over.

"MY YOUNG FRIEND, YOU HAVE SUCCEEDED. THE COUNCIL'S NAVY HAS WITHDRAWN AND SO HAVE ALL THE KREN HIVES," the queen reported in his ear.

"I'm glad to hear the good news Harriett, but what of the future? You warned me that asking all the Kren hives to take part in stopping this war, might cause many of the younger queens to decide that it was time for the Kren to rule the galaxy," Ogram asked cautiously.

"YOU'LL BE GLAD TO KNOW THAT WE KREN ARE A VERY PRAGMATIC SPECIES OGRAM. THE YOUNGER QUEENS CONSIDERED THIS OPTION FOR A FEW HOURS AND DECIDED THAT THERE WAS NO ADVANTAGE TO IT. ON THE CONTRARY, THEY DECIDED THAT ASSUMING THE POSITION OF DOMINANT SPECIES CARRIES WITH IT A GREAT DEAL OF RESPONSIBILITY AND RISK. THE KREN ARE HAPPY TO CO-EXIST WITH ALL OTHER SPECIES, SO LONG AS YOU LEAVE US FREE TO LIVE OUR LIVES."

"Amen to that Harriett! Thank you for helping us out with this crisis and thank you for telling my friends about my plan. You are far wiser than I'll ever be," Ogram remarked, glad that Harriett's decision had been instrumental in the success of Ogram's plan.

'YOU'RE WELCOME OGRAM, BUT AS FAR AS WISDOM IS CONCERNED, YOU HAVE IT TO SPARE. YOU ARE VERY YOUNG AND HAVE MUCH TO LEARN, BUT YOU ARE WISE BEYOND YOUR YEARS. BE WELL AND PROSPER MY YOUNG FRIEND, I LOOK FORWARD TO MEETING YOU IN THE FUTURE."

"Goodbye Harriet," Ogram said touching his temple. Tomorrow he'd have the extra cochlear implant removed. He suddenly realized how uncomfortable it felt.

Ogram looked around and saw that The Garden of Eden was being invaded by robo cams and media reporters, wanting to meet and talk to Ogram, Allondra, the Matriarch and Cardinal Richelieux. Ogram had programmed the robo cams that he and Allondra had released, to broadcast galaxy wide. He knew that the meeting with the Curia and everything else that followed had to be documented.

"Follow your hearts," Kelem had told him and the others. Ogram wondered what effect his decisions would have on the Church in the near future and beyond.

He sighed, straightened out his collar and turned to face the gaggle of media reporters waiting to talk to him.

CHAPTER 57

The End of a Very Long Relationship

Ogram and Allondra gazed out of the passenger window of the winged chariot taking them to the Heavenly Temple of the Kelemite Church and reminisced about their first meeting.

"I couldn't take my eyes off you," confessed Ogram, looking at his wife with the same appreciation of her exotic beauty as he had felt the first time he'd laid eyes on her.

"And I was nervous, trying to hide my attraction for you," she admitted laughing.

They had taken a three and a half month honeymoon after the incident at the Garden of Eden. They had met both sets of parents and then spent three weeks visiting other relatives and friends of Allondra's family. Ogram had been surprised to learn how big Tarsian families could get. In contrast, Ogram's family only consisted of his parents, two sets of grandparents, two aunts and uncles and a few nephews.

The rest of the time was spent trying to get away from flying robo-cams and being pursued by media hounds all over the galaxy. They tried wearing disguises and booking interplanetary flights under assumed names, but the sheer number of lookee-loos that followed them everywhere, thwarted every attempt at privacy. The broadcasted event at the Garden of St. Kelem had made them famous celebrities.

So when Cardinal Richelieux contacted them and asked them to return to the Heavenly Temple for a very important meeting, both newlyweds jumped at the chance to spend a few days in the relative privacy of the Holy See.

"What kind of meeting they want us to attend? Allondra wondered.

"It sounded serious. I hope no new threat to the galaxy has appeared. I'm done with adventure and danger for a while!" Ogram commented, hoping for the best.

The winged chariot banked left and approached Hangar 6, the very same hangar that had brought Ogram to the Heavenly Temple on his first visit. He smiled, remembering how nervous he felt disguised as a lay priest. This time was very different. Both Ogram and Allondra were dressed in expensive clothes purchased in one of Earth's fanciest boutiques.

Soon after their chariot touched down on the deck of Hangar 6, they were met by an enthusiastic group of nuns, priests and Heavenly Temple workers who had heard that they were coming. Ogram and Allondra laughed at the irony of it all. It seemed that the Church's clergy were as enamored of their celebrity as the secular world.

Bishop Mathias, the same priest that had worked as Bishop Kalduwan's assistant, came to the rescue and took them away from their religious fans.

"Welcome back blessed ones!" Mathias said excitedly, after the elevator door closed. "Her Holiness and his Eminence are waiting for you in the Matriarch's residence. You are welcome to stay at her Holiness' private residence for as long as you wish," the bishop commented with a smile.

"Thank you Bishop. By the way, do you know what this meeting we've been asked to attend, is all about?" asked Ogram, anxious to know what they were in for.

"It's all very hush-hush and I'm not supposed to tell anyone, not even you! But I can assure you that it doesn't involve a looming crisis or a crusade," he answered, chuckling a little bit.

"Oh, well, I suppose we'll find out soon enough," Allondra remarked, as the elevator doors opened to the Matriarch's private residence.

The moment that Ogram and Allondra stepped onto the main hallway, a platoon of the Matriarch's Gulax Guard approached them and all seven bowed respectfully at the couple.

"Welcome back Pavitraam!" Roko, the Guard's captain said, sporting a wide Gulax smile, showing a row of yellow sharp teeth.

"Thank you captain we are glad to be back," Ogram answered, shaking the Gulax's hand. Allondra obliged and shook the captain's hand as well. Both could tell that Roko was overwhelmed with pride for having been touched by them.

Mathias escorted them to the Matriarch's residence and didn't have the opportunity to touch the apartment's intercom to announce Ogram and Allondra's arrival.

The door swung open and Matriarch Vasilia came out and hugged both youngsters with great affection.

"Come in, come in you two!" the Matriarch said, drawing them into the apartment by their arms. "My, my, look at you two in your fancy clothes!" she gushed, like a proud parent welcoming back her children from a long absence.

"Are these the same two young people we met nearly a year ago?" Cardinal Richelieux, called out from behind the wet bar. He came out and hugged both of them at once. "I know it's only been a few months, but we've missed you terribly!" he told them with tears welling in his eyes. Ogram and Allondra suddenly realized that they had been missing them too. Now that they were back in the Matriarch's apartment they felt truly comfortable for the first time since they'd left. Both loved their families dearly, but this really felt like a genuine home coming.

Bishop Mathias excused himself and left them to their privacy.

The Matriarch and Richelieux insisted on hearing about everything that had happened to them since they left on their well-deserved honeymoon. They were surprised to hear their woes regarding their celebrity status and laughed with them, when the two recounted their misadventures and embarrassing moments trying to escape flying robo-cams and nosey reporters.

As he'd done before, Richelieux called for a toast, and the foursome emptied their goblets of Cointreau.

"Your Holiness and your Eminence, we're dying to know what this meeting you called us to attend is all about," Ogram asked, looking at the two of them.

Their faces turned serious and Matriarch Vasilia put down her glass down on the coffee table and looked at the two youngsters intently. "Tell me you two, what are your plans for the future?" she asked, with great interest.

Ogram and Allondra looked at each other and smiled. They had discussed this issue obsessively since they had left the Holy See.

"Well," Allondra said, speaking first. "I've decided to re-join the order. I came to the realization a few weeks ago, that the Church is my real home."

Both the Matriarch and Richelieux smiled with happy expressions and turned to Ogram with expectant eyes.

"And what about you Ogram?" Richelieux asked. "How do you feel about Allondra becoming a nun again?"

Ogram laughed and turned to Allondra. "I liquidated all my assets a month ago and put all my money in a trust fund for our children when they grow up. I want them to have the freedom to choose whatever career they want, regardless of the fact that both of their parents will be clerics in the Church of St. Kelem," he answered, waiting for the Matriarch's and Richelieux's response.

"Oh my! You mean that you have decided to become a Kelemite priest?" the Matriarch said, with her eyes filled with tears of happiness.

"Yes your Holiness. It took me a while, but eventually I got it. This has been my destiny all along," Ogram declared, with emotion.

Richelieux got up from his seat, walked over to where Ogram was sitting and the two men hugged.

"This is perfect Ogram! The Church is selling its interest in The Realm. That's why we asked you to attend this meeting. We are going to need ordained members of the Church to help make the transition to an all secular administration within the company. You two are the perfect individuals to take over that job. Are you interested?" the Matriarch asked.

Both Ogram and Allondra were shocked to learn that the Church of St. Kelem would no longer be a majority stock holder in The Realm!

"The Church is selling its interest in The Realm after nearly six millennia?" Ogram uttered, trying to recover from the surprising news. Once, not too long ago, he had been of the opinion that the Kelemite Church held too much wealth and power and that it should divest itself from owning majority stock in the most profitable business to ever have been created. But now, somehow, that idea seemed wrong.

"After the galaxy learned of the debacle at the Plantanimus CUBE and after trillions saw the broadcast you put in place to expose Kalduwan and her conspirators, public support for the Church's majority ownership of The Realm disappeared," Richelieux informed him.

Ogram felt as if the blood in his head had suddenly drained into his stomach. "But . . ., how will the church continue to finance its huge galaxy wide operation?" he asked, feeling as if he'd inflicted the Kelemite religion a mortal wound.

"Oh, don't worry about the church going to the poor house anytime soon my dear!" the Matriarch explained dismissively. "We will receive a humongous payment for the sale of our stock. The payment is so large, that we've agreed to take it over a period of one hundred years!"

"Oh!" Ogram expressed with relief, remembering that the number describing the total worth of The Realm Corporation ran up into the Tredecillions, a number with so many zeroes, that it had to be written with a ten, followed by forty-two zeros, (10/42).

"When is the transfer of ownership taking place?" Ogram asked, trying to calculate how long it would take him and Allondra to graduate from Kelemite seminary school before they could take on the job of managing The Realm's transition to secular ownership.

"It's happening today," the Matriarch replied casually. "That's why we asked you both to come. Your presence at the ceremony would be a great asset to all involved."

"Well, besides us wanting to give you two the job, The Realm's board of directors, asked that you be involved, particularly for the ceremony. The board has a very high opinion of Ogram and Allondra Zepol. They want the team that recovered the core from the hands of the Nadrogs and successfully returned it to the Plantanimus CUBE, to be in charge of the transition," Richelieux explained.

"Hold on, hold on!" Ogram interjected with alacrity. "You said that you wanted ordained members of the Church to take over the position! But your Holiness, it will take me and Allondra, at least three years to graduate from seminary school!"

Both Matriarch Vasilia and Cardinal Richelieux couldn't help but laugh heartily, almost hysterically. Ogram didn't think that his concern for propriety was so funny!

Controlling her laughter, the Matriarch shrugged and composed herself. "My dear honorable, kind and decent Ogram, for you and Allondra to attend seminary school now would be like asking St. Kelem himself or Sister Ornata to do the same!"

Ogram and Allondra exchanged glances, trying to figure out what both the Matriarch and Cardinal Richelieux were driving at.

"They don't have a clue!" Richelieux said to the Matriarch, unable to hide his amusement.

"It's very simple my dears. For all intents and purposes, both of you, and in almost the same measure, us" (the Matriarch added, pointing to herself and the Cardinal), "we are now considered living saints of the Church of St. Kelem! You are both ordained clerics of the Church by default!"

Both Ogram and Allondra went pale. His face turning white and hers light green.

"But . . .," "both mumbled, unable to speak.

"St. Kelem put his hands on your shoulders and said to the crowd that he had come to the garden named after him, to; *"bear witness and testify to this assembly and to legitimize the authority and true spirituality of these four individuals next to me."* The video clearly shows that he meant the four of us when he said those words," the Cardinal added, quoting Kelem's speech on that day. "Then, his auric glow spilled into our bodies and the rest you know. I have seen the video of the event over and over. It is quite impressive."

The Matriarch pulled out a folder from one of the small side tables around the large couch in the living room, then opened it and showed it to Ogram and Allondra. "I have already signed the decree making you two officially ordained members of the Church. Now, the only thing that you must accept my dear Ogram, is the fact that you will be wearing a vermillion cassock in public for the rest of your life!"

Ogram and Allondra looked at each other yet again and finally understood what had happened. They held hands and kissed each other on the cheek and knew that this was right.

They stood up and looked upon the Matriarch and Cardinal Richelieux. "We're ready, where are our vestments?"

Two hours later, the historic agreement to sell the Church of St. Kelem's entire portfolio of The Realm's stock was signed, with the galactic media recording the event for posterity and many important dignitaries in attendance. The ceremony took place in the Grand Reception Hall in the Matriarch's residence.

So ended the Church of St. Kelem's relationship to The Realm.

GALACTIC YEAR 10,148

CHAPTER 58

Kelem's Ascension

The Prophesy II landed softly about one hundred meters from the old house in the mountain, raising a cloud of dust from its landing thrusters.

"Good flight husband! Not bad for an octogenarian," Allondra quipped humorously.

"Thank you, but the ship practically flies itself my love. Still, if the automation were to fail, I could still fly this thing by hand," Ogram replied, confidently.

At eighty-five, Ogram looked and felt more like a middle-aged, man and Allondra, now aged seventy-nine, still possessed the same exotic beauty that Ogram had found so irresistible sixty-two years earlier.

"I'm going to go the med bed and check on her," Allondra said, unbuckling her safety harness.

Ogram shut down the ship's flight systems and went down to the lower deck to set up the floating gurney for their trip up the mountain.

When he came back to the main deck Allondra was waiting for him.

"How is she?"

"Still under Lectrosleep. I think its best we don't awaken her until we get to the top. Don't you agree?"

"Yes," Ogram answered, unable to hide his mood.

"What is it husband?" Your aura just darkened a bit," Allondra observed, concerned for his mental state.

Ogram sat on the pilot's chair and exhaled deeply trying to keep his spirits up. "It's the end of an era Allondra," he remarked sadly. "Matuch left us last year and now she's leaving us. I mourned the deaths of my parents, but when Matuch crossed over last year I was devastated!"

"I know my love. I miss him too, but the physical form is weak and mortal. How's that old joke go?" she mused, for a second. "I remember! *'When it comes to death, ten out of ten people do it'!*"

Ogram laughed, glad that Allondra could always find humor in everything.

"Don't dwell in the past, but live in the moment my love. Let us bring Vasilia to Kelem and Alpha. And as we trek up the mountain, we can recount her life and all the things that we love about her," she suggested reaching for his hand affectionately.

"You're right, I will stay in the moment," Ogram agreed, getting up from his chair and going to the back of the ship to change his clothes. Although Nobius was a warm planet and had a very mild winter in comparison to other planets, they'd be climbing to the top of the mountain where the temperature was chilly this time of year. In spite of their youthful energy, Ogram and Allondra had to make some allowances for their age, and wearing warm clothes in cold weather, was one of those adjustments that older people have to contend with.

Twenty minutes later, Ogram and Allondra were on their way to bring Matriarch Vasilia Bentara Rogeston to her final resting place. Both she and the recently departed Cardinal Matuch Richelieux, had chosen Nobius as their burial site.

The trek was arduous but not unduly so. Ogram and Allondra could still handle climbing the mountain without the aid of an antigrav harness. Perhaps in a decade or so, they'd be forced to use such devices, but not yet!

The floating gurney carrying Matriarch Vasilia in her med-bed was programmed to follow Ogram and Allondra automatically, as they climbed. The gurney's gyroscope kept her body level and safe as it climbed. This particular one was the same one they had used the year before to bring Richelieux's body up the mountain.

They arrived by mid-afternoon and were filled with delight when they saw Kelem's figure waiting for them by Alpha's massive roots.

"Welcome back Ogram and Allondra. It is good to see you in the flesh once again!" Kelem said, embracing them both at once.

Ogram and Allondra's spirits rose and their bodies suddenly felt young and strong with his touch. They took off their jackets and found the temperature quite warm, even though they were at three thousand meters elevation.

Kelem walked over to the floating gurney and touched the button to deactivate it. The device lowered itself and rested on the ground. The med-bed's protective canopy opened and Kelem reached in and touched Vasilia's hand.

"Awaken Vasilia," he said softly, and her eyes fluttered and opened.

"My lord! Am I dreaming, or is this real?" she asked, looking around.

"You are on Nobius and, yes, this is 'real'," he replied smiling.

"My lord, I am so pleased that I'm finally able to touch you in the flesh. I prayed that I would have the chance to meet you in person before passing on. Now that I've touched you and seen you with my eyes, I'm ready to go," she said, as tears fell from her cheeks.

Kelem reached out and gently wiped Vasilia's tears with his fingers. "Do not fret beloved Vasilia, death is but a step into another state of being."

"I do not fear death my lord, only leaving those I love behind."

"You take the love of those you've known with you and at the same time, your energy remains in the hearts and minds of those you've loved and served," Kelem assured her with tenderness. And as he soothed her and as comforted her with his words, his body began to glow and Vasilia's heart was filled with love and joy and her cares and worries faded away.

Ogram and Allondra's hearts were breaking with a combination of grief and joy and their eyes were also filled with tears.

"Sleep now sweet Vasilia, close your eyes and sleep. You have served others all your life and now your journey's done," Kelem said with a bittersweet smile.

Vasilia closed her eyes and Kelem picked up her frail thin body in his arms and carried her to Alpha's roots and laid her on the ground. He straightened her snow white hair and kissed her forehead and stepped away. Vasilia's chest rose once and then she was gone.

The Dreamer's vibrations soon filled the air, and their music rose in volume and intensity, shaking the very ground. Thin white tendrils appeared around her body and began covering her, until she could no longer be seen. Then, the music grew in power and Vasilia's body was absorbed into the ground, leaving no trace of her.

The music faded and all was quiet again. Ogram and Allondra had never seen this before. When they brought Richelieux to Nobius the year before, he was already dead and Kelem had simply dug a grave for him near Alpha.

"Why the difference?" Allondra asked, referring to the way Vasilia was interred.

"Vasilia's life energy was still inside her when Alpha absorbed her body. When Dreamers are able to 'take in' someone at the exact moment of death, they can hold a person's 'life hologram' in their consciousness. Unfortunately, Matuch had passed away hours before you got here. Alpha may not have been able to 'record' his 'life hologram'."

"Does that mean that she will be reborn, as you did?" Ogram asked, with anticipation.

"Hard to say," Kelem replied. "It is a personal choice. After I died on Plantanimus that first time, it took me a Plantanimus year in the Quantum Tide before I decided to re-incarnate as a Plantanimal. But, it also depends on the individual, whether or not they've learned enough life lessons over subsequent re-incarnations to be able to make the choice to re-incarnate in the same town, or sometimes the same family or in the same profession, etc. Most individuals do not have the choice to return to the 'old form' with all their previous life memories intact, because they need more life experience in a wide variety of situations before they burn enough karma to learn enough lessons to develop and move onto the next level of consciousness."

"What is the next level of consciousness for you Kelem? You've obviously been given the choice to return with the same personality and consciousness for millennia. And in this last incarnation, you have chosen your 'old form', or, can one say, 'your Kelem Rogeston 'life hologram'?" Ogram inquired.

"Ah yes, about that," Kelem said, looking a bit uncomfortable. We have to discuss something and now it's as good a time as any."

"What is it Kelem?" Allondra asked, sensing that she and Ogram were about to hear unwelcome news.

"Sit down you two, please," he asked, looking like a man about to unload a heavy burden.

Ogram and Allondra sat opposite Kelem and waited anxiously to hear what he had to say.

"Do you remember the conversation we had on the porch down by the old house, sixty-two years ago, the night before you returned to the Heavenly Temple?"

Ogram and Allondra searched their memories of more than six decades.

"Are you referring to my asking you what sort of being you were? Ogram commented, hoping his aging brain was serving him right.

"Yes. You said, 'Kelem, what exactly are you?' I gave you a short history of my many incarnations. Then you asked if the body that I was inhabiting, this body that I still inhabit, whether it was real, or a projection of some sort."

"Yes! Now I remember that conversation!" Ogram declared triumphantly. "You told me that your body was as real as mine or Allondra's."

"Correct, but I also told you that the universe itself is an immense hologram, that in a sense, we're all projections of consciousness. Do you remember me saying that?" Kelem asked.

Ogram nodded and looked at Allondra. Neither one liked where this conversation was heading.

And do you remember me telling you both why I came to Nobius in the first place?"

Both hesitated. Allondra spoke first. "Yes, you became depressed because your mate Anima had 'ascended', I believe you used that word to describe her passing on."

"I wanted to live my last human life and die of old age, which Alpha and the others let me do. However, they held on to my 'life hologram', unable, or, perhaps, unwilling to let me go completely. They kept me in Pralaya for thousands of years and decided to bring me back to life when the Kelemite Crusades began."

"Thank the Universal Mind God for that!" Allondra expressed with fervor.

"Yes, I'm glad they held on to me too. And I'm also glad that I remained in this form all these years, otherwise the Nadrogs might be ruling our galaxy now. But in a sense, I've been holding on to this realm of existence far too long, delaying the inevitable."

"What do you mean by that?" Ogram asked, wondering what Kelem meant by 'delaying the inevitable'."

"My mate Anima <u>had</u> to ascend. She had no choice, because she could no longer maintain her form, or her physical 'life hologram' if you will. Her spiritual vibration had become too rarefied and her higher body, or her 'soul', could not support a body in the physical world. She had to transcend."

"My lord, are you saying that you . . ., you're . . ., you're going to 'transcend'?" Allondra asked, with tears in her eyes.

"Yes, dear ones," Kelem said, with bittersweet sadness. "It is all I can do to hold on to this form with all my will, even as we speak!"

"But, can't Alpha and the Dreamers keep you whole? You said that it was their life energy that supported your physical form!" Ogram argued, feeling like he was losing Kelem forever.

"Even the almighty Dreamers lack the knowledge to hold on to me. They couldn't help Anima stay either. Just as a child cannot feed from the mother's breast all their lives, or the adolescent remain dependent on his or her parents forever, so must we all grow and develop and move on to the next stage of our lives. It is the order of things. It's how the universe works, dear ones."

Ogram and Allondra were overwhelmed with sadness and their hearts ached such as they never had before. They felt as if the spiritual center of their lives was being torn from them.

Kelem looked at Ogram and Allondra and his heart went to them. But his service in this realm of existence was over. "Now it's your turn to take my place," he said, reaching for their hands and holding them in his'.

"Take your place? Kelem that's ridiculous!" Ogram complained, wiping tears from his cheeks.

"You two have burned enough karma and have lived enough lives to take on the job! It is no accident that you have been part of everything that has occurred in the last sixty years. One day, many thousands of years in the future, you too will be giving this sad speech to other 'saints in training' who don't want to let you go!" It's your time to serve damn it!" Kelem said, with mock anger. "Let me go, please! You're only making it harder for me to leave."

Allondra rose to her knees from a sitting position and hugged Kelem, sobbing with great sorrow. "We will my lord, we will, but it's hard!"

Ogram reached for her and pulled her away from Kelem, then held her in his arms trying to comfort her, hoping that he would have the strength to stop crying and put up a brave front.

The ground began to vibrate and Kelem stood up.

"It's time," he said, and then moved away from them.

"Already?" Allondra asked, lifting her head and looking at Kelem.

"Come my love, let us dry our eyes and wish Kelem a safe passage into the next world. Let not our last moments with him be filled with selfish attachment. Let's open our hearts and send him off with joy and blessings, just like he taught us to give to others. Come, hold my hand and give the heart blessing."

Allondra stood up and held Ogram's hand. Both closed their eyes for a moment and then the sacred energy of Kelem's blessing spread from their chests to their entire bodies.

"Goodbye beloved ones. It has been a pleasure and a privilege to know you," Kelem said, as his body began to emit light.

It was then, that Ogram and Allondra finally understood that this was a wonderful thing and that they should rejoice in the mystery and magic of the universe. What they were witnessing was truly miraculous.

Music began radiating from Alpha's massive trunk, soon joined by all the Dreamers on the mountain and all the Dreamers in the galaxy. They were saying one last goodbye to the man that had awakened their ancestral species and given them a purpose in the universe.

"Farewell Kelem! Our love goes with you!" Allondra called, as Kelem's image began to pulsate and become transparent.

"Thank you for everything you taught us Kelem. We will honor your life with faithful service to others!" Ogram shouted, to be heard over the majestic symphony that was being played in Kelem's honor.

Kelem's image became a blur of multicolored lights that expanded and grew to encompass the entire mountain. It was as though Kelem's physical structure had been disassembled atom by atom and then into sub atomic and quantum particles of various shapes and colors.

The bubble of quantum dancing particles rose higher and higher, and then, as Ogram and Allondra looked up into the Nobius night sky, the particles began to sparkle, then slowly fade into the planet's upper atmosphere.

The Dreamer's symphony came to a loud crescendo that echoed around the mountain for a long time.

Ogram and Allondra looked at each other and then embraced, glad to be alive and thankful to have known Kelem.

It was too late to return to the Prophesy II and they realized that they would have to spend the night up in the mountain. They put their jackets back on and hoped that they could stay warm through the night.

"BELOVED ONES!" Alpha said in their heads, surprising them. "PLEASE COME CLOSER TO ME AND I WILL KEEP YOU SAFE AND WARM THROUGH THE NIGHT."

Ogram and Allondra laughed with relief and rushed to Alpha's trunk and entered his root labyrinth. There, the temperature was warm enough for them to take their jackets off and use them as pillows.

They lay next to each other and quickly fell asleep feeling like newborn babes in their mother's arms.

END

*Epilogue

To all my readers:

Thank you for reading The Holographic Saint. And my humble gratitude to those that have read the entire series, starting with the first four books; Plantanimus "Awakening", Plantanimus "Return to Mars" and Plantanimus "The Gulax War" and Plantanimus "Reunion".

When I started writing the first book, I had no idea that the "first book" would become a pentalogy. Nor did I imagine that twenty years would pass before I published an additional four books based on that original idea.

I'm not ashamed to admit that I shed a few tears when I typed the word "End", as I finished writing The Holographic Saint. Kelem Rogeston, the one character that ties all five books, became almost a real living, breathing entity for me. Like a close friend with whom one has shared many adventures. With the fifth book now finished, I'm going to miss him much like Ogram and Allondra felt when Kelem ascended.

I started writing Plantanimus "Awakening" in the summer of two thousand (2000) and finished the last book in January 2019. It took nineteen years to complete the saga. I never worked on any project for that many years and I feel proud that I stuck with it, day after day, and didn't give up on those occasions, when the writing wasn't so good or when ideas refused to manifest in my brain.

I look forward to taking a year off to concentrate on other creative pursuits. But, I have several unwritten sagas that have been simmering in the back burner for a long time. I'm a restless soul and I know that I might start writing one of those new books before that year is through.

Once again, thank you so much for reading the Plantanimus books. It's been a pleasure and a privilege to have written them and to have shared them with you.

Joseph M. Armillas

About the Author

A resident of Los Angeles California, Joseph M. armillas is an author, actor and film producer. Born in South America to show business parents and raised in the USA, Joseph is a US Army veteran and proud American. A science fiction fan since childhood, Joseph began writing short sci-fi stories while in high school. His love of the genre inspired him to write the Plantanimus Pentalogy. He is currently working on new stories to tell and on converting the Plantanimus Pentalogy into screenplays.

Printed in the United States
By Bookmasters